DAY OF WRATH

DAY OF WRATH

Daniel Easterman

BCA

LONDON NEW YORK SYDNEY TORONTO

This edition published 1995
by BCA
by arrangement with Harper Collins Publishers

CN 8284

Printed and bound in Germany
by Graphischer Großbetrieb Pößneck GmbH
A member of the Mohndruck printing group

In memory of My Father
David McKeown
1922–1995

For Beth, for making it
all worthwhile

ACKNOWLEDGEMENTS

My warm and undiminished thanks, as always, to my editorial teams in London and New York: Patricia Parkin and Mary-Rose Doherty, Karen Solem and Katie Tso. Brendan Munnelly provided such detailed and accurate information on Irish and related matters that I wish all my novels could be set in Ireland. Thanks, too, to my brother, David McKeown, for his unstinting help in checking details in Belfast, and to Joan McCaig for her comments and ideas. For research assistance on police and policing matters, I am grateful as ever to Roderick Richards of Tracking Line. My wife, Beth, took valuable time off from her own writing to read and comment on the manuscript and helped me see my way past innumerable obstacles. No one but myself is to blame for the use I have made of all this.

CHAPTER ONE

Belfast
16 August 199-

Donegall Place, the end of the day, the City Hall in tatters between sun and shadow, the shopkeepers shutting up and setting off home, shopgirls walking to the Central Station. An army Pig took the corner slowly, and headed left into Chichester Street. From the turret, an armed soldier kept watch nervously, trusting no-one.

Gearóid Lalor watched the armoured vehicle disappear from sight before driving off. In the seat next to him Seamus Lenihan stared out the window at the emptying streets.

He'd have gone down to Bangor that night, why not? Wee Fergie McErlaine and the gang from St Malachy's were going there to a disco, and he'd have gone with them if the call hadn't come that morning. They were terrible idiots the lot of them, but he felt like a bit of crack and a few laughs for a change. And maybe he could have gone up the Cave Hill on Sunday with Noreen. But it was no good, their commanding officer wasn't the sort to let his unit mess about.

'I could have been in Bangor the night,' he said.

'That so?' Lenihan did not turn his head.

'A bunch of fellas from the old school are going down in Fergie's car.'

'Fergie who?' They were turning into Donegall Street.

'McErlaine. You know, the wee lad from Eia Street. His auld fella used to have the fish shop on Duncairn Gardens.'

'Oh, aye, him. Sure he's a right buck idiot.'

'I know, but he's all right all the same. He keeps his mouth shut.

'He knows he'd have it shut for him if he didn't. All the same, you should keep well clear of him. I've seen him and his friends acting the fool more than once when they've been cut. Them ones are the kind of wee idiots that gets out of line, so they are. Your man Fergie'll get himself lifted one day and start talkin'. You understan' me?'

Gearóid looked at the dashboard.

'There would've been no harm in it. Going down to Bangor. It's just a bit of fun.'

'It'd be a waste of time. Bangor's fucked.'

'You're off your head. There's nothin' wrong with it.'

'They fucked it up when they built that marina business. I can remember when you could go down to Bangor on the train on a Saturday and go for a swim in the Pickie Pool. When you were finished, you'd head on to Barry's Amusements on the front. You could have a good time there for a couple of quid. There was decent dulse in them days too, not the shite they give you nowadays. The friggin' sea's half diseased, what with the shite and stuff they put in it. There's God knows what coming over from England. It's not enough they send in the army, they're trying to poison us now and all.'

'Do you like dulse?'

'I like it now and then, but it's years since I had some. You get better dulse in Donaghadee. But when was I last in Donaghadee?'

They were on the Antrim Road now, heading north. Seamus was Gearóid's senior by a good ten years or more, a man of respect who'd done time in Long Kesh and been in and out of Castlereagh nearly as often as he'd eaten dulse, the salty dried seaweed every Northern Irishman associated with days at the seaside. And here he was, talking about the Pickie Pool and the times he'd had as a youngster. It made him sound like an old man, thought Gearóid. His own brother had been the same way, before they shot him. He wondered when Seamus had ever had time for any of that.

Himself, he could remember nothing but the Troubles. There had been ceasefires, but they had passed him by, leaving him as he had been. And since he'd been big enough to join up, he'd known very little but the movement. All the same, he wouldn't have minded a trip to Bangor or Portrush or one of those places now and again. Just himself and a few of the lads.

But he wasn't going for a jaunt tonight.

10

'Have you any idea what's on?'

Seamus shook his head tetchily.

'You should know better than to ask. How the fuck should I know? I was told what you was told: be at the operations room by six o'clock and await orders. So that's what we'll do.'

Gearóid nodded. A volunteer never asked too many questions. It could get people talking about you, make some of them wonder if maybe you weren't a tout. 'Keep your gob shut an' obey orders' – that was the key to survival in this filthy business. If there was such a thing as survival. You kept yourself alive as best you could, for as long as you could, that was the way of it. And if you kept your nose clean and never touted or fucked up, they gave you a good funeral over at Milltown, with a beret and gloves on your coffin and a volley of gunshots over your grave.

They drew up outside a terraced house in a short street off the Antrim Road, in the New Lodge district. On a gable at the entrance to the street a mural showed a masked gunman against a map of Ireland painted in orange, green and white. Beneath it ran words by Pádraig Pearse: 'Ireland unfree shall never be at peace', and next to them others in the same vein: 'The fools, the fools, they have left us our Fenian dead'. It was an endless place, however changed, and the words on its walls and its people's lips endless. As enduring as the deaths they boasted.

The door was opened from inside as they approached. They stepped into a narrow hallway, half-dark and smelling of fried sausage. Colm O'Driscoll shut the door behind them. He was grim-faced as usual.

'Were yous followed?' the little man asked. He had a twisted hip, some said from an accident in a game of hurley, others from a long night in Castlereagh at the hands of the Special Branch. He'd been an athlete before that, a hard player at all sorts of games.

'No way,' Seamus answered. 'I'd my eyes peeled the whole time. If they were tailing us, they were smarter than the Holy Ghost.'

'Ay, well, nowadays that's just what the fuckers are. Come away on inside. Eugene's here already.'

He'd heard a poem once, thought Gearóid, a long poem in English that one of his teachers had read to them in school, Father McGiolla, a squat wee man with glasses half the size of his face.

It had been written by a man called Yeats, who was buried in Sligo. Gearóid had never been to Sligo, had never set foot in the South. Maybe one day, when all this was over.

> Out of Ireland have we come.
> Great hatred, little room,
> Maimed us at the start.
> I carry from my mother's womb
> A fanatic heart.

He had not understood the poem well, but McGiolla had spoken of the evil of great hatred, and his words had found some place in Gearóid's mind. The words had not been like the words of the patriotic songs his father had taught him, but they had their own resonance and spoke with their own voice. Perhaps he should go to Sligo soon, find time to read and think. At nineteen, he had never had time for anything but hatred.

Colm O'Driscoll, standing there in his Springfield Road shoes and stained shirt, would never have fitted into anybody's poetry book. He was a hard man, a man even his friends would take care not to cross. It was said he'd been to England before his accident and planted bombs in pubs and an army barracks, that the police on both sides of the water were mad keen to lay hands on him, but never had had a shred of evidence. He was a good man, all the same, with four weans, beautiful weans, the oldest nine, the youngest three. It was his sister brought them up now; his wife was dead, shot down by Loyalists a year gone, shot in the head while out shopping for milk. She was in Milltown cemetery with a headstone the size of a barn door.

There was food on the table, sausages and potato farls, nothing fancy, and scalding tea to wash it down. They always took plenty of tea before a mission, it kept you alert.

Eugene O'Malley was eating an iced bap, sitting in the corner as usual, tapping his foot to music he could hear in his head. He'd won first prize at the Fleadh last year, him on the tin whistle and Paddy Byrne on the guitar; and a couple of years before that he'd been the All-Ireland Whistle Champion at Boyle.

'How's about ye, Eugene? Have you brought your whistle along?'

'What do you think?' He nodded towards the door. 'There's

some champ in the kitchen if you'd like some. It'll still be hot. The scallions was fresh in today.'

'No, I'm all right, I had something in town. A cup of tea and a sausage'll do me rightly.' He poured himself a strong cup of tea.

'I was going to Bangor the night,' he said.

'You'll be lucky.'

The door opened suddenly. It was Conor Melaugh, the officer in command of their Active Service Unit. Immediately after him, a woman stepped into the room, a stranger. No-one moved. The woman was well dressed, out of place here. Her hair was auburn, cut in a low fringe. Conor would have to have a good explanation for bringing her here: it was a strict rule that the ASUs only ever had contact with outsiders through their OCs.

'Stay where you are, lads,' said Melaugh. 'I'd like yous to meet a friend of mine. This is Maureen O'Dalaigh. Yous'll have heard her name before this. I don't need to tell yous who she is. She has a few words to say before you go out tonight. I want yous to listen carefully.'

Gearóid whistled beneath his breath. Fuckin' right her name was familiar. Maureen O'Dalaigh was a leading member of the Army Council, one of the top people in the movement. What was she doing here in the New Lodge on a Friday night?

O'Dalaigh thanked Melaugh. She remained standing, looking at each of the men in the room in turn. She knew what they were thinking, that Headquarters had sent her in on a tout hunt, that there was an informer in West Belfast, and that Maureen O'Dalaigh had come to sniff him out. She was known for that, among other things. For laying the finger on traitors and seeing they were put out of the way. For interrogating any poor bastard that had given cause for suspicion, and getting the truth out of him whatever it cost. She was harder than any man among them. Her well-cut clothes and expensive hair-do had never stood in her way.

'You can put your minds at rest,' were her first words. 'I'm not here looking for anybody. What I am here for is to give you your orders for tonight's mission. In the ordinary way of things, that'd be the job of your OC, who'd get his instructions from the Brigade Adjutant. But this goes higher than Brigade level, and for reasons you'll understand in a minute, your orders have to come direct.

'Now, first things first. If anyone asks, I haven't been here tonight. You've never seen me, not here, not anywhere. You'll say nothing to anyone about the orders you're about to receive, or the mission itself. And I don't just mean outsiders, I mean any friends you may have in the movement, and your own families. Any hint of loose talk and the entire unit will be executed. Do I make myself clear?'

Gearóid felt a chill pass through him. She was not even offering them the option of leaving. They were soldiers fighting a war, and to leave would be desertion.

'Conor's got your weapons in a car outside. They're all clean as a whistle. I had them from a special shipment that was brought in yesterday. You don't need to know where they came from. But you can relax. They haven't been in a cache, and the Brits haven't come within a mile of jarking them.'

Jarking was an army term for tampering with illegal weapons, usually by planting small homing devices in the stock. The RUC or the army would get word of an arms cache, through a tout, and take the weapons off to be doctored. It had happened a lot in the seventies, less often of late. More than one volunteer had lost his life as a result of such tricks.

'The car was taken a couple of hours ago from outside a house on the Stranmillis Road. The owner's on holiday, so it won't be missed for a week or two. Conor has the man's driving licence and papers.'

O'Dalaigh paused and looked at each of them again. She was a cold bastard, thought Gearóid: you could see it right enough in her eyes. She spoke fancy too, with an accent, but better educated than the rest of them. He'd heard she was a lawyer or something. He wondered what the others were thinking. Something big was up, that was for sure. Jesus, and he could have been in Bangor.

'You are to drive down to Malone House in the south of the city. It's at the entrance to Barnett Park, near Shaw's Bridge. Conor here'll go over it all with you on the map. You'll be carrying FNC assault rifles with night-sights – Conor tells me you're all experienced in the use of them. You're to go out for a recce in half an hour, so you can see the place in daylight. Then you hold off until after dark.

'But I want you in position by eleven o'clock. Not a minute later – if you are held back for any reason and you can't make it by eleven, the mission's aborted. Is that clear? Good.

'Around twelve o'clock, you'll hear an army patrol coming down the Malone Road. One Shorland, no back-up. As well as the soldiers, there'll be four civilians in another vehicle. They're your targets. Once they're out of their car, you're to open fire. Shoot to kill, and take your time about it.'

She continued with the briefing, talking slowly, making sure they understood. None of them, herself included, would ever be sent out on a more important mission, and it was vital there were no slips of any kind.

'Right now,' she said, drawing to a close. 'I want you to listen carefully. After what happens tonight, you are dead men if you stay in Belfast. You have to disappear. No-one's to see hilt nor hair of you for a year at least. You'll be taken straight across the border tonight. I don't want anyone knowing where you've gone, and be sure none of you tries to get in touch with your families. They'll be told you're all right and still on active service. Once things settle down, I'll arrange for letters to be passed.

'Now, is there anything I've not made clear?'

There was a tense silence. It was hot in the little room. On the wall, a picture of the Sacred Heart glinted redly. From outside, the voices of children playing came in waves: the next generation of heroes and martyrs scrabbling on paving-stones, writing names in chalk that would one day be carved in marble. And a dog barking high and quickly, and the low, familiar growl of a Hotspur Land Rover on patrol.

'How long?' asked O'Driscoll.

'How long for what?'

'You know right enough. How long before I can see my weans again? They're just settling down now in school. It's barely a year since their mother was killed.'

It was Melaugh who answered him.

'Colm,' he said, 'I know well enough this is hard on you. But there's no choice. If the weans was to come after you, they'd be followed. You know that as well as I do. I'm sorry this was sprung on you, but we couldn't take any risks. I only knew myself earlier today. You don't have to come on the mission. There's no-one here'll think any the worse of you if you don't. You've given plenty to the cause.'

O'Driscoll looked steadily at his OC. He knew the man was talking a load of twaddle. You didn't walk away from a mission

15

at this level. If there was a word whispered about it anywhere, you'd be the first with a bullet in your head. And then who'd take care of the weans? He said nothing more.

Gearóid Lalor slumped back into his chair. He knew he was in some indefinable danger, that he was face to face at last with the brightness of martyrdom. This was something none of them would ever get out of. He looked across the room at Colm O'Driscoll and thought of another poem the man buried in Sligo had written. It made him want to weep, the beauty of the thing.

> The Horses of Disaster plunge in the heavy clay:
> Beloved, let your eyes half close, and your heart beat
> Over my heart, and your hair fall over my breast . . .

And he thought about dulse, and dancing, and fish and chips, and Noreen's hand and Noreen's lips and Noreen's breasts that he'd touched so rarely, and her heart that had beaten so seldom over his heart, wondering how it was that all things grew dark and ragged at the coming of night.

CHAPTER TWO

A light summer rain had come and gone, cutting the day in two, leaving the night humid and uncomfortable. The grass where they lay in wait was damp; not far away the river touched the air with a moist breath.

Conor Melaugh was grateful for the wet. In the summer months, the little park was popular with couples looking for a little more privacy than the average nightclub afforded. He had anticipated problems in setting an ambush even as late as this. Now, he was sure there was no-one within a radius of five hundred yards except himself and his men.

There was a rare silence all round them, into which random thoughts dropped, as though into still water. Melaugh watched clouds circle the moon. He imagined he could hear Seamus Lenihan breathing nervously a few yards away. Tension was building as midnight drew near.

Melaugh had been a full-time volunteer for seven years now, an officer commanding his own Active Service Unit for three. He had seen men come and go in that time – shot, arrested, taken for touts and executed, or just plain scared and running. Jesus, but he was scared himself tonight, who wouldn't be? He had never been given instructions like these before, had never sat through a queerer briefing.

But the queerness of the operation was only half of it. What bothered him most was the end of it, the thing he had to do, the thing that stuck in his throat like clay. But there was no way out, there never was. O'Dalaigh had driven the point home, as if it needed reinforcing. She was a hard bitch, that one, she'd put a bullet in your head as soon as shake your hand. Her reputation went ahead of her: she was not a woman to be crossed, not if you valued your life and the lives of your family. If he disobeyed orders, she'd make him an example people would remember the length and breadth of Ireland.

They lay in a flat semi-circle facing the front of Malone House. Melaugh held the centre, with Lenihan to his left and Colm O'Driscoll beyond him at the entrance. On the right were Eugene O'Malley, the music-man, flanked by young Gearóid Lalor. Maureen O'Dalaigh had laid on a sixth man to drive the van, parked several yards up Dub Lane, ready for a quick getaway through the Upper Malone and straight down Finaghy Road to Ladybrook.

Gearóid was still thinking of Noreen, and intermittently of the night out he had missed. Not that, in truth, he had ever enjoyed much of a social life. He belonged to a staunchly Republican family, one that had given martyrs to the cause, and his childhood and youth had been committed in one way or another to the movement.

He smelled the night air and thought of Noreen again, then found himself squirming to get comfortable on the wet ground. He'd been brought up to believe in destiny: the destiny of Ireland, that would one day be free, his own destiny as a soldier fighting for that freedom. But it was hard to think of the ballads and to picture yourself as a man of destiny, striding at the head of the masses with an Armalite held high, when reality was a wet field and your knees aching as you waited to kill a man or be killed in the doing of it. He held his breath against the raw damp and the muddy smell of the ground.

At thirty seconds to midnight, they heard a Norland approaching from the Malone Road, then turning into the short approach road that led down to Malone House. A much lighter vehicle accompanied it. Military precision. At midnight, the little convoy drew up at the front steps of the house, and the engines fell silent almost simultaneously.

The car was either a Jaguar or a Daimler, it was impossible to say which in the darkness. Nor did it matter. As Conor Melaugh watched through his night-sight, the rear door of the Norland opened and a patrol of six soldiers wearing flak jackets and carrying H & K MP5s jumped to the ground, two at a time. A detachment from B Company, attached to Belfast Roulement Battalion (OPCON BRB), or so O'Dalaigh had said.

As they got into position, the driver of the car got out and quickly opened the remaining doors. Four passengers stepped down, three men and a woman. Like the driver, they were dressed in civilian clothes. So far, everything was as Melaugh had been told it would be.

The four civilians started towards the house, and the driver started to close the doors of his vehicle.

Melaugh let a couple of seconds pass: he wanted the entire team to have a clear line of fire. He targeted the woman and eased back on the trigger. There was a sharp report and the woman jerked forward hard as though a brick had hit her. The men beside her started to turn, and they seemed to move in slow motion, each in a different direction, confused, their hands lifting, their heads turning, three stark silhouettes against a stone façade. And in mid-turn they twitched as though hidden fingers had pulled strings and hurled them to the ground.

Beside the Norland the soldiers stood and watched. Exactly as promised, they did not move a muscle, not even when O'Malley walked to the steps and riddled the prone bodies of the victims with round upon round of sub-machine gun fire. Melaugh saw the looks on their faces, distorted by the otherworldly glow of the night-sight. He was looking straight into their eyes, and they knew he was looking, and he knew they would kill him if they only could. Their faces were portraits of impotent rage and a terrible, deep hatred. Some of their fathers had fought in the long war too.

When the last burst of machine-gun fire echoed across the park, Conor got to his feet. He felt tired and he felt afraid. What if, after all, it was a double-cross within a double-cross? He wouldn't have put it past O'Dalaigh and her like to offer up an entire ASU as a sacrifice for whatever had been achieved tonight.

Eugene O'Malley rejoined the others.

'Let's get the hell out of here, lads.'

They regrouped and hared down the lane to the van. The engine was running, ready to take off. No-one wanted to hang around. Even if the patrol back at the house stuck by their agreement, there would soon be others, both RUC and army, who would cut them down without questions or remorse.

'It's to make it look right,' Maureen O'Dalaigh had said to Conor during the briefing that afternoon. 'It would never be believed that the army opened fire and hit no-one. They'll need a body to parade before the media, some sort of compensation for the unholy mess you and the boys will make.'

'You want to sacrifice one of our own volunteers just to save their face?' He had been deeply angry even then.

She had shaken her head.

'No, not to save face. To save the whole job from being blown. That one death will make it seem real, will convince the authorities that the Brits opened fire while you were there. It has to be like that, Conor. I'm sorry, but that's how it is.'

And that's how it was right now. As they came to the van, Conor was next to Gearóid Lalor. He'd seen they were together.

'Jesus, Gearóid,' he said, the words sticking in his throat. 'I've left the fucking Browning behind. Will you go back quick and get it for me while I get the lads into the van? You can't miss it: it's next to that big tree over there. The soldiers are watching us closely, they know who you are.'

'Right you are, Conor. I'll only be a wee minute.'

Conor didn't watch. But he heard the shots well enough when the bastards opened up. By the time they finished, they must have filled the wee lad with enough bullets to make a length of lead pipe. Conor felt sick and angry and confused.

'Let's get out of here,' he said.

And he could still hear Gearóid's voice ringing in his ears. 'I'll only be a wee minute.'

CHAPTER THREE

Area Metropolitan Police HQ
Harcourt Street
Dublin
4 September
0915 hours

Declan Carberry had woken with a headache for the fourth morning in a row. There'd been three the week before. Five the week
before that. 'The Grinder', 'The Thumper', and, more often than
not, 'The Detonator'. He had names for all of them, and he'd
started counting. Next thing he'd be keeping a log. Onset, duration, intensity, possible cause. He'd have to call on Brannigan
at this rate, but it was the last thing he wanted to do. Brannigan
was the sort of doctor who liked pushing people about. 'Take a
drop of this, swallow that, stop the other.' He'd be sure to order
Declan to take time off work, and that was something he could
not afford to do right now. And not next month. Or next year,
for that matter.

And, then, Brannigan was inclined to talk, to probe. 'Did anything happen before the headaches began?'. 'Is there anything in
particular that triggers them off?' The man fancied himself as
some sort of counsellor, in his old brogues and the Aran sweater
he wore in the surgery. 'Are you feeling anxious. Tense? Have
you any special worries? When did you last have sex?'

Jesus, Declan thought, leaning across his desk and picking up
the report on the bombing at O'Donoghue's, he knew perfectly
well what was wrong with him, and there were no nostrums
Brannigan could give him that would make things better.

A child could have explained Declan Carberry's headaches: a

21

wife he no longer loved but could not divorce; a tendency to overwork; and a job as head of the Special Detective Unit, the Irish Republic's Special Branch, with special responsibility for counter-terrorism. He was surprised it was only tension headaches. Men of his age, with his problems, dropped dead every day of the week from heart attacks. Maybe he had a brain tumour.

Even if they changed the law on divorce – which seemed as remote a prospect as ever – he would be none the better off. He still would not be able to divorce Concepta. It was bad enough that the woman had grown to be everything he detested – flashy and smug and wilful and self-pitying; but Concepta was the Taoiseach's sister. Or, to put it historically, her brother, Pádraig Pearse Mangan, had raised himself by slow degrees from chicken farmer to TD for Limerick West, to leader of Fianna Fáil, to Prime Minister.

So, even if divorce had been legal, Pádraig Pearse would never have permitted it for his sister. Concepta was one of the great man's brightest assets. She appeared at party functions, organized charity balls, entertained visiting statesmen and diplomats, and had very nearly taken up residence on the set of the Late Late Show. Gay Byrne loved her. Pat Kelly adored her. She was nearly as popular as the President. Every year at Christmas, the pair of them turned up at the family home outside Limerick, to be photographed with aged parents, cousins, nephews, and nieces.

Pádraig Pearse (he insisted on both names, and why not?) was a widower. The sainted Geraldine had been speeded to her eternal rest by cancer five years earlier, whereupon Concepta, ever with an eye to the main chance, stepped into the breach and sacrificed all for Ireland. 'My brother needs me' was her constant cry. Her only daughter was a grown woman, her husband was a busy man, so her brother and his party came first and last.

Declan sat still for a while until his head stopped spinning. When he was younger, he could at least put this sort of morning down to heavy drinking the night before; but he'd been going easy on the sauce for a couple of years now and hadn't touched so much as a drop last night. Maybe that was what was wrong. Maybe it was time he went back to the bottle after all. His body was telling him something, that was undeniable. More's the pity that it chose to speak in a foreign language.

Seven dead and thirty injured, and all Declan Carberry could think about was that his wife did not love him. He groaned and started going over the report for the fourth time.

The bomb had gone off in O'Donoghue's bar in Merrion Row at a couple of minutes after nine two nights ago. To make matters worse, the place had been packed with tourists, Americans and English among them, and the fallout from that was only beginning. He had meetings to come at the British and American embassies, and if some of the injured died, you could add the French and Dutch to the list. Over at the Department of Foreign Affairs on St Stephen's Green, the new Minister, Ciaran Clark, was fielding enquiries from all sides. He'd been on the phone to Declan a dozen times the day before, asking for assurances.

'Assurances?' Declan had protested. 'What the hell do you mean "assurances"?'

'That there'll be no more incidents. That you have the situation under control. Jesus, man, this could kill the tourist trade for the rest of the season. And there's the presidency of the European Commission coming up next year. We have to be able to tell people abroad this won't happen again.'

'Ciaran, I'm not Jesus Christ.'

'I never thought you were. But you are the head of the Special Detective Unit, and it's your job to keep terrorism off the streets.'

Declan had taken overall responsibility for the investigation, rather than leaving it in the hands of one of his superintendents. Two of them, Coyle and Grogan, were working closely with him, and he himself was reporting directly to the Garda Commissioner; but he'd made the bombing his personal responsibility, and he was regretting it already.

A patrol car left Area Headquarters with its siren blaring. Declan sighed and tossed the report aside. He couldn't concentrate. If it wasn't Ciaran Clark, it was his blessed brother-in-law. P P had been on the phone a few times yesterday. He was never as demanding as the Foreign Minister; but then he didn't need to be.

The phone rang, and Declan braced himself for another day spent fending off enquiries. It wasn't real police work, and he wanted to be out at the scene of the crime or wherever else the investigation was leading. He could feel the headache moving up a gear.

Meanwhile, seven innocent people were lying in coffins, and

23

thirty more were in hospital, some without faces, some without limbs, several without any hope of coming out alive. He had their names and ages and photographs in his report, he had details of their injuries, and they were whirling in his head like pieces of dust in space. Some of them had been younger than his daughter, Máiréad. And they all had families. He picked up the phone.

'Carberry.'

'Declan, this is Austin McKeown. Have you got a wee minute?'

Declan sat up straight. Austin McKeown was head of the RUC Special Branch's E3 Division, responsible for intelligence within Northern Ireland. He and Declan met regularly to review cross-border security, and over the years they had become close friends. Not too close, of course; as Declan had been reminded more than once, the Taoiseach's brother-in-law chooses his friends carefully.

Austin had already been in touch within an hour of the bombing. The RUC had set afoot their own investigation, since it was almost certain the bomb had been planted by a Loyalist group based in the North.

'How's about ye, Austin?' Declan always enjoyed mocking the other man's Northern accent.

'I'm well enough, Declan. Listen, are you free today round lunchtime?'

'I can make a space, certainly.'

'I'll be coming down. I'd like to see you.'

'Well, a meeting would be useful at this stage. Why don't you just come over here to Harcourt Street?'

There was a brief hesitation. When he spoke, Declan could detect an unaccustomed nervousness in McKeown's voice.

'I'd rather see you alone, Declan, if you don't mind. Is there somewhere else we could meet?'

Declan thought quickly.

'Be at Bewley's on Grafton Street at one. Downstairs.'

'I'll be there. And, Declan – please don't mention this to anyone.'

The nervousness again, as though he was watching over his shoulder.

'Is this about O'Donoghue's, Austin?'

'I can't speak on the phone. I'll tell you when I see you.'

The Northerner hung up. Declan put down his receiver gently

and sat back. He had never heard Austin McKeown so tense before. What was going on?

The phone rang. Declan felt his headache return with renewed vigour. He picked up the receiver.

'Carberry.'

'Daddy, it's me.'

He relaxed. It was always a pleasure to hear Máiréad's voice. He heard it too little these days. She'd left home a year ago, after finding a job with Bord Fáilte, the Tourist Board, and had settled happily into a little flat in Ballsbridge. He'd wanted her to go to college, but she'd preferred the independence of her own income. Anyhow, she'd said, people these days started university later, and a little experience of the world never did anyone any harm.

'How are you, love?'

'I'm fine, Daddy; but I'd like to see you.'

He groaned inwardly. There was nothing he'd like better than to see Máiréad, but he already had his plate full for today, and the rest of the week was likely to be horrendous, especially if Austin McKeown turned out to have a lead for him.

'I'd love to, Máiréad, but you know I'm tied up with Monday night's bombing.'

'It'll only take a few minutes, half an hour at most.'

'Darling, I don't know when I was last this busy.'

'You were busy last month, then there was the gun-running thing in June.' She paused. She sounded tired and close to tears. 'Daddy, I need to see you.'

'Is something wrong, Máiréad? You sound upset.'

'I'm all right. But this is important. I get off work at five. Can I see you then?'

He sighed.

'I'll pick you up.'

He could have picked Austin McKeown out anywhere, even in a smoke-filled room. The Ulsterman always wore the same suit when he came to Dublin, he'd been wearing it ever since he and Declan first met. It was a green suit, cut by a tailor in Limavady, Austin's home town, and it made the poor man resemble a farmer out for the day at the Balmoral Show. Declan had always pitied him for the suit, but he liked the man too much to tell him so.

Bewley's was crowded, but they managed to squeeze

themselves into a corner. It looked as though half of Dublin had packed themselves inside and as if the rest were in the queue waiting to get in.

'I'll say this for them,' Austin said, as he manoeuvred himself onto his chair and his tray onto the table. 'They make a grand loaf of bread here. I bought one the last time I was down, and the wife never stopped about it for weeks. "When are you in Dublin again?" she kept asking me, "I'd like another of them loaves."'

They talked of bread and cakes for a while, and sipped hot tea while they played with the food on their plates. Neither man was hungry, and Declan's headache had settled down to what he called 'The Grinder'. He was hoping it would stay there; stage two, 'The Thumper', was a killer. Ciaran Clark had been on the phone three times, the Justice Minister twice, and the Taoiseach once.

'What brings you to Dublin, Austin?' he asked at last.

McKeown drained his tea and set the cup down ringingly on its saucer. He was a farmer's son, thin, with a scrawny neck that would have looked equally at home in a dog collar or an Orange collarette. His loud countryman's voice drew attention at nearby tables.

'I've heard the grounds of Trinity College are very fine at this time of year, Declan.'

'They are indeed, though it's hard enough to see them for tourists. Would you like me to show you round?'

'I'd appreciate that.'

It was a short walk. Austin said nothing until they were through the main gate of the college and into the first courtyard. Students preparing for the September examinations mixed with tourists in search of the Book of Kells.

'I'm awful sorry about the cloak-and-dagger stuff, Declan, but I'd rather we kept on the move.'

'There's no need to apologize. We're in the same business. I'd be nervous if I was in your part of the country.' Declan's Special Detective Unit had until a few years earlier been known as the Special Branch, and its work paralleled that of its Northern equivalent and others on the UK mainland: the surveillance and prevention of internal subversion and terrorism.

'Look, Declan, before I tell you what's on my mind, I need

your agreement that you'll make no effort to trace my source or do anything that might jeopardize me or my colleagues.'

'For God's sake, Austin, that goes without saying . . .'

'And that you'll say not a word of this to anyone else. If it gets out that I tol' you . . .'

Declan shook his head.

'I can't promise you that, Austin; you know I can't, not if it has to do with national security.'

McKeown hesitated, then nodded.

'Aye, right you are. As long as you're careful, then. Don't go shooting your mouth off.'

Declan tried to look wounded by the suggestion. Around them, grey buildings stood like monuments against a cracked sky. A young woman went past them carrying books, her hair tied back with a red cord. And a boy in slacks watched her from a corner and did not take his eyes away until she was gone through an open doorway.

'It's about O'Donoghue's, isn't it, Austin?' Declan asked, trying to ease his friend into whatever it was he had come to say.

The thin man nodded slowly and knotted his hands. He looked uncomfortable in his winter suit. A beleaguered Protestant in the land of the Papists, at bay and without resources.

'You'll mind,' he began, 'that there was a shooting in Belfast a couple of weeks ago, on the sixteenth of August. Three men and a woman, and one Provisional IRA gunman caught in the crossfire.'

Declan nodded.

'Yes, I know of the incident. Near the Lagan, wasn't it? We have men looking for the ASU in all border areas.'

'I doubt you'll find them. They'll be deep under cover by now. It wasn't an ordinary shooting.'

The official story fed to Declan through RUC headquarters at Knock was that the four victims had been civil servants from Ofwat, the body responsible for supervision of Britain's regional water authorities. They had been in Belfast to set up a nitrate-testing programme, and it was thought they had been mistaken for off-duty soldiers.

'I'd already guessed that much,' said Declan. 'For one thing, I never believed the army patrol just happened to be passing at the time of the ambush.'

McKeown nodded unhappily. He hadn't been responsible for the cover story, and he'd known it wouldn't withstand even casual scrutiny.

'I presume,' Declan went on, 'that the four victims really belonged to a more elite organization than Ofwat. I'd put my money on 5, since 6 doesn't seem to be getting up to much in the province these days.'

'Well, you're right. And not just common-or-garden MI5 neither. The woman was the Deputy Director-General herself, Jean Whitmarsh. The three men were from T Branch – the Branch Director and two former F5 officers.'

Declan grasped his meaning at once. MI5's increasingly powerful T Branch dealt in the main with counter-terrorism. Among the old divisions it had taken over had been F5, originally responsible for monitoring Irish terrorism.

'They'd been flown in to attend a meeting at Malone House,' McKeown continued. 'I'm told they were due to meet a group of Loyalist leaders, half politicians, half paramilitaries. There was to be a deal set up. I don't know the details, but the bottom line was to guarantee a British military presence in the North for the foreseeable future, at least ten years more.

'The Loyalists were to drop any idea of pulling Northern Ireland out of the United Kingdom. In return, MI5 would supply their paramilitaries with high-grade intelligence on Republicans in general and the re-formed IRA in particular. It had been done before, but this was to be much more sophisticated. They reckoned they could wipe out the IRA within three years.'

Declan whistled.

'Would it have worked?'

McKeown shrugged.

'Hard to say. But it would have stood a good chance.'

'How reliable is your source for all this?'

McKeown rubbed his chin.

'As good as they come. His code-name's Drummer. He belongs to an Orange band, plays the Lambeg drums. Terrible things them, they'll cut a man's hands raw to the knuckle. I've been running him for seven years now, never known him to go wrong.'

'He wouldn't feed you false information?'

McKeown shook his head.

'Never. He's more frightened of me than he is of Old Nick.'

28

'No wonder the IRA risked the ambush. Didn't they try to hit the Loyalists while they were at it?'

'They weren't due for another thirty minutes. And the Provos'll have known well enough that taking out half the Loyalist leadership like that would have led to reprisals they couldn't handle.'

'But O'Donoghue's was a reprisal, wasn't it?'

'Aye, of course. That's why I'm telling you this. I'm warning you not to poke about too deeply. If you dig up too much it could turn nasty.'

'It's nasty already.'

'It could get worse. I'm just suggesting you go through the motions for the moment. When we're able, we'll find somebody suitable for you to pin it on.'

'You're warning me off the top people, is that it?'

Austin shook his head.

'Don't misunderstand me, Declan. You've always dealt fairly with me in the past, and I hope I've been as straight with you. I'm not warning you off anybody. I'd like to lay my hands on those bastards myself, believe you me. But this is something that could blow up in both our faces. I can't prove it, but I'm certain the army patrol guarding the victims had been given orders to stand aside. The forensic evidence doesn't match up. But try sticking your finger into that pie.'

'That's precisely what I have to do, Austin. It's what I'm paid to do. The same as you.'

'No, men like you and me, we're paid to keep the peace, not to go poking our noses where they aren't wanted. Believe me, probing into this business could spark off a backlash you wouldn't believe. On both sides of the border. If you'll take my advice, you'll concentrate on tracking down that ASU and leave these other boyos to me and those that know how to deal with them.'

'What if one thing just leads me to another?'

'You don't get it, do you, Declan? Next time it won't be a bomb in a pub. Next time it could be you they go for.'

'Let's say they do. And let's say I come out of it alive. Who do I go to for more information? You?'

McKeown shook his head hard.

'I'm keeping myself out of this from now on.' He hesitated. 'But if things get out of hand in any way, there is one man you could go to.'

29

'Who might that be?'

The Ulsterman hesitated again.

'Declan, if I give you this man's name, you have to promise me not to write it down and not to pass it on to anyone else. Anyone.'

'All right. I'll keep it to myself.'

'His name's Wetherell, Captain Richard Wetherell. He's with British military intelligence, with 14th Int at Lisburn. I'll give you his direct number. About a year ago he was given a special brief to look into this sort of thing. Give it a wee while, Declan. Let things cool down. And for God's sake, be very careful how you make contact with him.'

CHAPTER FOUR

Dublin
4 September
1748 hours

'I'm pregnant, Daddy.'

The words hung in the air like little bombs, primed to go off. He closed his eyes, holding on for a precious few moments longer to the belief that his daughter was still a child and that the problem she'd come to speak to him about was no more than a telling off from one of the Sisters at school.

He opened his eyes, and she was still sitting there, across the table from him, not a child, but an anxious young woman in a grey suit, in need of his help and understanding. He wanted to reach out and hold her, tell her everything would be all right, that he would look after her. Paradoxically, his mind filled with words like 'slut' and 'whore', but he realized they were in his own father's voice, and he shut them out before they could do further damage.

'Who's the father?' he asked. 'Michael?'

She nodded and put down the long spoon she had been holding. He had picked her up at the main Bord Fáilte office in O'Connell Street and taken her to a small ice-cream parlour nearby. He understood now that it had been an unconscious gesture; it was a place he had taken her often as a child.

'You'll be getting married then?' He felt disappointment rise up in him as he said the words. Michael had never impressed him much, he was not the sort of man he had envisaged for his beloved daughter.

Máiréad shook her head slowly and lifted one hand to brush

the long hair out of her eyes. He could see that she was close to tears.

'No, Daddy, we're not planning on getting married. In fact, I'm not sure we'll be together that much longer. We're not really suited to one another.'

'Jesus,' he exclaimed, 'it's a bit late to be thinking about that now, isn't it?' But he felt relief wash over him all the same.

She looked at him candidly, knowing he must already be kicking himself for what he'd just said.

'Is it, Daddy? Better now than later on. Don't you think?'

He said nothing. She'd had to live most of her life putting up with his own failures in that department.

'Look, Daddy, I want this baby. I'm excited about it, really I am. I just don't want to marry Michael. The reason I'm telling you now is to avoid problems later. Mother would have me off to England for an abortion, but I don't want that. Uncle Pádraig – well, he won't want me around in case the press get hold of the story. You'll remember he made that speech to the Dáil earlier this year, condemning one-parent families as unnatural.'

'Indeed, I do. Fornication, contraception, abortion, and one-parent families. I believe the eating of ice cream is high on his list too. Ah, well, but he's very fond of you. I'll have a word with him. It's your mother I'm worried about. She'll hit the roof. But, then, you know that yourself.' He paused. 'When's the baby due?'

'The first week in February.'

'You've known for four months, then?'

She shrugged.

'More or less. It hasn't started to show yet. But it will before long, and I'm worried Mother will guess.'

'I'll have a word with her tonight.' He hesitated. 'Máiréad, you won't like this I know, but I think going to England may not be such a bad idea. You should think about it. Is there any hope of your getting a transfer to Bord Fáilte's London office?'

Austin McKeown changed into second gear, ready to stop at the checkpoint ahead. He'd had a long drive back, and he still had a meeting tonight at Army HQ in Lisburn. There'd been a diversion after Dromore, but he expected to be turning back towards Hillsborough any minute now.

All the way back, he'd been thinking over his conversation

with Declan Carberry. No-one in his own office knew he'd gone down to Dublin, and there'd be awkward questions if they did. But he couldn't have left things to sort themselves out. Carberry was sharp, and he had good investigators working under him. If anything, Southern intelligence was better than that in the North. Austin McKeown was one of the few people who knew just how badly the Chinook disaster back in June '94 had been for Northern Ireland security.

The helicopter had crashed on the Mull of Kintyre, en route to a conference in Inverness. It had been carrying six MI5 officers, including the Deputy Director-General; ten RUC officers, including an Assistant Chief Constable and two Detective Chief Superintendents; and eight soldiers, including the Assistant Chief of Staff at Army HQ, one colonel, two lieutenant colonels, and five majors. Between them, they had carried a wealth of intelligence data and irreplaceable inside knowledge. The system had never recovered from their deaths.

That had left the field open to mavericks like the bunch of MI5 operatives who'd tried to set up the deal with the Loyalist paramilitaries. And Austin knew that, if Declan Carberry and his team started digging into the real facts behind the bomb in Dublin, they couldn't help finding leads that would take them to the guilty men, if only because security was so poor. He also knew that, if Declan got that far, the Taoiseach wasn't the sort of man to let sleeping dogs lie. Except that these were dogs that would tear a man's throat out without a murmur.

He saw four Ulster Defence Regiment soldiers up ahead, standing in front of their Land Rover. Glancing in his rear-view mirror, he noticed to his surprise that the small queue that had been behind him since Dromore had disappeared. Up ahead, the road was empty.

Jimmy Bryce quickened his step. He didn't want to be late for the meeting, didn't want to draw particular attention to himself. Half his mind was on that, and the other half on the job that was waiting for him in Glasgow, if he could get the wife to agree to the move. She wouldn't like it, she hated change of any kind, but if he could get as far as Glasgow he could maybe move down to England after a while and get himself clear of everything once and for all. By 'everything', he meant his double life as a quartermaster for the Ulster Defence Association and a police informer.

He thought Austin McKeown would let him go, maybe even help him out. Hadn't he passed on enough information to the man over the years? And hadn't that recent stuff on MI5 been worth something?

He turned into the Woodstock Road. He'd seen no-one he knew out on the street tonight, save Mrs Maguire on her way to the off-licence. His eldest son had a good job with a firm of engineers in Glasgow, and he'd written a couple of days ago to say they were in need of a competent electrician. He'd have to let Brian know by the end of the week, they wouldn't hold the job for ever. His mind was as good as made up; he'd go if he could talk Annie round and get his bill of leave from the peelers. They'd squeezed him dry, they owed him a new life. He was only fifty-one, he had years in him yet.

The door opened at his knock and he went straight inside. There were four of them in the little room, Cairns, Brown, Massey, and Martin.

'What's up,' he said. 'Yous all look like yous've swallowed a lemon.'

Tommy McCracken closed the door behind him.

'Sit down, Jimmy,' he said. 'There's a few questions we'd like to ask you.'

Declan sighed. All round them, couples and families talked and laughed while they spooned up ice cream from tall glass goblets. The lighting was bright, everything glistened.

'Go to England? Jesus, Daddy, you'd think this was the nineteen fifties.'

He looked round. He'd come to the same ice-cream parlour as a child. It had not changed much.

'In some ways it is,' he said. He glanced in the mirror opposite, saw a man on his own, dressed in an anorak. Was it his imagination, or had he been watching them?

'We'll speak to her together,' he said. 'But your timing couldn't be worse. Your mother and I had a flaming row yesterday. I've told her I'm thinking of moving out.'

'Oh, for heaven's sake, Daddy, not again.'

'It's bad this time, love. If it weren't for the blessed Pádraig and the impact it might have on the next election, I think she'd have me out bag and baggage.'

'Uncle Pádraig wouldn't try to stop you, would he?'

'Not in so many words . . .'

Declan glanced in the mirror without moving his head. The man in the anorak had changed tables. He was closer to them than before. Declan changed his own position imperceptibly, so he could watch without making it obvious he was doing so.

'Would you mind stepping out of the car, sir?'

Austin reached inside his jacket for his ID papers.

'My name's McKeown,' he said. 'Detective Superintendent, Special Branch. I'm late for a meeting at Thiepval Barracks.' He handed the papers to the soldier by the open window.

'I'm sure you are, sir. Now, would you mind stepping down?'

The man wasn't local. McKeown could tell from his accent that he came from Belfast. Hadn't been in the regiment long either, by the look of him.

He opened the door and stepped onto the tarmac. It was a narrow road, bordered by elms. On a tree opposite, someone had nailed a tin sign on which were painted the words: JESUS IS SAVIOUR.

'Who's your commanding officer?' he asked. 'This roadblock hasn't been set up properly at all.'

The soldier ignored him. Austin looked round. It was strange. There should have been more traffic on a diversion between two busy towns.

'Where are you coming from, sir?' asked the soldier.

'That's classified. Now, I don't have any more time to waste. Hand back my papers and let me get on to my meeting.'

The soldier shook his head.

'That won't be possible, sir.'

'What the hell do you mean?'

In answer, the soldier raised his weapon. It was a sub-machine gun, but one of unusual manufacture, being, if anything, shorter than an Uzi. Wherever it had come from, it wasn't standard issue. The soldier took the gun in both hands and opened fire. The last thing Austin McKeown saw was the sign on the tree opposite, tilting and then spinning away from him into a red field.

The soldier emptied his magazine, turned on his heel, and

35

walked slowly back to the vehicle in which he and his companions had come. High above, a helicopter circled, then dipped and sped off into the distance.

He felt numb. He wanted to be sick, but the numbness got in the way. The other men in the room were all his friends, but he knew that not one of them would lift a finger to help him. They'd known the lot. He'd caught sight of a thick RUC file with his code-name on it, 'The Drummer'. It would all be in there, every last detail of the information he'd passed on to Austin McKeown, the name of every man he'd ever betrayed to the security forces. It was pointless even to ask for mercy.

'It won't take long, Jimmy,' said Billy Cairns. He'd known Billy all his life, since they were wee lads playing football together on the Ravenhill Road. 'Don't make it hard on yourself. It's not easy for us either, you know that.'

'Am I . . . Am I allowed to write something? A wee word for Annie and the boys.'

'I don't think there's time, Jimmy. I'm sorry.'

The door opened and a tall man walked into the room. Jimmy had expected him. His real name was Raymond Hughes, and he was a plasterer by trade; but in the UDA he was known as the Hangman. He nodded at Jimmy as he entered. Jimmy had seen him at work more than once, he knew exactly what was coming. It was the worst feeling in the world, to be here and to know that he would not leave this horrid little room alive.

'Would you mind taking off your tie, Jimmy, and unbuttoning your collar?'

His shaking hands did as he was told. The next moment, the men on either side of him had pinned his arms behind his back.

'I won't make a fuss,' he said, though he badly wanted to.

'That's good, Jimmy,' said the Hangman.

From his pocket he drew out a length of thick piano wire, its two ends soldered to metal handles.

'Don't worry, Jimmy. This'll be quick.'

But nothing in Jimmy Bryce's life had ever taken as long.

The man moved to the next table. He had no ice cream in front of him, no coffee. He started to unzip his anorak.

Declan stopped talking and leaned forward.

'Don't ask questions, Máiréad. When I tell you to, just get up and go ahead of me to the door.'

'Daddy, what's the matter?'

'Just do as I say. Get up now.'

Declan stood. Máiréad hesitated, then followed suit. Out of the corner of his eye, Declan could see the man pulling his anorak open. Máiréad was in the aisle between them and the next table. Declan turned and saw the man pull a small sub-machine gun from a pouch inside the anorak.

Without thinking, Declan hurled himself on Máiréad, throwing her hard to the ground. Half a second later, a burst of automatic fire swept the space where they had been standing. Bullets bounced off the marble-topped tables, spilling milk shakes and ice creams. Others thudded into flesh. People were screaming, some trying to get out from the cages of chairs and tables within which they were sitting, others pushing their children down. The man in the anorak ejected a magazine and rammed a fresh one into the gun.

Declan twisted, pushing Máiréad further beneath the nearest table. As he did so, he could see the gunman's legs, swivelling as he turned in their direction. The man took a step forward. A teenager near the door got up to run for help. The gunman let off a burst of rapid fire that took him in the back, throwing him against a mirror in a shower of splintering glass. Declan reached inside his jacket and pulled out the Browning HP automatic he carried everywhere.

He rolled, shouting to draw the gunman's attention away from Máiréad. He saw the man's legs turn again, then, taking careful aim, fired twice, taking the man in the upper thigh.

The gunman fell heavily. Declan twisted, pushing himself upright with his left hand, keeping the gun steady in his right. Getting to his feet, he was disorientated. All around him was a scene of chaos and terror. He looked down at the spot where he had expected the gunman to be. It was empty.

Turning, he saw the man in the next aisle, rising on his good leg, balancing with one arm on a chair while he raised the gun with the other. Declan raised his pistol just as the man started to fire again. The first burst went wide, then the gunman retrieved his balance and got off a single round that took Declan in the left arm. Declan still had control of the Browning. Using his right hand, he fired twice in quick succession. The second shot hit the gunman's wrist, knocking the gun from his hand.

Declan shouted, instructing the man to put his hands to his head. At that moment, a small boy, terrified by the shooting, ran between them, howling for his mother. The gunman saw his chance and took it, limping for the door. No-one tried to stop him.

Declan raised his gun, intending to fire, but there were too many people round the entrance. Swearing, he ran after the man, only to see him stumble across the pavement straight through the open door of a waiting car. Declan opened fire as the car accelerated away from the pavement, smashing the rear window and ripping the brake lights to smithereens. But it was useless. The car was already out of reach, weaving through the early evening traffic. Moments later it was out of sight. In the distance he could hear the sound of sirens heading in his direction.

Putting the gun back into its holster, Declan returned to the ice-cream parlour. Chairs and tables had been overturned, glass lay in heaps everywhere, like diamonds on a jeweller's counter, the dead and wounded were strewn across the floor like slaughtered sheep. He picked his way through the mess to the table where he and Máiréad had been sitting. Their ice creams sat incongruously on the table-top, melted but otherwise untouched.

'Máiréad,' he said, bending down, 'it's safe to come out now. He got away, but he won't come back.'

There was no answer. The pain in his arm was starting to burn. He got down on both knees. Out of the corner of his eye, he caught sight of her grey suit. He crawled closer.

'Máiréad, you can get up now, he . . .'

His voice trailed away. With a shaking hand, he reached out to pull away the long spear of glass that had broken from a mirror in the ceiling and gone hurtling, point first, through his daughter's throat. The floor seemed to move beneath him. He tried to call her back, to hold her steady against the dip and swell. But she had gone somewhere he could not follow, somewhere beyond the reach of his voice or his heart.

CHAPTER FIVE

The night passed, dreamlike, but without dreams. The sea was always in the background, its movements guarding his thoughts, its regular murmur insinuating itself into memories of carnage. Short periods of sleep would come, from which he would be snatched by anxiety or pain. Waking at intervals through the night, he would walk across the garden to the edge where it plummeted to the water, and gaze out into the darkness while he listened to the night breathing.

There were lights all along the bay. People lying in bed reading, nurses watching at the beds of the dying, lovers in one another's arms, children mastering their fear of the dark. And ghosts: there would be ghosts down there, pale and trembling, lonely, ill at ease, watching the living as they slept or made love or prayed or slipped close to death, or woke from the endlessness of sleep, or went back into it again. But none of them knew what he knew, that something had come among them blacker than the blackest night. He shivered, but did not think once of going to bed or going indoors for a coat.

Inside, Concepta – the wife who did not love him, whom he did not love – lay awake with her own thoughts. She'd been at a reception when news of Máiréad's death had come through. Declan had not told her. He'd been busy until after midnight, first having his arm seen to in St Laurence's, then at his own office with his colleagues, fighting against grief while he went through the events that had led to Máiréad's killing. Three other people had died in the shooting, and seventeen were wounded, none seriously. To Concepta, they were of minimal importance; all that mattered was that her only child had been murdered.

Her brother Pádraig had brought the news in person, at

Declan's request. The reception had been at Paddy Quinn's, the head of the Electricity Supply Board, and there'd been great excitement at first, when word went round that the Taoiseach himself had come. The gaiety had turned to a frozen silence as those on the fringes of the party saw P P Mangan's face and guessed that there had been a tragedy.

She'd been standing at the centre of a gilded room, a champagne glass in her hand, when she saw him coming towards her, and she'd known at once, she'd dropped the glass to the marble floor, instinct had told her that her daughter was dead. She lay fully dressed on her bed now, clutching Máiréad's favourite doll to her breast, listening to a high sea and the night tide turning. A piece of glass, an invisible thing, had snatched her only child from her. And slowly, slowly, she tore the rag doll to pieces, unaware she did so.

Imperceptibly, the darkness altered. Dawn was not far away. Declan didn't think he could face a new day. His arm would heal, the wound had been a clean one; but the centre of his universe had received a blow from which he knew it would never recover.

The shooting had not been random, he was sure of it. The gunman had been sent there or had chosen to go there for the express purpose of assassinating Declan Carberry. All the other deaths, Máiréad's included, had been incidental. He had spent the night trying to come up with a motive, without getting anywhere. The gunman's face was fixed on his memory, but so far he had been unable to identify him in the files of suspect photographs through which he had ploughed that night until they sent him home.

A footstep crunched on the gravel behind him. He did not look round. Concepta sat on the bench next to him. The sky ahead of them had started to grow pale. The lights of a ship appeared, out past Dalkey Island.

'I couldn't sleep,' Concepta said. They had scarcely spoken since he got back home.

'No,' he said. 'It's hard to sleep.'

In the garden behind them, the smell of night-scented stock was almost overpowering. A bird sang briefly, then another.

'Do you think they'll let me see her?' she asked. 'Before the funeral.'

He nodded.

'She wasn't badly hurt,' he said. 'There'll be no problem. If that's what you'd like.'

'Yes. I'd like to see her.'

He looked round. In the growing light, he could just make out the shape of the house. It seemed massive, massive and empty.

'How's your arm?' she said. 'I never asked.'

'It'll mend. The bullet went through a fleshy part, there's no permanent damage.'

'That's good. I'm glad.'

There was no irony in her voice. Its absence surprised him.

'I could have saved her,' he said. 'If I'd acted sooner, gone for him before he could get his weapon out . . .'

'Shhhh,' she said. She put her arm round him. 'You mustn't blame yourself. You can't know what would have happened.'

'It was me he was after, Concepta. If I hadn't been with her, Máiréad would have been safe.'

'You can't know that.'

'Oh, use your head, woman. Who else in that place was a likely target?'

'Máiréad herself. She was Pádraig Pearse's niece. But please let's not argue.'

'No, you're right. I'm sorry I spoke like that. It's a bloody business all the same.' He paused. 'How's Pádraig taking it?'

'Badly. You know how fond he was of her.'

The Taoiseach had never had children of his own, and from the day she was born he had treated Máiréad as though she were his own daughter.

'I'll see him later today. But I have to go in to the office first.'

'Surely you're not going to work today, Declan?'

'I've placed myself in charge of the investigation. I saw him, I was face to face with him. Believe me, Concepta, I'll not rest till I bring him in.'

She said nothing. She would like to be there, she would like to see his face as well. If she had a gun, she would shoot him.

The paleness in the east was becoming light. In a few minutes, the sun would be with them again.

'Declan,' she whispered, 'I don't want you to go. We were both angry when we talked about separating. But this isn't the time. I'd like you to stay here.'

'This hasn't changed anything between us, Concepta. Máiréad's death won't bring us together.'

'No, I understand that. But . . . for the moment. It's bad enough without the thought of you leaving as well.'

He turned to her. Unconsciously, his hand went to her cheek. It was wet. He stroked it gently. Should he tell her that Máiréad had been pregnant?

'Come inside,' he said. 'You're getting cold.'

CHAPTER SIX

Area Metropolitan Police HQ
Harcourt Street
Dublin
5 September
0845 hours

'This came through first thing this morning, sir. I thought you should see it.'

Tim O'Meara handed Declan a print-out. The message had come through a secure computer link-up connecting Garda HQ with its RUC equivalent.

Declan scanned the page quickly and let it fall to one side. He was so dull this morning that it took several seconds to sink in properly. Austin McKeown had been found riddled with bullets on a side-road near Hillsborough.

He looked slowly round his room. Máiréad's photograph looked down from one wall. On another wall hung a photograph taken at a joint security conference held in Newry five years earlier. Austin McKeown stood in the row just behind Declan, two to the left.

He stood and went to the door.

'Tim,' he said, 'would you mind coming in here a moment?'

A few heads turned. The mood in the office was tense and unsettled. Most of the staff close to Declan had known Máiréad, some since she was a little girl.

'Close the door, Tim. Look, there are a couple of things I'd like you to check for me, only I don't want anyone else knowing about it at the moment.'

'Understood, sir.'

'First, I'd like all you can find out about Austin McKeown's murder. But for God's sake, make it look routine. We don't want anyone to know we've a particular interest in him or his death.'

'Right you are, sir.'

'Second, I want anything you can dig up about a Loyalist informer called The Drummer. The code-name is all I know about him, that and the probability that he was run by Austin McKeown. Be extremely careful how you go about this one. If The Drummer's alive, I want to be able to get to him without exciting suspicion. And if he's dead, I want confirmation as soon as possible.'

'Anything else, sir?'

'Yes, one last thing. Will you ask Grainne to run a search for all ex-MI5 and ex-SAS operatives who may still be active in the North, either on their own account or working for one of the agencies. That includes people known to have connections with one or more of the Loyalist paramilitaries.'

'Looking for anything in particular, sir?'

'I want photographs. The moment she has some, she's to bring them to me.'

'May I ask if this has any connection to . . . to the case we're working on, sir?'

Declan looked at him sympathetically. Tim had been with him a long time. He'd known Máiréad, and he'd known what she meant to Declan.

'No, you may not. If there are any connections, you'll be notified in due course along with the others. Now, get on with it – and make sure you keep your tracks well covered.'

'I want him dead. Not maimed, not beaten, not imprisoned and out again with remission in five or six years, but dead. Hunted down like a rat and killed at the bottom of a wet field. Do you understand me, Declan?'

The Taoiseach thumped a closed fist on his desk to help get his point home. An almost-empty bottle of Bushmills and a dirty glass shook with the force of the blow. Declan didn't need them to tell him that Pádraig Pearse had been drinking heavily. They were in the Taoiseach's office in the north wing of the Government Buildings on Merrion Street.

'Sit down, man, sit down,' Mangan thundered.

Declan sat down. 'It's no more than I want myself, Pádraig.'

'I know it is, Declan, I know.' He stopped abruptly, his voice shaking, looking away until he could find control of himself. 'Jesus, Declan, she was a grand girl. What are we going to do? What are we going to do?'

'I don't know, Pádraig. I can't believe any of this is happening.'

The Taoiseach got up and walked across to a window, his thick figure reduced to a blur by a nimbus of morning light. Pádraig Pearse Mangan was a heavy man who found shaving and keeping his hair in place a strain. The unkempt look endeared him to the farmers and turf-cutters who formed his chief constituency. Declan's brother-in-law was fifty-five, glum-faced, and permanently dumbstruck to find himself sitting in the Taoiseach's office. He was living in a dream, and sometimes it showed.

'Have you any leads yet, Declan?' he asked, turning from the window.

'I have one or two.' Declan was still unsure just how much he should let the Taoiseach know. 'The thing is . . .'

'Yes?'

'It could turn out difficult. Politically, I mean.'

'It was you he was after, is that what you're getting at?'

Declan shook his head.

'No. More than that. I think they were after me on account of something I know. And I think someone else was killed last night for the same reason. The thing is, if I'm right and there is a connection, killing this man isn't going to be the end of it. You may have to make some painful decisions.'

'Well, the investigation has my personal support. If decisions have to be made, I'll make them when the time comes. There'll be a report on my desk every morning until this man is found.' He paused and went back to his seat. Unscrewing the bottle, he poured what was left into the glass and drained it.

'Will you join me in a glass, Declan? There's plenty more where that came from.'

Declan shook his head. He wanted to keep his mind clear.

'Suit yourself.' Pádraig Pearse opened a drawer and took out another bottle. 'Tell me, how's Concepta taking it?'

'Brannigan was over this morning again. She won't have any tranquillizers, but he left some all the same. He thinks she may need a few to tide her over the funeral. We'd like it to be a quiet affair, Pádraig. Just family.'

'That's understandable. I'll see it's taken care of.'

'I want it over with. I want my daughter buried so I can get down to the job of finding the killer.'

Pádraig Pearse seemed ill at ease suddenly. He got up and crossed to the little Georgian fireplace near the door.

'That's what I wanted to talk to you about, Declan. There's a little problem. I had a visit from Seán Roche this morning.'

Roche was the Justice Minister, with responsibility for the Gardaí and Declan's ultimate boss. Declan waited.

'He's taking you off the investigation, Declan.'

'What? But you just said . . .'

'Forget what I said. It's what I want, but you won't be the man to do it. Seán's right. You're personally involved, and that makes you dangerous. You've just told me this could get us into political difficulties.'

Declan clenched his right fist.

'For God's sake, Pádraig, this is outrageous. I'm already in charge of the investigation into the bombing at O'Donoghue's. There may be a link between the two cases. Jesus, I have a right to lead the search.'

Mangan shook his head. He went back to his desk and put the bottle and glass away. The leader of the nation was about to assert his authority.

'Ah, Declan, it's no good, you're wasting your breath. Sure, if you had any common sense at all, you'd know this is the one investigation you can't be involved in. Joe Healy's been put in charge of the O'Donoghue's investigation. Timothy Breen is taking over the other case. He has a team working on it already. Your team has been assigned to other duties. I'm sure Breen will be glad of any lines of enquiry you can suggest to him.'

'And what am I to do when I've made my suggestions? I can't sit about idle.'

'You won't be asked to. The last thing you need at the moment is to be sitting on your backside. I have a job for you, and to tell you the truth, I'd have taken you off the other investigation anyway so you could do it. You're to take charge of security for the Muslim Leaders' Conference next month.'

Declan's mouth opened.

'You can't be serious. Dear God, Pádraig . . .'

'Shut up a minute and listen. This is important to me, Declan. Hosting the conference is the biggest diplomatic initiative this country has pulled off in God knows how long. If it goes well, the benefits could be enormous. It'll raise our stature in Europe, and it'll give us a lead in trade relations with Islamic countries.

'The thing is, you know we had to persuade the participants that the security situation in the Republic was better than average. But the bombing earlier this week and last night's shooting have changed that. There's already been talk of people pulling out. It could be a disaster. That's why I want you on top of it, from now until it's over. After that, I'll see if I can't persuade Seán Roche to reconsider your involvement in the investigation. And don't forget that the post of Garda Commissioner comes vacant when Pat Devlin retires next year. If the conference goes off without a hitch, you'll be the man of the moment.'

'I couldn't care less right now, to tell you the truth.'

'Don't you think I know that? If I weren't Taoiseach, I'd be out in McDaid's or somewhere drowning my sorrows along with you. But I have the interests of the country to look after. Will you at least take a few days off? Think it over, and let me have your decision after the funeral.'

Declan stood.

'There's no need for that, Pádraig. You've left me with no choice. I'll look after your bloody conference. But I want your promise that Tim Breen will let me know of any major developments in the search for Máiréad's killer. I have as much a right to be informed as you.'

Mangan hesitated, then nodded.

'Fair enough, Declan. I'll see that's done. And thanks for agreeing to the other.'

He stood and they shook hands. Mangan accompanied Declan to the door. As he opened it, he paused.

'Declan, there'll be a briefing on the conference in this office in a week's time. I've asked the Lebanese to let us have one of their people. They're sending a woman, an expert on the Islamic terrorist outfits. It'll be like old times for you.'

Fifteen years earlier, Declan had served with Irish military intelligence at their Headquarters in Tibnin in southern Lebanon. He had been posted there with the Irish contingent of the UN peacekeeping force, UNIFIL, and during that time he'd worked closely with Lebanese intelligence.

Pádraig Pearse's words hit him like a blow in the stomach. He found it hard to ask the simplest of questions.

'What's her name? Can you remember?'

'Just a minute, I have it on my desk. I scribbled it down earlier.' Mangan walked over and opened a file. 'Looks something like "Bushavi" – would that be right?'

Declan did not move from where he had been standing.

'Bustani,' he said, more to himself than to the other man. 'Amina Bustani.'

The Taoiseach looked up at him in surprise.

'That's right,' he said. 'How on earth did you know?'

Back at Harcourt Street, most of the team had already dispersed. Some were working with Breen, others had been posted to a surveillance job in Cabra. Tim O'Meara was packing his briefcase as Declan entered.

'I'm sorry about this, sir. We're all sorry. We'd have given anything to go on working with you on the case. But you needn't worry, we'll find the bastard.'

'I know you will,' said Declan. 'Tim Breen's a good man, and his judgement won't be clouded by personal factors. The best of luck.'

Just then, Grainne Walsh passed with a trolley of files.

'Grainne, did you find those things I asked for?'

'They're on your desk, sir.'

'Thanks.'

'What will you be doing now, sir? We all think you should take some time off.'

'I'm on my way home now, but it's just for a few days. Then I have a security job. I'll be back in next week.'

He went to his office and closed the door. The files were on top of his desk. There were not many. He sat down and began to read through them, concentrating on the photographs. It took him three minutes to find him.

His name was Peter Musgrave, age thirty-four, born in Oldham, divorced, two children, one boy, one girl. Ex-SAS corporal, ten tours of duty in Northern Ireland between 1988 and 1993, known contacts with MI5, a close friend of Ulster Defence Regiment members convicted of membership in illegal Loyalist organizations.

He glanced down the internal telephone directory to find Tim Breen's number. His hand reached for the phone, then drew away again. He remained sitting for over a minute, then closed the file and slipped it into his briefcase.

CHAPTER SEVEN

Dublin
12 September

The weather all the next week was exceptionally fine. Monday, the day of Máiréad's funeral, was marked by glorious sunshine. All that day, and the next, and the day after; and then rain so heavy it made the city dark from morning to night. The funeral had been closed to all but family and friends, and yet the torrent of people all round them had been past counting. Declan had never known she had so many friends, and he was comforted by it.

No-one but he knew of the child she had been expecting, and he considered it best to leave things that way. Nevertheless, he thought of it all throughout the funeral, his unborn grandson or granddaughter, his dead future. He had never experienced thoughts like those before, had never felt so close to oblivion or paralysis of the will. Only the thought of revenge kept him going, and that he found ugly and demeaning, to make a life for himself out of something so sordid.

He held Concepta's hand throughout the Mass and the burial, comforted her, talked with her when she needed to talk, sat with her in silence to receive condolences. Something had been spirited out of her by Máiréad's death: old anger, old resentment, old frustration.

Almost for the first time in their long marriage, it seemed that he was sufficient for her as he was. It did not matter that he lacked ambition, that he did not want to be Garda Commissioner, or Justice Minister, or enter the Dáil or the Senate. A long silence grew between them that had something in it of love, and a little of compassion. Máiréad's death would not heal the deep rift between them, but for the moment it lay like a bridge across it. It seemed the rankest injustice that, throughout all this, he should be kept awake at night by the thought that he would soon be seeing a woman he had not met in fifteen years.

On Thursday morning, he turned up for work as usual. His new team was ready for him, but before meeting them he went through his papers, tidying up items left over from his work on the pub bombing. He sent several files down to Tim Breen's office with a covering note, and suggested a meeting to go over things properly.

On his desktop lay a slim file left behind for him by Tim O'Meara. It contained what little was known to Dublin SDU about a Loyalist informer called Jimmy Bryce, otherwise known as 'The Drummer'. On a separate note was a brief inscription to the effect that Bryce had been found dead on the morning after Austin McKeown's murder.

There was also a full report on the circumstances of the Detective Superintendent's death. Declan read it through carefully. The ambush had been laid squarely at the door of the IRA, though without any evidence beyond McKeown's having been a senior member of the security forces. Significantly, or so it seemed to Declan, the IRA themselves had not laid claim to the killing.

One point struck him at once. The bullets and cartridge cases collected from the Hillsborough ambush had been 9mm Parabellum, manufactured by Remington. That matched the ammunition fired by the gunman in the ice-cream parlour. The gun he had dropped before making his escape had been a little unusual, a short-barrelled American sub-machine gun known as a Viking.

The Viking is even shorter than an Uzi, with a total length of only fourteen and a half inches with the stock retracted. It is manufactured by Viking Systems Inc at a plant in Londonderry, New Hampshire, and has a good reputation as a sturdy and efficient law enforcement weapon. Declan had never heard of any Vikings having been found previously with Irish terrorist organizations, whether Republican or Loyalist.

The configuration of trigger strikes on the bullets used to kill Austin McKeown showed similarities to that on the ammunition fired in the Dublin ice-cream parlour. It was at least possible that

Vikings had been used in both incidents. It was a small point, but Declan knew that, if it could be proved, it might serve as evidence of a connection between the two events. He made a note of the fact and continued reading the report.

When he had finished, he put it in the drawer along with his file on Peter Musgrave. He did not look at Musgrave's photograph again. He did not have to: the killer's face was etched on his brain, and would remain there for the rest of his life.

He sat quite still for several minutes, as though thinking something over. Then, reaching a decision, he leafed through a small notebook until he found a telephone number. He punched the number slowly and waited.

Two rings, and a man's voice answered. English, a public-school accent, confident.

'Wetherell.'

'Captain Wetherell? My name is Carberry. Can we talk?'

There was a brief pause.

'I know who you are, Mr Carberry. And I can make an educated guess at how you came by this number. As for talking . . . I would prefer to see you face to face. Can that be arranged?'

'I think so, yes.'

'Good. Leave it with me. Don't contact me on this number again.'

'How am I to get in touch?'

'You aren't. I'll contact you. Goodbye, Mr Carberry.'

Declan put the phone down. When he took his hand away, it was shaking.

They were waiting for him downstairs. Earlier that morning, he had read the briefing paper prepared for him by the Foreign Minister. The Muslim Leaders' Conference had been Ciaran Clark's brainwave, and he was anxious to ensure it went smoothly. It was to be held in October at Castletown House, a stately home near Celbridge, a few miles west of Dublin.

'We've all worked together before,' he began, 'so there's no need for introductions. Some of you have been taken off important operations in order to work with me on this job. You may be feeling some displeasure at having been assigned to a routine security exercise. Let me dispel that illusion at once. It isn't going to be routine, and I can assure you that it won't be easy.

'So far, all that any of you have been told is that this is a regular security operation, providing cover for foreign VIPs attending a conference at Castletown House next month. What you have not been told until now is the real nature of the conference and how important it is to this country that it goes ahead without a hitch. What I'm about to tell you is top secret, and I want it kept that way.'

He looked slowly round the room. There were ten of them, all hand-picked, experienced, and loyal to him. He could depend on them for the job in hand, and he could rely on them to help him with any information-gathering he might want carried out into the ice-cream parlour shooting.

'Next month, the Irish government is due to host a secret conference at which representatives of the United States and the European Community will meet with leading Muslim clergy from several countries. On the agenda will be issues of mutual interest: Palestine, security in the Gulf, Bosnia, terrorism. Before the meeting, there will be a series of private sessions at which the Muslim leaders will try to knock out a joint policy on most of these issues. Once they have agreed on as much as possible, they'll go into discussions with the US and European diplomats. Later, there'll be a public conference designed to quieten fears about growing confrontation.

'The reason for the conference is simple. In 1993, the Israelis and Palestinians were able to sort out most of their differences. There was a serious prospect for peace in the region. The following year, the West Bank was handed back to Palestinian control. But the Muslim fundamentalists wouldn't accept it. They weren't willing to talk to the Israelis at all. The various heads of state in the Arab world are aware that, if they're going to get anywhere in the long run, they have to settle some of the religious issues. Hence this conference.'

Dominic Lawlor raised his hand. He was an old friend of Declan's. They had been together at Dungarvan harbour when they had intercepted a shipment of arms bound from Czechoslovakia in 1979.

'This is all very well, sir,' he said, 'but I can't see what on earth it has to do with Ireland. The average Paddy thinks the Middle East is somewhere in County Wicklow.'

'Well, and aren't we a nation of innocents,' retorted Declan. 'I hope the rest of you keep more abreast of current affairs. Ireland's an obvious choice for a meeting of this kind. The one thing almost everyone knows about this country is that we've never been imperialists. On the contrary, we've a long history of being colonized, and that's something that goes down well with modern Muslims.

'So far, the IRA have benefited from that sympathy a good deal more than the law-abiding people of the country they claim to represent. The Libyans have supplied them with arms, and the Palestinians have provided them with training facilities from time to time.

'But that's going to change now. You may remember that the Israelis and Palestinians held their first talks outside the Middle East, in Norway. The Norwegians were able to use their history of neutrality to bring them together. Now we're going to do the same thing on a broader scale.

'There are other factors that make this an ideal venue. We have close ties to the United States. We're well liked in Europe. As a Catholic country, we're trusted by the French, the Italians, the Spanish, and the Portuguese, and we carry weight at the Vatican. For all our differences, we have close relations with England.'

He paused. It was beginning to sink in that they were being given responsibility for a security operation of above-average importance. He could see them begin to settle. Perhaps this assignment was not going to be as boring as it had at first promised.

'However,' he went on, 'we have a problem. As you can imagine, one of the biggest obstacles to holding the conference here was the bad press this country gets as a result of the situation in the North. The government had a hard job persuading some of the delegate organizations that our security situation is totally different, and that we're capable of stopping the violence there crossing the border.

'As you all know only too well, the past ten days have shown that claim to be hollow, and as a result there's now talk of some of the delegates pulling out. The Foreign Department is working flat out to stop that happening, but they desperately need a concrete security proposal from this room in order to show round the table.'

At that moment, the door opened and a uniformed Garda officer came to the front.

'Sorry to interrupt, sir, but I've got a woman in the lobby down-stairs asking to be allowed up to see you. She has a pass from the Oifig an Taoiseach, sir, but in view of the circumstances . . . Well, I thought it best to check with you in person first, sir.'

'Did she give her name?'

'Yes, sir, she did. A foreign name it was, sir. Bustani or something. Would that be right?'

CHAPTER EIGHT

She was waiting on a chair near the entrance, apart from everyone. Dressed in a light red suit, with a blue scarf at her neck. Not very tall, her body unchanged, her features well-defined, as though carved rather than moulded, her hair cut short, streaked with grey.

Perhaps it was the shadow in which she stood that betrayed him. Perhaps the light at this time of the morning was too weak for his tired eyes. And perhaps it was just the shadow of too many years blinding him. But as he came within the last few feet and dared to look her in the face, he saw at last what he had missed at first. A young woman in battle fatigues, sitting on a cold hill above Tibnin, waiting for a raw young Irish lieutenant to make his first rendezvous.

'Hello, Amina,' he said. 'Welcome to Ireland.'

She stood and looked at him before replying.

'Hello, Declan. It's been a long time.'

'I added it up just now,' he said. 'Fifteen years. Can you believe that?'

'I'll believe anything. It's good to see you, Declan.'

'It's good to see you too. Listen, if you're here for the briefing, we needn't go up yet. I've told the team they can take a couple of hours off. I'd rather speak to you first. Not here, somewhere a bit more personal. We could take a stroll through the Green and have a coffee in the Shelbourne.'

She smiled.

'I'm here on business, Declan.'

'Well, this is Ireland. You'll find we're very relaxed.'

'A quick coffee, then. We'll talk about your plans for the conference.'

They had met fifteen years earlier when Declan was serving with UNIFIL, the United Nations Force in Lebanon. Amina had been seconded from Lebanese intelligence to the Irish Battalion HQ as an advisor and interpreter. A Sunni Muslim and the daughter of a government minister, she was a graduate of the American University of Beirut, with degrees in Arabic and Middle East history. For six months in the winter of 1981, she and Declan had been lovers. And not merely lovers in the physical sense, but deeply, hopelessly in love with one another.

Their affair had ended abruptly when Declan was sent back to Dublin in the spring of 1982, following an incident involving relatives of Nabih Birri, who had recently been re-elected head of Shi'ite Amal. Tibnin was not just IRISHBATT headquarters, but Birri's home town and a Shi'ite stronghold. In the course of the incident, Declan and his operation had been irretrievably compromised. There was no question of his remaining in Lebanon.

On the night before his departure, he and Amina had stayed awake until dawn, talking and talking, not knowing what to do, as hopeless as any woman and her lover on the eve of his deportation. In the end, they had decided that she would follow him to Ireland at the earliest opportunity. He would leave Concepta and they would move to England to start a new life. She had been to England, to a language school in Cambridge, and together they constructed a dream of living there in a country cottage on the edge of town. She would teach Arabic at the university, he would take a law degree. Had they guessed, even as they talked their last night away, that their ordinary lives could never have accommodated so rich a dream?

Later the same morning, Declan returned to headquarters for his bags and was driven directly to Beirut airport. There was shelling as they neared the city. Everywhere, groups of militia stood by roadblocks, young men locked into a tense, hate-filled world. The air had been filled with the sound of sirens and, once or twice, the rattle of heavy gunfire far out in the hills.

Back in Dublin, he did not tell Concepta about Amina as planned. Her mother, to whom she had been deeply attached, had died at Christmas. Her father was in hospital, seriously ill. She had been prescribed tranquillizers, carelessly, by her GP, and was becoming dependent on them. He decided to wait for a better moment, for the right time, whatever that meant. Amina wrote to him through a Post Office box in town. He left the army and joined the Gardaí, moving into Special Branch soon after. Concepta had her third miscarriage. Máiréad started nursery school. Pádraig Pearse was elected to the Dáil for the first time.

In June, the Israeli army invaded southern Lebanon. The PLO were pushed out. Hizbollah and Islamic Amal became more active. The spiral of civil war spun faster and faster and widened by the day. Amina wrote to say that she could not leave until the Israeli threat had been removed. As time went by, her letters became less frequent. In the last, she wrote that she could not abandon her people in a time of desperation.

There was never a right time to tell Concepta, never a time in Lebanon that was not one of desperation. Months passed and became years. He had no reason now to go to Beirut, she could not leave for Dublin. Their dream of a new life was clouded over with the ordinary obsessions of the old. The inertia of separation took hold of both of them. And fear of change, and loyalty, and guilt. They were in that gulf of things, where passion does not hold. Only the saintly can be lovers at a distance, lacking passion – and they were not saints or passionless. In time her letters stopped. He did not know if she was alive or dead. When he wrote, he knew his letters would go unanswered, perhaps unread, unopened; Amina, whom he still loved, had entered an underworld of intrigue and bloodshed.

In the end he too stopped writing. Sometimes, for an hour or two hours at a time, he would watch the mist gather on a low sea and think of her. Or see his reflection caught in a mirror and think that he had aged, and brood a little on what time had done. But as the years passed more and more quickly, so his thoughts grew less urgent, and his need for her less frequent, less intense; but his love undimmed.

And now, on a cold morning between summer and autumn, the years had slammed suddenly together again.

They walked together through the park beneath a sky marbled with cloud. At a discreet distance, his bodyguard, one of a team appointed to watch over him since the attempt on his life, walked behind them like a chaperon.

'I heard about your daughter,' she said. 'I'm truly sorry.'

'You never met her,' he said. 'It's a terrible shame. You'd have liked her, and I know she'd have liked you.'

'Even if she'd known?'

'What? About us? Máiréad would never have let a thing like that bother her.'

'You used to talk about her in Lebanon.'

'She was nearly three. I missed her. But not half as badly as I miss her now.'

She found his hand and squeezed it, then let go of it.

'It's lovely here,' she said. She gave a half smile, then looked away. 'I'd almost forgotten what a civilized city could look like. You never saw Beirut at its best.'

'This isn't Dublin at its best either,' he said. 'The developers have been trying their hardest for years now to demolish most of the buildings round the Green. But you're right, it's still a lot better than Beirut.'

They walked a little further. Statues and busts lined the pathways: poets, rebels, heroes, heroines – all changed, all turned to stone . . .

'Why were you chosen to come here?' he asked.

She shrugged. He remembered the gesture well. She had taken life as she found it, day by day.

'You know I've worked with Irish detachments serving with UNIFIL. I know several people in Irish intelligence. I know you. And much of my work in Lebanon since the mid-eighties has involved keeping tabs on Islamic groups. Hizbollah. Islamic Jihad. Shi'ite Amal. Someone decided I was the right person for the job. So here I am.'

'How long are you staying?'

'Until the conference is over and they've all gone back home.'

'How important is it really – this conference?'

This time she did not shrug.

'Extremely. If it goes well . . . I think it could change the course of history in the Middle East. I don't mean it would bring peace overnight or anything like that. Just that it would provide so many opportunities for change.'

'And if it goes badly? Or if something goes wrong?'

'It could set things back fifty years. The political situation is still volatile. A lot of innocent lives depend on what happens next month.'

She hesitated.

'Declan,' she said, 'I know you don't want this job. I know you were taken off the investigation into your daughter's death, and I can understand why that would take priority for you. But this conference is genuinely important. You weren't selected for the job just to keep you occupied. I asked for you. You're the best, and I trust you. There are several groups who would like to see this conference fail. Some of them are very powerful, all of them have the means to pose a serious threat.'

'Will you explain all this to my team this afternoon?'

'Of course. Will I have to speak to them in Irish?'

He laughed.

'Of course not,' he said. 'We choose our people more carefully than that. They're all fluent Arabic speakers.'

This time she let the smile happen. It transformed her face, throwing him back through fifteen years like a rubber ball caught and hurled through the still air.

'You've changed,' he said.

'You too.'

'You look . . .' He did not know how to finish. He shrugged. 'I don't know,' he said. 'Different. You were . . . softer before. You seemed vulnerable then. Now . . .' He shrugged again. 'You seem harder to reach, better guarded, more finished.'

'Thank you,' she said. 'That's what I've become. What I had to become in order to survive. It's what the war made of so many of us. Those of us who lived were changed. Irrevocably. It's twice as hard – no, ten times as hard for a woman. I don't mean to survive, we are better at that than you men. But to come through intact, to go into the heart of so much hatred and come out again without real damage, that is very difficult. And when we are damaged, it is more . . . devastating.' She paused, in search of the right words. 'It is something we experience more deeply. If we have children, they are damaged too.'

She laughed suddenly, breaking the mood she had created.

'I'm sorry,' she said. 'Here I am making speeches, and we've barely been together half an hour. You'll be wondering "how can I get away from this terrible woman?"'

He shook his head, smiling.

'Quite the contrary,' he said. 'I like listening to you talk. Your voice hasn't changed a fraction.'

She reddened and glanced away from him.

'It's something we should find time to talk about,' he continued. 'Things have happened to you. I'd like to know about them. What you say sounds very familiar. It's a bit like that in Ireland too. Not here in the South, but in the North. The same kind of hatred. I've seen old friends there changed by the Troubles.'

'You've changed.'

'It was a long time ago,' he said. 'Fifteen years.' He slowed his pace, then stopped to look at her.

'Has there been anyone else?' she asked. He noticed the tension in her voice, the anxiety behind the question.

'Concepta,' he said. 'If that means anything. And you?'

'My parents wanted me to marry,' she said. 'They were growing ashamed of me, staying single so long.'

'I didn't mean marriage,' he said.

'No. Of course you didn't.' She raised her eyes. 'I had lovers, certainly. Some of them are dead now. But there was no-one permanent. Nothing is permanent in Lebanon.'

He looked at her.

'Nothing is permanent anywhere,' he said.

The phone rang at eleven o'clock that night. Richard Wetherell wanted to meet. There was an unapproved road between Dundalk and Newry, a scenic route that overlooked Carlingford Lough for part of the way. Could Declan make it there unobserved?

'When?'

'Soon. I'll be in touch.'

CHAPTER NINE

Dublin
13 September
1320 hours

He had wanted to have lunch with Amina, but at the last moment a message had reached him from Martin Fitzsimmons, the head of C3, Ireland's small national intelligence agency, asking to call him urgently. Martin wanted to talk, face to face, and alone. They were old friends, and Declan agreed to meet right away, at Martin's office in the Red Building at Garda HQ, across the city in Phoenix Park.

Fitzsimmons was a tall man, affable, at ease with himself, a soft man by all appearances. Yet Declan knew he was ruthless in the war he waged against terrorism. His agency was the smallest of those engaged in the fight against the subversion of the Irish state, but under his management it had become a finely-tuned weapon that chose its targets well and seldom missed. He was one of the few people in the security hierarchy to whom Declan would have trusted his life.

'Cigarette, Declan?' he asked, holding an open box.

'No, thanks. I haven't touched a cigarette in six months, as you very well know.'

'I'm always glad of company,' said Martin. He took a cigarette from the box and lit it. There had been any amount of 'No Smoking' ordinances passed round his department, and he had treated every one with the contempt of a man born to the sound of matches striking.

'How's Concepta?' he asked.

'Well enough. It's early days. Early days for all of us.'

'Give her my love.'

'You weren't at the funeral.'

Martin shook his head.

'No. I sent a letter – you'll come across it when it's time for that sort of thing. I loathe funerals. They depress me for weeks afterwards. You'll not mind, surely, that I wasn't there?'

Declan shook his head.

'I'd as soon not have been there myself.' He shifted, inhaling smoke from Martin's cigarette. 'Maybe I'll have one of those after all,' he said. Martin passed the box.

'Now,' said Declan once he had lit up. 'What did you want to see me about?'

'What's going on, Declan?'

'I don't understand.'

'Oh, come on, man, of course you do. You were with Austin McKeown the afternoon of the sixth. That evening, he was killed. The same evening, his chief Loyalist informer, a man called Jimmy Bryce, was shot in Belfast. And in Dublin, a man tried to kill you and succeeded in killing your daughter and some other people.'

'Coincidence, Martin.'

'Don't give me that. What did Austin come down to talk to you about?'

'He had a lead for me on the bombing at O'Donoghue's.'

'He didn't have to come all the way to Dublin to pass on a lead. There are channels for that sort of thing.'

'Don't be naïve. None of us uses official channels for anything but routine stuff.'

'So, this wasn't routine.'

'It was . . . sensitive.'

'Did he believe he was in any danger?'

'We're all in danger, Martin.'

'I asked you, did Austin McKeown think he was in any special danger?'

'Is this an interrogation?'

'Just answer the question, Declan.'

'I believe so, yes.'

'Did he mention The Drummer to you?'

'Who?'

'Come on, Declan, you know perfectly well who I mean. His informer, Jimmy Bryce.'

'He may have done.'

'The bombing was the work of Loyalists: is that what he was telling you?'

'Martin, I'm not working on that case any longer. I've passed on everything I know to Joe Healy. He has my files: you can ask him.'

'I already have done. There's no record of your meeting with McKeown.'

'Isn't there? I must have forgotten to put it in. Jesus, Martin, Máiréad was killed that same evening, and you're asking why I haven't got my records up to date!'

Fitzsimmons raised a hand.

'I'm sorry, Declan. You're right. It's just . . . To tell you the truth, I'm a bit worried.'

'Worried? About what?'

'Someone's asking questions about you. They're generally buried among a lot of other routine stuff, but they're there all right. And not all of them are coming through routine channels. As you say, people in our trade often use unorthodox means of going about their business.'

'Who's asking?'

'It's hard to tell exactly. Whoever's doing it is clever, spreading the material across several agencies. But if I had to guess, I'd say MI5.'

Declan nodded.

'How high up?'

'Hard to say. It could go quite high.'

'What do they want to know that they can't find out from existing files?'

Martin shrugged and sucked hard on his cigarette. He reached into the box for a replacement and touched it to the glowing end of the first.

'What you know,' he said, exhaling. 'Specifically, what you know about the bombing at O'Donoghue's. Theories, leads, who you've questioned so far, what you've passed on, what you may be keeping to yourself. All of it spread about, you understand. A question here, a question there.'

'Why are you telling me this?'

'I should have thought that was obvious, Declan. We're old friends, we don't have to play chess with one another. I know you're under strain, but the people asking these questions don't give a toss about that.'

'Well, I'm grateful for the information, Martin. I'll bear it in mind.'

Declan stubbed out what was left of his cigarette in a large ashtray on the other side of the desk, and stood to go.

'Declan, I'm asking you to treat this as a warning. Someone's got an unhealthy interest in you.'

'Jesus, Martin, half of Ireland has known that since the shooting in O'Connell Street.'

'It might help matters if you were to tell me just what it is you do know. If I knew that, I might be able to help.'

Declan hesitated. It would be an enormous relief to share his knowledge with someone, not least someone on whom he could depend implicitly. But there was no getting away from the fact that, were Austin McKeown's information to fall into the wrong hands, however innocently, the consequences could be disastrous.

'I'll be in touch, Martin. Keep me informed if you hear of anything else.'

He left, taking care to close the door behind him. His fingers were still warm from holding the cigarette.

1559 hours

Richard Wetherell drove through the crested metal gates and up the drive, turned left along the school's long brown and cream façade, and nosed in to a space reserved for masters. They let him leave the car there as a special privilege, on account of his need for additional security. He'd still have to check the Astra before leaving, it was a standing order any time you left a car unattended; but it reduced the chances of his finding a little black box taped to the underbody.

The little car park was almost empty. It was Friday, and school had been out for almost an hour; any masters not involved in extra-curricular activities had gone home. Wetherell came here about twice a term to talk to the senior members of the Combined Cadet Force, fourth form and upwards. None of the boys knew what he was up to, of course. They thought he was just regular army, some poor sod of a subaltern sent in to do a bit of public relations work and maybe encourage a few of the sixth-formers to think harder about a career in the military. Not even the master in charge of the CCF knew his real job, nor the true purpose behind these visits.

Wetherell was a long-serving officer with 14th Int, the British army's 14th Intelligence Company, popularly known as 'The Detachment'. It had developed out of an earlier undercover operation known as the 4 Field Troop, and was permanently based at army HQ in Lisburn. Its members were recruited from the intelligence corps and trained at Hereford by the SAS.

Wetherell's purpose in visiting the school was straightforward. He was keeping a sharp eye out for senior boys who might prove suitable for work with the Detachment or, failing that, another section of military intelligence within the province. Those he considered likely candidates would join the army in the regular fashion – pre-Regular Commissions Board test, then down to Westbury to the RCB itself, three days to prove themselves, then on to Sandhurst and, if they stuck the course, a commission as second lieutenant at the end. But the Intelligence Corps would have had them down to Ashford long before that, just to see what they were made of. They'd have a spell there, then nine months with an infantry battalion in Northern Ireland, then back to Ashford and Hereford for further training. In the end they'd be shipped back to Ulster ready for their first tour as undercover operatives.

14th Int needed local talent badly, and Richard Wetherell was its chief talent spotter. Selection was from a very small pool of boys chosen from the province's top schools. The Royal Belfast Academical Institution – sensibly shortened to Inst – was, along with Campbell College on the east of the city, one of his main hunting-grounds. The reasons were simple.

Inst, though it no longer took boarders, was a long-established public school whose headmaster (known, for some reason, as the Principal) was almost always an Englishman. It was Ireland's top rugby school, eschewing both soccer and Gaelic football. From its pupils were drawn a high proportion of Ulster's ruling class – its civil servants, high-ranking police and military, lawyers, judges, bankers, scientists, doctors, and businessmen. Boys and staff alike were, almost to a man, Protestant and middle-class. And the school was one of the very few with a Combined Cadet Force. With a little careful vetting, members of the Force could turn out to be perfect material for undercover work that called for a convincing regional accent and sound local knowledge.

As he headed for the CCF hut down near the cricket nets, Wetherell saw Paul Mercer hurrying towards him from the rear of the school hall. Mercer was a Latin master, a protegé of the brilliant but infamous Charles Fay, whose reign of terror in and beyond his department was still a legend in the school. A Scot by birth, he was second-in-command of the CCF, and had himself served with the Intelligence Corps before taking up teaching.

They shook hands warmly. Though he did not know Wetherell's exact position, Mercer was privy to the real reason behind his visits. He, rather than Chris Abernethy, the senior CCF man, helped weed out the most promising of each year's possible candidates.

'I'm glad I caught you,' he said. 'Alcorn's taken the boys in to the gym today. We'll have your talk there, once they've finished and changed.'

'Don't the poor bastards get enough PE in school as it is?'

Mercer laughed. They set off for the gym, next to the modern languages block.

'More than most would like. But they've got a tough route march in the Mournes on Saturday, and Chris wants them in shape.'

They reached the gym. Mercer seemed on edge about something.

'What's the new senior intake like?' asked Wetherell.

'Very good. I've got some promising lads for you to have a look at. We can go through them later.'

He opened the door that led into the changing-rooms, ushering Wetherell in ahead of him.

As Wetherell stepped through, he did a double take. Something was wrong, but it took a couple of seconds before he saw what it was, seconds that were to cost him his life. There were no clothes on the benches or hanging from the hooks above them. And no sound of pounding feet from the gymnasium beyond.

'Put your hands behind your head and keep them there,' ordered a clipped voice by his side. Out of the corner of his right eye he caught sight of a hand holding a gun pointed at his head. He raised his hands slowly, turning his head slightly as he did so, in order to get a clear view of his assailant.

'Eyes forward!' commanded the voice in military fashion. The accent was English. Was this some sort of stupid schoolboy joke dreamed up with the help of a moronic NCO, Wetherell wondered.

'Mercer, take his gun. Do it quickly.'

Paul Mercer stepped in front of him, his eyes averted, sweat on his forehead. He frisked him quickly and took the Browning automatic he always carried.

'Start walking,' ordered the Englishman, pushing Wetherell in the small of the back, towards the gym.

Mercer went ahead and opened the door for them. Inside, the gym was quite empty. This was beginning to seem less and less like a joke or an initiative test. And what sort of teacher would set up an initiative test pitting one of his boys against a trained soldier carrying a loaded weapon? He began to think furiously of how to turn the tables in his favour.

'Over there!'

He was prodded across the floor until he stood hard in front of the opposite wall, which was covered with wall-bars almost to the ceiling.

'Hands to your sides.'

He did as he was told. The next moment, a hood was pulled down hard over his head. Then he was being spun round, pushed roughly up against the wall-bars, and next thing his arms were being lifted and strapped to the bars. He was completely helpless now, and he realized, as panic began to grow in him, that he might be only moments from death. He hoped so, since the alternative for an intelligence officer was prolonged torture. A hand took his ankles one at a time and, splaying his legs, strapped them to the bars as well.

'You,' he heard the English voice order, 'get out of here. Make sure no-one comes in. I'll be with you as soon as I've finished in here.'

There was a sound of footsteps hard on wood, then the door opening and closing. It left a small echo in the huge, empty room.

'Take the fucking hood off,' said Wetherell.

'Sorry, sir,' came the voice, almost apologetic. 'Best not to. Best

68

you don't see none of what happens. I'll try to make it quick when the time comes. But the first few, sir, they need to be done while you're alive. For the forensics. So it looks like the Paddies have been asking you questions.'

'Who the hell are you? Who sent you?'

'Best you save your breath, sir. Here, sir, slip this between your teeth. Something to bite on. They say it helps.'

He felt the hood partly lifted, then something pushed into his mouth. A rubber plug. The hood was dropped again.

In the echoing gymnasium, smelling of sweat and dried blood, he could hear the sound of a naked blade being sharpened.

CHAPTER TEN

Castletown House
Celbridge
6 October
1811 hours

Declan had wanted a last look at Castletown House when there
was no-one else around, to get a feel for the place in its own
right. Tomorrow night's reception would mark the beginning of
the conference, and weeks of intense activity. Preparations were
still going on inside the house, but outside the gardens were
deserted.

He had spent the day with Concepta, their first full day alone
since the funeral. It had not gone well. They had not quarrelled,
but they had not really been at ease in one another's company.
Through the day, his head had grown steadily more and more
painful. He tried lying down after lunch, but it only made it worse.
In the end, a call from Grainne Walsh had given him the excuse
he needed to get away. Before leaving, he had asked Amina to
come with him, ostensibly to cast a professional eye over the
security arrangements with him, but really in the hope that there
might be time to talk.

In the past few weeks, he had experienced two sets of very
contradictory emotions. While grieving inordinately for his
daughter, he had found himself spending more and more time
in the company of the one woman he had ever truly loved, and
who had loved him with the same intensity. At times, he had
had to stop for breath, like someone who has been running too
hard or who is being stifled.

Being with Amina had reminded him of what he had lost.

Whatever confusion he had felt previously about his lack of love for Concepta had hardened into certainty. And with the loss of Máiréad, he no longer had a substitute on whom to lavish his feelings.

It was still too early to say what might happen between Amina and himself. Certainly, they had not become lovers again. He had made no advances, she had given no sign that she might be open to any. In all likelihood, she would return to Beirut at the end of the conference, leaving him truly alone and doubly bereft. But he had some small hope of persuading her to stay on: he could think of any number of pretexts.

A cold wind had risen just after lunchtime, and there were signs that a storm might be on the way. Below the house, the Liffey ran between green banks, in its last stretch of freedom here before it entered the city and came finally to the sea. They wandered down to the river's edge and found a narrow path winding eastwards, towards Leixlip.

Amina had been analysing the threat of an attack by Muslim terrorists, based on the latest briefing she had received from Beirut. Several members of Hizbollah's covert action group, al-Jihad al-Islamiyya, were thought to be in Europe. Two hitmen, known to have worked with Shi'ite Amal, had been seen in Oslo.

They halted by the riverside, taking shelter from the wind in a clump of ancient trees. There was wind on the water, and the face of the river was drawn and puckered with waves. High above their heads, clouds scudded across a barren sky. A heron swooped, shimmered a moment, and was gone. A very great silence was with them, in which the wind and the waves were little more than measures against which it might be laid. The light did not seem to come down from the sky, but to be there, quiet, within the stones and the water, not bright, but dimmed by the trees and the tall, swaying grasses.

She took his arm and they began to walk again. They passed a small boat moored to a wooden jetty. A bird cried plaintively from the reeds behind them.

'Do you still love Concepta?' It seemed such a stupid question, hackneyed, trivialized by innumerable cheap romances, worn threadbare by the agony columns of every magazine she had ever read. And yet she had been unable to stop herself asking it. She needed to know, whatever might happen.

He did not answer right away. There were no words for what he wanted to say, no easy words. He had articulated so little of it to himself, and all that unexpressed, misexpressed confusion threatened to tear him like blades the moment he dared give it speech. Just holding Amina was the most dangerous thing he had ever done.

'I loved Máiréad,' he said. 'I would have died to save her.'

'That isn't what I asked.'

A trick of the silence made it seem that her voice came from far away, from the other bank. He wanted to kiss her, to pull her down upon the damp grass and make love to her. But her voice seemed to hang in the cold air, mocking him.

'I've never loved Concepta,' he said. 'I've admired her, cared for her, pitied her – all sorts of things. She's part of me, I can't dig her out without hurting myself. But I've never loved her.'

'Why have you stayed with her so long?'

'This is Ireland. Divorce is next to impossible. And she is the Prime Minister's sister. You were in Lebanon. Máiréad was still growing up. I made what I could of things.'

'You should have come back.'

'To Beirut?'

'Yes.'

'You know that wouldn't have been possible. For either of us.'

'Is it possible now?'

He gazed past her at the troubled water.

'No,' he said.

'I could stay here.'

His hand stroked the back of her head.

'Let's walk on a little bit,' he said.

They joined hands again and continued along the path. Above them, the sky was blotted with cloud and growing dark at the edges. There was none of the rushing twilight of the Mediterranean here, just the steady dulling of the light and the unpatterned falling of night. It was as if she had always been here, as if her life in Beirut had been a dream, and a dream not even her own. She remembered a poem by Yeats, that she had first heard read in a class on English literature years before she had met Declan or spoken with him about Ireland. She had learned the poem by heart, and now as they walked she recited it in a slow, inflected voice.

O'Driscoll drove with a song
The wild duck and the drake
From the tall and the tufted reeds
Of the drear Hart Lake.
And he saw how the reeds grew dark
At the coming of night-tide,
And dreamed of the long dim hair
Of Bridget his bride.

He listened to her voice among the reeds, remembering the same verses in another time. He knew how the poem ended, how O'Driscoll's bride was taken by a young man of the Sidhe, the host of the air, never to be seen again. Amina came to the last verse.

But he heard high up in the air
A piper piping away,
And never was piping so sad,
And never was piping so gay.

The words were whipped from her by the wind and tossed on the grey water. They stood facing one another, as though waiting for the sound of piping to come down to them from the heights of the wind, but there was no music, only the rush of the growing storm through high, bending branches. He bent forward and took her in his arms, as though for the first time, and kissed her, a long kiss in which everything was forgotten and everything was remembered.

When they drew apart at last, the darkness was deepening upon the river.

'Where can we go?' she asked.

'Come with me,' he said.

He took her hand and led her a little way further along the river, then off the path into a plantation of tall fir trees. It was quite sheltered here, and dim beneath the dark branches. There was a small clearing carpeted with pine needles. Beyond the magic ring of trees, the rising wind boomed across the water, but inside all was silence again.

When he touched her, he knew that love was more important than duty or kindness or pity, that he could no longer compromise or go on paying the high price his heart demanded in exchange for putting up with things. He had never felt so filled with regret or so betrayed by the passing of time.

He undressed her quickly, without breathing, as though she might vanish in a puff of smoke. How strange that he had known of this place, though he had never been here before with a woman. As though it had been waiting for them all these years. He removed his own clothes and laid her on a bed of their summer coats above the soft needles. It was only a lot later that he noticed his headache was gone.

Afterwards, they lay together for warmth and listened to the storm grow beyond the trees.

'Do you love me still?' he asked. It was dark, and he could see her only as a shape beside him.

'I never stopped,' she said.

'I want you to live here with me,' he said.

'We'll see.'

'I may be able to get an annulment. Pádraig Pearse has influence in the right quarters. He'd prefer a quiet annulment to a scandal.'

'We'll see.'

'I wish you wouldn't keep saying that.'

'What else can I say? You abandon me for fifteen years, then expect me to give up my life and my home to live here with you. It's not that easy, Declan. Really it isn't.'

'But you do love me?'

She pulled him to her, thinking of all the times she had lain in the darkness thinking of him, when he was not there to be touched.

On the opposite bank, a hidden watcher spied on them through a high-resolution night-sight. The name he used Ezekiel. He was not a voyeur, not by any stretch of the imagination. Like Declan, he had come for a last look at Castletown House before the conference began. He recognized Assistant Commissioner Carberry from his photographs, but the woman was unknown to him. He made a mental note of her face, then went on with his surveillance of the perimeter.

CHAPTER ELEVEN

Castletown House
Celbridge
7 October
1853 hours

It was a perfect evening for a reception, Declan thought. He lifted his head and looked out across the lawn, down to the Liffey, remembering the previous night. There had been a storm in the end, and they'd both gone back to Dublin soaked, but it hadn't mattered.

Now, a cool breeze had come up from somewhere, as though God looked after His own. The wrong God, of course – but Declan Carberry had never been one to quibble at theological niceties. There was a low mist on the river, as though hinting at the coming of autumn.

A cool night, then, but warm enough for guests to walk about the grounds or down by the river without catching a chill. The sybaritic urge had taken most of them, though the more steadfast resisted it and stayed together in small, earnest cliques. They would be the diehards on Wednesday morning. There was no alcohol, of course, nor would there be any pork on the dinner menu, nor were there many women present – but that was as far as the asceticism had been allowed to go.

Men came and went on the wide terraces or walked softly through gilded rooms lit by chandeliers. They carried glasses brimming with exotic fruit juices, calpis, or iced sherbet imported from Tehran and smelling of roses. The curious glanced with pretended insouciance at the menu: soufflé suissesse, ballotine of Irish salmon, gateau of artichoke (the word 'Jerusalem' discreetly

75

omitted), noisettes of Irish lamb in a tarragon sauce, Dublin Bay langoustine tails served with grated truffle in ravioli. Someone had sat up all night translating everything into Arabic and Persian.

The chefs had been wisely steered clear of trying to tackle Middle Eastern dishes. All the meat was guaranteed *halal*: there were men with beards in the kitchens to see that it stayed that way and that no wine or spirits were slipped in by any of the cooks.

The few Western guests were all seasoned diplomats. The alcoholics among them had come well fortified beforehand and were equipped with hip flasks to see them through the evening. Those who were gay knew better than to cruise the representatives of Islamic piety. Those who were gay and knew what they were doing had already made their arrangements with the assistance of a sweet young First Secretary at the Turkish embassy. Those who were straight had wives and mistresses tucked up in bed back home, deeply grateful all of them for a night off. Nobody much minded.

Ciaran Clark floated among them all like a swan on a river, the embodiment of grace and quiet bonhomie. He shook hands, he simpered, he made introductions, he tried out his ten words of all-purpose Arabic, he knew everybody's name, he had everybody's number. This was his moment, before the Taoiseach and President Fallon arrived.

He had been Foreign Minister since April. Kerry born, Dublin bred, Harvard polished. Turfed cottage and Ivy League had combined in him to produce the very model of the new Irishman. Like his mentor the Taoiseach, he had his eyes set firmly on Europe. He wanted to remake the land of Cúchulainn and Finn Mac Cumaill in his own image: confident, entrepreneurial, clear-eyed, and undistinguishable from anywhere else.

Declan watched him pass, black-suited and confident in himself. Sometimes he wondered whom he feared the most: Sinn Féin and their mad IRA boys with guns, driven by their vision of an Ireland that had never been and could never be, or Ciaran Clark and his Armani-suited wonders, content to look on while the country sank into a grey sea of their own banality.

Clark reminded Declan of a bird, though whether one of fine plumage or of prey he could not quite decide. It was too early to

76

know what lay behind the fine gestures and easy smiles. Clark's face was sharp, hawk-like, tense, the head poised on a slender neck. The eyes observed and recorded, but gave nothing away.

The two men had spent the morning arguing about the finer points of security at the reception. Clark had restricted the number of men Declan could deploy, and had banned random searches. Declan had told him he could not guarantee the safety of the delegates under those conditions. And he had asked to be allowed to keep an armoured unit of the Fiannóglach – the Army Ranger Wing – on the perimeter of Castletown House. Clark had turned him down point blank. Discretion was the order of the day. It would not inspire trust in the delegates if they were made uncomfortably aware of a police and military presence in their midst. Political and diplomatic considerations had to take priority. Declan would have to make do with twenty Gardaí and fifteen Rangers, kept well away from the guests.

The only military visible inside the house were Lieutenant General O'Rahilly, Chief of Staff of the Irish Defence Forces, and his Adjutant General, Major General Walsh. O'Rahilly had served with UNIFIL in Lebanon in the eighties and had spent a year as Chief of Staff of the UN Truce Supervision Organization. He knew a great deal more than anyone from the Department of Foreign Affairs about the problems of keeping the peace in the Middle East.

The other military were outside, keeping a low profile. On the front terrace, Declan Carberry was sharing a gripe with Captain Tommy Murtagh, OC of the Ranger Wing. Neither man was happy.

'I'm sorry about this, Declan,' Murtagh was saying. 'I'd have fifty men here if I could. But my hands are tied. I've done the best I can. I've cancelled all leave at the Curragh and put all sixty of the men back there on yellow alert. They'll get here fast if we need them.'

Declan looked behind him at the vast house, then round again at the wide, encircling grounds. Plenty of cover out there for an assassin. He'd wanted to keep the guests inside, but the warm evening had brought them out on to the terraces.

'Let's just hope we don't need them, Tom. Tell them they can all have a round on me once this is over.'

Murtagh smiled at him.

'You must be a wealthy man, Declan Carberry, the price Guinness is these days.'

Declan smiled back, but it wasn't much of a smile. His dinner suit had been hired for the evening. He shook his head gently.

'No, Tom. I'm not a wealthy man at all. I'm married to a wealthy woman. There's a difference.'

Ezekiel had his men in place and linked up through a trunked UHF communications system. They were dressed for action: one-piece Nomex suits over ballistic vests, black anti-flash hoods, gas masks. Each man carried two weapons: an H & K MP5 for the operation proper; and a semi-automatic rifle. The semi-automatics were fitted with Laurgage night-sights equipped with third-generation image intensifiers, the most expensive on the market. Too much depended on them to tempt him into the economy of first- or second-generation models. With these, a sniper could acquire a man-sized target at three hundred metres in low light conditions.

He looked at his watch: eighteen fifty-three hours. This whole thing depended on timing. The diversion, the perimeter penetration, the operation itself. If all went well, they would go into action as the light began to fade. The final phase of the mission could then be carried out under cover of darkness. The element of surprise would not be enough in itself. They needed darkness and speed as well.

He felt the skin grow tight across his scalp and a thin, nervous sweat on his palms. This was always the worst time: the moments leading up to an operation, the enforced idleness, the adrenalin building up in the bloodstream, adrenalin that could not yet be discharged.

There were still some minutes to go. He lowered himself to his knees and whispered into the mike built into his gas mask.

'Let us bend our knees in prayer,' he whispered. He could not see them from where he knelt, but he knew they were out there, bowing their heads. The sounds of the forest came to him, cautious, gentle sounds of a world preparing for the coming darkness. He remembered his first hunting trip in the Rockies, back when he was ten. His father had taken him on a deer-shoot, armed with his first gun, an old .22 Hornet that had belonged to his grandfather and was really unsuited for anything but varmint shooting. He still remembered the smell of the woods, the cracking of twigs beneath his inexperienced feet, the stars at night like broken glass from horizon to dark horizon.

'Lord, hear us.' He spoke softly, knowing the mike would transmit his voice undistorted to each member of his unit. 'We are gathered here in Your sight tonight . . .'

And the deer falling as he fired, mortally wounded, threshing in a field of bracken at dawn . . .

'. . . in these last days, seeking Your blessing and Your assistance. Our spirits are weak, shelter us with Thy Spirit.'

And the red blood, and his father standing and taking aim to finish it . . .

'Our hands are weak, strengthen them with Thy mighty Hand.'

And the deer jerking once more and lying still, the bracken suddenly silent, no birds, no squirrels . . . no God . . .

'Our eyes are weak, sharpen them, we beseech Thee; and grant us inner sight, like the vision Thou hast granted Thy servant David, that we may see and know and understand.'

And the tears he could not hold back, and his father's voice, rough and angry, like something biting at him: 'Act like a man.'

'And grant us courage in what we now begin, knowing that what we do, we do in Thy name. And if any perish, let him die a martyr in Thy holy cause. We ask Thy strength and Thy protection in this, our hour of trial. All this we ask in Thy Son's name and in the name of David, whom Thou hast sent to us. Amen.'

He fell silent. The rifle felt good between his fingers, heavy and dark and silent. It would speak only once tonight. He took a magazine from his belt and rammed it home. It held five 7.62 Glaser rounds. But one would be enough.

Declan looked at his watch. The Taoiseach and the President would be on their way now. He'd suggested that they should arrive before the light faded, but they had a prior engagement with the British ambassador, and he reckoned it would be nearer nine than eight o'clock when they got here.

Someone coughed gently behind him. He turned to see Concepta. She was wearing an elegant white outfit that had been specially designed for the evening. Hours of thought and discussion had gone into it, directed as much by politics as by fashion. It was striking as evening wear, yet unlikely to outrage any of the guests. A long white scarf covered her head. She was very lovely, he thought, and for the first time he understood why she was so much in demand at these events. This evening, in company, the mood between them was less tense.

'You look stunning,' he said.

'Thank you. I'm doing my bit. Wait till you see Sheilagh Burke. She's got up like a sister of St Peter Claver.'

He laughed. Sheilagh Burke was a silly woman whose husband ran Pádraig Pearse's chicken farms in County Limerick.

'All the same, Concepta, you should have stayed away. Pádraig Pearse had no right to make you come tonight. It's much too soon.'

'You're here.'

'I have to be. I wouldn't choose to be at a party.'

'Pádraig thought it would do me good to get out. And Brannigan thinks work will help keep my mind off things.'

She held out one of the glasses. 'I brought you something. It's called calpis.'

He looked at it.

'What is it?'

'It has lychee juice in it. Something else – I forget.'

'I'm on duty.'

'Jesus, Declan, there's not a drop of alcohol in it.'

It was the wrong time and the wrong place, but he could not help himself.

'Concepta,' he said. 'I've been thinking. When all this is over – this conference, I mean – I think I should move out after all. Find a place of my own, the way I was planning to do before . . .'

'She's barely been dead five weeks. Christ, Declan, I told you I need you to stay.'

'You'll be all right. We'll see each other. I just need to be on my own.'

He wondered if that was honest or fair. Even yesterday morning it might have been true; but now? He thought he was being disingenuous.

'What about me, Declan? Do you ever think of anyone but yourself? I'll be on my own in that tomb of a house. No husband, no daughter, no life to speak of.'

'I'll stay a little longer. But this can't be put off indefinitely. Maybe you could go down to the country for a while and stay with your family. It would do you good to get away from Dublin for a while. And they'd like to have you.'

'You've found someone else, haven't you?'

It seemed almost ridiculous. He'd found Amina fifteen years ago.

'That's nonsense,' he said.

'It's true though, isn't it? Why else would you want to clear out? Jesus, Declan, if you think I'm going to let you run off with some tart from Ballymun, or wherever else it is you pick them up, you can think again. It's not just me you'll have to contend with. Pádraig Pearse will roast you alive if you so much as mention it to him.'

At that moment, Ciaran Clark appeared behind her. He fixed a suspicious eye on Declan. With him was a tall man with a heavy beard.

'Concepta,' he said, 'I'd like to introduce you to Professor 'Abd al-Halim 'Abbud, head of the Egyptian delegation.'

She turned her back on Declan, stretched out her hand, and smiled.

'*Masa' al-khayr*,' she said in her most charming tones.

Declan watched her go without saying a word. The Foreign Minister nodded politely, then went off in search of another VIP. Declan was about to go when he felt a soft tap on his arm. He turned to see Amina smiling at him. At once, all the anger and tension left him.

'You don't know how glad I am to see you,' he said.

'That was Concepta, wasn't it?'

He nodded.

'She's very beautiful. You never did her justice when you used to speak of her.'

'I couldn't think of her as beautiful,' he said. 'Not when I was with you.'

She blushed.

'We're here on official business, Commissioner.'

'We were on official duties in Lebanon too, as I remember. Not to mention last night.'

She smiled, still embarrassed. She was dressed very differently to Concepta, in a European style trouser suit, her short hair uncovered.

'Does Ciaran approve of the way you're dressed?' he asked.

'I'm a modern woman,' she said, an edge to her voice. 'This is how I like to dress. In Algeria, fundamentalists like some of these people here tonight have slit the throats of schoolgirls for no other reason than that they were not wearing *hijab*. So I refuse to wear *hijab* either, in their honour. Do you object?'

He shook his head.

'How's she coping?' she asked, trying to change the subject.

'Concepta? Not very well. I think I told you that she was very bad when her parents died. She's taken Máiréad's death very badly too. I've had to leave her on her own a lot, organizing this conference.'

Amina said nothing, but she knew that wasn't entirely true. A lot of his evenings had been spent with her. Not that she blamed him: he'd had his own grief to cope with, and being with her had helped, or so he'd said.

'She seemed upset just before I came over.'

'Yes. That was my fault. I'm not very good at choosing my moments. I told her I want to move out, find a place of my own in town.'

She reddened again.

'Don't you think that's being rash?'

He shook his head.

'I'd already raised the idea before you arrived. It's something I have to do, whatever happens.'

'Wouldn't it be better . . .'

Declan's two-way pocket communicator suddenly beeped loudly. He pressed the receive button and spoke.

'Carberry.'

'Declan? This is Tommy Murtagh. We've got trouble, Declan. I just had a call from Curragh Headquarters. Half the Wing's been pulled out.'

'Pulled out? What do you mean?'

'There's been an alarm on the road west of Lucan. The British ambassador was on his way to dinner with the President of Maynooth College. His car's been ambushed.'

CHAPTER TWELVE

Tommy Murtagh had gone, taking his fifteen-man unit with him. The entire Ranger Wing at the Curragh had been placed on red alert. Other units were on their way from the camp to the scene of the ambush.

Declan Carberry lost no time in taking charge. Overriding Ciaran Clark's voluble protests, with Amina's help he got all of the guests inside, concentrating them in the ballroom on the first floor. It was the worst thing he could have done, but he had no way of knowing it at the time.

Rather than alarm anyone, they kept the ambush quiet. Declan swore to himself that heads would roll. He had not been told that the British ambassador was planning to pay a visit to St Patrick's, a theological seminary located at Maynooth, only about four miles north of Celbridge.

The decision to move people inside was explained in terms of the fading light and the growing breeze. The president and the Taoiseach would not be arriving now, of course: Declan had made that his first priority the moment he heard of the ambush. He could not rule out the possibility that the target for the ambushers had, in fact, been the presidential car, and that the attack on Ambassador Reynolds had been a ghastly if providential mistake.

Providential in the short term, at least. Declan shuddered to think what the fallout might be if Reynolds had been hurt or worse. Anglo-Irish relations had taken a severe pummelling following the murder of Christopher Ewart-Biggs, London's ambassador to Dublin, in 1976. Another assassination was unthinkable, not least in its consequences for the head of Special Branch. Declan felt another headache beginning.

Once the guests were back at their canapés and lychee juice,

Declan rearranged his team. He stationed ten men as a cordon along the inside of the perimeter fence, five outside the house itself, and five at strategic points inside. They would do until reinforcements came in from Dublin. Amina, Declan's principal liaison with the Muslim guests, discreetly alerted the various delegation bodyguards to the situation and asked them to be extra vigilant.

Outside, it was unnaturally quiet.

Ezekiel looked at his watch. Nineteen-fifteen. The ambush had been perfectly timed. That was a great weight off his mind. Tomorrow, the IRA accountant in New York would receive a slip of pink paper notifying him that a payment of one million US dollars had been made to a bank in Zurich. He would think the money came from Noraid. It did not. The chauffeur at the British embassy had already received ten thousand pounds. He thought it came from the IRA. It did not. Both men would keep their mouths tightly shut. What else?

He watched as the Transaif carrying the Rangers swung out of the gates. Time to act. His assault team consisted of twelve men and himself. Men of power. Men of God. The first step was to get them into position. He whispered into his laryngophone.

'Set jammers.'

At the signal, six of the team switched on jamming devices locked to the frequency of the perimeter alarm's r. f. transmitter. Nothing would happen at the command centre back in the house. The alarm would be dead, but nobody would know that. The instrument panels would show it working perfectly. And that was exactly how he wanted it, because it meant that nothing would happen once they crossed the line. Or so he prayed. If the alarm had not been deactivated after all, then he would have to abort the entire operation. Unless Garda bullets aborted it first.

'Go!' he said.

Silent figures began to move through the trees. They passed the perimeter. Ezekiel watched through powerful glasses for a reaction at the house, a sign that the alarm had been triggered.

'Hold still,' he whispered.

From his vantage point he could see at an angle of almost thirty degrees across the long front. The Garda commander had posted one man at the front corner of each wing, two on the front terrace, and two more lower down on the drive. That accounted for six, but he still had to know how many there were behind the house. He could not afford any mistakes.

His plan allowed him a maximum of four casualties before it became unworkable. The decision to work within such fine margins had not been reached lightly. In the end, he had calculated that the risks of going in with more than twelve men far outweighed those of losing too many in the assault. If he got men in, he had to get them out before reinforcements came from Dublin or the Curragh.

No response. So far, so good. The guards down below watched, on the alert. But no signal came from the command centre. They'd know what was happening soon enough, he mused.

'Move to your positions.'

The last of the sunlight lay lightly on the uncrushed grass. The world began and ended here in the forest, among the trees, in a realm of moving shadows. He could hear his own breath, dark behind the mask, a soft reminder of mortality: each breath that much nearer the last. He had worked it out once as a child. An average of fifteen breaths per minute. Twenty-one thousand six hundred per day. Five hundred and fifty million three hundred and sixty-eight thousand if you lived to be seventy.

As his men came out of the trees, they flattened themselves against the ground, crawling forward into a rim of low bushes.

'*Five in position . . .*'

'*Three in position . . .*'

'*Ten in position . . .*'

The voices broke into his consciousness as he shuffled to his own position, snagging his rifle on a low branch. Within moments everyone was in place. Number six – that was Capaldi – gave him the lowdown on the layout at the rear of the house.

'*Four more guards. Two at the wing corners, two at the rear entrance. They're all clearly visible.*'

'What about the roof?'

'*Nothing.*'

'OK. I'm going to number from the man on the drive nearest my position, moving clockwise as arranged. This is routine, no need for anybody to get flustered. Everybody takes a target except six and seven. One and twelve are long shots – nearly three hundred metres – two and eleven are medium-range – I estimate

85

one fifty to two hundred metres – and the rest are under a hundred each. I don't want any misses, so let's get the two long targets established first.'

That meant him and Ross. He raised himself on his elbows, manoeuvring the rifle into the firing position. The PSG1 weighed in at over eighteen pounds with the suppressor – he was glad he'd be ditching it after one shot. But the weight made it an ideal sniper's rifle, lending it stability. He lowered the tripod and swung the rifle down, away from the house. The cheek-piece felt cool against his face. The fingers of his right hand curled easily about the grip. He took slow, deep breaths and told himself there was no hurry.

As the rifle swivelled, he felt it begin, the strange symbiosis between himself and the weapon. In his mind, he hated it, loathed what it could do, what it could turn him into. But in his heart, he and the rifle were one. It was an extension of his deepest self. He hated killing, but he believed himself forgiven and empowered. A surgeon and his scalpel will cause pain, he thought, but if they heal the sick, what sin is there in spilling blood?

The world he saw in his sights was not the real world. The light-intensified images were ghostly things, shapes from a parallel universe. He could see long black cars like beached whales, shining and unreal. And the gravel of the drive, drained of all colour, like a pebbled beach without a sea. And then his target – not a man at all, not a human being with so many counted breaths left to breathe, but a ghost that lived in the little world of his rifle. A man could kill such phantoms with impunity, could kill them and go to his God smiling, running to His embrace.

The guard's head seemed to drift into the crosshairs. He steadied his finger against the trigger, holding his breath. '*Don't move*,' he murmured.

'Number one targeted,' he whispered into the mike.

'*Twelve targeted*,' came the response.

It was nineteen-nineteen.

Inside Declan was speaking on his mobile telephone with Garda Headquarters.

'I don't care if you have to bring in the reserve! Just get me all the men down here you can, and get them here now.'

86

'Sir, I need . . .'

He switched off the phone and looked out the window onto the terrace. This was the front room on the west wing. His mind was racing. According to the British embassy, the dinner at Maynooth had been a last-minute affair arranged between friends. The ambassador had been expected earlier, but the Taoiseach had invited him in for a few words with himself and the President. It made it all the more likely that the real target of the ambush had been Pádraig Pearse and Fallon. Except that . . .

If the ambush had been the work of the IRA – and he could not see who else might be responsible – it would not have been aimed at Ireland's two most prominent statesmen. The IRA's own Standing Order No. 8 was quite explicit about not engaging the military or the police of the Republic.

The more he thought about it, the more the timing and the location seemed too good to be true. It was starting to look like a set-up job. A diversion. The President and Taoiseach had not left Dublin. But the delegates were still here at Castletown House.

It looked quiet enough outside. In the distance, tall trees reflected the light of the dying sun. A bird trembled through the wind-tossed air. On the terrace, Paddy Delaney and Jim Costello guarded the main entrance. Further down the drive, Martin Kavanagh and Seán Maher were keeping an eye on the main gate. They were among his best men, all hand-picked for the squad and carefully selected for this week's special duty.

A peacock strutted on the lawn, barely visible against the twilight. It walked through its own world, untouched by the trivial concerns of the man who watched it, a thing of beauty merely.

In a split second, the whole scene changed. As Declan watched, the four Gardaí jerked sideways simultaneously and fell to the ground suddenly, like puppets whose strings have been cut. The peacock screamed, shrill and precise. Silence dropped again. The peacock spread its fan against the coming darkness.

With fumbling fingers, Declan pressed the button on his communicator.

'This is Carberry. I want a report on what's happening out there. Over.'

Silence. He held his breath. Silence.

He pressed the button a second time.

'Come in Team A. Over.' He realized his voice was shaking.

Silence.

'Is there anyone there for God's sake?'

He felt as though his heart was breaking. He pressed the button again.

'Team B. Can you hear me? Are you there, Conor? Over.'

'This is Conor. What the hell's going on, sir?'

'Keep your men on alert. Get the guests into the Long Gallery, but for Christ's sake don't panic them. Report to me at once if anything happens. Over and out.'

He ran to the control room. There was nothing he could do for any of the men outside: they had been dead before they hit the ground, the very precision of the shots had told him that.

The man at the console was desperately twisting dials. In front of him, eight monitors flickered soundlessly with lines of bright interference.

'Jesus Christ, what's going on?'

The operator turned.

'All the screens went dead, sir. About a minute ago. I can't get any of them back into action.'

'Did you see anything before they went off?'

'On the screens, sir? No. It was completely quiet out there, sir.'

'Well, it isn't quiet now. Someone's just gunned down Team A. Leave this fucking thing and get upstairs on the double. Report to Lieutenant Dunn.'

The man stared at Carberry. His face had gone white.

'Jesus, man, don't stand there gawping like an idiot! Move!'

The guard snatched up his Steyr AUG and dashed through the door into the broad entrance hall. He went through a pair of unfluted Ionic pillars and turned left towards the staircase. And then, gently, like a dancer who slows to execute a step of greater than usual complexity, he hesitated and began to twist his body round. His arms swung backwards in an arc and his rifle fell clattering to the black-and-white tiled floor.

Declan watched him fall, watched his blood spread like dark wine across the whiteness of the pillar, heard him cry out once – or was it just an echo in the empty, marbled hall? He looked up towards the main door. A man was outlined against the twilight. He was dressed from head to foot in black. Only his eyes were visible behind the glass of his respirator. He was staring straight at Declan. And he was holding an MP5 sub-machine gun pointed directly at his chest.

CHAPTER THIRTEEN

The assault had been rehearsed so many times, the real thing came almost as an anticlimax. They had built mock-ups of the house and grounds using recent photographs and interior plans taken from guide books. But only in the past day had there been any chance to estimate the possible strength of the resistance they could expect to meet.

At nineteen twenty-two four men secured the ground floor. The remaining eight threw aluminium ladders up against the windows of the Long Gallery on the first floor: seconds later they were at the windows, poised to enter. At a signal from Ezekiel, the two end men smashed a pane each and lobbed stun grenades into the room.

The grenades exploded simultaneously, blinding and deafening everyone in the gallery. The end men followed up the pyrotechnics with rubber ball CS gas grenades. Within seconds, the room had started to fill with thick, choking fumes.

While this was going on, the six men in the middle were using long-handled axes to hack their way through the wood and glass of the window frames. It did not take more than a few seconds.

The end men covered the guests inside with their MP5s while their companions clambered through. At that moment, a door in the west wall opened. A Garda officer ran into the room, his Steyr raised ready for firing. A wisp of gas stroked his face, choking him. Instinctively, he lifted a hand to wipe his eyes. And in that split second the gas seemed to explode as a hail of bullets tore both hand and head apart. A second burst of fire across the door deterred any further attempts to enter the room by that route.

Suddenly, in the midst of the gas, someone began to dance, turning and twisting without music, a shadow in the swirling

90

smoke. His name was Brendan McGlinchey, and he was one of the Gardaí sent to protect the guests in the Long Gallery. He had been thrown into utter confusion by the flash and roar of the stun grenade. But he had kept tight hold of his Steyr assault rifle, as though the weapon had become his anchor in a universe lurching out of control. His eyes and nose were streaming, it felt as though the gas were shredding him inside, a million tiny knives lacerating his lungs. But somewhere in his mind a stronger force was keeping tight control, telling him what was happening, what he had to do. He knew he had to locate the windows and fire.

He forced himself to open his eyes against the gas. The smarting was terrible, making him cry out in pain. He closed his eyes again. All around him was a world in madness, the sounds of animals caught in a stinging trap: baying, barking, snarling, without thought of grace or hope of redemption. And the sound of his own voice among them, crystal clear, humanity stripped clean away. He had a full magazine, thirty rounds. If only he could fire even a few of them off.

So many moving shapes, so much smoke, so little time. He brought the rifle round. His limbs felt heavy. He moved like someone in slow motion.

Another smashing of glass. Brendan steadied himself and pointed the rifle in the direction from which the sound had come. He pulled back hard on the trigger for full automatic. There was a loud blast of undirected fire, delivered in a broad, sweeping action. Every bullet hit the ceiling. The last man through the windows raised his own gun and shot him through the neck with a single round. A cloud of CS gas presented no problems of visibility. The raiders wore night-vision goggles: they could recognize a man-sized target three hundred metres away in starlight. Recognize it, acquire it, and hit it square.

All eight raiders were in the room now. There was a sound of rapid firing from behind the doors, accompanied by hoarse shouts. The remaining Gardaí were putting up a fierce resistance to the small assault team moving up from the ground floor.

Leaving two men to cover the rabble that a minute earlier had been a glittering collection of VIPs and their bodyguards, the leader of the raiding party directed the rest to the main doors. A stun grenade here would be counter-productive: it would affect his own men as they fought their way up the stairs as much as it would disorient the Garda force. Ezekiel instructed his men to set their weapons to single-shot firing. With his thumb, he slipped the firing lever on his own gun from 'F' to 'E', the single-shot position.

On the other side of the door, the chatter of gunfire continued. It was like listening to a television blaring in the next room. That made Ezekiel feel more unreal than ever, as though none of this were happening. He prepared to remake his reality in a mould of flesh and blood. To share the sacrifice, the act of immolation; to take on himself the sweat and blood and nails, to become one with his God: that was the heart of this thing. It was the Lord's Supper, with a gun for a chalice. For the second time in his life, he had entered the fire and the smoke in search of love. He lifted his foot and kicked the door open.

He fired twice in quick succession, hitting a policeman with each shot. Two of his men slipped through under his covering fire. But as the third reached the door, a burst of automatic fire threw him back bodily into the room. Of the seven Gardaí who had been defending the stairway, only two were still alive. The one who had just fired dodged behind a marble pedestal that held a pale Georgian bust. Ezekiel heard him ram a fresh magazine into place and stepped back as the man fired across the doorway again. There was a single shot from an MP5 and the Steyr fell silent. Ezekiel moved back out onto the landing. At that moment, the last of the Gardaí threw his weapon down and stepped out, holding his hands high. Ezekiel dropped him where he stood, a single shot to the forehead, clean and sacrificial. They could not afford to take prisoners.

In the Long Gallery, pandemonium was turning to cowed submission. It was nineteen twenty-four. A sharp through-draught blew across the room, dispersing the gas rapidly. The guests, dressed for a warm evening, were shivering. Several were bent over, throwing up. Concepta Carberry had found a chair and was sitting on it, wheezing hoarsely. Nearby, Ciaran Clark was doing what he could to distance himself from his guests. Amina was with a group of Muslim women, trying to calm them. She had already dumped her gun in an empty vase: years of experience told her when it was worth fighting back and when it was better to wait.

Ezekiel turned back to the room. Out of the corner of his eye, he caught a small movement. An Algerian bodyguard, recovering his wits, was reaching for the gun he had secreted beneath his dinner jacket. Ezekiel took two steps in his direction, aimed, and fired. The man dropped to the ground kicking. Ezekiel fired again. This time the bodyguard was still.

'Rodriguez, Nielsen, frisk the rest. Anyone with a gun is a bodyguard. Line them up over there.'

He paused, then unclipped a two-way handset from his chest.

'This is Homeboy. Come in Roadrunner. Over.'

There was a crackle, then a voice answered.

'*Roadrunner. Everything quiet out here.*'

'Get your asses down here now. We'll be ready to go in four minutes.'

'*We'll be there in two. Over and out.*'

He replaced the handset and spoke again into the laryngophone.

'Freeman? Robbins? How are things down there?'

'*Ground floor is secure. We have one prisoner. Not an Arab.*'

'Send him up here with Freeman. Robbins, you stay there and keep a lookout till we come down.'

He checked his watch.

Rodriguez and Nielsen had lined up seven men. Their guns were on the floor. Ezekiel came across.

'That's all?'

'All that had guns.'

'Shoot them. Rodriguez, you take care of it. Nielsen, check the exit.'

The bodyguards were no use to them. Worse than that, they could cause trouble in the retreat. Rodriguez went about his task with the unhurried efficiency of a slaughterman killing cattle. He loaded a fresh magazine: to stop half-way through in order to reload would have been unprofessional and cruel.

'Lie down!' he ordered.

One man did so, the others looked at him, confused and uncomprehending. Few of them understood a word of English. Rodriguez motioned them to their knees. One by one they knelt. Then he made them lie flat, face down.

He walked along the row, firing into the heads, two shots each. There were no survivors.

As the shooting died away, one of the party from the ground

floor entered, bringing with him Declan Carberry. In his evening dress, he looked just like another diplomat.

'Put him with the others,' ordered Ezekiel.

It was nineteen twenty-six. Ezekiel stood in front of the delegates.

'All Irish citizens step forward,' he commanded. His voice was magnified grotesquely by a device built into the mouthpiece of his mask.

No-one moved.

'I don't want any heroes,' he said. 'I want only the Muslims. The rest of you are free to go.'

No-one stepped forward.

Ezekiel had no time to waste. He strode into the crowd and came out dragging Ciaran Clark behind him. His face had been familiar to Ezekiel from press photographs. The Foreign Minister whimpered as he was brought to the front.

'I want you to identify your people,' he told him. 'If you hesitate, I will kill you. If you try to include any Muslims, I will also kill you.'

His eyes streaming, his throat on fire, Clark did as he was told. This was not his sort of battle. Let someone else go in with flags flying. He pointed out members of his staff one by one, and they were pulled out by the raiders and sent to stand in the middle of the room. The Irish military men, O'Rahilly and Walsh, were easily recognizable in their dress uniforms.

Clark caught sight of Declan Carberry. He was tempted to leave him behind, but he knew it would not wash – Carberry did not look remotely Middle Eastern. And, in any case, Ciaran needed a suitable scapegoat on whom to lay the blame for tonight's fiasco. He pointed a finger at Declan.

Doing so, he remembered Concepta, huddled out of sight near the back with the group of Muslim women, in her long dress and headscarf. Ciaran stepped forward and made to bring her out. As he did so, Ezekiel shook his head and pushed her back.

Before anyone else could move, Amina hurried across to Concepta and brought her back to the front.

'You stupid fool,' she shouted at Ezekiel. 'Can't you see she's not a Muslim? Her name's Concepta Carberry, and she's the Prime Minister's sister. If you take her, there'll be hell to pay.'

Ezekiel hesitated, then nodded and told Concepta to join the Irish.

'What about you?' asked Ezekiel, grabbing Amina by the upper arm. 'You're not a Muslim?'

Ciaran Clark stepped forward, shaking his head.

'Her name's Amina Bustani and she's Lebanese. Check the guest-list if you want.'

Ezekiel looked more closely. He remembered her face from the night before, down by the riverside with the head of security. The other woman must be his wife. So who was this? Not a delegate, by the look of her and her behaviour yesterday evening. Garda posing as an Arab? Or something more interesting? He nodded, and she was pushed back into the group of hostages.

'For God's sake, she isn't a delegate,' came a shout from the rear. Declan darted forward in an attempt to pull Amina to safety. The raider nearest him turned and swung the butt of his MP5 against his temple.

For a moment, Declan's headache cleared miraculously, then Castletown House came crashing in a heap all around him, crushing him helplessly beneath its weight. Marble and glass and gilded cornices became darkness as heavy as lead.

CHAPTER FOURTEEN

Dublin
8 October
1045 hours

The streets through which they drove were ordinary streets, the people on them ordinary people. Or so it seemed. Declan could not distinguish any longer between the ordinary and the grotesque. In his head, a dull ache reminded him of the blow he had received over fourteen hours earlier. At St James's Hospital they had shaved a circle of hair away and stitched the wound. His hand kept straying to the dressing that covered it, as though about to tear it off. The throbbing in his skull was less severe than most of his headaches. They had given him painkillers at the hospital, but warned him against using too many, or repeating the dose too often. As if he cared.

Someone had been there waiting for him when he came round. Not one of his own men, but a grey-suited type who looked and acted as though he belonged to intelligence. A lot of use they would be now, thought Declan. But he said nothing.

How many had died last night? Twenty of his own men, certainly. All officers he had known personally, good men for whom he considered himself accountable. And he had watched them kill the bodyguards, seven of them, all strangers, all his responsibility. And after he lost consciousness? He had no idea. He only remembered waking up in a stark white hospital room, his head aching and his thoughts in a mess.

The man in the suit had refused to answer any of his questions. He had waited patiently while Declan was taken for X-rays and subjected to a range of tests. When they gave him a relatively clean bill of health shortly after ten, the man had asked that he be discharged immediately. The doctors would have preferred to keep Declan in for further observation over the next twenty-four hours, but the man insisted and got his way.

Now, they were driving down Nassau Street, with the long grey wall of Trinity College on their left. There was nothing intimidating or official-looking about the black Volvo, but the late-morning traffic seemed to melt away from it as though by magic. Dublin had never seemed more unreal to Declan, more insubstantial. He guessed where they were headed, more or less.

The car slowed at the government offices in Merrion Street, turning into the ministers' driveway alongside the north wing. They turned left into a covered archway, where Declan's minder hurried him out. A lift took them to the first floor. It was only a short walk to the Council Chamber. Two Rangers armed with Steyr automatics stood on guard outside the panelled door. The man in the suit flashed a pass and the door was opened.

A square table took up most of the room. On the walls hung portraits of historic figures, brooding over the present. At the far side of the table sat Pádraig Pearse Mangan, looking more haggard than Declan could have imagined him. Near him were grouped seven other men, all of whom Declan recognized. Lieutenant General Denis Quaid, army Chief of Staff; Tómas O'Sullivan, like Declan an Assistant Garda Commissioner; Martin Fitzsimmons, head of C3; Seán Roche, the Justice Minister; Pat Devlin, the Garda Commissioner; Eoin Ceannt, Ireland's representative on the European Commission for Terrorism; and Ciaran Clark, white-faced and still clearly stunned. A stenographer sat at one end of the table, ready to take notes. By the look of it, they had all passed a sleepless night.

Ciaran Clark got up and ushered him to a seat. Pádraig Pearse glanced at him once, then looked away awkwardly. There was a stiff silence, then the Taoiseach seemed to pull himself together.

'Thank you for coming, Mr Carberry. I'm sorry we had to drag you out of hospital. But we have a crisis on our hands here, and we need to ask you some questions.'

'Questions? What about? I don't even know what happened. I've been trying to find out since I came round this morning.'

'Assistant Commissioner,' interrupted Roche, 'perhaps you

could begin by going with us over the security arrangements you made for the conference at Castletown.'

Declan turned to his brother-in-law.

'Pádraig, for God's sake, won't anyone tell me what happened last night? Is Amina Bustani alive? What about my men?'

'Will you answer the Justice Minister's question, please, Mr Carberry? There are things we need to know.'

Declan looked round the table. His companions were all stony-faced, their faces giving away nothing.

'Please tell them what they want to know, Declan. It's for the best.' Tómas O'Sullivan looked embarrassed.

Declan wanted to hit out. Why were they keeping the truth from him? Was he suspected of collusion with the terrorists who had attacked the conference? Could they be that dense?

'There's a file in my office giving details of the arrangements,' he said. 'You can consult that if you need to.'

'We want to hear your own version of how the security arrangements were made. We need to know who had access to what. If there was an informer inside the Special Detective Unit, we have to track him down. Quickly.'

'There was no informer. All the men involved in the operation were there that night. As far as I know, they are all dead. If you want to know what went wrong, you might begin by asking Mr Clark here who was responsible for restricting the security force to thirty-five men and refusing to allow checks.'

Pat Devlin, the Garda Commissioner, leaned forward. He was an old friend. But his manner was cold.

'I understand those decisions were yours. Apparently the Taoiseach and Mr Clark tried to persuade you to increase security, but you chose to ignore their recommendations.'

Ciaran Clark was earnestly inspecting the top of the table. Pádraig Pearse stared ahead, saying nothing.

'That's a deliberate distortion of what happened. I . . .'

'Mr Carberry, I would warn you against trying to shift the blame for your own operational weaknesses onto the Taoiseach and a member of the cabinet.' Devlin was a hardliner, very close to the Prime Minister, brought up on the struggle with the IRA. Declan knew he was not a man to go up against lightly.

By now, he knew what was going on. They were looking for a scapegoat on whom to pin the blame for last night's fiasco, and who better than the Taoiseach's brother-in-law? What better sacrifice, what brighter evidence of the government's pure intentions?

'I deployed the number of officers available to me from the Gardaí, and I was allowed fifteen soldiers from the Sciathán Fhiannóglaigh. There were to have been three rotating watches. Watch B was on duty at the time of the raid.'

'Under your direct command?'

'On that occasion, yes.'

'What was the chain of command?' asked Roche.

The questioning continued without pause for over an hour. By then Declan's head was spinning and he had started to feel nauseated. They were stitching him up, and he had no means of defending himself. People more powerful than himself had decided that his head should roll to save their own.

'Mr Carberry,' Pádraig Pearse began haltingly, 'I very much regret this, but it has been decided that you should be suspended from duty pending an official enquiry into last night's killings. As the police officer with overall responsibility for security, you cannot be absolved of blame for what happened. It will be for the enquiry to determine whether or not there was a leak, and, if so, how and when it occurred.

'We shall want a full report on the security measures taken at Castletown House, the failsafe procedures designed to operate in the event of an emergency, and a thorough analysis of what went wrong. You'll have it on my desk first thing on Thursday morning. Is that clear?'

'Yes, sir.'

'We know this must come as a blow to you on top of everything you've been through, but you will appreciate that we have no option. Thank you for coming here straight from hospital. I'm sure the gesture won't be forgotten by the board of enquiry.'

The stilted formality of Pádraig Pearse's language alerted Declan to the fact that the man was in a deep funk. The repercussions of last night's raid, not to mention the ambush of the British ambassador, both coming on top of last month's bombing and Máiréad's killing, would not be easily deflected. More heads than Declan's would roll. More careers than his would be at stake. For all he knew, the entire government would be on the carpet in a matter of days. No wonder they were rushing to cover up what they could while they could.

He got to his feet. For a moment he swayed, and Tómas O'Sullivan reached out a hand to steady him.

'I'll be all right,' he said. 'I'll see myself out. I know the way.'

'One of the Rangers will show you to the door. Go home and get some rest.'

He turned at the door.

'Now we've got that over with,' he said, 'perhaps one of you will tell me what happened after I was knocked out last night.'

But no-one answered him. The door opened and he was ushered out in silence.

CHAPTER FIFTEEN

Paddy O'Leary was waiting for him half-way down the corridor. He had been the Taoiseach's private secretary for some years before Pádraig Pearse entered office. A fourth-generation Republican, he had voted Fianna Fáil soon after the Official IRA abandoned its policy of abstaining from elections. His past was murky, but he had the reputation of a hard man who looked after his master like a hawk. He and Pádraig Pearse had been friends since school. According to Concepta, he was the only person her brother really trusted.

'Mr Carberry,' he said, 'would you step this way, sir?'

'I'm finished here,' said Declan. 'I'm on my way home. For God's sake, Paddy, I'm half-dead one way or the other.'

'It's the Taoiseach's special orders, sir. If you don't mind.'

The Taoiseach's special orders. Just what the hell sort of game was Pádraig Pearse playing? Declan hesitated, then followed Paddy down a side corridor. The Ranger did not come after them.

'If you'll wait in here, sir,' said Paddy, showing him into a small office, 'the Taoiseach won't be long.'

'Can you tell me what's going on, Paddy?'

'No, sir, I can't. I only know there's been terrible trouble and that there's more to come. That's all I know, on my honour. I'm sorry.'

Pádraig Pearse turned up twenty minutes later to find Declan unscrewing the top of the bottle of painkillers.

'I'll get Paddy to bring you a glass of water for those,' he said, slipping out again briefly. When he came back in Declan could see that he was washed out, the control he had displayed during the past hour and more slipping at last.

'Holy Mary, Mother of God,' he exclaimed as he took a seat

opposite Declan. The office was sparsely furnished with a few uncomfortable wooden chairs and a table in the corner that could be pulled out for committee meetings.

'I want to go home, Pádraig,' Declan said.

'Stay in your seat for God's sake, Declan. I haven't finished with you yet.'

There was a knock and Paddy O'Leary appeared with a tray. It held two glasses and a bottle of Ballygowan water. Declan took the tablets and set one of the glasses on the table.

'Jesus, Declan, I'm sorry about what just happened. There was nothing I could do, believe me. You can hardly credit the pressures . . .'

'Spare me the recital, Pádraig. And at least tell me what happened last night. I seem to remember that Concepta got out all right. But what about the others? Are they all alive?'

'Alive? Possibly. Dear God, I hope so. Here, will you take a look at this?'

He drew a folded sheet of paper from his pocket and passed it to Declan. His hand was shaking. He reached for the second glass on the tray, took a hip flask from his pocket, and half filled it with whiskey.

'Mother of God,' he blasphemed again, lifting the glass to his lips and downing the contents in a single swallow. Declan said nothing as he refilled the glass.

'I don't suppose you're allowed this stuff.'

Declan shook his head. He unfolded the sheet and spread it out. It was plain white typing paper, A4, 80 gsm, the sort you could buy in any stationery store. A typewritten message sat square and undecorated in the centre of the page.

'The prophet, which shall presume to speak a word in my name, which I have not commanded him to speak, or that shall speak in the name of other gods, even that prophet shall die.' Thus has God spoken. Praised be God. His word is the truth, and it endureth forever.

Declan looked up.

'What is this, for God's sake?'

'It was in my mail this morning. Paddy found it. Delivered by hand. The quotation at the beginning is from the book of Deuteronomy.'

102

> The Lord has seen, and the Lord has heard great wickedness among the nations and the sons of men. Praise the Lord, and praise His Son. Hallelujah. I came out of the flames, and they did not devour me. 'When thou walkest through the fire, thou shalt not be burned; neither shall the flame kindle upon thee' (Isaiah 43:2). I came out of the smoke, and it did not blind me. 'And there arose a smoke out of the pit, as the smoke of a great furnace' (Revelations 9:2).

'Jesus, Pádraig, this is a load of nonsense. Don't tell me you've started listening to street-corner preachers.'

'Just keep reading, Declan.'

> The abomination of Arabia shall perish by the sword. The following are with us and are at all times subject to the fear of death, for the Lord is not merciful to them that do not fear Him or dread His wrath. 'For the fierce wrath of the Lord is upon you' (2 Chronicles 28:11).
>
> From the Children of Egypt, two. From the tribes of Arabia, likewise two. From the Sons of Lebanon, two, and from Syria likewise. From them that dwell in Algeria, two, and out of Libya, two. From the inhabitants of the land that lies upon the two seas, where holy Constantinople once stood victorious, two. From the Medes and Persians, two. From the bazaars of Pakistan, two. From the tents of Afghanistan, two. From the shores of distant Malaysia, two. Of women, we have six.
>
> They are companions of the devil, and their lives are nothing in the eyes of the Lord. Remember them when you enter the Council Chamber (and take counsel, but the best counsel is with God). 'The counsel of the Lord standeth for ever, the thoughts of his heart to all generations' (Psalms 33:11).

Declan laid the paper gently on his lap.

'Tell me what you know,' he said.

Pádraig Pearse gazed at him intently for several moments, as though trying to read his thoughts.

'While you were unconscious, we were able to get statements from Ciaran and his staff. They were all left unharmed. Concepta, as you say, was allowed to go. She's all right, but I've sent her down to the country. God knows, she needs a rest.

'The only casualties were your men and the bodyguards. The delegates were taken by the raiders and the Long Gallery was locked on the others. But they saw what happened through the windows.'

He took a deep breath and a sip of whiskey.

'There was a coach with blacked-out windows waiting on the drive. The hostages were bundled on board along with the raiders and then driven off at top speed. They'd been gone about eight minutes before the first relief unit arrived at Castletown. By the time the house was secured and they reckoned it was safe to release the survivors, another ten or more minutes had passed.'

'What happened to the British ambassador? Was that just a decoy?'

'Oh, the English gentleman was ambushed all right. No doubt about that. He's not hurt, but he's badly shaken. There was a terrific firefight, guns blazing just like in a Western. One of your man's bodyguards was killed, and the driver was hurt. The attackers were gone by the time the Rangers got there. As you say, it was all a diversion to draw the Rangers off from Castletown and to get more in from the Curragh. To tell you the truth, it was very successful.'

'IRA?'

'Ah, well now, let's not be jumping to conclusions. That's what Downing Street is saying, and I'll not argue with them: they're the obvious candidates, them or the INLA. But that note on your knee was never written by a Sinn Féiner.'

'You think this is genuine? It could just be a hoax.'

'Hoax my arse. That's the real thing all right.'

'You're sure of that?' The painkillers had started to work. Declan's head was beginning to clear. He wondered if they'd let him have another bottle when this was finished.

'To begin with, not a word of all this has been breathed to the press. Nor will it be. The whole thing is being kept under tighter wraps than the Secret of Fatima. Thank God we had the wit not to allow any reporters in to Castletown last night. No-one need know a thing.'

'Jesus, Pádraig, you don't seriously think you can keep a thing like this buried for long, do you?'

Pádraig Pearse shook his head. He seemed very tired. More than that, he seemed to have aged. He raised the glass to his lips and filled his mouth with whiskey.

'Of course not. But the longer it stays out of the papers the better. The last thing we need is half the television crews in the world descending on Dublin. I've given strict orders that there's to be a blackout, and I believe there will be one for a while yet. Anyway, as I was saying, it means that whoever wrote that little *billet doux* knew exactly what had happened. Which means it was not a member of the general public.'

Declan waved the sheet in the air.

'For Christ's sake, Pádraig, this is the work of a maniac.'

'Is it now? I'm glad you're so sure. From what I've heard so far, last night was the work of professionals. I doubt you'd find cooler heads in the Jesuit Order. It isn't maniacs we're dealing with here.'

'What, then? What's the motive? The point of the thing?'

'Oh, now, I've no doubt we'll find that out soon enough. For the moment, all we know is that someone has taken our delegates hostage, that they're holding them in a safe location, and that they've got in touch with me.'

'That's not all,' Declan said.

'What else?'

'We know they're not Muslims. The note proves that. It wasn't the work of jealous rivals or what have you. I doubt very much if it came from one of the Middle East secular opposition groups. If you ask me, it sounds more like the Christian lunatic fringe.'

'Mother of God save us from that crew. But you could be right. I'll have it looked into.' He lifted the glass and took a small mouthful.

'Pádraig, you haven't finished telling me what happened after the coach drove off. There must have been a good description. Wasn't it stopped at a roadblock?'

'There were blocks up inside an hour. Every road out of Cel-bridge for a fifty mile radius. No sign of the bus. There are two possibilities: either they're holed up somewhere inside that radius, or they managed to dump the bus and got the hostages out some other way.'

'I'd go for that. You'll find the coach in a barn or a lock-up.'

'We're looking.'

Pádraig drained the last of the whiskey and set the glass aside. He had always known when to control his drinking.

'Declan, Ciaran says that Concepta told him that evening you were thinking of leaving her. I pray to God that's not true.'

'It is true, Pádraig. We've come to the end of it.'

'Ah, sure I can't believe that. Not you and Concepta. You were always the great couple.'

'That's a load of nonsense, Pádraig, and you know it. It's not too late for either of us. If we lived in a normal society we could do it legally, but as it is we'll just have to put up with it.'

'Well, don't be hasty, Declan. Don't be hasty. Wait till this business is over. And a while after that. It would be cruel to leave her after what she's gone through over Máiréad.'

'It's you she needs, Pádraig. It's you she's always needed.'

'She needs us both. But let's talk about this another time.' He looked at his watch. 'I've got to go in a few minutes. There's a meeting with the National Security Committee.'

He paused.

'Declan, I really am sorry you were put through all that, but it was necessary if you're to be any help to me at all.'

'Help? I thought I was being kicked out.'

'Don't be so gormless, man. Would I want you out at a time like this? Sure, we all know you weren't responsible for the lack of manpower last night. Though I doubt very much whether twenty or thirty more men would have saved the day. That's not important now. What is important is what's likely to happen in the next few days and the next few weeks.

'You'll have guessed that we have a hostage situation on our hands. There'll be demands pretty soon, and God knows what else. A ransom, or political concessions, or an exchange of hostages for prisoners in Cairo or Tehran. We're already coming under considerable pressure from the governments of the hostages themselves. There have been meetings with ambassadors in Dublin, and more are flying in from London today.

'I'm doing what I can to keep the operation in Irish hands, but you know as well as I do that however mysterious the ways in which God works, leaving it to the Irish isn't one of them. I don't expect to hold out more than forty-eight hours, probably a good deal less. All the major security agencies have been alerted. Obviously, we'll want to cooperate with them, especially at the European level. But this is an international crisis, and you can bet everyone and his uncle will want a hand in it.

'That's why I moved you sideways. I'm sorry the meeting had to be so rough, but the other agencies are sure to want a transcript of it, so I had to make it convincing. Roche knows what's going on, and so do Ceannt and Fitzsimmons. I thought it better if the others were left in the dark for the present.

'Declan, I want you to run your own operation independent of the SDU and any other agency that may be brought in. You'll be kept abreast of all that happens – you have my word on that. I want this thing cleared up by ourselves, not some interfering pricks from MI5 or the CIA.'

Declan felt a headache starting again, in spite of the tablets he'd taken. Whatever his feelings about carrying the can for last night's disaster, they had been mingled with a sense of relief at getting out at last. Now, Pádraig Pearse was drawing him in deeper than ever.

'Pádraig, I have a report to write. It's going to take all my time.'

'Jesus, Declan, if I didn't know you better, I'd think you were soft in the head. The report will be written all right. It has to be written. But you needn't give it another thought. I have a man in an office somewhere with a dozen pints of Guinness and a typewriter. Relax, man – you won't even know you've written it.'

Declan stared at him. There was desperation written all over his face. Declan was tempted to play the thing for all he could get out of it. But he was too tired and too old for that sort of nonsense. Screwing was a young man's game.

'For goodness' sake, Pádraig, you can't expect me to take on an operation like this on my own. The investigation could stretch anywhere.'

'You can choose your own team. A dozen of the best men, more if you need them. You'll have the use of a suite of offices on Merrion Square – Paddy will give you the details. There will be a direct secure line to my office and another to Martin Fitzsimmons. He already has men installing a computer system. You will have direct access to Garda and government intelligence files. Talk over any details with Martin. He has my authorization to give you whatever you want.'

'I haven't said I'll do it yet.'

'You'll do it. Declan, I want you to find the people behind this business, and I want you to put them behind bars for a very long time. If that isn't possible, I don't think anybody is going to worry about the body count. Most important of all, though: I want those hostages out unharmed and back with their families. Otherwise . . .'

Pádraig Pearse shivered.

'Otherwise what?'

'If anything happens to them, Declan, we'll all go down with them.'

The Taoiseach stood.

'Go home, Declan, and get some sleep. You've got a long day ahead of you tomorrow.'

CHAPTER SIXTEEN

Killiney
Dublin
8 October
1855 hours

Day had come and gone, night was descending. Declan sat in the garden of his empty house, high above Killiney Bay, overlooking the dark incoming, outgoing sea. He had sat there, on and off, for hours, motionless as the tide turned and turned again, concealed by tall trees and the shadows they cast on the dappled grass.

The garden was growing cold. A sharp wind had moved in from somewhere across the sea, stroking the leaves on the trees. Until Máiréad's death, he had not sat on the old wooden bench for years, nor watched the sea, nor been physically alone. Now, he could barely pull himself away. He sat like an older man, waiting for night to fall.

Sleep had not come all day, as though his mind, fearful of oblivion, craved wakefulness. Guilt sat in him like a Sunday-morning priest. And remorse, and sorrow, and a growing dread. He had been unable to keep down food or drink. Outside, light drained from the sky. The sea grew black.

Inside, the house seemed deserted without Concepta, something he had not expected to feel. She had not spent much time there in recent years, but the place had always retained a sense of her presence. Strangely, her absence made all the more acute his sense of Amina's loss. He had only just regained her, and now she was further away than she had ever been. Knowing she might soon be dead, might already be dead, he felt desolate, caught between empty rooms and the sea.

He went inside. As he entered the kitchen, the phone rang. He crossed quickly to the table on which it sat, catching it moments before the answering machine cut in.

'Declan?' It was Martin Fitzsimmons.

'Who did you think it would be?'

'I thought you should know that they've found the bus. It had been abandoned in a barn on the outskirts of Naas. The farmer's being questioned, but it's ten to one he knows nothing about it. The barn was out in a back field, one he seldom used. The Gardaí have men here now going over it for fingerprints.'

'Tell them to call it off. They're wasting their time.'

'There may be prints.'

'Of course there'll be prints. What do you expect to find on a bus? If it was ever in public use, which I'm sure it was, there won't be an inch of it without fingerprints. I can't believe the raiders would have cleaned it down before the operation and then proceeded to smear every last inch of it with clues for the police to find. And something tells me you won't find any of their prints on your files.'

He paused.

'Do you know yet what they did after dumping the bus?'

'There's evidence they had cars hidden in the barn. Plenty of tyre-tracks inside and out. They'll have bundled the hostages into them and driven off.'

'In one direction?'

'Only as far as the main road. They got onto the N7 just above the Newhall crossroads, on the Drogheda side. There's mud where they came through. But after that some went right and some left, and from then on they could have gone in twenty different directions. They'll have done that at any rate. You can be sure they won't have travelled in a convoy. Better to have risked the bus than that. Once they were well enough away, they'll have headed to wherever it was they had for a rendezvous.'

Declan thought about that.

'How can we be sure they didn't have a dozen different destinations?' he asked. 'For all we know, they're keeping the hostages in more than one place. Maybe a dozen places or more.'

'Jesus, Declan, I hadn't thought of that. It would make the job of finding them a real terror. But all the same, it would increase the risk of someone stumbling across them.'

'Only for that one hiding-place. The others would remain as untouched as ever. Well, it's only an idea. A single hideout would be easier to control.'

'I'll mention it to Pat Devlin all the same. But I'll have to tell him it came from me. He doesn't know you're in on this.'

'Tell him what you like. He isn't going to be the one to find them anyway. I am.'

CHAPTER SEVENTEEN

Baalbek
Lebanon
9 October
0700 hours

Morning prayers had just finished at the al-Rida mosque. The cramped and battered building was the most important of the numerous Shi'ite places of worship in the town, the headquarters of the Lebanese branch of Hizbollah. Outside it, the streets were draped with red-and-black and yellow-and-green flags. Inside, bearded men stood in groups talking. Some shook hands as they took their leave, heading off to open shops and offices. Others renewed old acquaintances. One or two stood apart, reciting supererogatory prayers. A row of old men, their fingers twisting strings of prayer beads, sat at the front. Here and there were little knots of teenagers, their beards sparse or not yet grown, watching their elders, learning how to conduct themselves in adult society. A few children, all boys, played quietly around their fathers.

At the mosque entrance, armed militia in khaki shirts and camouflage jackets watched every passer-by. These were not the young men who normally patrolled the mosque precincts, but senior militiamen, long-standing Hizbollah fighters who had seen action during the civil war and still led the struggle against the Zionist regime to the south. A little further out, checkpoints had been set up to stop cars and trucks entering the streets around the mosque. No-one would get within five hundred yards of the mosque who was not known to the tightknit community of worshippers whose spiritual and material needs it served.

Inside, a few latecomers went through their prayers alone,

heedless of the conversations taking place around them. At the centre of every group could be seen the black-and-white turbans and black robes of the *ulama*. Several were Iranian, representatives of the government of the Islamic Republic, or emissaries for leading *mujtahids* at the theological seminaries of Qum, Karbala, or al-Najaf. Many of them were young men who had barely finished their *Dars al-kharij* year. Some held Qur'ans, others books of sermons. There was an air of expectation among them. Every few moments, someone would lift his head or turn and look towards a low door at the rear of the building.

There was a flurry of voices at the front, just inside the entrance; a hush began at the door and passed rapidly through the mosque. A group of women entered and made their way towards the female section, a narrow area cordoned off from the rest of the *masjid* by sturdy grey curtains. Their faces were heavily veiled and they were dressed uniformly from head to foot in black. The first to enter were the *'Ara'is al-Damm*, the celebrated Brides of Blood, virgins who had dedicated their lives to Husayn, the Prophet's grandson and the Prince of Martyrs. All had taken vows to offer their lives when the time came, by carrying out suicide attacks on the enemies of Islam. Most were members of the Sayyida Zaynab Brigade, a commando squad for women financed and run by Hizbollah, the chief Iranian-sponsored organization in Lebanon.

After them came thirty or so women of varying ages, also in black. These were mothers, sisters, aunts, grandmothers, and cousins of those Brides of Blood who had already given their lives for the cause. They walked quietly, anxious not to disturb the men at their prayers. No-one greeted them. They would come and leave in silence.

As though at a signal, the men and boys began to sit down in rows facing the *minbar*, the high stepped pulpit normally reserved for the Friday sermon. *Saqis* started to pass among them, carrying trays with tall jugs and beakers. They poured out glasses of rose-water *sharbat* and passed them round with murmured blessings.

Word had gone round late the night before that Sayyid Muhammad Husayn Fadlullah was going to deliver a sermon after the *fajr* prayer. The leading authority within Hizbollah and its religious mentor, he seldom made public appearances now. For some of those present, it would be their first opportunity to hear him speak in person. For others, a chance to listen once again to the voice that had inspired and guided them in their struggle through civil war and invasion.

The door at the rear opened and two young clerics came out, followed by the shaykh himself. He was sixty now, grey-haired and serious, but he walked like a much younger man and his eyes shone with barely contained emotion. He wore his black turban high on his head like a crown. While his two assistants took their positions on either side, he mounted the stairs of the pulpit and sat down on the last step but one.

No-one spoke. No-one moved. All eyes were on Fadlullah.

'Bismillah al-Rahman al-Rahim,' he began. *'Al-hamdu li 'llah rabb al-'Alamin, wa sala 'llah 'ala sayyidina wa mawlana Muhammad wa alihi al-tahirin, wa la'natu 'llah 'ala a'da'ihim wa ghasibi huquqihim wa nasibi shi'atihim wa munkiri fada'ilihim min al-jinn wa 'l-uns min al-awwalin wa 'l-akhirin ila yawm al-din . . .'*

The exordium finished, he fixed his eyes on the congregation. From his expression and the tone of his voice, they had already guessed that whatever news he might have for them was grim.

'I congratulate you, people of God. You have been steadfast and loyal, firm in the true faith. Lovers of the Prophet, peace be upon him, lovers of the holy Imams, lovers of the martyred Husayn. We have shared a thousand griefs together. We have watched a thousand rivers of blood spill upon the sands of our homeland: the blood of our sons and daughters, of our brothers and sisters. Lebanon has become a plain of Karbala for our sacrifice. Beirut has been turned into a graveyard for our children.'

He paused and looked towards the long grey curtain that cordoned off the women.

'Among us today are the *'Ara'is al-Damm*. May God and the Imam of the Age be pleased with them. May the Prophet and his daughter Fatima shower blessings upon them. They have shamed our menfolk with their courage. I congratulate them: may God soon deliver the keys of paradise into their hands.'

A small shiver went through the women's section. There was no mistaking the meaning of the shaykh's words: very soon the volunteers would be called to action. Of those now standing behind the curtain, some would soon be dead.

'The duties incumbent on all believers are few in number. To pray, to observe the fast, to go once on the pilgrimage to Mecca, to give alms, to avoid whatever is forbidden, to cling to whatever is good. But in these days another duty lies on us collectively: to wage *jihad* against the enemies of Islam until the earth returns to God. *Wa qatiluhum hatta la takuna fitnatun wa yakuna 'l-din li 'llahi.* "Wage war with them until mischief is at an end and the religion belongs to God." What the word of God has promised will undoubtedly come to pass.

'But today a great dagger has been thrust into the heart of Islam.'

A seamless silence, a sea of faces without motion, breath held in every chest, every eye on the speaker's lips.

'The delegates who had gone to attend the conference of Muslim scholars in Ireland have been taken hostage by a gang of Crusaders and Zionists. Among them was my friend and teacher, the luminous pearl of faith, the father of virtues, *Fakhr al-Milla wa 'l-Din*, Shaykh Mu'in Usayran. All here know him and love him, even as I do. At this very moment, his commentaries on the Word of God are to be found in the homes of believers everywhere. But even as I speak with you, his life hangs by a thread. His life, and the lives of his companions.

'People of God, I wish you to return to your homes to pray for the lives of our hostages. There are to be no demonstrations. Publicity will only put lives needlessly at risk. What will be done must be done quietly. We are not without resources. Even in our weakness, we have the strength of thousands. As God has written: *in yakun minkum mi'atun yaghlibu alfan min alladhina kafaru bi-annahum qawmun la yafqahuna.* "If there be one hundred of you and you remain patient, they will conquer a thousand of them that have disbelieved, for they are ignorant people."'

The shaykh fell silent. Here and there throughout the mosque, people were crying out. Tears for the martyrs, imprecations against the enemies of the Imams, threats of vengeance against the opponents of Islam. All their grief, all their anger, all their frustration in life had been newly awakened by this latest calamity. Stillbirths and cancers and the losses of war, hunger and poverty, the daily rage of exile, the repeated indignities of life in the villages of the south or the slums of Beirut, failed crops, failed marriages, failed examinations, failed lives: all burst forth in a tide of lamentation over the fate of men and women of whom they knew next to nothing.

For centuries, the Shi'a of Lebanon had been walked over and spat upon. The prosperity of more recent decades had all but passed them by. They had watched as their homes and farms and businesses were torn to pieces, and all they could see behind the bloodshed were Israeli planes and American warships and Russian guns. These were the wretched of the earth. They had nothing to lose that they had not lost already.

As the cries subsided, the shaykh stood and descended the steps of the pulpit. Men pressed forward to clasp and kiss his hand. He greeted those he knew, blessed the children they pushed before him, smiled benignly on everyone who came to him. It took over twenty minutes before his hard-pressed aides managed to get him to the door through which he had entered. While one of the assistants opened it, the other helped the shaykh slip through. The door closed, shutting out the hubbub in the mosque.

They were in a small, scantily furnished room. One wall bore a huge poster with a photograph of Imam Khomeini, another the image of the vanished Imam Musa al-Sadr, Lebanon's revolutionary Shi'ite leader who had disappeared on a visit to Libya many years earlier.

On a tubular steel chair, a tall man was seated. When Fadlullah entered, the man got hurriedly to his feet. He came forward, bending low, and took the shaykh's hand, raising it to his lips.

'Abu Hida,' murmured the shaykh as he took the man's hand in his own. 'I am overjoyed that you have come. My anxieties are at an end. I will ask for coffee to be brought. Then we shall talk. There is work for you to do.'

CHAPTER EIGHTEEN

Merrion Square
Dublin
9 October
0830 hours

Declan had spent most of his life on the edge of terror. When he was eighteen, the Troubles had started in the North, and before long they had cast their shadow into some parts of the Republic. Entering the police on leaving UCD, one of Dublin's universities, he had soon been transferred to Special Branch, where he worked in Department 6, the section responsible for monitoring IRA activity in the South.

He had been one of the first on the scene when UDA bombs killed twenty-five people in Dublin in 1974. For many years after that he had lived, like so many of his countrymen, with the dread that the conflict in the North would escalate and drag the South into a cycle of terror and retaliation, and, finally, civil war. His grandfather had been a fighter in the twenties and had seen at first hand how internecine strife tore families and towns apart. Declan had never forgotten his warnings. The danger had receded, but the threat was still there, unspoken, unacknowledged, behind everything he said and did.

There had been all kinds of madness down the years. They had paraded before his desk like figments of the most debased imagination. But this was something different. He knew it. He smelt it. What had happened at Castletown had not been the work of the IRA, the INLA, the UVF, or any of the other terrorist groups Declan had fought against in the past. This was something alien, performed for reasons he could not even begin to guess at.

The Lord has seen, and the Lord has heard great wickedness among the nations and the sons of men.

He had arrived at his new office at eight-thirty. It was an underground bunker, built several years ago to accommodate members of the cabinet and senior civil servants in the event of a nuclear attack. For some time now, it had stood abandoned and without purpose. The entrance was through an antiquarian bookseller's shop on Upper Mount Street, from whose basement a tunnel led under the road. Steep steps led into the bunker, which lay beneath the small park at the centre of Merrion Square.

The bookseller was a brother of Martin Fitzsimmons, a man whose discretion was total. No-one much came to his shop. His stock was dull and grotesquely overpriced. Those few bibliophiles who ever found their way to his door generally left soon afterwards without having made a purchase.

Declan's only regret was that they were so close here to the government offices on Merrion Street. He could not help wondering what sort of scenes were being played out over there at that very moment.

Paddy O'Leary had given Declan's list of twenty-five men and women to Martin Fitzsimmons, and Martin had seen to it that they were all transferred to 'special duties' without further explanation. Declan knew them all, and welcomed them as they arrived. By eight-fifty his team was in place.

The telephones, faxes, and computers had all been hooked up. A secure modem link allowed access to the national police computer and, through it, wider access to European security files. Three operators were set the task of monitoring everything that the Gardaí, Special Detective Unit, and C3 came up with on the hostages. He did not want to duplicate their efforts.

At nine o'clock, Declan assembled the team in the large room that had been designated as operational headquarters. On his instructions, they had all turned up for work in civilian clothes: he did not want someone wondering what was going on when a crowd of uniformed Gardaí arrived in force at Dublin's least frequented bookshop. *The Herald* would be sure to publish conjectures about a pornographic book ring. It was, after all, what half the city had been hoping for for years.

'I want to thank you all for agreeing to take part in this operation. It's only fair I should tell you right away that we're going to be working outside the strict boundaries of the law. Properly speaking, the Taoiseach has no authority to order a secret operation without consent or knowledge of the Dáil, the Cabinet, or the National Security Council. Officially, I am no longer head of the SDU, and I have, in fact, been suspended from duty. So, just by standing here and giving you instructions I am already breaking the conditions of my suspension.

'Now, it's more than likely that, if anything should go wrong with this operation, the Taoiseach and anyone else involved will deny all knowledge of it. If we fail, we needn't expect forgiveness from that quarter. You might well face suspension or even dismissal from the service, in all likelihood the latter. If this causes problems for anyone here, they're free to leave now. Because, once you're in, you're in. No second thoughts. To tell you the truth, I'd go myself if I weren't in it up to the neck already.'

He glanced round the room. There were smiles at his last remark, but no overt expressions of unease. In the room were several men and women with whom he had worked closely in the past. Dominic Lawlor. Tim O'Meara, who had lost an eye in a raid on a bomb factory in Glasnevin in 1983, and whose career had been saved only by Declan's personal intervention. Maire O'Brien, with whom Declan had spent six months tracking down a kidnap gang operating out of a village in Offaly and responsible for the abduction of half a dozen industrialists and the death of two. They all kept their eyes fixed on him. No-one moved. No-one showed any sign of wanting to. He had chosen well.

'Thank you,' he said. 'I hope none of you will have cause to regret your decision later. Now, before we go on with this briefing, there are some ground rules we need to establish. First, this is a twenty-four-hour operation. All leave is cancelled until further notice, and all personnel are confined to this bunker while the operation lasts. The bedrooms will need a bit of an airing. I've asked for fresh bedclothes, towels, and so on. It won't be the Shelbourne, but it's a lot better than being out on surveillance.'

A series of low groans passed round the room.

'I told you, once you're in, you're in. You can make phone calls home after this and cancel any engagements you may have. But I need you here in case of emergency. Dominic Lawlor will draw up a shift rota this morning and assign individuals to teams.

Grainne Walsh will be my second-in-command. If we need additional personnel, they can be brought in; but I'd prefer to work with the smallest number possible. That means I want twice the work and twice the commitment out of every one of you. If I find anyone slacking, he won't need the Taoiseach's blessing to find himself picking spuds in Galway.'

He paused. No groans this time.

'Second, this operation is several degrees higher than Top Secret. You are to say nothing about this job to anyone, and I mean anyone. That includes wives, husbands, girlfriends, boyfriends, parents, the postman, even your priest, if any of you are in the habit of going to confession. If any of you feels an overwhelming need for absolution, I'll bring a priest in here for your private use and keep him locked up in the back.'

There were smiles. Sin was not a major preoccupation for anyone here. They had all seen enough of human wickedness to render minor transgressions matters of little moment.

Declan now explained as best he could what had happened at Castletown House. It was the hardest part of the briefing, and he had been dreading it all night long. The officers who had died in the raid had all been known personally to the members of his team, and some had been close friends. When he came to an end, many were in tears. But he knew he could depend on them now, whatever happened, however many nights they had to spend in this place. They would all risk far more than their jobs to strike back at the killers and bring them to justice of one kind or another.

He took a sheet of paper from his pocket.

'This was sent to me this morning via the Corea fax system,' he said. 'The original had been delivered to Iveagh House during the night by a man on a motorcycle. Only the night porter saw him come, and he didn't even bother to get the registration. So far, the kidnappers have had it pretty much their own way. Security is now being tightened at all government offices where letter drops may be made. We need to make it difficult for them, force their hand.'

He unfolded the paper and began to read.

Who we are and what we are is unimportant. What matters is that twenty-eight lives are in our hands and that they will begin to die if our demands are not met. What we ask is simple justice.

First, that in Arabia the ban on all religions but Islam be lifted and public worship for Christians permitted.

Second, that in Iran all property be returned to the churches and conversion from Islam to Christianity be made legal.

Third, that those responsible for the persecution of Christians in the southern part of Sudan be found and punished, and all attempts to impose Islamic law on non-Muslims be abandoned.

Fourth, that restrictions on the building of churches by the Copts in Egypt be lifted, and that those Muslims who have carried out attacks on Christians in Asyut and elsewhere be arrested and tried.

Fifth, that Christian missionaries be accorded the same rights in Islamic states that Muslim missionaries are accorded in the West.

Sixth, that all restrictions be lifted on the import, printing, and sale of the Bible in Islamic countries.

Once these demands have been met, we shall release our hostages unharmed. It is your responsibility before God to ensure that our lawful requests be presented to the governments concerned. As a token of your cooperation, you should place a statement in the classified columns of the *Irish Times* tomorrow morning. It should read as follows: 'In God We Trust'. That will be sufficient. Should it not appear, it will prove necessary to put the first of our hostages to death.

You will be contacted by telephone tomorrow at nine pm. We pray God that good sense will prevail and that we may be enabled to exercise mercy. If not, His wrath is sudden and His vengeance swift to fall.

There was a long silence. Declan folded the paper and returned it to his pocket. At the back someone summoned up the courage to ask the question that was on everyone's lip.

'Did the statement appear, sir?'

Declan closed his eyes briefly, then opened them. He was tired. They could see the signs of his ordeal at Castletown House.

He shook his head.

'No,' he said. 'The porter didn't bother telling anyone about the note until they turned up for work this morning. Copies of the *Times* were already on the streets by the time we even knew about it.'

CHAPTER NINETEEN

Office of the Director and Co-Ordinator
of Intelligence, Northern Ireland
Stormont Castle
Belfast
9 October
0955 hours

'You should get a wife, Perkins. They do that sort of thing for free.'

'Yes, sir. So I've been told, sir.'

Perkins had been seen in a club on Belfast's Golden Mile, consorting with a lady of questionable morals. By no means the greatest of offences, and not one about which Willoughby would have thundered back home. But in Belfast, an MI5 officer did have to be careful about the sort of company he kept. Honey-traps were sweet and frequently deadly, if not always to the victim, then to someone else he blabbed about.

'You do realize you'll have to go, don't you, you stupid man? Stain on your character. Could scarcely be worse.'

Perkins nodded shamefacedly.

'Yes, I rather thought so, sir.'

'"Rather thought so." You acted like an imbecile. What got into you anyway? I didn't know you were soft in that department.'

'No, sir. Not ordinarily, sir. It was just . . . I'd had a bit to drink, sir, and this woman . . .'

'Yes, well, I don't think I want to listen to this drivel, Perkins. This will go on your report, and I don't mind saying it will have a wounding effect on your career. If I were you, I'd think about another job. Now, have you got the O'Dalaigh file that I asked for?'

Perkins brightened, thinking he might yet get away with a flea in the ear and no more said about it.

'Here it is, sir,' he said, passing the file over.

'You say she was sighted yesterday. Why am I only hearing about it now?'

'Bit of a hiccough in communications, sir.'

'Meaning what exactly?'

'Not sure, sir. That's what I was told.'

'Well, find out and make sure it doesn't happen again. Now, get out of my sight and send Harker in.'

Geoffrey Willoughby leaned back in his chair and scanned the report. He had been MI5's Director and Co-Ordinator of Intelligence in Northern Ireland for three years now, but he still felt as if he were sitting on a knife-edge, that he was no more in control of events now than when he had arrived, and that at any moment all his plans could blow up in his face. Quite literally.

But the real danger here lay less in bombs and bullets than in the insidious spread of cynicism. It grew like rust, even on the most shining metal. He had watched them all over the years, politicians and academics and soldiers and spies, bright with their new schemes and flawless plans, go aside rusted one by one. Back home in London, it had seemed a rather pointless game, but a game nonetheless. But out here he no longer had the luxury of distance. He had started to want and to feel disappointment, and he could see the first stains of rust on his own armour. Laying hands on Maureen O'Dalaigh and her boys was his one hope of bringing back the polish before it was time to go home.

The door opened and Anthony Harker came in. He closed the door as though shutting out everything that lay behind it: the Department, Stormont Castle, Belfast, the whole of Northern Ireland. Not that he needed a door. His whole manner acted as a sufficient barrier between himself and the world.

Willoughby smiled and asked him to sit down. Harker was in his forties, with the physique of a much younger man. But it was not the physique that first struck or held the attention. Harker's face drew your eye, not all at once, but with increasing power, because it gave so little away. Nothing altered his expression, the power of self-containment was a thing so developed in him that you knew instinctively he was a man capable of anything.

Harker restored the DCI's self-confidence, made it possible to believe in victory of a sort, or, if not victory, an honourable way out of this mess. What Harker was, what Harker had been, were mysteries even to Willoughby, who was, in name at least, his boss. Soon after his arrival in the province, Willoughby had learned that, whatever else he controlled here, he did not control Harker. Harker was something special, something set apart, untouchable, almost holy. He had always been there, he would remain there when Willoughby left and a new DCI took his place. Harker was the heart of the Department, and its brains, and, if it were to die, he would be its ghost.

'O'Dalaigh's surfaced,' Willoughby said.

'So I understand.'

'You've seen this, then?'

'A few minutes ago.'

'You think it's reliable?'

'Oh, no doubt of that. Pierce is very dependable. Eyes like a hawk. But it's not just the sighting. Something's up. Some of their top people are on the move.'

'It's not their top people I want. It's O'Dalaigh. You know that.'

'Nevertheless, she's part of whatever's going on. My men have their ears close to the ground. The RUC are bringing in their best touts. Give it a day or two. We'll have her.'

'Good. Don't let me down. And make sure you bring her in alive. I want the rest of that ASU. Every last one of them.'

'I'll do my best.'

There was a pause, and with it a change in mood. In Anthony Harker, Willoughby had found a path to the darkest corners of the Northern Irish jungle.

'What about that other business?' the DCI asked. 'Has it been taken care of?'

'Wetherell? I've seen to everything. It went very smoothly.'

'Does that mean that everything's secure again?'

Harker shook his head.

'Not quite. There's still Carberry. He's a very difficult target. The repercussions would be appalling if it were ever brought back this way.'

'I'm perfectly aware of that. Do what you can. Make sure there are no further leaks.'

'Is that all?'

Willoughby shook his head.

'There's this,' he said. 'It arrived from London this morning.' He took a slip of paper from his desk and passed it to Harker without comment. Harker read it and passed it back.

'It's started, then,' he said.

'I think it's time for you to go to Dublin. Things will get out of hand otherwise.'

'Very well. And if I'm needed here?'

'I'll take care of that for the moment. You've done a good job so far. I'm at ease with things.'

Harker half rose, as though about to go, then sat down again.

'Should I tell Mangan about Scimitar?'

Willoughby shook his head.

'Not at this stage.'

'It would help him understand . . .'

'No. Later, if things get stuck. For the moment, he has no need to know. And if he goes, better he knows nothing. For his own sake.'

'Very well. I'll arrange to be in Dublin early this evening. Let them know I'm on my way. And that I have your authority.'

Harker stood without ceremony and left. Willoughby shivered slightly, then took a small notebook from his pocket. Consulting it, he punched a number into his telephone. It rang a few times, then someone answered.

'Ciaran Clark? This is Geoffrey Willoughby. I'd like to speak to you in private if I may.'

CHAPTER TWENTY

Dublin
9 October
1005 hours

'I hate to say this, sir, but they could have a point.' Dominic Lawlor spoke hesitantly, but with the doggedness of someone who has a point and insists on getting it across, come what may. 'About the Muslims, that is. The way they behave. You know – the way they throw their weight about. Executing people they don't approve of. Stoning women. We are Christians after all, sir. Isn't that right?'

Declan looked at him evenly. Dominic had always seemed to him a fair man, a calming influence on his subordinates, a good policeman with a great dislike of bigots.

'Does anyone else think this way?' Declan asked.

No-one answered, but he sensed agreement here and there in the room. He had known from the beginning that this was not going to be an easy operation.

'All right, then, I'd better make myself clear. If that's really what you think, Dominic – that the terrorists have a point – then I'd rather you left now. And anyone else who thinks the same way. I'll give you time to think it over, all of you. But I don't want anyone on my team who thinks even for a moment that the people we're after may be right, or that there may be some sort of justification for their actions, or that their victims may have been asking for it. Have I made myself clear?'

Lawlor's face was ashen. He had not expected such a rebuff. But he knew Declan was not bluffing. His own choice was simple: he could stick to his guns and leave, or he could think things through. If it had been anyone else but Declan Carberry, he would have had no hesitation in getting his coat and going home.

'Right,' said Declan. 'I think this meeting has gone on long enough. If anyone has problems, they can speak to me later.'

He knew that the only way to stop the team brooding about what they were being asked to do was to get them straight to work.

'Most of you have jobs to do. I'd like your preliminary reports on my desk by one o'clock. Liam, Grainne – I'd like to see you both in my office now, please.'

Liam Kennedy and Grainne Walsh had belonged to the Special Support Unit of the police Special Task Force, a rapid-reaction squad set up in the seventies to respond to a spate of kidnappings in the Republic, many of them engineered by the Provisional IRA. The SSU had worked with the task force in an undercover role, providing them with electronic surveillance expertise. Now disbanded, some of its members were still with Special Branch.

Declan closed the door.

'I'm glad you're with me on this job,' he said. 'You have the right experience. You've done things like this before. But I want to know that you're not going to let me down. I don't want anyone on this team who isn't going to see it through.'

'It's not straightforward, is it, sir?' Grainne had studied law at Trinity for a couple of years before giving it up and joining the police. Her decision to leave had not been based on problems with the work – passing exams had been effortless for her – but from a growing conviction that, once graduated, she would find herself on the wrong end of the legal system. She was one of the sharpest minds on the force, and Declan was desperate to keep her. He knew that any attempt to gloss over the difficulties would have her back in Harcourt Street by lunchtime.

'Straightforward? No, it's not,' he replied. 'And it isn't going to get any easier either. I don't even know if the Taoiseach is doing the right thing, or if I'm right to go along with him for that matter. All the same, I trust his judgement. Between ourselves, he gives a very good impression of being an idiot at times. But what politician doesn't? Pádraig Pearse is far from stupid. And in matters of this kind, he has a certain skill.

'The trouble is that even he can only do so much. If this operation isn't to grind to a halt the moment the Brits and the rest get in on the act, we can't rely on information being passed on from the Taoiseach's office or the intelligence services. If we want to know what's going on, we'll have to get the information for ourselves. And the sooner we get our surveillance equipment in position the better. By this time tomorrow, we'll have about as much chance of installing a line-tap in Ireland as we have of persuading the Pope to wear a condom.'

'Who exactly are we expected to bug, sir?' Liam was a Kerryman, from Kenmare or Sneem, or one of those places. Declan knew that he had never been happy about some of the work he'd been asked to carry out for the SSU in the old days, when the unit was used to monitor non-violent political groups.

'Anyone you can think of,' said Declan. He began to tick off a mental list he had made earlier. 'I want a tap on Garda Síochana Headquarters in Phoenix Park and Metropolitan Area Head-quarters in Harcourt Street. The Taoiseach's office, naturally. Iveagh House. The intelligence service. Army intelligence. All Middle Eastern embassies. And the British embassy for good measure. But the ones I've listed will do for the moment. Unless you can think of others yourself.'

Grainne grimaced.

'What's wrong, Inspector Walsh?' asked Declan. 'You don't have any objections, do you? Of the legal or moral variety? You're my second-in-command here: I want to know I can depend on you to carry out my orders or act on your own initiative.'

'No, sir, that's not the problem. It's just that the targets you've just named won't be easy. Most of them carry out regular anti-bugging sweeps. And it could be very difficult keeping that number of surveillance operations going simultaneously, sir. With the limited manpower we have here, that is.'

'You're right. We'll probably need some more experienced monitors. I'll leave that to you to arrange. What sort of equipment will you need?'

'Well, to start with, I'd like to install an ICR. That's an Inter-national Communications Recorder. It can record conversations on one hundred and twenty lines at once. It's not a lot of use on its own, but if we can get hold of a Racal Timesearch unit to go with it, we're in business. The Timesearch will scan the tapes automatically at six hundred times normal speed. It takes two minutes to read twenty-four hours' worth of tape. We can code it to watch out for key words or phrases. "Hostage", for example.'

'Right. Where can you get one?'

'They have one in the Post Office building.'

'Fine, I'll write out an authorization. As far as putting the taps in place is concerned, I'd like you to use your discretion. There are people you've both worked with at Telecom Éireann: they'll cooperate if you put suitable pressure on them. Handle anybody else with more tact. You'll know yourselves who you can talk to and who not. Tell them as little as possible, but get their cooperation. Work on their nationalist sentiments or something.

'I'll give you a list of people who know about this operation. Go to them first. They'll give you any assistance you need. Even when the Europeans take over, we can expect help from some of our own people.'

At that moment the phone rang. Declan picked it up. He listened carefully. They could see the expression on his face change as he did so. Had he not already been pale from his ordeal, they might have seen the colour drain from his cheeks.

He put the receiver down gently. For a moment he stood looking at the surface of his desk. Then he looked up at them.

'They've killed the first hostage,' he said.

CHAPTER TWENTY-ONE

Phoenix Park
Dublin
9 October
1030 hours

Martin Fitzsimmons was waiting at the Park Gate entrance. Phoenix Park lay beyond, green, wet, half-hidden behind a faint mist. Garda Headquarters was just visible behind the People's Garden. Declan had come here more often than he liked to remember; but today was different.

'It was over here we found him,' said Martin without preamble. 'One of the Egyptian delegates, a man called 'Abd al-Halim 'Abbud.'

'You're sure? You're certain that's who he is?' The name meant something to him, he could not quite remember what.

They were walking over the damp grass towards the Wellington monument. Declan scarcely noticed the parked Garda cars, the men in black uniforms, the ambulance waiting to take the body away. It was all depressingly familiar. And yet, in the space of a day, he had learned to view it all as if from a great distance.

'He was identified half an hour ago by an attaché from the Egyptian embassy. You can speak to him if you like. His name's Hafiz.'

Declan shook his head.

'I'm not interested in the hostages individually. Who this 'Abd al-Whatever was or did won't help me find his killers. I just want to see if there's anything – a clue, a hint, a mistake – something that might lead me to them.'

'They have a sense of humour, that's one thing.'

131

They had reached the foot of the monument. It soared above them, two hundred and twenty feet from the ground, the world's tallest obelisk, its grey stone flat against the sky. The body lay huddled on the steps at the bottom, dwarfed by the massive pillar, like a sacrifice to a pagan deity. It seemed unnecessarily cruel to have left him here, away from the warm sun, crumpled under mist. He had a bearded, gentle face. Declan remembered him now, the man Ciaran Clark had introduced to Concepta. He had been the head of the Egyptian delegation. Declan wondered if he had had a wife and children.

'Humour?' he said. 'I see nothing funny here.'

'Well, not humour, that's not what I meant. But this . . .' He indicated the obelisk. 'It seems . . . well, chosen for its aptness.'

'An Egyptian at the foot of Dublin's one and only obelisk. Is that what you mean?'

Fitzsimmons nodded. He wished he'd said nothing about humour. He hated this sort of work. This was not his strength, investigating corpses in cold parks. He was not a policeman, after all. From the beginning he had been an ideas man, a man for behind the scenes.

'Who found him?'

'A Garda patrol.'

'By chance?'

Fitzsimmons shook his head.

'Not at all. Someone rang. A call-box in Trim. There are men out there now. The call came straight through to Garda Head-quarters.'

He nodded at the long building on their right. The spot was appropriate in more ways than one, thought Declan. Behind them, on the other side of the main thoroughfare that ran through the park, Chesterfield Road, lay Army headquarters, housing the Ministry of Defence. Further along was Aras an Uachtarain, the president's official residence, the old Viceregal Lodge. Opposite that stood the American ambassador's residence. And below that again, nearly completing an ellipse back to the monument, rose the tall cross that had been erected to mark the visit in 1979 of Pope John Paul II. All tokens of the Irish state and its foreign relations. Had the symbolism been intended, or was it just in Declan's head?

'Has the body been touched at all?'

'Not yet. There's the risk of a booby trap. If it's the IRA.'
Declan shook his head.
'It won't be booby-trapped.'
'We've had to increase security for the President and the US ambassador. This is too close.'
'That's not what they're after. Have them pull their extra men off the American. I don't want him getting suspicious, asking what's going on. There'll be time enough for that yet.'
He looked round. In the distance, a couple were riding across the grass, near the polo grounds. The woman's hair rushed out behind her like a short banner. She rode a grey horse. Once, on a rare holiday in Lebanon, he and Amina had ridden for miles along a beach in sunlight. He closed his mind to the thought.
'Did they say why? They gave us no time to react to their demands. We don't even have a means of communicating with them.'
Fitzsimmons looked at the body, only feet away. The Egyptian was soaking wet from the dew and the mist. He had been a good-looking man. They did not know yet how long he had been dead.
'I didn't hear the call, and there's no recording of it. It wasn't expected, after all.'
'Jesus, Martin, there's supposed to be twenty-four-hour monitoring.'
'I'm telling you what I was told. Maybe it was recorded, I don't know. The caller said that we needed to know they meant business. That a hostage would die every day until their demands were met. He told the girl on the switchboard that there was a body at the feet of the Iron Duke. Then he hung up.'
They went across to the body. 'Abd al-Halim's hands had been tied behind his back with cord. He was wearing a white *gallaba*, and around his head was wrapped a plain white cloth. The cloth was stained on one side with blood that had seeped from a bullet-wound in his left temple. On his feet were thin leather slippers. He lay awkwardly, like a child asleep. His eyes were wide open, staring at the grey stone. Declan reached out a hand and closed them.
Without a word, he bent down and moved the body, straightening it. It moved easily, and he guessed that rigor mortis had already come and gone.

There were no further wounds. Declan swiftly examined the hands, arms, legs, and feet, but there was nothing unusual. He would have to leave the body to more skilled hands and a proper postmortem examination. But as he began to straighten, he noticed something. The wristwatch looked out of place on someone so plainly dressed. Declan bent again and lifted the arm. It looked ordinary enough, but the strap was bright red, and around the face was an inscription: 'One Hour Nearer the Lord's Return'. The strap had caught Declan's eye.

He took the watch off and turned it over. It was made of stainless steel, a cheap watch without pretensions other than the enormity of what its face proclaimed. The second hand moved round the face at its appointed speed, as though in mockery of the watch's wearer. On the back, in small letters, was the maker's name: EndTime Products Inc, Decatur, Illinois.

Declan slipped the watch into his pocket and lowered the dead man's arm to the position it had been in before. Fitzsimmons pretended not to notice. As they walked back to the road, Declan turned to him.

'They're going to have to get their act together pretty quickly if they don't want many more of these.'

Fitzsimmons nodded.

'The Taoiseach has called a meeting with representatives of the countries involved. Some are flying in from London this morning. The others are using embassy staff here in Dublin.'

'I want to hear as soon as the kidnappers get in touch again. Make sure all lines in and out of government offices are monitored and recorded.'

'I'll do my best. Declan, I was wondering – how do you think they chose which one to kill first?'

Declan shrugged.

'At random probably.'

'I just thought . . .' Fitzsimmons's voice trailed away. 'His name began with "A".'

The thought stabbed Declan through like a knife. Amina Bustani would always be towards the front in any queue.

'Perhaps,' he said. 'It doesn't help us, though.'

'I thought it might help the Taoiseach. If we knew which governments to concentrate on, whose hostages were most at risk.'

'They're all at risk, Martin. They'll kill a few now, then play for time. Unless one of us finds them first.'

'There's a massive search on already, Declan. They'd be wonderful clever if they could keep that many hidden for long.'

Declan shook his head. They had reached his car. He opened the door. The mist was growing thicker around the pinnacle of the obelisk. A flock of migrating birds circled impatiently above the Zoological Gardens. Everything spoke to him of the coming of winter. He couldn't face it without the hope of Amina.

'They'll have thought of that, Martin. You can be sure they'll have thought this through to the end.'

CHAPTER TWENTY-TWO

He sat on a hard rock, facing the open sea. The air was filled with its smell. From behind him, a cold wind came out of the east and passed on to a darkening horizon. Every breath he took reminded him of long days spent on another shore. Another time, another place, another world. He wondered if he would ever see America again. It really did not matter – his Father was with him everywhere he went, after all. But he felt an affinity for the place, and he believed he still had a special mission there. He still dreamed of returning home in triumph, of building his New Jerusalem in the desert.

A seagull passed over his head with a raucous cry. He shivered slightly, bracing himself against the wind as it came in from the west. There was a sound behind him. He turned and saw Ezekiel coming across the beach. He recognized him from the red baseball cap and green windcheater he wore. He watched him come to him, his footsteps growing firm as he reached the hard-packed sand of the shorefront. Seaweed-studded rocks lay scattered across his path. Between them were pools of salt water, abandoned by the outgoing tide. Ezekiel moved over them, agile and full of grace. When he reached his Master's side, he was breathing unhurriedly. Only his eyes gave away the slight tension he felt.

'We've got trouble. I reckon you should come see for yourself.'

'I told you I wasn't to be disturbed.'

'I'm sorry. But it may be important. It's not something I want to handle on my own.'

He pursed his lips, torn between irritation at being interrupted and gratification at the deference shown him by his lieutenant.

'What is it?' he asked. The disciples had come to him like this the first time, on the shores of the Sea of Galilee. He pictured them now, walking to him while he stood at the water's edge, Peter and James and Andrew. Perhaps when all this was over he would do just that, travel to Israel and live with his disciples on the shores of Galilee.

'One of the Algerians. Says he's ill.'

'Says he is? Well, is he or isn't he?'

'I guess. He doesn't look none too good to me.'

They returned together to the low barn-like structure in which the hostages were kept. There was a single entrance, guarded day and night by men carrying AK-47s. The few windows had been boarded up. The interior was lit by a string of bare electric bulbs, powered by a petrol generator located in a nearby hut.

The two men stepped inside. The bulk of the building had been divided laterally, with a broad aisle down the centre. It was laid out in the form of a military barracks, except that the beds had been divided from one another by heavy wooden partitions, creating two rows of open cells. The partitions were obviously of much later construction than the building itself. The barn – originally used to house cattle and fodder in the winter – had been built from local stone and at one time roofed in thatch. The thatch had long since rotted and collapsed, and had been replaced by panels of corrugated iron. The wooden partitions had been installed at the same time.

Each of the cells thus created held one hostage. The women were kept in a separate section at the far end, divided from the men by a sturdy door; they had their own toilets and washing facilities, and were guarded at all times by two armed men. There were no women among the guards. The Master had considered and rejected the idea, believing it would lead to difficulties with discipline. He had had problems with women before.

The Algerian was in a bed in the third cell on the right. Beside him on the edge of the bed sat one of the two Saudi delegates, Shaykh Hasan al-Turki. He had been untied and allowed out of his own cell to act as an interpreter. He and the sick man had been able to communicate in standard Arabic, a version of the classical language used between the educated, however divergent their own colloquial form.

The Algerian's name was 'Ali Bouslimani. He was in his late fifties, a philosophy teacher at the University of Algiers, and the leading theorist of the FIS, Algeria's Islamic Salvation Front. His face was ashen, and he was breathing with difficulty. Al-Turki was holding his hand and speaking to him gently.

As the Master and Ezekiel appeared at the opening to the cell, the Saudi got to his feet. His face was flushed, and he was angry.

'This man has to be removed from here at once,' he said. 'If not, he will die.'

The Master pushed past him and went to the head of the bed. He looked down at Bouslimani. The Algerian stared up at him with unfocussed eyes.

'What's wrong with him?' asked the Master.

'He is suffering from *khunaq*. I am not sure what is the English for it. A heart disease. It is very serious. His medication is in his room at Castletown House. The distress he has suffered from the raid on the house and his treatment since then have made him extremely ill. He has to be taken to the nearest hospital.'

'That's out of the question,' the Master snapped at him.

'Then a doctor. You must do something. If he is not treated he will die.'

'I'm sorry,' he said, 'but I can't permit that.'

'Are you telling me that you have made no medical provision for your hostages or your own people?'

'God is our doctor,' was the only answer.

'You speak of God? What God kills innocent people? Takes them prisoner? Leaves them tied up like animals?'

The Master turned to Ezekiel.

'Take him out of here,' he said. 'I'll deal with this.'

Al-Turki moved back towards the bed.

'Let me stay with him,' he said. 'And let me have a pen and paper. He wants me to write to his wife and children in Algeria.'

'No-one's writing any letters. Now, I want you out of here.'

Al-Turki stood his ground. He was a short man, without great physical strength. His white *dishdasha* was stained with the blood of a policeman he had tried to help before being dragged from Castletown House.

'We all have families,' he said. 'It is unjust and cruel to leave them without news of our condition. Surely it will do no harm to let us write to them.'

The Master hit him hard across the face. Al-Turki staggered back, then recovered and straightened.

'You will be judged,' he said.

'I do the judging round here. Ezekiel, get him out of here.'

When they had gone, the Master bent over the sick man. Bouslimani reached out a hand and clutched his wrist. He spoke no English.

'*Ana marid* . . . ,' he whispered in Arabic. '*Utlub li tabiban* . . . *Ana ma'it* . . .'

The Master laid his hand over the sick man's. He could not understand a word he was saying. But he guessed it was a plea for help.

'We'll pray together,' he said. 'I'll ask Jesus to give you healing. You only have to believe in him. Let him take your sins away, let him make you whole.' He paused. 'Let me give you life.'

He spent over an hour by the dying man's bedside, his head bowed in prayer, his lips moving with supplications for healing and salvation. From time to time an armed guard would pass and glance curiously into the cubicle. Sometimes one of the other hostages would shout out in English or Arabic or Persian. Sometimes a dense silence would fill the entire building, and people would hold their breath, waiting for something indefinable. Behind the door, a woman wept. No-one came to comfort her. And a man who thought he was Jesus Christ and sometimes thought he was God mumbled prayers into the ear of a dying man.

CHAPTER TWENTY-THREE

St Stephen's Green
Dublin
9 October
1835 hours

Declan glanced at his watch and looked up at the sky. It was growing late. Seamus Cosgrave should have met him half an hour ago. It was not like him to keep Declan waiting. They had spoken briefly on the telephone three hours earlier, and Cosgrave had promised to be at the Green shortly after six. It was not their usual meeting-place, but Declan had made it clear he would be on a seat near the bullrush fountain. Cosgrave could hardly miss him.

Declan got up and walked around. He had brought no-one with him to watch his back. If he was being followed, he would have to find out for himself. He headed down towards the lakes, scanning between the trees for a sign of someone watching. Nothing seemed out of place.

He caught sight of Cosgrave coming over the bridge. They passed one another without acknowledgement. Both men knew the drill. Cosgrave kept on walking in the direction of the fountain. He had made no sign that they should call it off. Declan took the long way round, back to where he had started, checking that Cosgrave had not been followed.

Cosgrave had found a bench and was waiting for him, a copy of *The Herald* open in front of him. Declan sat down at the other end of the bench.

'You're late.'

'Jeez, Mr Carberry, this is a public place. I had to check it out. If anyone saw the two of us together . . .'

Seamus Cosgrave had been Declan's principal informer inside the IRA for a long time. Declan had arrested him eleven years earlier on a charge of smuggling arms, and then gone to work on him. A little digging had thrown up several more serious charges. There had been no hard evidence, but Declan had succeeded in convincing Cosgrave that he had enough to make the charges stick.

It might not have worked, but for the fact that Cosgrave had married a year earlier. She was a nice girl, Teresa, and Seamus was besotted with her. He was over thirty then, had been in the movement all his life, and had been starved for female company. Now he had started resenting time spent away from his Teresa. An IRA man in love – how the lads had laughed about that in the interrogation centre. But Declan had not laughed once. Love had given him power over Seamus Cosgrave.

To make things harder, Teresa had just given birth to a child, Joseph, and the Cosgraves were already talking about brothers and sisters. Seamus, himself the youngest of twelve, was a family man at heart. A killer, certainly, and a diehard Republican, but a loving husband and tender father at home. Ireland's tragedy, Declan thought, was that he was far from unique.

It did not take Declan long to show his prisoner just how much trouble lay in store if he did not cooperate. With the charges available, he could be put away in Kilmainham for a long time. A very long time. Joseph would be a grown man by the time he came out. Teresa would have long ceased to be the slim and vivacious woman whose bed he now shared. Declan hinted at acts of infidelity, at the untrustworthiness of other men.

Seamus had tried to buy himself off with odds and ends of information, but Declan had wanted more. Much more. He had wanted Seamus for himself, for life. A marriage, in short, with the price of infidelity life itself. They had settled on a year in prison and a debt to be paid slowly over the coming years, a debt that Seamus was still paying. And that Declan was still collecting in person. Seamus was his source, his tout, his treasure-trove, and he would hand him over to no-one else.

Two priests walked past, deep in conversation. A group of children with a football that had seen better days. A young woman in a powered wheelchair, her face tight with pain. Water rose from the sculptured bullrushes and fell endlessly into the pool. In the sky, grey clouds hung heavy over the city.

'How's Teresa?' Declan asked.

'She's well. Did you know her mother died a few months back?'

'I did. I was sorry to hear of it. Was she very old?'

'She was over ninety. She saw them read the Proclamation from the Post Office in the Rising. So she used to say. A fine woman. Very regular at Mass she was until the last year or so. She's sorely missed.'

'And the children, how are they?'

'They're getting on fine. Joseph won a prize for Irish the other week. He's looking for a holiday in the Gaeltacht next year. The Brothers have a place in Galway.'

'I've heard of it.' Declan paused. They had not looked at each other once. So much subterfuge, Declan thought. And for what?

'I heard about your daughter, Mr Carberry. That's a terrible thing. You must be broken-hearted.'

'Worse than that, Seamus. But let's not talk about it.' He paused. 'What can you tell me about Monday night?'

'Monday night? What happened on Monday night?'

'You know well enough, Seamus. Was it your own people or the INLA?'

'The Ambassador? Is that what you mean? It was men from the Dublin battalion. Special orders.'

'What was the plan?'

'There was no plan. Army Council had a leak from the embassy. They knew where Reynolds was going to be that night and they put an ambush together. To show him he's vulnerable. There was no plan to kill him or hold him to ransom.'

'Why wasn't I told? Why didn't you warn me? It wasn't a minor incident.'

Cosgrave shook his head.

'Sure, I only heard about it this morning myself. You've been keeping it quiet enough yourselves.' He shook his paper. 'There's not been a word in here about it. Or anywhere else. What's going on?'

Declan glanced at the informer. Cosgrave was looking old, he thought, though he was only in his early forties. His cheeks were pale. He looked tired and on edge. A lifetime in the movement had brought him little peace. Declan thought he might be telling the truth.

'What about Castletown?' he asked. 'Was that a Dublin

battalion job as well? I didn't think you had the muscle to pull something like that yourselves.'

Cosgrave lowered the paper and looked at Declan.

'Castletown? Where the hell's that?'

'Out at Celbridge. The big house there. Castletown House.'

'When was this?'

'The same time as the ambush. Monday night. And don't tell me nothing happened, because I was there.'

Cosgrave laid *The Herald* beside him.

'There was only the ambush, Mr Carberry. I swear to God, there was nothing else.'

'You just told me you only heard about the ambush this morning. Maybe you just aren't in on Castletown.'

'Was it a big job?'

Declan nodded.

'Very big.'

'Then I'd have heard something. Honest to God, Mr Carberry, I would. I was with Gerry Noonan just this morning, and we talked about the ambush right enough, how it went well and no-one but an English bodyguard was killed and that. He said nothing to me about no raid.'

'Seamus, the ambush was just a decoy. It was nothing in itself, just a lot of shooting and carrying on that drew all the nearby Garda and Ranger units in that direction. While it was going on, a group of armed men attacked Castletown House and took some very important people hostage. You're to tell no-one I told you that. Do you understand me, Seamus?'

Cosgrave swallowed and nodded nervously.

'Right you are, Mr Carberry. I never heard nothing.'

'Now, Seamus, I'm not a believer in wild coincidence. Two major terrorist incidents did not just happen to take place within a few miles and a few minutes of each other. There was some sort of pre-arrangement. Am I making sense, or would you like me to talk more slowly?'

'Perfect sense, Mr Carberry. Sure, you're a man of great sense, haven't I always said so? But I know nothing about no raid, that's God's truth, and I'll swear no-one else in the movement does.'

'Nevertheless.' High above, hidden by cloud, an aeroplane growled past. 'There was a connection between the events. I want you to find out for me what the connection was. I want to know

143

who benefited from the ambush, and in what way. Was it money, a publicity stunt that went wrong, was there political kickback? You'll have the Christmas presents for the family bought and paid for if you can get this for me.'

Cosgrave had grown restless. He darted nervous glances right and left. If he were discovered speaking to the head of the SDU, his life would be worth nothing.

'Jeez, Mr Carberry, it's a great deal you're asking. I could get myself topped, honest I could. This ambush was top secret.'

'Sit down, Seamus, and listen to me. I need to have this information. I need it badly. People died at Castletown House. Gardaí mostly. My own men. A lot of other lives are in danger. Bring me what I need in the next twenty-four hours, and you'll be well paid. Let me down, and I'll dust off my file on you.'

'Twenty-four hours? Holy Mother of God.'

Declan did not move. He watched Cosgrave out of the tail of his eye, while remaining alert for anyone who paused too long, showed too much interest in two men sitting side by side on a park bench. He knew what Seamus was thinking, knew him as well as his own heart. Any moment now the question would come popping out.

'Is this the one, Mr Carberry? Would it make us quits? That's the best Christmas present I could have.'

Like all touts, Seamus Cosgrave dreamed of the day when he would be free, when the last item of information was handed over and the reins taken off. For eleven years now, he had lived with the daily expectation of exposure, torture, and death. And only one man, Declan Carberry, could lift his burden and set him at liberty.

'Maybe it will be, Seamus, maybe it will. If what you bring me's good enough, if it gets me close to the people I want, I'll call it quits right enough.'

'Who is it you want?'

'Whoever's behind the attack on Castletown House. I want them badly, Seamus. You can't imagine how badly I want them. As much as I want whoever killed Máiréad.'

'I'll see you get them, then.'

He got to his feet. When he bent to pick up the copy of *The Herald* he had brought with him, he noticed that Declan had substituted for it a copy of the *Evening News*.

'Don't ring me on the usual number, Seamus. That's no good now. You'll find another number inside the *News*. You can get a message to me anytime, day or night. Be sure I hear from you within twenty-four hours. I won't wait longer than that. Get on with you now. I'll watch your back to see you're not followed.'

Cosgrave put the paper in his pocket and headed off towards the bridge. Declan watched him go. All he could think about was Amina.

CHAPTER TWENTY-FOUR

Oifig an Taoiseach
Dublin
9 October
2100 hours

The telephone rang at nine as promised. Pádraig Pearse let it ring three times before answering. His hand shook as he lifted the receiver.

'This is the Taoiseach,' he said. 'Who am I speaking to?'

There was a brief pause. The room was filled with quiet men, some of whom were bent over a variety of listening devices. The call was being monitored, taped, and traced. In rooms nearby, experts were waiting to analyse the voice and to sift the message for any clues it might throw up. Around the country, Garda leave had been cancelled, and all units had been put on round-the-clock alert.

'My name is not important. I am that I am.' The voice was abrasive and mechanical, disguised by some sort of scrambling device.

'Listen, mister,' murmured Pádraig Pearse. The Biblical reference had not been lost on him. 'I don't care if you're God Almighty in person – this thing has got to stop. Your damned message got to us too late. But you still went ahead and killed an innocent man.'

'No-one is innocent. We are born in sin, and we die in sin, unless we have the Lord. Have you found Jesus, Mr Prime Minister? Have you let him into your heart?'

'If we're going to talk, let's talk about how we're going to resolve this thing. Anything else you have to say, you can say later.'

'I say what needs to be said. My voice is the voice of Jesus. My words are the words of God. Don't try to bargain with me, don't think you can play games. I am that I am. I will do what I have said I will do.'

Mangan looked round at Commissioner Devlin, who was seated next to him. He slipped his hand over the receiver.

'Jesus, Pat, the man's mad. I'll try to keep him talking. Have your boys got a trace on him yet?'

Devlin shook his head.

'Any minute now. Keep at it.'

Mangan removed his hand.

'I need a number where I can reach you,' he said. 'To avoid further mistakes.'

'There have been no mistakes. I will contact you whenever it is necessary. Things have started badly, but I hope they will go better. For your sake and the sake of the men and women in my care. First of all, I wish to know whether you are willing to act as my intermediary with the governments to whom I am putting my demands.'

Devlin slipped a note across Mangan's desk.

Got him. Call-box in Mountcharles, Donegal. Garda unit on the way.

Mangan nodded, then returned his attention to the phone.

'I can only agree to speak to them in a private capacity. Beyond that, I have no authority. My government can take no responsibility . . .'

'Just give them my demands. What they choose to do is their own responsibility. But please stress to them the consequences of even a short delay. To make things easier, I will insist on only one demand at a time. That will help the children of Satan to reach an agreement.

'We will begin with our demand for the open import, publication, and sale of the Word of God in Muslim countries. I'm willing to accept an initial agreement to this restricted to Saudi Arabia, Iran, and Malaysia. They have until tomorrow night to comply. A statement acknowledging their acceptance of this demand must appear in the Friday morning issue of the Arabic-language newspaper *Al-sharq al-awsat*, which is published in London. If it is not there, the next hostage will die.'

The Taoiseach put his head in his hands. He had never felt so powerless. Pat Devlin leaned over. There was a line of sweat on his forehead. He could not ignore the presence of Anthony Harker, seated by the wall, watching, and saying nothing.

'What's he up to?' the Chief Constable whispered. 'He must know we've traced the call by now.'

Pádraig Pearse shrugged.

'He seems to like the sound of his own voice. How far are your men?'

'They have to drive out from Donegal town. Not long now. Keep him talking.'

'There are some things we have to establish,' said the Taoiseach. He had been carefully coached for over an hour by an expert in hostage negotiations from the Ranger Wing. The whole thing stuck in his throat, but he went on swallowing.

'Go ahead.'

'First, we need to have a code-word. In case news of the kidnappings leaks out. Once it does, anyone could ring me and claim to be speaking on your behalf. All sorts of cranks would try to get in on the act.'

'Agreed. I will introduce myself using the code-word "Carmel". Only I and my second-in-command will know that.'

'Second, we can't afford a repetition of what happened last night. If your courier delivers any written messages to the gate outside my office, you have my word that he will not be apprehended or followed.'

'Not acceptable. You're no longer in charge. Even as we speak, you're being watched. Your word isn't worth a red cent. Next request.'

'But where will messages be delivered? We have to know in advance.'

'They'll be delivered where and when I say. Next question.'

Devlin scribbled a note on a slip of paper and passed it across the desk.

They have the call-box in sight. There is someone inside. Keep him occupied.

'Very well,' said Pádraig Pearse. His heart was beating fast, as though he himself were there in Mountcharles, in at the kill. He could not believe that it had been so simple. 'I have another request. We need to know that the hostages are alive and safe. You must furnish us with proof. Photographs. Letters written by them. Anything. I need proof to take to . . .'

Suddenly, the Taoiseach's expression changed. He glanced at the receiver, frowning, then laid it gently on the desk top.

'It . . . went dead,' he murmured. 'Just like that.'

Round the room, heads were lifted. A man in a slate-grey suit and yellow tie came across and picked up the Taoiseach's receiver. He put it to his ear, then gestured to another man at a low console on the other side of the office. The second man twiddled some dials, pressed several buttons, then shrugged and removed the headphones he had been wearing.

'What's going on?' asked Pádraig Pearse. He turned to Devlin. 'Pat, what the hell's happening?'

Devlin frowned.

'I don't know, Pádraig. They'll have made an arrest by now. We're trying to get through to the unit now.'

'The line went completely dead,' said Pádraig Pearse. 'As if someone cut the wire. I think something's wrong.'

'It'll be all right, Pádraig. They were on top of him. Maybe one of them cut the wire. He'll never have got away.'

No-one had moved. In one corner, a technician was speaking frantically into a handset. One of the men in suits was whispering instructions into a mobile telephone. Harker watched in silence. The door remained shut. No-one came in. No-one went out. The man in the yellow tie replaced the receiver on the Taoiseach's desk.

A long time passed; many minutes. Pádraig Pearse rose from his desk and crossed to the window. It was pitch dark and unnaturally quiet. Tonight, this had ceased to be his office, his city, his country. He was part of a brave new world, he and his people, all alike now. He turned as the door opened.

Tómas O'Sullivan entered. He saluted the Taoiseach before crossing the room to Devlin.

'This just arrived, sir.' He passed a note to the Commissioner. 'I thought you should see it right away.'

Devlin bent his head to read it. Pádraig Pearse joined him. He could see the blood leave his old friend's face.

'What is it, Pat? Haven't they caught the bastard?'

Devlin shook his head. His face was ashen. The Taoiseach noticed that his hand trembled.

'There was a back-up unit,' he said. 'From Ballyshannon. They arrived at Mountcharles a few minutes ago.'

149

'Well?'

'The call-box must have been booby-trapped. A bomb of some sort. A big one from the sound of it. The unit from Donegal town was wiped out. Five men. They're all dead.'

CHAPTER TWENTY-FIVE

Dawn lay on the eastern horizon like a half-washed rag, pale, and sloppy, and drenched in dirty water. If you were close enough, he thought, you might smell it. It bore no resemblance to the startling dawns he had seen in the New Mexico desert, or the golden sunrises of his native Texas.

When they had rowed out about a quarter of a mile from the shore, he told Ezekiel to ease up.

'Right about here should be far enough,' he said. 'Can you see which way the current's headed?'

'Should carry on out past that island and all the way down.'

'That's fine. Just fine. Let's get on with it.'

He sat in the prow of the little, bobbing rowboat. Looking back, he could make out the short beach from which they had set off, and behind it the sloping ground beyond which lay the barn and outbuildings he had chosen for his headquarters.

'Don't you think you should say a prayer?' Ezekiel asked.

He shook his head.

'Be no good,' he answered. 'He's in hell already. Be there for another million years. And another million after that. No way he'll get out now. I hate to think of it, him burning in hell, I truly do; but it's done, he's made his choice. I preached to him, you know I did. I offered him the joy of knowing Jesus. All he did was pray to Mahomet and ask me to fetch him a doctor. Couldn't make his mind up which he wanted more, a doctor or the devil.'

He laughed, amused by his own joke. Ezekiel smiled. A tense smile, love and anxiety mixed.

The thought of the fire upset him. A million years burning, without respite. His own wife and children had died in a fire, had been burned to death along with dozens of his closest friends. It had lasted a short time, but they had suffered more than it was right for anyone to suffer. He looked down at the water, let it quench the thought of flames that so tormented him.

'Then he upped and died,' the Master went on. 'And went straight to hell. They got no doctors there, that's for sure.' He paused. 'Lot of abortionists, though.'

Ezekiel smiled weakly. He hated to think of anyone in hell.

The crumpled remains of Ali Bouslimani lay on the bottom of the boat. He had died painfully in the middle of the night.

'We could still use his body,' Ezekiel ventured. 'In case they don't accept our demands and we have to give them another corpse.'

He shook his head. Not far from here, the great Atlantic swells began. He could scent the ocean vastness behind him, as though immensity and depth were qualities of smell.

'If the Saudis say "no" – and they will – one of the hostages must die. I gave my word. No substitutions, no cheating. Their lives are measured. Not even I can lengthen what God has cut short.'

Ezekiel knew better than to argue. He had seen his master switch moods before, like a broken light that flickers on and off. Anyone who argued with the man could find himself in the same stretch of sea as Ali Bouslimani. Anyone at all. Ezekiel glanced at the bulge under the other man's anorak. The gun never left him day or night.

'You don't think they'll accept our proposals?' he asked.

He grinned. Still affable.

'They don't have to,' he said. 'That's the whole idea.'

'I don't understand.'

'You should by now, Ezekiel. They're all going to die. Don't you see that? Our demands will be unacceptable. I've seen to that. The corpses will pile up, they'll get more and more frantic, but all the time they won't be able to swallow what I offer them. Satan can't afford to compromise. He knows and his servants know that freedom for the Church would be an axe at the root of his rotten tree. That's the one thing he can't afford. Beside that, a million deaths would seem like nothing. Ten million. So they'll go on saying "no" until all the hostages are dead. And it will all be over. You and I will go home. The waves will wash a faceless body ashore.'

'They'll call them martyrs, David. I've seen it on television. They dress up in black and wave banners. They're mad for martyrs – it only makes them stronger.'

The Master smiled. Not a nice smile. The boat lifted and fell. In the bottom, the body lay like lead. A wan light crept from the east across the changing sky, turning the waves a dirty grey.

'Stronger, yes. And weaker. If we push them hard enough, if we rattle them, they'll give us martyrs too. A harvest, Ezekiel, like fruit falling from a high tree. The blood of martyrs was the seed of the church. If we provoke Satan, he'll give us more. And our people back home will lift a cry loud enough to split the sky above Washington. There'll be no choice but to go to war. The last Crusade, Ezekiel. Think of it. I will be there at the head of my armies to wage war against Satan until he is chained and cast into the pit. We are truly in the last days.'

As if in answer to his words, a shaft of sunlight broke through the dense clouds above. He watched it, saw it flicker and fade. A sense of imminent triumph surged through him.

'Time we put this one to bed,' he said.

He bent down and got his hands underneath the corpse's armpits.

'Take his feet and help me toss him over. Careful we don't capsize the boat.'

It was trickier than they had thought. Ezekiel had to sit back at one side in order to balance the little vessel. They got the head and shoulders over the gunwale. The boat tilted precariously. The further the corpse slipped over, the sharper the tilt. Just as it seemed they were going to topple after all, the body shifted and flopped over the side. There was a dull splash, the feet seemed to kick convulsively at the last second, then the dead man was gone and there was only a thrusting of cold water against the side of the rocking boat.

CHAPTER TWENTY-SIX

Dublin
10 October
0800 hours

Declan had called an early morning conference with Shift A and was now regretting it. The top of his head seemed to have lifted off and gone elsewhere. He had passed a sleepless night and the headache had come on around four. Neither it nor his nerves were improved by the thought that at any moment he could expect to receive orders shutting his operation down. He had never felt so helpless in his life: forbidden to track down his daughter's murderer, unable to find and rescue Amina.

'I hope you all slept well,' he said, looking round a roomful of men and women who looked anything but rested. It made him feel a little better that he was not alone. 'I'm sorry the accommodation here isn't exactly what you're used to. I did suggest moving the operation to the Shelbourne, but I'm told there are budgetary considerations which make that inappropriate for the foreseeable future.'

The remark sparked off a few wry smiles, but no-one laughed. There were no prizes for jokes about budgetary considerations.

'Last night,' Declan went on, 'there were two developments that concern us closely. The first was a move by MI5 to take overall responsibility for the crisis here, while leaving day-to-day running of police and special operations activities to our own government. A man called Harker, of whom most of you will have heard, met with the Taoiseach early yesterday evening. He had full authority to act on behalf of the Director and Co-Ordinator of Intelligence, Northern Ireland. We don't know how

Willoughby came to be informed about the hostage crisis, but that's now academic.

'Obviously, MI5 have no jurisdiction here. But Ireland is a member of the European Community, and there are numerous European agreements on fighting international terrorism. The Trevi group of ministers, which co-ordinates working groups on terrorism and organized crime, has considerable influence. MI5 has much closer links than we do with the different European intelligence agencies. All Harker had to do was dangle the threat of joint European action over Mangan's head. Better from our point of view to deal with MI5 Northern Ireland than get drawn into an international operation within which we'd lose every last shred of national autonomy.

'This means that, as of eight o'clock yesterday evening, our semi-legal operation passed completely outside the law. We are more on our own than before, although clandestine contact with both C3 and the SDU will continue for the foreseeable future.'

He paused. From their faces, he could tell that it was at last sinking in that they could all end up in serious trouble.

'Second: yesterday evening the hostage-takers made contact with the Taoiseach in person. I have here a transcript of the conversation between Mr Mangan and a man who appears to be the leader of the kidnapping group.'

He read it through quickly. No-one interrupted him. There were no questions.

'I don't want to talk about this just yet,' he said. 'We'll get back to it later. First of all, I need to tell you why the conversation was broken off so abruptly.'

He told them about the explosion that had killed five Gardaí at Mountcharles.

'I have just received details of the initial forensic examination of the site,' he said. 'We now know two things. First, that the figure sighted in the call-box was a shop-window dummy; second, that the telephone had been attached to a short-wave radio receiver. Whoever spoke with the Taoiseach was not in the phone box. If he had a powerful enough transmitting device, he could have been anywhere in the country.'

'Or outside,' said Liam Kennedy. 'He could have been transmitting from the North, or from Scotland. Even further afield if he used satellite communications.'

155

'That's a good point. I'm certain the hostages have not been moved outside this country. But there could well be a control group organizing the hostage-takers from mainland Britain or even the continent. However, I think we should act on the assumption that the people we're looking for are wholly or mainly in Ireland. Anywhere else, and it really does become a job for our friends from the Trevi Group.'

He paused to consult the papers on the desk in front of him.

'You said you were going to come back to the conversation the Taoiseach had with the leader of the hostage-takers,' said Grainne Walsh. Grainne looked fresher than her colleagues. She was one of those insufferable people who can spend six months in a Thai jail or travel through China by train and come out looking as though they have just been to a beauty parlour.

Declan nodded.

'Thank you for reminding me, Grainne. You're obviously the only one of us who got a decent sleep last night. I hope you won't mind brewing me a pot of coffee after this.'

'Will it be one sugar or two, sir?'

'None. I'm on a diet. Yes, the Taoiseach's conversation. There were one or two matters that deserve a closer look. I'm sure the competition are on to them already. First of all, the fact that the man who spoke with the Taoiseach felt it necessary to disguise his voice. There could be several reasons for that, but the most likely is that he thought someone might recognize it. We need to find out why.

'Another thing about the voice. It could be that the caller had an accent. That raises all sorts of possibilities.'

Declan pressed the button on his desk intercom.

'Myles? Could you come in now, please?'

The door opened and a curious little man stepped diffidently into the room. He was short, with wispy reddish hair and a flat nose, dressed in tweeds and an Aran waistcoat. Declan motioned him to a seat near the front.

'I'd like to introduce Professor Myles O'hUiginn,' he said. 'Myles is an old friend of mine. He's head of the Department of Religious Studies at Trinity College. I've told him the nature of our problem, and he's agreed to be part of our team for the duration. I think we'll have need of his brains before this is finished.'

He paused and glanced at O'hUiginn.

'Myles, I've just been telling them about the business of the accent. Maybe you can say a bit more on that.'

O'hUiginn nodded. He looked uncomfortable. This was not his world. Until now he had passed his life without undue alarm or incident. Yet in the past ten years and more he had seen his field of studies become crucial to the politics of more than one region of the globe. Now, finding himself at the centre of the stage, he was nervous lest his expertise reveal itself to be no more than an irrelevance.

'Well now, yes,' he began, not knowing quite in what language to address the present company. They were not the age of under-graduates, yet they were not colleagues from whom he could expect a measure of common knowledge and trained understand-ing. 'I have to say – that is, you'll understand that this is all quite provisional. We have little enough to go on. Almost nothing, really. That is . . .'

'Get on with it, Myles. This isn't a seminar. Just tell them what you told me.'

'I'm sorry, Declan. I'm not accustomed to what I suppose you call briefings. But I'll do my best.'

'Good man, good man.'

'The business of the accent is interesting,' O'hUiginn went on, 'mainly because I'm certain that we are not dealing with an Irish group here. For one thing, there are very few Protestant sects of any size in this country. A great deal more if we include the North, of course, and I'm not ruling out that possibility. Most of the larger cults have some sort of operation down here – the Moonies, Transcendental Meditation, Baha'is, and so on – but I'm confident none of them have had a hand in this.

'Both the written communications from your kidnappers and yesterday's telephone conversation strongly suggest a right-wing Christian grouping. But from what I've been told about the scale of what happened, I can't believe that any of the small sects here is behind it. None of them have that sort of capacity in terms of money, manpower, or training. Of course, several have inter-national connections, and that's something we should look into; but they wouldn't be my first choice here. None of the Irish sects has a background in violence, and as far as I know none is connected to foreign groups with such a history.

'If I were looking for a right-wing Christian sect with the money, personnel, and organizational skills to carry out a raid of this kind, I'd go straight to the United States, where there are several groups meeting the right description. That hunch would seem to be backed up by a couple of things. First of all, at one point last night's speaker said to Mangan: "Your word isn't worth a red cent." Next, there's this.'

He took from his pocket the watch that Declan had found the day before.

'This is a watch that was removed from the wrist of the dead hostage from Egypt. It seems to have been put there as a kind of statement. It's of American manufacture, and I happen to know that they're not uncommon among fundamentalists over there. I understand that Mr Carberry plans to look into the sale and distribution of watches from this manufacturer.

'Well, that's about it for the moment. As I said, we don't have much to go on. I dislike conjecture, and ordinarily I wouldn't . . .'

'Thanks, Myles. I want you to stick around so you can comment on further information as it comes up. If we can identify who these people are, we may find it easier to track them down.'

O'hUiginn got to his feet. At the back a young computer operator named Tim Donnelly raised a hand.

'Professor,' he said. 'Could you tell us if the code-word chosen by our man last night has any significance?'

O'hUiginn shook his head.

'Not yet. It's too general. Mount Carmel's a well-known Biblical location. It's where the prophet Ezekiel defeated the priests of Baal. And, of course, it's situated in the modern state of Israel, overlooking the port of Haifa. Obviously, that could have significance in the present context. Or perhaps it has some meaning more personal to our friend on the radio. We'll see.'

'Does anyone else have questions for the professor? No? Very well, we'll let him get back to work.'

'Declan, if you need me I'll be in my room upstairs all day. There are materials I have to consult. By tomorrow I'll have a list of other items I need. You'll have to get them for me: the university library system will be too slow. A lot of them can be transmitted through the internet. Can you handle that?'

Declan nodded.

'There should be no problem. I'll keep in touch.'

When O'hUiginn had gone, Declan got back to business.

'Don't discount him because of his manner. He's sharp. He'll see things none of you will see, make connections you couldn't begin to make. The absent-minded professor bit is largely a front. Myles is one of the best. And we need somebody on our team who can interpret the statements the hostage-takers send us.'

'Won't the official investigation try to pull him in?' asked Grainne.

'They won't find him. He won't be leaving this building until the whole thing's over. I've got his word for that.

'From what he says, there's a good chance that the leader of the hostage-takers is American, and it's likely some or all of his team are also from the States. Agreed?'

A few people nodded.

'All right. It's as good a lead as we have. I want Pronsias and Brendan to get on to this right away. You're to check on all Americans entering Ireland over, let's say, the last three to four months. Narrow it down to any that have stayed on. When you've got your shortlist, we'll see how many are still at the addresses we have for them. My guess is that the organizers will have come in a while ago to set things up, but the rest of their team could have flown in weeks or even days before the raid.'

The telephone rang. Declan picked it up. It was Pádraig Pearse.

CHAPTER TWENTY-SEVEN

Belfast
10 October
1130 hours

The plane landed at Aldergrove airport on time, dropping from a dim blue sky across a frayed expanse of ploughed and unploughed fields. On the previous day, Abu Hida had flown from Beirut to Athens, and from Athens to Amsterdam. He had carried with him false papers supplied by Hizbollah's operational intelligence unit in Sidon. From Schiphol airport he had gone to a café in the centre of Amsterdam, where a Malaysian supporter had provided him with fresh papers and a large sum of money in used UK banknotes. The Malaysian also lent him a razor with which to remove his beard.

That evening, Abu Hida had taken an Air UK flight to Newcastle in England. Since the flight originated in another EC country, there had been no customs check, and passport clearance had been virtually automatic for anyone who, like Abu Hida, held an EC passport. He was met at the airport and driven straight to a terraced house in Benwell in the west of Newcastle, where he made contact with a group of Iranian students. In the morning, he flew to Belfast, carrying documents that identified him as Ghiyath Shafique, a Pakistani grocer resident in Gateshead.

The morning flight from Newcastle had been diverted from the harbour airport to Belfast International in the mountains outside the city. Its passengers were made up mostly of reps and buyers in Marks & Spencer suits. 'Ghiyath Shafique' did not merit a second glance. The security men at both airports let him through with no more than routine questions about the reason for his visit. Their targets had names like Liam and Brendan and came from Turf Lodge and Ardoyne, not Lahore or Rawalpindi.

He was not very tall, not very handsome, not very well dressed. But no-one would pass him in the street without registering his presence. Above all, it was the eyes, with their innerness, their olive-blackness, their immensity, their awareness of everything. And the mouth, firmly set, and tense, as though at any moment he might smile or burst out laughing, as though all the energy of his face was there, coiled in those lips. If Anthony Harker had been on duty at the airport, he would have recognized what he was at once. They were brothers, after a fashion.

Outside, he took the first taxi in line and asked to be taken to an address near the city centre. The road from the airport was secured by a permanent RUC checkpoint, but the taxi-drivers – Protestants to a man – were known to the police. The duty sergeant threw no more than a cursory glance at Abu Hida. A nod and they were through.

As they pulled away, the driver glanced in his mirror and started up a conversation. Being friendly with strangers is the Ulsterman's traditional compensation for hating his neighbour.

'Your first time in the province, is it?' he asked, betraying his religious affiliation the moment he opened his mouth. No Catholic would have spoken of the six counties as 'the province', any more than he would have called Derry 'Londonderry'.

'Yes,' murmured Abu Hida. 'My first visit.'

'Well, don't mind the peelers, son. They're only doing their job. Keeping us out of trouble.' He turned a sharp bend and suddenly they could see the city below, spread out along an expanse of sparkling water. 'From the mainland, are you?' the driver went on.

'From England. I live in England. Gateshead.'

'That so? My youngest went to university near there, so she did. The University of Newcastle. She did sociology or whatever they call it. Still, she's back here now. A lot go over and never come back. But it's not as bad as it was. Northern Ireland's just like anywhere else, sure. You can live here for years and never see hide nor hair of trouble. You wouldn't want to believe all the things you see on television. It's not like that at all. Sure, there's an odd killing, but it's not like it was ten years and more ago. I hear tell there's more crime on the mainland than over here.

That's God's honest truth. What line of business did you say you were in?'

Abu Hida found it hard to keep up with the rapid flow of heavily accented English. He spoke the language well enough, but this was like being in a foreign country.

'I'm sorry,' he said. 'I did not understand.'

'What's your work? Your job.'

'I own a shop. A grocery shop. But I also rent videos.'

They joined the M2 motorway at Templepatrick. The car picked up speed, heading towards the coast.

'I've heard there's a lot of your people own shops now in England,' said the driver. 'It's a pity all the same you can't be at home in India. You'd get a lot of sun over there, so you would. We could do with some here.'

'I come from Pakistan.'

'Aye, well, it's the same thing only different, isn't it?'

Abu Hida watched the city fold round him. For years he had heard people speak of Belfast as the Beirut of Europe. He had expected to find it war-ravaged, patrolled by rival factions, a place of devastation; but instead he saw the dull streets of a provincial European city.

'You're a Hindu, then, are you?'

'Muslim.'

'Is that so? I had Salman Rushdie in there where you're sitting, as big as life. True as God, I did. But tell me something – are you a Catholic Muslim or a Protestant Muslim?'

It was an old joke and one that Abu Hida could never come near to understanding.

'I'm sorry, I don't . . .'

'It's all right. Sure, I'm only having a geg.'

They came to a large roundabout, then turned off onto Glenmachan Street. There was another police checkpoint, but again they were waved through. The driver turned left into Tate's Avenue, heading east towards the university.

There were armoured cars on the roads, and once or twice Abu Hida caught sight of a military patrol edging its way along a pavement; but he saw no signs of shelling or bombardment. Whatever war they were fighting here must be strictly contained, he thought, its deaths mere rituals that had no other purpose than to avoid the compromises peace would bring.

They drove through ordinary streets, past ordinary houses, and he wondered why he had been sent here, wondered how he might find his destiny in such a place. Unexpectedly, he felt drained of hope.

'Now, sir, I think this is the place you're after.'

They had pulled up in the Stranmillis Road, outside an Indian restaurant called The Imambara, the name written in heavy gold letters above an elaborate arched door that seemed grotesquely out of place in a terrace of plain Victorian town houses.

'You have friends here, then?' the driver asked.

'Friends?'

'You know – family. Relations.'

'Oh, yes. I'm staying with my cousin.'

'Well, I'm sure they're very happy in Belfast. No-one will trouble them here, not like over the water. Everyone's welcome in Northern Ireland. Black, brown, yellow, it makes no difference. As long as you're not a Catholic, eh?'

He paid the driver and went inside. It was already lunchtime, and the restaurant was filled with customers, many of them students from the nearby university taking advantage of special midday rates. A waiter wearing a long white coat and red sash approached him.

'I'd like to see Mr Shafique. Tell him it's his cousin from England.'

Shafique owned the restaurant. He arrived moments later, smiling fiercely to cover an underlying nervousness. Although he reached no further than Abu Hida's chest, he looked at least twice his weight. An exaggerated politeness tainted his every movement and thickened his voice with unctuous insincerity. Abu Hida saw in him at once a twin of the taxi-driver. Both men were desperate for reassurance. They needed above all other things in life to be liked, and Abu Hida surmised that they would sacrifice anything to that end, even the opportunity to be themselves.

'You are very welcome,' said the little man. 'Please, you must be hungry. I will tell the kitchen to prepare lunch for you. All our food is *halal*.'

Abu Hida shook his head.

'This place is too public. Do you not have a private room?'

'Of course, of course. I am so sorry. We will go upstairs to my office.' He picked up Abu Hida's bag and preceded him through a side door. The smell of cheap curry followed them.

The office was a cramped room at the top of the building, packed with cardboard boxes containing spices and bags of linen waiting to go to the laundry. The walls were festooned with framed prints of badly-executed Arabic calligraphy and garish pictures of the Kaaba done in silver foil. Above the desk was a coloured photograph of a building bathed in Indian sunshine. Shafique pointed it out as he set down the bags.

'That is the Great Imambara in Lucknow. A very holy place for the Shi'a, as you know. I named my restaurant after it. My grandfather used to go there on the festivals and at Muharram. Our family lived in Lucknow until the partition. Of course, I have never been there myself.'

Abu Hida had no time for reminiscences.

'I wish to be left alone,' he said. 'When I have finished my prayers, I will eat. At two o'clock a man will come here for me. He will give his name as 'Ali. Send him to me as soon as he arrives.'

CHAPTER TWENTY-EIGHT

The man whose name had been given to fat little Shafique as 'Ali arrived shortly after two. Abu Hida had prayed and eaten and rested. He was ready for the hardships that lay ahead. They were part of his *jihad*, his personal struggle against the realm of un-belief, both in the world and within himself.

'Ali was an Arab like himself, an Iraqi from the south. He was not like Mr Shafique: not round, not nervous, not content to build a life around icons of family piety or relics of a forgotten past. He wore cheap, simple clothes. His face was bearded and his hair fastidiously trimmed. His bearing impressed Abu Hida the moment he set foot in the dingy room.

He knew that 'Ali had fought against Saddam Hussein in the marshes of southern Iraq during the Shi'ite uprising of 1991. Before that he had been a student at the theological seminary of al-Najaf, and he had led a *halaqa*, a cell of the Shi'ite Da'wa Party, in his home town of Suq al-Shuyukh, a centre of resistance to Saddam and the Sunni-controlled Baathist dictatorship. He had close links with some of the smaller resistance groups: al-Afwaj al-Islamiyya and the Jund al-Imam. Following the crushing of the rebellion, he had fled the country on the orders of one of his teachers, Hujjat al-Islam al-Ghaffari. He had been in Northern Ireland for five years now, working on a doctorate in Islamic studies at Queen's University. In that time he had not been idle.

Shafique left the two men alone. When he had gone, Abu Hida turned to 'Ali.

'Can he be trusted?'

'Adequately. He knows the price of betrayal. His cousin, the one whose papers you are carrying, is a believer, very active in the movement in England. Several other members of the family are good men, true Shi'is, lovers of the Imams. Shafique has no reason to betray you.'

'Perhaps not deliberately, but he is capable of making mistakes. He may open his mouth at the wrong time, say the wrong thing. You will keep a close eye on him. Speak to his cousin, make sure he understands the importance of my presence here, but give him no details. See that he impresses on our Mr Shafique the consequences of a loose tongue to himself and his family.'

He paused. Even had he not been fully briefed on his background, he knew instinctively that 'Ali could be trusted. Abu Hida had lived his life among men committed to a cause, men willing to die for what they believed in, for whom any form of compromise was a betrayal of absolute truth. He too carried it inside himself, the knowledge of his own triviality, the transcendence of total commitment, and he could recognize it in others, as though something in them spoke to what was in him.

'However – Shafique is not important. Have you made contact as asked?'

'Ali – his real name was Abu Ahmad al-Rikabi – nodded.

'They are expecting us. The rendezvous and time still have to be decided on. I'll take you to my place and we can wait there until they ring. My flat's only round the corner in Pretoria Street.'

'Do they know what they are doing?'

'I think so. Some of them are very experienced.'

'We shall see. Will the equipment I asked for be there?'

'Most of it. The guns certainly: they have assured me they will supply you with what you want.'

'We shall see.'

'The rest will be delivered to you soon after you make contact with the group who will be working with you. I am sorry, but it was not physically possible to bring everything in at such short notice. My people are doing the best they can.'

'As long as I am armed. That is the first essential.'

'Ali glanced at his watch.

'I think we should go. Is this all your luggage?'

Abu Hida nodded. 'Ali bent to pick up the bag, but his companion took it from him.

'No,' Abu Hida said gently. 'You are not my servant. I will only ask you to do what I cannot do myself.'

'Ali smiled.

'They told me you'd be hard to handle.'

Abu Hida held his gaze.

'Harder than you can imagine,' he said. Without another word, he headed for the stairs.

Dublin
1628 hours

The door opened and Grainne Walsh glanced in. Declan started. He had been thinking about Amina.

'Sir? I think you should listen to this.'

He stood and went to the door. Several members of the team were gathered round a desk at the far end of the next room. A radio was playing. Declan glanced at his watch: it must be the half four news. Someone turned up the volume.

'... will take place next Wednesday. The factory in Limerick closed last February with the loss of sixty workers, but Mr O'Sullivan now says that he intends to relocate by the New Year. A union representative interviewed this morning said that the offer was unacceptable and that their protest will continue.

'And now we go back to that report I mentioned earlier, concerning claims that a hostage crisis is developing here in Ireland. I have Siobhan Coyle on the line from London. Siobhan, have there been any further developments?'

'Not as yet, Raymond. Spokesmen for the main Arab embassies here deny that there is a crisis and insist that the conference is continuing as planned. At the moment, all we have to go on are rumours originating with a handful of fundamentalist organizations in the Middle East, who claim that their delegates are missing and that Western intelligence communications reveal details of a conspiracy to kidnap and possibly assassinate them. I understand that evidence is to be passed to the Reuters agency in Beirut this evening.'

'Thank you, Siobhan. Meanwhile, here in Dublin, the Foreign Minister, Ciaran Clark, issued a statement denying that the delegates were in any danger. He suggested that rumours of a raid on the conference were simply disinformation designed to throw the negotiations into confusion. These rumours were probably the work of several extremist groups who had been refused permission to take part in the talks. According to a spokesman at the

Taoiseach's Office, the conference continues at Castletown House under conditions of tight security.

'And now, the latest sports news . . .'

CHAPTER TWENTY-NINE

Belfast
10 October
1910 hours

The war zone of West Belfast is little more than a leisurely stroll from the leafy avenues and stockbroker homes of the Malone Road. Walk down Balmoral Avenue and along Stockmans Lane under the new motorway, and you will find yourself in a sprawl of Housing Authority estates, where the accents are different, the houses smaller, and the cars – those there are of them – older. Walk where you like now, it is all one: a vast Republican ghetto that runs from the east of Dunmurry through to Clonard and the lower Falls on the west of the city centre. The names are familiar from a million television screens: Ballymurphy, Turf Lodge, Andersonstown, the Falls. This is a world within a world, impoverished, besieged, patrolled day and night by the soldiers of what its inhabitants consider an army of occupation. It is the West Bank in another place. No-one really wants to be here, no-one dares live anywhere else.

'Ali drove without hesitation, down Stockmans Lane, along Kennedy Way, past the eastern edge of Ladybrook, into Andersonstown. The phone call had come twenty minutes earlier, giving a time and place for the meeting. He knew his way there as well as any local. Almost from the day of his arrival in Belfast, the young Iraqi had busied himself forging contacts with Republican groups. He and they had nothing in common but a hatred of British imperialism, but that was enough to give their alliance a veneer of meaning.

Rain had started to fall, a little uncertainly at first, then with sullen persistence. An armoured car went past; from its turret, a British soldier looked out, his rifle pointing menacingly towards them.

They moved deeper into a network of sad, haggard streets where men with wary eyes watched on the corners and teenagers huddled in doorways, their collars turned against the drizzle, waiting for night. The fronts of the little shops were barred or shuttered, every other wall carried slogans of defiance and dogged idealism, evoking memories of an impossible past. Outside the bars, closed circuit TV cameras kept watch for random killers. There were almost no cars, and those there were were battered and rusted. The year-old Escort in which they drove seemed brash and out of place. At last Abu Hida began to understand what he was doing here and how, in spite of everything, he might yet come face to face with destiny on this rain-soaked island.

There was an Arabic word, *al-mustad'afin*. 'The miserable', 'the poor', 'the downtrodden' – it had innumerable translations, but they all amounted to the same thing: people from whom everything had been crushed but hope and defiance; Fanon's 'Wretched of the Earth'. For centuries, the Shi'a had regarded themselves as the downtrodden, and now they had risen up to claim what was theirs.

In all his years of struggle in Beirut, Abu Hida had visualized the West in monochrome: a bright land of richly-dressed tyrants bent on the destruction of all he held dear, profiteers manipulating an international trade in drugs, pornography, and weapons. He had known his vision to be a lie, a gross oversimplification, but it had served him better than any truth. His hatred of cruelty and deceit had strengthened him to carry out the most terrible acts of war. He had clung to his canting images of Western arrogance to fuel his hatred.

But here, driving through these shabby streets, past the young men in their cheap anoraks, the women with their limp shopping-bags, the children with their hollow faces and empty eyes, he understood that there were *al-mustad'afin* here too. He was not to know that there were Protestant streets just like these in other parts of the city, that there were poor and wretched people throughout Britain, that the real enemy everywhere was not the English or the forces of imperialism or armies of occupation, but insidious, grinding poverty, and that it blighted the lives of anyone it touched, regardless of creed.

They pulled up outside a two-storey house in Clonelly Avenue. 'Ali glanced round carefully, then stepped out and went to the front door. The house looked like all the others in the street. A child's bicycle lay rusting in the front garden. A satellite dish jutted out from one corner. The woodwork had not been painted in years and was visibly rotten.

The door opened a fraction. 'Ali spoke earnestly to someone in the narrow hallway. Nearby, a dog barked listlessly as though unnerved by the silence. Moments later, its voice was drowned as a helicopter passed by overhead: eternal vigilance, but without freedom. 'Ali turned and came back to the door. The silence returned.

'They're waiting for you,' he said.

CHAPTER THIRTY

They were in the front room, two men standing and a woman in a chair. The call house had been requisitioned half an hour earlier from the Cronins, a Catholic family who had lived here all their lives: he was unemployed, his wife cleaned at a day centre for pensioners, they had five children. They were over in Turf Lodge with her sister for as long as the house was needed. They would not have dreamt of complaining: no-one would. Giving up your house at a moment's notice was a necessary part of life, like hiding a gun or a box of fuses or a man on the run.

'Ali introduced the men as Desmond McCormick and Con McKearney. They were in their mid-thirties, with wide, dreamless eyes and dry, humourless mouths the colour of weathered brick. Abu Hida shook hands, weighing each man up in turn, knowing that his life and the success of his mission might depend on their reliability and strength.

The woman sat in a low chair apart from the others, and Abu Hida might have ignored her, partly because she was a woman, partly because she did not conform to any of his stereotypes of a fighter. In his own cause, the women wore either veils or army fatigues. Make-up, perfume, fine clothes belonged to the enemy. But this woman wore a quiet suit, her hair was well cut, and she smelled faintly of roses.

'Ali brought Abu Hida to her. As they approached, she rose slowly and stretched out a well-manicured hand.

'This is Dr Maureen O'Dalaigh,' said 'Ali. 'Dr O'Dalaigh – this is the man I told you about.'

Abu Hida took her hand. And as he did so he sensed at once what he had not sensed in either of the men: strength, hardness, the determination of a killer. The clothes and make-up were camouflage or a mockery. He pressed her hand and she returned the pressure.

'I'm pleased to meet you,' she said. "Ali's told me a lot about you. He says you're a hero where you come from.'

'That is not for me to say. We do not have heroes. I am a fighter, a *mujahid*. I do not fight for myself, but for the Imams.'

'Of course, you're a Shi'ite. Am I right?'

'Yes. A Muslim who loves the Family of the Prophet.'

He paused. He realized that he still held her hand in his. Embarrassed, he let it go.

'I understand,' she said. 'The *ahl al-bayt*.'

'Yes,' he said, surprised. 'You are very well informed.'

'Och, I read an awful lot. We're not all ignorant savages here, you know. Not like them pair of morons in the corner,' she said, smiling at her companions.

'Dr O'Dalaigh has a doctorate in law from Queen's University,' said 'Ali. 'She's a clever woman. You'll have to watch what you say to her.'

Abu Hida smiled. If she was a lawyer, it explained the clothes and the hair. But not the strength.

'On my way from the airport,' he said, 'my taxi-driver asked if I was a Protestant Muslim or a Catholic Muslim. It seemed a stupid question, meaningless.'

She smiled, and he wondered if she was laughing at him, as she had just laughed at her friends. She seemed very self-possessed.

'Oh, I don't know,' she said. 'It's all the people here understand, all half of them ever think about. There are two camps, and they're lost if they can't put you in one or the other. "Which foot do you dig with?", that's the usual question. It's no use saying you've got three feet or four or none at all, they know that can't be true. If you're not a Protestant, you're a Catholic, even if you're a Jew or a Hindu. And vice versa.'

'Leave the poor man alone, Maureen.' Desmond McCormick came over and took Abu Hida by the arm, leading him to a chair.

'Would you like a drink?' asked McKearney.

'Tea or coffee would be fine.'

'Nothing stronger?'

'I'm sorry?'

'A beer maybe? Or a whiskey. There's some Bushmills in the kitchen.'

Abu Hida shook his head.

'I do not drink alcohol.'

'Sorry,' said McKearney, 'I was forgetting . . .'

'For God's sake, Con,' Maureen O'Dalaigh interrupted, 'will you stop wasting time? The man's here to talk business, not sit around drinking Guinness. Sit down and let's get on with it.'

McKearney sat sheepishly in a chair next to Abu Hida. 'Ali remained standing.

'I have the things you wanted,' said McCormick. He was an agitated man, his drabness shot through with some sort of nervous energy that seemed to give him no rest. Bending, he unzipped a large sports bag at his feet. He took out a gun and handed it to Abu Hida.

'It's not loaded,' he said.

Abu Hida hefted the weapon in both hands, running his fingers along the barrel with the delicacy of a doctor examining a limb that may be minutely damaged. The gun was a Heckler & Koch sniper's rifle, identical to the one he had used back home. McCormick next handed him a Franchi 12-bore automatic. Abu Hida checked this second weapon carefully and laid it beside the first.

Apart from this, the bag also contained a Heckler & Koch 9mm P7M8 automatic pistol equipped with a Soginco laser targeting device, a SIG-Sauer P–226 pistol capable of taking 15-round magazines, a Steyr AUG assault rifle, two night-sights, and several boxes of ammunition.

'These are very good,' said Abu Hida. 'You have been extremely efficient.'

'They had to be brought in special,' said McKearney. 'At short notice. I hope it's worth it. We could do with guns like those ourselves.'

'Shut up, Con; you're giving me a headache,' snapped O'Dalaigh.

'I was only saying, like.'

'Well, don't. The go-ahead for this was given by General Headquarters yesterday. It was ratified by the Army Council this morning. Or perhaps you'd like to put them right. I have Dan Hughes's number here if you'd like to give him a ring.'

'Leave him alone, Maureen,' pleaded McCormick. 'There's no need to be arguing among ourselves.'

Abu Hida interrupted.

'Mr McKearney, you can have as many guns like these as you want. If your people play their part, I give you my word that you will have guaranteed shipments of anything you need. You have had dealings with 'Ali before. You know we can keep our promises. These guns are necessary for the task I have been sent here to carry out. Now, if you have no objections, I would like to discuss the arrangements you have made.'

'Before we do that,' said Maureen O'Dalaigh, 'I'd like to know what evidence you have that someone is holding your people hostage. According to the radio, the conference down South is going ahead as planned. All this talk about hostages is no more than a rumour.'

Abu Hida shook his head.

'The conference was attacked by armed raiders on Monday evening. That is not a rumour, it is fact. The intelligence services of at least three Arab states have intercepted a series of coded communications between European anti-terrorist agencies. These provide detailed reports of the raid and subsequent events. I shall continue to receive details of further intercepts through 'Ali. With their help, I hope to locate and rescue the hostages.'

'Why not just let the Irish security services do the job for you?'

'The Irish are not in charge any longer. The security operation has been taken over by MI5. I think you will agree that they are not to be trusted.'

'Are you to be trusted?' Maureen looked at him hard, as though she could, with a little effort, read his thoughts or, deeper than that, his soul.

He was not accustomed to dealing in such an open fashion with a woman, a woman who asked questions, demanded answers, put men in their place. And the knowledge, the inner conviction that she was as strong as himself, perhaps even stronger made it hard for him to treat her as anything but an equal.

'We have to trust each other,' he said. It was personal, then. The organizations behind them could fence as they liked, but they would have to find trust on an individual basis. 'If not, I shall do this alone. It will be harder, and almost certainly I shall not succeed; but I have no choice.'

He knew he had to win their confidence. At home, he had proved himself in all the ways that mattered. But here, among strangers who did not even share his faith, he found himself adrift. He looked round the cramped, untidy room, at its pathetic ornaments and cheap wallpaper, at the holes in the carpet and the tears in the furniture. All they had in common, he thought, was their poverty and a notional hatred of an all-pervasive enemy with many names. He could get by with that if it were not for the woman. Her clothes and manner and quiet cleverness intimidated him, that and her being a woman in the first place.

'I need your help,' he said. 'I don't know your country, I don't know where to begin to look for the hostages. All I have is second-hand access to communications between the security services, and even that is limited. I have very little faith in the ability of the anti-terrorist agencies to track down the raiders in time. Without your help, I will be seriously handicapped.'

He paused. Rain fell outside almost without a sound. It was growing dark. Another helicopter passed overhead. The room smelled of stale food and sweat.

'What I am asking is not without risks. But whether we succeed or fail, your people are guaranteed the support of every organiz-ation with hostages on this island. You will have the weapons of your choice. All the explosives you may need, here or in England. Training for your soldiers at our expense.'

Maureen O'Dalaigh watched Abu Hida carefully. His hands, his feet, the way he moved, his manner of speaking. Without wanting to, she found herself admiring him. Physically, he attracted her strongly; but it was not that, and she knew it was not that. She sensed in him an almost elemental force, but she sensed too that it was wholly under control, that he would never be careless or wanton or undirected. If only she could have a few men like him, she thought, enough to bring this senseless war to some sort of conclusion. The calibre of the average IRA recruit was abysmally low. She wept every time a bomb went off prematurely, every time innocent victims died. It was something she could live with, they were casualties of war, but she took no pride in it. A thought began to form in the back of her mind. Why bother sending men like Con McKearney to Lebanon or Iran for training when Abu Hida's people could send her a handful of men like him for a year?

'There's one thing I'd like to know,' she said. 'Are you here to set these people free, as you say? Or have you been sent as their executioner?'

176

She was astute, he thought, and he realized that there would be little he could hide from her.

'Shaykh Mu'in Usayran is my father. His life is of very great importance to the Shi'a of Lebanon.'

'That does not answer my question.'

'I have come to Ireland to rescue the shaykh. Your task is to take me to him. His kidnappers will be punished. The other hostages are not my concern.' He paused. 'Nor are they your concern.'

Con McKearney stood and went to the window. He looked out anxiously, up and down the darkening street, as though worried about something. Above them, the helicopter was circling. He left the window and returned to his seat, still restless.

O'Dalaigh hesitated, then shrugged. Why should she quibble about the deaths of foreigners if she was willing to accept Irish fatalities in the interests of the struggle?

'Very well,' she said. 'Where do we start? We are willing to assist you as far as our resources allow. The British army and MI5 have the largest intelligence-gathering network in Ireland. The army 125 Intelligence Section operates a computer known as Crucible. It has access to one of the biggest data banks in existence. They have a direct link-up to the mainland R2 computer and its database. There are connections to European and international intelligence databases. It's very impressive.' She paused. Beside her McKearney was whispering to McCormick. He turned and looked at her, and she continued.

'But there's one thing they don't have,' she said. 'I expect it's the same where you come from. They don't have the people, nor their hearts, nor their minds. The Republican movement has no computer databanks, no satellite stations, and no Tinkerbell system to tap telephones with; but it does have the cooperation of thousands of ordinary people throughout the length and breadth of this island. We have eyes and ears everywhere. Believe me, nothing much happens that we don't find out about soon enough. That's how we're going to find your hostages for you. And we'll find them before the security services get so much as a whisper.'

Abu Hida nodded. He felt reassured by the woman's directness and common sense. Somehow, he was sure she was not just boasting when she said her organization had the resources to track down the hostages.

'I'm grateful,' he said. 'But I need to know how many men you can spare to go with me.'

Maureen turned to McCormick.

'Dezzy,' she said, 'will you tell him what we have planned?'

McCormick took a deep breath. Abu Hida sensed that he was uneasy. His manner towards Maureen O'Dalaigh was deferential, as though she was his superior. There was such a difference between them, Abu Hida thought. It was not his shabby shoes or threadbare clothes that manifested the difference, but his whole bearing.

'Well,' McCormick began, 'what it is, like, we've decided the best thing is for you to work with an Active Service Unit. They can give you the back-up you need during the search, and if you have to take military action, like, you'll have trained men to go in with you. Usually the ASUs are needed for general operations here in the North, but one unit was taken out of action a wee while back. They're down South at the moment, and they've been given orders to act as your support team.'

He hesitated, as though he had something difficult to say.

'The thing is,' he went on, 'they're all Northerners, all Belfastmen, and none of them knows the South that well. So the Chief of Staff has decided to place them under the overall command of someone familiar with the country as a whole. He chose Dr O'Dalaigh here.'

'I don't understand,' said Abu Hida.

'It's very simple,' said Maureen O'Dalaigh. 'The lads in the ASU are all good men. They're well trained, they're experienced, and they're hard. But take them outside Belfast and they're about as much use to you as a bunch of wee girls from the blind school in Jordanstown. They need someone with them who knows their way round. And that happens to be me. Being a lawyer, I get around a lot. And wherever I go on legal work, I'm sure to have work for the cause as well.'

'Who exactly are you?' asked Abu Hida. 'What position do you hold?'

She smiled.

'Well, that's supposed to be something of a secret. But seeing as Dezzy and Con here both know, I may as well tell you. I'm

178

an executive member of the Army Council. Does that answer your question?'

'I want to know why your people thought they had a right to offer me a woman. This is man's work. There may be killing.'

She flushed, angered even though she had anticipated his rejection.

'And I suppose your famous Brides of Blood just sit at home and paint their frigging toenails. Listen, mister, you don't have a choice. We're doing you a favour as it is, arms or no arms. Without me, you don't stand a chance. You're . . .'

On the table in front of her, a mobile phone rang. Once, twice, three times.

'For God's sake, answer it,' shouted McKearney.

O'Dalaigh picked it up.

'Yes?'

She listened, and Abu Hida thought her cheeks went pale.

'I understand,' she said and finished the call. Without speaking, she stood and crossed to the window. The helicopter above was louder than ever. Night was falling.

'That was Jimmy Kane,' she said, her words almost indistinguishable. 'He's just got word that an army patrol's moved into this area.'

She turned and looked angrily at Desmond McCormick.

'What happened to your fucking lookouts? Eh? They were supposed to be there. What the fuck happened to them?'

At that moment, there was a loud crackling noise outside. The helicopter lifted and moved away. As the sound of its engine receded, a megaphone boomed into the stillness. An English voice, precise and patrician, echoed through the rain-washed street and bounced off the walls of the little, unhappy houses.

'Maureen O'Dalaigh. Desmond McCormick. Con McKearney. The house you are in is surrounded. You are under arrest. I want you to leave any weapons you may have behind. Come out with your hands on your heads and you will not be harmed. You have my word. Any attempt at resistance will render you liable to return fire.'

And silence came afterwards and rested on the street for a little while until the helicopter returned, booming and thudding out of the hollows of a grey sky from which almost all light had gone.

CHAPTER THIRTY-ONE

'You brought them here! You fucking shites, you brought them here!' Con McKearney ran at Abu Hida, his hand raised to strike. The Arab did not move, did not attempt to ward off the coming blow.

'For God's sake, Con! Leave it!' Maureen O'Dalaigh moved between them, facing down her subordinate.

'They're touts for the fucking Brits,' spluttered McKearney. 'They fucking set us up.'

'We'll deal with that later, Con. All right? All right?'

Ignoring Abu Hida, she turned to McCormick.

'Is there a back way out of here, Dezzy?'

'There's open ground between here and the Glen Road,' he said. He was shaking visibly. Outside, the roar of the helicopter threatened to cover his words. 'Down over the playing field by the Christian Brothers school. If we could get across the road, we could go past St Theresa's and over to the Black Hill or down to Turf Lodge. I don't know. I don't fucking know.'

'Right,' said Maureen. 'They'll have soldiers out there, but if we split up they may not have enough on the ground to cover us all. It depends on how quickly the raid was put together. I'll try to head over towards Whiterock. Dezzy, you go the other way, down to the Glen – if you can make it to Andy Doyle's house he'll get you out in his car.'

She turned to McKearney.

'Con, you go on down to the church on the other side of the Glen Road. There's a Ford Escort parked in front of it. A red one. Here's the key.' She tossed a car-key to him. 'Head on up the Glen Road out of town and dump it as soon as you get a chance.'

She looked at them in turn.

'Have you both got guns?'

They nodded. McCormick had an automatic pistol, McKearney a revolver.

'Right, then. We'd better get moving.'

'What about them? Yous aren't going to let them walk out of here, are you?' McKearney raised his gun and pointed it, first at 'Ali, then Abu Hida. 'They fucking got us here with a cock-and-bull story. They're just waiting for us to leave before joining up with them SAS butchers out there.'

He held the revolver steady, aimed at Abu Hida's head.

'Well, if yous aren't going to do anything about it, I fucking am.'

Con McKearney was an experienced killer. He had murdered at least fifteen men and women in his time. An off-duty policeman playing with his children in the Ormeau Park. Three road sweepers drinking in a pub in Donegall Pass. A schoolgirl who got in his line of fire once outside the King's Hall. A soldier shot from behind in the markets. And others much the same. It was a tawdry list of casual deaths easily come by in the world he inhabited. A list to make a hero from a straw man.

He took a step nearer Abu Hida, in order to make sure of his target. Both hands on the gun now, ready to fire.

'Fucking bastard tout,' he shouted. 'And you're next,' he said, glancing at 'Ali.

It was the last thing he did. No-one even saw the ashtray leave Abu Hida's hand, but they all heard the crunching sound it made as it shattered the front of Con McKearney's skull. He swayed for a moment, still holding the gun towards his intended victim, then his legs crumpled and he fell to the floor in a heap. The revolver bounced at Abu Hida's feet. The ashtray, a round dish of heavy glass, was still rolling across the carpet as he fell. It came to a halt, tottered, and dropped onto its base. 'Murphy's Stout' it said in large red letters.

Dezzy McCormick dropped to his knees beside McKearney.

'He's dead,' he yelled. 'You fucking killed him.'

'Leave him, Dezzy. You can do nothing for him.' Maureen took her colleague by the arm and raised him to his feet. She looked at Abu Hida, almost with understanding. His face was completely expressionless, as though Con McKearney's death had found no rough surfaces within him to which it could cling.

The megaphone burst into life again.

'This is my second appeal to you. I shall not make a third. You are completely surrounded. Leave your weapons in the house and give yourselves up. You have my word that you will not be harmed.'

'Get going, Dezzy.'

Maureen pushed McCormick through the door of the little room and followed him towards the kitchen at the back. As she reached the kitchen door, she felt a hand on her arm.

Abu Hida was standing beside her. He shook his head.

'You will be committing suicide,' he said. 'They'll be expecting you to make a run for it. Don't give them the chance. Stay with me. I will get you out.'

McCormick had already opened the kitchen door. He looked back at her.

'Come on, Maureen,' he pleaded. 'What are you waiting for?'

She looked again at Abu Hida. The Arab was calm, calmer than anyone had a right to be under such conditions. What if Con had been right? she wondered. What if the two Arabs were no more than fifth columnists infiltrated by the Brits' 14th Intelligence Company? Abu Hida did not put pressure on her. It was her choice. She took a deep breath, made her mind up, and stepped towards him.

'If you're with the Brits,' she said, 'I'll have you. Do you understand? I don't care how long it takes, but I'll see you crucified.'

She turned to McCormick.

'Hurry up, Dezzy. I'm staying here to hold them off. Good luck. I'll see you in McD's tomorrow night. You can buy me a pint.'

Dezzy hesitated. It would not be easy on his own. He sensed that he was being used as a decoy, but he had little choice. He'd rather take his chances in the dark than get trapped here as reinforcements came in to tighten the cordon round the house.

'Right you are,' he said. His voice was unsteady. All that was left was false bravado. 'I'll see you around.'

He stepped outside. Maureen closed the door behind him and ran back to the living room. The lights had been switched off, and the only illumination came from the last of the sunlight and the orange glow of a streetlamp.

'Ali had been busy. He had taken three of the guns from the bag and loaded them – the H & K sniper's rifle, the Steyr AUG assault gun, and the Franchi 12-bore automatic. The first two he had fitted with night-sights, Rank Pullin SS20s, capable of identifying a target at a range of three-hundred metres – more than adequate for present circumstances.

Abu Hida took the sniper's rifle. He handed the Franchi to Maureen O'Dalaigh.

'Can you use one of these?' he asked.

In reply, she unfolded the butt, drew back the cocking handle, and swung the gun under her arm.

'I'll take the rear,' said 'Ali. He carried the assault rifle. 'When you're ready to go, let me know and I'll cover your get-away.'

There was a sound of shooting from the back, and they guessed that Dezzy McCormick was making a stand. None of them expected him to hold out long.

'Ali took a spare box of ammunition and disappeared through the door.

'Stay down here,' ordered Abu Hida. 'Once shooting starts, fire in short bursts to hold them down. Move after each burst, otherwise they'll pin you down from your muzzle flashes. I'm going upstairs. Don't shoot until I'm ready.'

She looked at him as though seeing him for the first time.

'We're going to die here,' she said, matter-of-factly. They were in an impossible situation, and she knew there was no way they could fight their way out.

'No,' he said. 'I have done this before. Many times. Trust me. I will get you out of here. After that, I depend on you. We have to do this together.'

'What about him?' she asked. She nodded in the direction 'Ali had taken.

"Ali? He will die.' Abu Hida's voice was without emotion.

'Just like that? He gives his life so you can get out of here. And you let him.'

Abu Hida nodded.

'You would not easily understand. And I do not have time to explain. It is our destiny, that is all. Without it, nothing would have meaning.'

She looked round her then, at the unlovely room and, by inference, the squalid streets to which it belonged, the steady rhythms of unchanging poverty, the hatred, the resentment, the soldiers ringing them about.

'Does this have meaning?' she asked, as if formulating the question for the first time.

'Yes,' he said. 'In the eyes of God.'

'I don't believe in God,' she said.

'Then nothing can have meaning. Least of all your anger.'

The shooting at the rear stopped abruptly. At the front, the officer with the megaphone reached his decision.

'One of you has been shot. Any further resistance will result in my men taking retaliatory measures. I have issued orders to advance on the house. My men will shoot anyone who opens fire on them.'

Abu Hida had reached the front bedroom. He opened a window and tore it bodily from its hinges. The rotten wood gave with little difficulty. On the street outside, the glare of the lamp made it hard to see properly. Kneeling, he took quick aim and shot it out.

He closed his eyes to let the image of the light fade. When he opened them, he could see men moving on the other side of the street, dark shapes, soldiers in battledress. He knew they would not want to move in too quickly, that they would be watching for the first direct shots.

A round of rapid fire came from the rear. It was repeated, then several short bursts followed. Abu Hida was certain he could rely on 'Ali, that he would hold the rear as long as he could.

The helicopter was still circling, but he knew they would not use its searchlight for fear of illuminating the soldiers and making them easy targets. Nevertheless, he would have given much for an SA-7 shoulder-launched missile, capable of bringing a helicopter down. If it picked them up as they made their escape, it could make life difficult.

He had three main objectives. If he could carry them out, he and the woman might stand a chance of getting away. He removed the night-sight from his rifle and used it to scan the street below. If they could see him, they would not feel immediately threatened, though they would guess he had a low-visibility sight. He did not think they knew about either him or 'Ali, though it remained a distinct possibility that British intelligence was better than he imagined. If they did not suspect their presence, they would be expecting resistance from Maureen O'Dalaigh and

Con McKearney – Dezzy McCormick would have been identified by now. That gave Abu Hida a large element of surprise.

His first target was standing in a narrow passage between two pebble-dashed houses thirty-yards to his left. He continued scanning. Target number two was in the open doorway of a house directly opposite. Number three could not be identified, but Abu Hida was certain he was there. It did not matter – he would appear if the first two were hit.

He replaced the night-sight and swung back to the first target, the unit signal's officer, whose job it was to relay messages between the unit and base. It had to be a quick shot, before someone noticed the rifle and opened fire on him. The soldier was wearing a flak jacket and helmet and was only partly visible behind the wall against which he was crouched. Someone like Con McKearney could never have hit him, not even with an anti-tank missile.

He aimed at a spot between the man's shoulder and the top of his head. *Keep still*, he thought. A voice below shouted 'Rifle in upper window!'

Abu Hida breathed out gently and brought the trigger towards him. The soldier's head jerked up and back. In the next instant, Abu Hida threw himself sideways out of the line of fire, dropping behind the window ledge. He was barely in time. A fusillade of shots shattered what was left of the window and ripped through the ceiling and the back wall of the little bedroom.

In the half silence that followed, he shouted again.

'Dr O'Dalaigh! Cover the street! From left to right.'

She opened fire, and he stood and aimed and fired. Straight ahead, an easy shot. The man in the doorway jerked and fell forward onto the front path. The megaphone he had been holding fell from his lifeless fingers and clattered on the concrete. Abu Hida drew back again. There was a cry outside.

'Captain down!'

Abu Hida crept to the other side of the window and took a firing position against the wall. A soldier opposite had moved behind a fence and was kneeling, firing repeatedly into the living room. Abu Hida shot him between the eyes. He swung the rifle and shot another as he moved back towards a Shorland parked on the corner. That was when he caught sight of his third target, the unit's point man, responsible for co-ordinating fire against the house. He was crouched on the other side of the Shorland, speaking into a hand-held transmitter. As he moved out to help pull the latest casualty back to the shelter of the armoured car, Abu Hida shot him in the neck.

By now it had begun to sink in that the troops were up against more than a couple of armed and half-trained thugs. Sustained firing still came from the rear of the house. Abu Hida guessed that 'Ali would have inflicted a few casualties on his opponents by now.

He crept to the bedroom door, got onto the narrow landing, and ran down the stairs. In the living room, Maureen O'Dalaigh was loading a fresh magazine into her Franchi. He moved inside, crawling to stay below window level, slung the bag over his shoulder, and turned.

'We're leaving in one minute,' he said. 'Will you be ready?'

She nodded, paused, and fired a short burst.

Abu Hida crawled out under a hail of bullets. Once through the door, he stayed low in the hall. Some high-velocity bullets were punching straight through the thin partition wall of the living room. Once out of their reach, he stood and ran to the kitchen, where 'Ali had made a bunker for himself from a washing machine and a fridge turned on their sides.

Abu Hida joined him.

"Ali — we're going to try to go through the front. Can you cover us?'

'Ali nodded. He fired several rounds into the darkness, emptying his magazine. There was no answering fire.

'They're re-forming,' he said. 'Let's go before they decide to move in.'

As he turned to leave, he rammed a fresh magazine into the gun.

'This is my last,' he said. 'You'd better be quick.'

Abu Hida reached into the bag and took out the SIG-Sauer pistol and a magazine.

'Here,' he said. 'Don't let them take you alive.'

'Ali put his hand in his pocket and brought out the keys to his car.

'Here,' he said. 'You'll need these.'

They could barely see one another. Still kneeling, they embraced.

'Your name will be remembered for this, *shahid*,' Abu Hida said.

'Bring my greetings to the Prophet. And ask his grandson to lend me his strength.'

'Ali, weeping, kissed him on both cheeks. Then, pocketing the pistol, he crawled into the living room. He took Maureen O'Dalaigh's place and told her to go. As she reached the door, she heard a shot and a cry as another soldier fell.

Abu Hida placed the sniper's rifle in the bag and took out the H & K pistol. 'Ali had loaded it earlier. Abu Hida slipped two more magazines into his pocket.

He knew that, even without radio back-up, the unit's HQ would already have despatched reinforcements. The helicopter could see what was happening on the ground and would soon be joined by others. He and Maureen would have to clear the area quickly. His chief worry was the helicopter, but he trusted to the woman's knowledge of the area to make it possible to evade it long enough to break clear.

He handed her the keys to 'Ali's car.

'The car is to the left near the gate. They haven't tried to move it. Let me deal with anyone trying to shelter behind it. You should concentrate on getting in and driving. Get us to someone who will know how to take us out of Belfast tonight. Can you do that?'

'Yes,' she said. 'It's already set up. Standard procedure.'

'Good. Are you ready?'

She paused.

'He was my brother-in-law, you know,' she said.

'Who?'

'McKearney. He'd have killed you.'

'I know. I'm sorry for your sister.'

'You needn't be. She left him years ago. And you needn't be sorry. He had it coming.'

He squeezed the cocker mechanism to arm the pistol.

'How did you know he wasn't my husband's brother?' she asked.

'You have never been married,' he answered. 'And you would never have married into any family he belonged to. Now – are you ready?'

He had a cheek, she thought. She would love to bring him down a few pegs. But this was hardly the moment. She nodded.

'Now,' he said.

CHAPTER THIRTY-TWO

Dublin
2010 hours

Ciaran Clark rang just after dinner. A secure line, or so he said. Declan doubted it – MI5 would treat all communications to and from the Foreign Minister's office as top priority. Pádraig Pearse had told him of Harker's arrival, and it had done nothing for Declan's peace of mind, let alone his headaches. He had heard the name mentioned more than once, had overheard tales of the power he wielded. Their paths had never crossed directly, but from time to time Declan had felt the other man's shadow fall across him. A mission aborted here, information withheld there, a death that could not be explained somewhere else – and always anxious whispers, fragile rumours from a world not quite contiguous with the one he inhabited.

'Declan, it's Ciaran. We're on a secure line. I had it checked half an hour ago.'

'Don't bet on it, Ciaran. There's more than one way to tap a telephone.'

'For God's sake, Declan – you'll be making me as paranoid as yourself in a minute.'

Declan sighed.

'What do you want, Ciaran?'

'Just a chat, that's all. You'll be in need of a spot of conversation. Tell me, have you got any leads on this thing at all?'

'Nothing you don't have, Ciaran.'

'Your brief was to find out what we couldn't. Have you no ideas at all where they might be? Wild guesses, anything? We're under terrible pressure here, Declan, I swear to God we are. We can't just keep on denying these rumours, they're asking for proof the delegates are safe. But that's the one thing we can't give them. The press are on top of us, the radio, the television people – you've no idea. Jesus, Declan, we need something we can tell them. Anything, just to show we're making progress, that we haven't been sitting around idle.'

'We' – the word cropped up in almost every sentence. It wasn't Ciaran Clark's style. He was strictly a child of the 'Me' generation.

'Are you alone, Ciaran?'

'What?'

'Is there anyone there with you?'

A short pause.

'Of course not. No-one else knows I'm speaking to you. Jesus, hardly anyone knows you're still working for us.'

'Have you spoken to Pádraig Pearse at all today?'

'Yes, I have, once or twice. He's a worried man. Jesus, we're all worried.'

'I know. Listen, Ciaran, I've got nothing you can give to the press at this stage. You'll have to stall. Feed them a line – you're good at that. You've got the touch, Ciaran, believe me.'

'We need to know, Declan.'

'Who exactly is "We"?'

Ciaran did not answer.

'I'll be in touch as soon as I have something, Ciaran. I promise.'

'We . . .'

There was a pause at the other end. Total silence. Declan had the distinct impression that Ciaran was listening to someone else. His manner was stiffer than usual, like that of a man taking orders.

'I'll get back to you, Declan. In an hour or so. I'd be grateful for anything at all; we're not the church, we aren't looking for miracles.'

He hung up. Declan paused, pressed the rest, and keyed the private number Pádraig Pearse had given him. It rang twice. Paddy O'Leary answered.

'Paddy? This is Declan Carberry. Can I speak to Pádraig?'

There was a barely perceptible pause.

'Well, Mr Carberry, he's in a meeting at the moment. It was called at the last minute. I'm sure you can guess what things have been like round here lately. I'll tell the Taoiseach you rang. I'm sure he'll get back to you as soon as he can.'

Paddy hung up. Declan looked at the receiver as though it had betrayed him personally. Paddy O'Leary had never spoken to him so formally before. 'The Taoiseach' indeed – weren't they all old friends, and wasn't Pádraig Pearse Declan's brother-in-law? What was going on? Pádraig Pearse had made it clear that Declan would be put through to him at any time, even if he had to interrupt other business. Had Paddy been trying to protect Declan? Or had this been a brush-off? If so, what was it in preparation for?

He replaced the receiver. On his desk, the second hand of his clock moved round remorselessly. He hated the silence. The clock did not even tick. As though time had lost something of great value.

CHAPTER THIRTY-THREE

Belfast
2115 hours

They had made it, but with little to spare. Without Maureen
O'Dalaigh, Abu Hida would have been trapped. She had got them
clear of the tangle of streets to the south of the Glen Road, out
onto the Andersonstown Road where it turns down towards the
Falls. That had been the easy part. The next thing was to choose
a route that would not lead them straight into a roadblock or
reinforcements on their way from Fort Whiterock. The troops
would come in along the Monagh Road by-pass, then west into
the Glen Road. All the time, the helicopter flew above them,
monitoring their progress. Abu Hida knew they would be in contact with their base, directing the nearest patrols to cut them off
at the next turn.

Maureen guessed there might be roadblocks where Kennedy
Way joined the Glen Road and the M1. That cut them off to both
north and south. She could cut north across Turf Lodge, but that
would bring them within an unhealthy distance of Fort Whiterock
barracks. They could keep on down the Falls Road, but just where
it joined the Glen at Milltown Cemetery was the site of an RUC
station: there was certain to be another roadblock there. And that
was the direction she had to go in if her plan was to work.

As she drove, she spoke quickly into a mobile phone. The
British were capable of tapping the call if they could lock onto it
with a Celltrack unit, but she was laying her life on their not
guessing she had the phone in the first place. The mobile did not
belong to her, was registered in the name of a well-known and
politically clean solicitor, a member of the Rotary Club and the

Linenhall Library who had offices on the Malone Road and clients who included top civil servants, judges, and senior members of the security forces.

She switched off the phone and slipped it into her pocket.

'They're ready for us,' she said. 'Listen hard now while I tell you what we're going to do.'

Above them, the helicopter came swinging low across the trees in the cemetery, sweeping its searchlight like a wand behind them.

She came off the Andersonstown Road at Dunmisk Park, swinging northwards back through Andersonstown and down onto Fruithill Park, exiting just below the roundabout at the Glen Road. Heading towards the motorway, she pulled back into the eastern section of Andersonstown and drove through to the top of the Falls Road. A short drive took them just above the RUC station. She could see the roadblock in the distance.

'This is where we get out,' she said.

Milltown Cemetery was on their right. The white headstones, carved with the names of so many nationalist dead, stood out against the blackness. They scrambled up the fence and down the other side.

'Keep close to me,' she whispered. 'If they saw us coming, they'll be all over this place in minutes.'

They walked quickly between the graves. Abu Hida felt the warm familiarity of the place. The dead were all alike. In the end, nothing else mattered.

They came out on a path opposite the Falls Park. A car had been parked some yards away, a green Datsun. The roadblock was just on their left. Even as they got in and Maureen switched on the engine, Abu Hida could see policemen turning and looking in their direction. She put the car in gear and drove off, passing the park and the much larger Belfast Cemetery on the left.

Turning into the Whiterock Road, she went as far as Britton's Parade. Just before a bend, she stopped outside a large school.

'This is St Peter's,' she said. 'It's where we get out. I'll take your bag from the boot. You keep the one you've got.'

She had taken charge, but he was willing for her to do that.

The wrong sort of pride could get him killed here in someone else's territory.

Leaving the car behind, they doubled back to a fence. Some distance behind it stood a building on a hill, its windows brightly lit. Around them, the darkness was complete. Someone had managed to extinguish all the streetlamps in the area. Even with its sophisticated equipment, the helicopter would find them difficult targets to pick out.

'This is Our Lady's Hospital,' Maureen said. 'It's a geriatric hospital.'

'Will it be safe?'

'We're not staying there. It's just a way out of here.'

They helped one another to climb the high railings. Maureen knew her way through the grounds without hesitation. She led Abu Hida to the hospital garage. The doors were open, and an ambulance was already half-way through them. A shadowy figure moved out from the unlit building and approached them.

'Yous the ones the Brits are looking for?' he asked.

'We are,' Maureen answered. 'You Gerry?'

'I am.'

'Can you get us out of here?'

He looked at her steadily for several seconds then nodded.

'I can get yous as far as the Royal,' he said. 'After that yous are on your own.'

'You get us there,' said Maureen, 'and I'll handle the rest.' She looked round. 'Isn't there supposed to be a nurse with you?'

'Eileen'll be over in a wee minute. We'll be out of here as soon as you're in place. Who's the fellow with you?'

'That doesn't concern you. Help us in.'

The space underneath the bench in the ambulance had been rebuilt to allow two people to crawl in, one after the other. Abu Hida went first. It was cramped and dark, with only the most basic form of ventilation, and he was crushed hard against some sort of bulkhead at the far end. His bag lay heavily across his legs. Maureen O'Dalaigh pushed in after him, her head against his feet. The man who had met them closed the door and they were swallowed up by darkness.

*   *   *

In the sky above the hospital, a second helicopter joined the first. They both swung their searchlights over the ground, crossing and recrossing as they kept track of their quarry.

As the ambulance pulled away down the long drive that led to the upper Falls at Clowney Bridge, the 'copters pulled round in pursuit of it. But at that instant the headlights on the Datsun came alive. There was the sound of an engine racing, then the car burst away in a squeal of tyres. The second helicopter hesitated, dipped, and turned back to follow the car along Britton's Drive and abruptly south again into Whiterock Gardens.

The ambulance passed the leisure centre and came out onto the Falls Road. It turned left, heading down towards the Royal Victoria Hospital. The driver did not use his siren, but he drove quickly, a bit over the speed limit.

There was a roadblock across the Broadway, cutting off the road to the motorway. Another had been set up a few yards further along the Falls, above the children's hospital. Two Sankey 'Flying Pigs' stretched across the Falls, their square wings fully extended. Armed RUC men were distributed behind the wire wings and on both sides of the road. The ambulance drew up short of the checkpoint. Two policemen armed with sub-machine guns approached it cautiously.

'Will you step out of the vehicle, sir?'

The driver stepped down and turned to one of the policemen, a tall man with heavy eyebrows.

'Can you tell me what's supposed to be going on now? I've been followed all the way from the hospital by thon friggin' helicopter, so I have. I've a sick man in the back that's being took to the Royal.'

'Will you open the rear of the vehicle, please?'

'Do it yourself.'

'I asked you to open the vehicle. I won't ask a second time.'

The driver went to the back and pulled the doors open. Inside, a nurse sat alongside an old man on the bed. Blankets were drawn up to his chin.

The tall policeman stepped up into the ambulance.

'Have you any identification on you?' he asked the nurse.

She indicated the plastic-covered card pinned to her left breast.

It carried her name and hospital details alongside a coloured photograph. The photograph and face matched.

'What's wrong with him?' The policeman pointed at the old man.

'You can see for yourself,' she said. 'He's had a turn and we're taking him to the Royal to have him checked over. We don't have the facilities at Our Lady's, as well you know. Now, will yous let us go on? He could get worse if he's not seen to soon.'

The policeman hesitated and looked at the man on the bed. He looked around ninety, with a thin, pain-streaked face and a head dappled with scanty white hair and liver spots. His blue eyes were watery and unfocussed. He had not been out on the streets fighting a gun battle. The policeman drew down the blankets as far as the old man's waist. He was dressed in thin cotton pyjamas with a stripe. The drawstring on the trousers was slack. An unpleasant smell rose from him.

'Hey, leave the auld man alone, will you? He'll get a chill.'

The policeman shrugged and pulled the blanket up again. He could not understand it. The helicopter pilot had been so sure. But neither the nurse nor the old man were among those he was looking for.

The Datsun pulled away down Whiterock Gardens and into Whiterock Road with the helicopter in hot pursuit. At the next corner, it all but slammed into a Shorland in the middle of the road. Reinforcements had come in at last from Fort Whiterock. The driver of the Datsun swerved, flung the car up onto the pavement, scattering soldiers, and skidded past with a scream of burning tyres.

The next moment, firing broke out from all sides. Bullets piled into the car, it went into a locked skid, and for three hundred yards it went on spinning out of control. As it came to a halt, armed soldiers converged on it from back and front. They were prepared for gunfire, but no shots came from the car. Slowly, the soldiers closed in.

The passenger door opened and someone started to get out.

'Hold your fire,' an English voice shouted. 'We want this bastard alive.'

The passenger stepped out, staggered two steps, and fell on his side. Seconds later, he was surrounded by men with assault rifles.

Simultaneously, others covered the figure slumped over the steering wheel.

A bright light illuminated the figure on the ground. One of the soldiers rolled him onto his back.

'Christ, sarge, it's just a frigging kid.'

The passenger was unquestionably young – twelve or thirteen at most. He had been wounded in several places, but was still alive. Just. His lips moved.

'We . . . wasn't . . . doin' nothin'.' He retched and tried to get to his knees, then fell back. 'Just joyridin', mister . . . Kevin's brother sent us out . . . Said there was a car we could have . . . We was just havin' a ride . . . That's all . . . Just a . . . wee ride.'

CHAPTER THIRTY-FOUR

Dublin
2140 hours

Pronsias Donnelly and Brendan Cahill arrived with an interim report at nine-thirty. They looked exhausted. Declan spoke with them briefly, then called the team together. When they were all ready, Pronsias came to the front. He was compact and tiny, with delicate, shiny hands; his pretty features showed the ravages of his profession. Cahill stood behind him, his thin, grey skin almost transparent in the unnatural light. Pronsias cleared his throat, as though removing the dust accumulated there during a long day buried among archives. He had, in fact, spent his time in front of a computer screen.

'Well now,' he said. 'If you've ever been to America, you'll know there's more Irish there than here, though the devil a one of them would like to live in what they call the "old country". But they do like to visit it. This year alone, it's expected that almost half a million Americans will arrive in Ireland, most of them tourists. Between the first of May and the end of August, which is the period Brendan and I were asked to check, two hundred and sixty thousand Americans and Canadians passed through Irish customs, most of them at Dublin or Shannon airports.

'Out of these, two hundred and forty-seven thousand came as tourists, a great many of them on world tours or tours of Europe or the British Isles. Eight hundred arrived to take up employment with American or Irish companies, eleven thousand were students here for summer courses, six hundred had come for longer periods of study. In addition, there are several much smaller

197

categories, all of which are being checked out: academics here for conventions, Catholic religious visiting mother houses in Ireland and so on, members of other religions attending summer schools or other events, military personnel, musicians, writers, and so on. Many of the tourists had relations of some sort here, so we don't always have exact details of the addresses they've stayed at. Visitors don't require visas, and they don't have to report their whereabouts to the Gardaí, which leaves us in the dark about most of them until they turn up at the airport again on their way out. A lot of the time, that's our only check.'

He paused and consulted the file in front of him. Lifting his head, he looked at Declan.

'Sir, I'd like to ask Brendan to take over here. He did most of the work on tracing those who've stayed on.'

Brendan Cahill got to his feet. He was a thin man, prematurely bald, with large eyes sensitive to light. As he spoke, he moved on the edges of his feet, as though seeking for balance.

'As far as we can tell, of the two hundred and sixty thousand who arrived between May and August, two hundred and forty-five thousand have already gone home or on to other destinations. The main tourist season is over and all the summer courses have ended. Most of the business visitors came and went in a matter of days, and almost none of those who arrived at the end of August are still in Ireland. So that takes care of the majority of our visitors.'

He coughed nervously and looked round the room, then down at the notes he held in his hand. Delivering reports always reminded him of presentations at school back in Kilgarvan. He wished he was back there now, helping his brother in the fields. There was talk of Japanese coming to Killarney, setting up a computer factory. Maybe it would soon be time for a move.

'Now,' he continued, 'that leaves us with a handful of tourists who've stayed on into September, some full-time students doing a year abroad, and employees on long-term contracts. We still don't know exactly what it is we're looking for, and we don't have the manpower for a proper search. We need Garda back-up, men on the spot who can check if somebody is where he's supposed to be. That's the only way we have of eliminating suspects.'

'And women on the spot too,' said Grainne. 'Don't forget we have Bhangardaí as well.'

'Ah, well, women. Sure, and if they're all like yourself it's the suspects I'm sorry for.'

She grinned and made a discreet V-sign.

'Regardless of all that,' said Declan, 'how long do you think it would take to trim that list down? Assuming we had cooperation from Phoenix Park and Harcourt Street.'

Brendan shrugged.

'Two days? A lot have gone out to the west, fishing and so on. They're maybe not easy to find. And there are some that don't want to be found. They're in Ireland to get away from it all.'

'Well, one or two won't matter. We're looking for a pattern. A group of people in one place. Tourists who haven't stayed in any hotel or registered at any camp site. I don't know.'

'And if we don't get help from D Branch?' Pronsias was still on his feet.

Declan felt another headache coming on. Right behind the eyes this time, like thunder just out of sight on the horizon.

'Then we're scuppered,' he said. 'We can't do this alone. Maybe it isn't worth it. Maybe this American thing is a red herring.'

'I thought we were guaranteed cooperation with this, sir,' said Liam.

'We were. But I don't know how long it will last. Too many people know about this operation. Once it leaks out, we'll be wound up. I warned you all at the start.'

The meeting dispersed. Declan went to his office. One or two of his colleagues went back to their desks. Several went to bed. Grainne Walsh headed for the television room. There was a news flash at ten, confirming that the delegates had been taken hostage. An ashen-faced Ciaran Clark spoke of the pressures the Irish government was coming under from the Arab world. He was followed by the Minister for Home Affairs, who described the steps being taken by the security forces to find and release the hostages. All governments involved had agreed not to negotiate with the terrorists responsible. No mention was made of the presence in the capital of British security officials. The Taoiseach did not make an appearance.

The report lasted for almost twenty minutes. A fuller feature devoted to the crisis was promised for midnight.

There followed a brief but curious item.

'There was a call this evening from TD Brian O'Mara for an

immediate investigation into allegations that the Taoiseach has been implicated in a conspiracy involving the misuse of government funds. At a press conference at his Lifford constituency this evening, Mr O'Mara said that papers had come into his possession earlier today which supplied evidence of a massive fraud. It is alleged that payments have been made from official funds to several countries in the Middle East in order to guarantee contracts for Mr Mangan's Limerick-based meat export company, EuroChick. A spokesman for EuroChick, which has branches in France, Belgium, and Germany, said this evening that there was no foundation to the rumours. Mr Mangan was not available for comment. Mr O'Mara is expected to make a further statement in the Dáil tomorrow.

'The . . .'

Grainne switched off the set. As she turned, she saw Declan standing in the doorway. His face was ashen.

'I'm sorry . . . I didn't know you were there, sir. I . . . Did you want the rest of the news?' She was embarrassed. After all, it was her boss's brother-in-law they had just been accusing of fraud.

'That's all right, Grainne. I've heard enough.'

'It can't be true, I'm sure. What they said about the Taoiseach.'

Declan shrugged. He was no longer sure what could and could not be true. He remembered his conversation with Ciaran Clark, the sense of another presence in Iveagh House, the stiffness with which Paddy O'Leary had prevented him speaking to Pádraig Pearse, the arrival in Dublin of the man called Harker. It looked as though they had wasted no time.

'It could be true,' he said. 'Pádraig Pearse was never the most scrupulous of men. But he was never really dishonest. I don't think he would have used public funds in that way. I think you'll find there's a kernel of truth in it all, and that someone has manufactured the rest.'

'Manufactured it? What on earth for?'

Declan managed what he hoped might pass for a wry smile.

'For? I would have thought that was obvious. To get him out. To put someone in his place more willing to cooperate with whatever it is they're planning here. I'd put my money on Ciaran Clark.'

He looked at his watch.

'It's time we were all in bed. We've got an early start in the morning. The night watch will let us know if there are any developments.'

He held the door open for her. As she went past, she turned.

'We don't have much longer, do we, sir?'

He shook his head.

'I'd give us twenty-four hours, maybe less. With Pádraig Pearse gone, we'd have no authority.'

'We'd just drop it then, would we, sir?'

'The investigation? Probably.'

'Even if . . .' She shook her head. 'I don't know, I'm just inventing things.'

'Even if what?'

She hesitated.

'Even if it meant the hostages didn't get out alive?'

He did not answer her. The thought never left him, day or night.

CHAPTER THIRTY-FIVE

Belfast
2150 hours

While the nurse went inside with the old man (who would be admitted, checked over, and sent back to Our Lady's in the morning), the driver stayed with the ambulance until the coast was clear. The helicopter was still circling the area, and from time to time it let the powerful beam of its searchlight pass over the top of their vehicle. A second ambulance came in, several others left in a rush. They would be returning before long with casualties from Andersonstown. The driver did a quick check.

'Yous can come out now,' he said, banging on the bottom of the bunk.

Maureen came out first, then Abu Hida.

'Jesus!' she exclaimed, moving stiff limbs in an attempt to get the blood circulating properly again. 'That was never built for two people. I'd as soon be picked up by the peelers as go back in there again. And you,' she went on, turning to Abu Hida, 'you could have kept still. You kept sticking your big feet in my head.'

He smiled at her, the first time he had been anything but serious. The expression transformed his face. Maureen felt a lump tighten in her stomach.

'Your head's hard,' he said. 'I think my feet came off worse.'

'There's no time to stand around here gegging,' the driver said. He was a grumpy little man, displeased to be mixed up in business of this kind, but fully aware of the price he and his family would pay if he refused.

'We're going,' she said. 'As soon as you get this crate out of here. Maybe the Brits'll follow you instead of us.'

'Aye, well, I hope not. I've a family to get home to. I don't want pulled in and questioned the night.'

'You did well, Gerry,' Maureen said. 'Just keep your mouth shut. And see your woman does the same.'

'Eileen? She's all right. She'd be one of yourselves if it weren't for the job she does.'

'I'll bear that in mind. Now, away on off with you.'

He drove off, leaving them exposed on the drive outside the main doors. As the ambulance turned through the gates, they could hear the sound of sirens drawing nearer.

'Put that coat on,' whispered Maureen.

Gerry had left them two white coats with stethoscopes in the pockets. They fitted well enough and made them both look the part from a distance.

They walked to the main gate. As they reached it, the roar of sirens grew deafening. A white ambulance swung into the open-ing, its blue light spinning like a top. Maureen and Abu Hida had to jump aside as the driver rushed on towards the casualty entrance. A second ambulance came behind, and a third could be seen in the distance, coming towards them at full speed.

Just as they prepared to slip through the gate, a man in a white coat came running from the side of the building.

'Where the hell do you two think you're off to? Can't you see there's an emergency on? There's been a major incident in Andersonstown. Get the hell in here and lend a hand.'

'For God's sake,' protested Maureen, 'we've just come off duty. I'm flat out.'

The doctor, a middle-aged man with a red face and bristling hair, screamed at her.

'I don't care if you're fucking dead. We need everyone in casualty now. There's a hell of a flap on.'

'I'm sorry,' she said. 'I've got better things to do.'

The red-faced doctor looked as though he would soon need emergency treatment himself. He stepped up to Maureen, spitting in her face as he shouted at her.

'I can't believe what I'm hearing. You bloody little bastard, who the hell do you think you are? If you don't get yourselves over to casualty this minute, you'll . . .'

His voice was drowned by the wail of a siren as the third ambu-lance turned in at the gate. Maureen took a step towards the doctor, smiling, and as she did so slipped one hand under the coat. As the ambulance passed them, she glanced round. Everyone had gone inside to help. She pulled out a pistol, rammed it into the doctor's ribs, and fired twice. The shots were drowned by the passing siren.

Abu Hida caught the man from behind as he slumped away from Maureen. Together, they dragged him across to the railings and left him face down in a corner away from the entrance.

'Let's get the hell out of here,' exclaimed Maureen.

They came out onto the Grosvenor Road. The little knot of people on the pavement opposite did not look at them twice. Two doctors carrying bags, going home for the night.

Above them, the helicopter turned, joined moments later by a second. Maureen led Abu Hida to the right, towards town, walking at a moderate pace.

'Keep your coat on till we get clear of the hospital,' she said.

They crossed the road and went up Servia Street. It was darker off the main thoroughfare, and many of the streetlamps were broken. They stripped off their white coats and dumped them in a doorway.

'Down here,' she said, walking more quickly now. There was a sound of military vehicles approaching behind them along the Grosvenor Road. A sound of brakes and then hard-soled feet on the roadway. Voices shouting orders.

'Keep your head,' she said. 'Just keep walking.'

'Where are we going? If they cut this area off they can work their way through to us in their own time.'

'Trust me,' she said. 'I told you I was going to get you out of here, and that's what I'm going to do if you give me half a chance.'

A helicopter went past, covering the lozenge of little terraced streets between the lower Falls and the Grosvenor Road. Maureen knew they could get cut off in here as Abu Hida feared. But if they could just make it to the other side of the Falls they would almost be where she wanted. She headed down towards the Divis Flats. The streets were emptying as word passed that the army was out in force. People were heading to get indoors before the searches started. She moved a little faster. The sound of cars moving at speed on the Westlink came to them across the fluttering of the helicopter. Maureen knew that the 'copters had high-powered night-sights on board, that if they were tracking them darkness would be no obstacle.

They reached the Falls. There was a roadblock on Northumberland Street, army this time. Turning right, they got into Percy Street and continued to head north. There was a sound of Shorlands screeching to a halt along the Shankill, right ahead of them. She was sure they had sighted them, that the troops were moving in to cut them off.

'Down here,' she said urgently, pressing him into an opening on his left. The street they had entered was a short cul-de-sac of shabby houses with windows covered by steel mesh grilles. At its bottom was a twenty-foot high fence. This was part of the so-called 'peace line' that divided certain Catholic sections of the city from their Protestant neighbours yards away. For two-thirds of its height, it consisted of grey concrete, on top of which was a fence of solid green steel. It was too high to climb and too thick to penetrate.

Several of the houses nearest the fence had been left abandoned. Maureen pushed open the broken door of the third from the end.

'Get inside,' she ordered. 'Hurry up!'

There was no light. But their eyes had already had a chance to adjust to the dark. The house was empty, stripped bare years before during a riot. Maureen did not hesitate. She led Abu Hida to the back, into what had been a little scullery. A sink still clung to the wall, white in the darkness, like a tombstone. Maureen went straight towards it, gripped it by the front, and pushed it away from her.

The sink moved, pulling with it a large slab on the floor beside it. As Maureen pushed, the hole widened until it was large enough for a man to climb through.

'In there,' she said.

From outside, they could hear the sound of armoured vehicles close at hand.

'I'd rather stay here and fight,' he said, 'than hide in a cellar till they find me.'

It was his greatest fear, one he scarcely admitted even to himself, to be trapped like that, in a closed room or a place deep beneath the earth.

Maureen shook her head angrily.

'Get in, you great lump. That's not a cellar. That's our way out.'

CHAPTER THIRTY-SIX

11 October
0215 hours

Sometimes he spent whole nights in prayer or reading the scriptures. Tonight, he had sought guidance from one end of the Bible to the other and found none. Sometimes the nights were so long and so dark he thought he would never see another dawn.

He crossed to the window where there was no light, no light anywhere. Not even a ship passed on the grey sea, bringing light with it. The distance dragged him down like a weight. No light, no guidance anywhere. Tonight he was tormented by doubts. Had he done the right thing to let others use him in this affair? What should be his next step? How should he bring this thing to a conclusion, without also calling down destruction on himself and his people, as he had done once already?

He did not doubt his own Messiahship, his superiority to other men, even his divinity. Nor did he doubt that the world would end and be reborn, soon, very soon, or that he would then reign in his new Jerusalem, the world's king, God's Son on an angelic throne. He doubted nothing in himself, only in others, and he feared the consequences of the world and the world's traps. He had been trapped before, dreadfully. Now he needed to be certain before he took another step.

He picked up his Bible from the table beside his bed. The limp cover and sweat-stained pages felt heavy in his hand. If only he could creep inside it and take refuge from the doubts that assailed him here. He opened it and looked down at the page and read.

His heart leapt. God had not left him without guidance after all. It was simple and blindingly obvious what he should do. He closed the book and held it steady for a moment. It felt light now, as though God had lifted something from it. With a smile, he returned it to the table.

Zechariah, Ezekiel's second-in-command, was in charge of the guard division tonight. Five members of his personal bodyguard, all armed and watchful, two inside with Zechariah, three on the perimeter. The hostages were locked in their cells without light or food. Several prayed, chanting verses from the Qur'an. The Devil's book in the Devil's tongue. He let them chant. He liked to hear them, it hardened his resolve. One of the women wept. Another sang to her, alone in her own darkness.

He found Zechariah by himself in the operations centre, reading the Bible. They exchanged greetings.

'I want everyone up now,' he said. He was growing excited by the prospect of what lay ahead. No more indecision. 'Everyone, including our prisoners and the Englishman.'

Zechariah looked at him in surprise. He glanced at the clock.

'Isn't it late? Why not wait till morning?'

'No, now, this can't wait. God wants me to speak to them right away. And to act right away.' He glared at his subordinate. 'Don't cross me, Zechariah,' he said. 'Don't ever stand in my way or act as though you're going to, or I'll crush you. Do you understand?'

The slow Texan drawl had grown harsh and dangerous. Zechariah nodded tiredly. He had been through moods like this before, many times. A rush of elation, a sudden plunge into depression. Enthusiasm, tears, rages, sexual binges. His Master was wholly unpredictable. At such times not even Zechariah's love and loyalty were wholly equal to the strain.

'Get your men in,' he said. 'The entire bodyguard. There's to be a meeting in the dining hall. Bible study. I want them all present, even the Babylonians.'

It was his code-name for the unbelievers, the ones God hated, whom He had cast out.

Zechariah groaned inwardly. Some of the Master's Bible studies went on for hours at a stretch. Twelve hour sessions were not uncommon. They consisted of little else but the Master preaching, giving his latest interpretations of scripture. Anyone falling asleep or showing inattention faced the threat of immediate punishment. Zechariah knew better than his leader just how tired the men were, how badly they needed what little sleep they could snatch here. The preparations for the raid, the raid itself and the escape that had followed it, the constant vigilance since then had all taken their toll.

Zechariah sighed and got to his feet. There was no point in wasting time. The Master always got his way, and Zechariah had been with him long enough to know that nothing was to be gained by trying to stall. He found the two guards watching the interior and told them to bring their colleagues in from the cold. Their leader was already on his way to the dining room, where he would get himself in the right frame of mind for the coming session. Zechariah felt nervous, as he always did before Bible study. These sessions were frequently the occasion of some announcement: a new insight, a fresh revelation, something God had told the Master the night before. The consequences were often devastating.

The north end of the barn had been divided roughly in two, a large dorm for the bodyguard, and a smaller bedroom for the Master. He was the only one on the whole compound who had his own bathroom, small and uncomfortable though it was. Zechariah left the control sector where the prisoners were kept and entered the dorm. They would hate being wakened, but he knew they would obey his orders. There was no choice, none that made sense anyway. Without their leader, they were nothing, worse than nothing. He had stripped them of ties, removed them from their former lives, given them in exchange himself and the promise of heaven. That was all he had himself, all he asked.

He flicked a switch and four rows of fluorescent lights flickered lazily into life.

It took over half an hour to fill the dining hall. They had had to handcuff the hostages and take them there in pairs. The dining hall was the southern end of the barn, corresponding to the sleeping quarters. The cells lay between. There was a large kitchen behind the dining area, on the east. The arrangement was arbitrary, dictated by the uncompromising shape of the original structure. Outhouses served for ablutions and toilets, an armoury, and a communications hut.

He just sat watching them come in. The expression on his face never changed. He was seated on a sort of dais he had had erected for precisely this purpose. There was a microphone on a stand in front of him, and two tall speakers on either side, ridiculously large for the relatively small area of the dining hall.

At his request, the hostages sat in the front rows, his own people behind or standing at the sides, guns at the ready. He called Ezekiel to the front and whispered to him gently. Ezekiel's back was to the audience, and no-one saw his face turn white as he spoke to him.

'You're sure about this?' he asked finally.

The Master nodded. He had never been so sure of anything.

'Yes, absolutely sure. Tonight. Go and get what I need. Then wait until I tell you to bring it in.'

Ezekiel nodded and stepped down from the dais. Without a backward look, he went through the door and into the corridor that led to the outside.

Silence fell over the audience – it was hard to think of it as a congregation, he reflected, with so many of the Devil's children there. He looked at them one at a time. His hand-picked body-guard and the prizes they had taken.

He smiled and stepped down from the high stool on which he had been sitting and strolled down to the front of the dais. It was raised about three feet off the floor – high enough to elevate him above the heads of a seated audience, not so high as to distance him from them.

He knew most of those listening would not understand. 'Hear ye indeed, but understand not; and see ye indeed, but perceive not.' But if the apostles could speak in tongues, if men now living had the gifts of the Holy Spirit, then might he not call on God tonight to drive understanding into the hearts of these unbelievers?

'You think you're clever,' he began, using a low nasal voice, the words drawled out. 'You think you're smart, you think God smiles on you. Well, I'm not clever and I'm not smart, hell no, but I know you're all full of shit.

'That's what I said. Don't you think I should say that? Don't you think a preacher, a prophet ordained by God should use words like that? Is that what you think?'

He had seen them jump, the few that had understood. They

had grasped this much by now, that the man in charge of their abduction was considered holy by his followers. Of course, none of them had remotely guessed his true identity, and none of them would ever grasp who he really was – the true David, the King of Israel, the Son of God, the Lamb, Jesus Christ returned to usher in the last days.

He smiled at them. They did not smile back. What were they thinking? What were they waiting for? For Allah to come to their rescue?

'You're full of shit,' he went on, his voice gaining clarity, 'because you all believe in a false God, a God of lies and iniquities. You heard me. That isn't blasphemy, that's the truth. Your God is Satan in person, even if you call him Allah and get down on your knees to him morning, noon, and night.

'There's only one true God, and only one true Son of God, and you can choose to come to them or you can go to hell. It's as simple as that, God's truth is always simple, and His word is always the same.'

He paused and looked round the room. His bodyguards looked tired, his prisoners disoriented. He possessed them, he could offer them life or death as the spirit took him. Life, death, anything in between.

He reached inside himself for the light, the light he knew dwelled within. It was covered at times in so many darknesses, he hardly knew if he would find it again each time he peeked inside. But it was there, dully glowing, waiting for him to blow it into flame.

'The prophet Daniel was told that the books were closed. "And he said, Go thy way, Daniel: for the words are closed up and sealed till the time of the end." And the Lord Jesus repeated God's warning about the books, when he read from the Book of Isaiah in the synagogue. It says so in Luke: "And he closed the book, and he gave it again to the minister, and sat down."

'Hell, that's why I was sent. To break the seals on the book. To unloose the seven seals on the seven scrolls. "And I saw in the right hand of him that sat on the throne a book written within and on the backside, sealed with seven seals. And I saw a strong angel proclaiming with a loud voice, Who is worthy to open the book, and to loose the seals thereof?"

'Well, I'm telling you who's worthy. I am. Only the Lamb can break those seals, only God can tell you what's inside the books. Only the true David can let you into the secret of what God means to do.'

CHAPTER THIRTY-SEVEN

Amina stared with mounting horror at the man on the dais. Since the raid and their abduction, she had concentrated her energies on helping the other Muslim women understand just what was going on. None of them had particularly fluent English, and they had been unable to grasp in any detail what was happening to them. Amina had been able to explain, up to a point.

Now, watching and listening to this pale, arrogant creature, she began to feel a sense of real panic. All that had occurred until now had seemed, in its fashion, rational. A gang of terrorists had taken a group of VIPs hostage. There was nothing unusual in that, nothing to engender particular fear. There would be demands, negotiations, compromises, payments, and a final release. They would want money or arms or a release of prisoners, nothing that could not be talked towards an agreement. It was not, after all, as though they were in Beirut or Tehran. She herself might very well be in a position to help negotiate some sort of deal, once she was sure it was safe to make her real identity known.

She had told everyone she had spoken to that there was little to worry about, that even now the Irish authorities would be actively engaged in the search for a solution. They were honourable men, she said, they would be sure to do all in their power to secure the release of the hostages. She had started to sound like an official communiqué. But she believed it all herself, she really did.

Until now. Now she had started to understand the true horror of the situation. Nothing rational was to be hoped for. The man into whose hands they had fallen was, she did not doubt, quite insane. He might want the moon or peace on earth or a throne by the side of God, and not even Pádraig Pearse Mangan could grant him his wishes. She looked up. He was still speaking.

'It's in the book of Ezekiel, that's where God says what He means to do. Since most of you here tonight don't know your Bibles, I'll just have to read it for you.'

But he did not open the Bible in his hand. There was no need. He had all the scriptural passages he would ever have call for right there in his head.

'"And I will set up one shepherd over them, and he shall feed them, even my servant David; he shall feed them, and he shall be their shepherd. And I the Lord will be their God, and my servant David a prince among them; I the Lord have spoken it."'

He raised the Bible as if about to hurl it at them. In a way, that was just what he wanted to do: to turn the word of God into a missile aimed at the heart of unbelief. He had always told his followers to arm themselves with two weapons: an AK-47 and the word of God.

Amina watched him, mesmerized, the fear growing inside her that she would not come out of here alive.

'Have you read the story of David and Goliath? How the boy David took a sling and slew the champion of the Philistines, struck him dead right there in front of the army with a little pebble? Maybe you've heard the story, and maybe you've wondered what it really means, what God is trying to tell us in a story like that. Some preachers say it's just a way of teaching us the lesson that the meek can stand up to the strong, that a boy with faith in God can bring down a giant in armour.

'But if that's all the Bible had to tell us we might as well not call it the word of God. Hell, we don't need the Bible to tell us something like that. I can read about the meek and the strong any time I like in the *Reader's Digest* or in some New Age book from Dalton's bargain counter. There's more to God's word than Sunday-school stories, you better believe it.'

They watched him together, in silence, all of them, most of them without the least comprehension of his words. A few murmured invocations inaudibly. Across a single room, two angry gods confronted one another.

'I don't know about you, but I sure as hell don't see no point in reading about some old battle took place thousands of years ago in Israel. That's just history, dead and gone. What matters is what it means, and what it means nobody knew until God opened the seals on the books.'

He looked over their bewildered, anxious faces, felt their anger, tapped their despair. His eyes moved on to his own people in their fatigues. His bodyguards were tired, but he saw them listening hard all the same. They knew better than to fall asleep in a Bible study. He saw the woman in the second row, saw the way she was watching him. She would be more frightened than the rest, he reasoned. He knew her name and who she was. Ezekiel had found out, and he had told him soon after they got here. She was the lover of Declan Carberry, the head of Ireland's equivalent of the FBI. He had not really noticed how pretty she was before. Older than he liked, but nubile. She had good breasts. He would ask Ezekiel to bring her to his room tonight. But first he had to get this done.

'As you all know, this was a fight between the Children of Israel and their enemies, the Philistines. "For Israel and the Philistines had put the battle in array, army against army." David stood up in front of the Israelites, and he turned to face Goliath, and what he said was "I come to thee in the name of the Lord of hosts, the God of the armies of Israel, whom thou hast defied."'

He paused, relishing their confusion. They had to follow him, had to hang on his words, if they were to make sense of anything. It was the high he had always looked for, almost better than sex, the exaltation of knowing that others depended on him for their sense of meaning, for worth, for salvation.

'Look at the story again,' he went on, 'not with your eyes, but with mine. I'll show you what to look for, how to understand. David says he's fighting in the name of God, so we know Israel must stand for the whole of mankind, since God is the God of everyone, not just the Israelites. And mankind isn't in danger from a mortal man called Goliath. No, the real enemy is Satan, Satan and his army of evil. Man's only hope is for a saviour to stand up and face up to Satan. We know who that saviour is, we know that he is Jesus Christ. And we know, because it's there in the Bible right in front of our eyes, we know that Jesus Christ and David are one and the same person. "And I will set up one shepherd over them, and he shall feed them, even my servant David."'

She felt bewildered. This logic that was no logic was unutterably alien to her. Although a Muslim, she had been brought up in what had once been the most ecumenical of Arab countries, in close proximity to Maronite Christians. Later, after the civil war broke out, she had regarded an understanding of Christianity as essential to her work in bringing peace between the warring communities. There was much she found to admire in Christian teaching; but this was beyond all sense, beyond all reason. Knowing that made everything worse: she was going to die because a madman had driven reason out of the world.

'Now, the scriptures are always clear to them that have pure hearts. In the story of David and Goliath, we know that the army of Israel is an antitype for mankind and the Philistines an antitype for the forces of Satan, just as the Assyrians in the book of Isaiah stand for the United States and the two tribes for the Branch of David. But those of you who know your Bible also know that the word of God has many meanings. Goliath is an antitype of Satan, but he also stands for the Beast, the Antichrist who will appear in the last days. And who are the Philistines?'

He paused, catching the eye of the five or six Arabs who understood him. Had they understood? Were they afraid of him yet? Truly afraid?

'If you get a good dictionary, you'll understand how God's word fulfils itself in every age. The land of the ancient Philistines is what we know today as Palestine. Falistin they call it in Arabic.' He smiled. 'Isn't that right?'

No-one answered. He went on.

'The army of the Philistines is an antitype of the modern Palestinians. And they stand for the Arabs, who stand for the followers of the false Arab prophet, Mahomet. And this is how everything becomes crystal clear. Because if we look at the book of Daniel, we find it full of prophecies about the last days. Listen to what God says near the end of that book, two verses after He tells Daniel that the words are closed up till the time of the end: "And from the time that the daily sacrifice shall be taken away, and the abomination that maketh desolate set up, there shall be a thousand two hundred and ninety days. Blessed is he that waiteth, and cometh to the thousand three hundred and five and thirty days." And then God says: "But go thy way till the end be."'

216

'I needn't remind you that, as it says in scripture, we should count "each day for a year". One thousand, three hundred, and thirty-five years. Does that mean anything to you? It didn't to me, not at first, not until God sent a light into my heart and showed me the truth in His words.

'The setting up of the abomination that maketh desolate occurred in the year 622, which is the beginning of the Muslim calendar. The Arabs invaded Palestine and built a great mosque on the site of God's Temple in Jerusalem. And they stayed there, Satan's great abomination, ruling over the Holy Land, for one thousand three hundred and thirty-five years. Not Christian years. Muslim years, according to their calendar, which follows the moon like the old Jewish calendar.

'The year 1335 of the Muslim calendar fell alongside the year 1917 in ours. That was the year the Turks were driven out of Palestine, the year the Muslims ceased to rule over the Holy Land. God's word could not have foretold the future more clearly. But no-one saw what God had revealed until I came and opened the seals.

'Now, Satan was driven out, but not entirely. The Mosque of Omar still stands on the Temple site. The Holy Land is still encircled by the armies of unbelief. 1917, as we all know, was not the end of time, but the beginning of the end. And we are nearing the end now.

'If we read the book of Daniel, chapter nine, we see that God has determined a period of seven years – "one week" – immediately before the last coming. I can tell you when that last week of years began. It began in 1993, the year of my great suffering. Not long after that, the government of Israel signed a pact with the Palestinians – the Philistines, whose head is the Beast. Well, that was no more than a simple fulfilment of the prophecy in that same verse of Daniel: "And he shall confirm the covenant with many for one week." And that same verse goes on to say that "in the midst of the week he shall cause the sacrifice and the oblation to cease."

'The midst of the week is three and a half years, which brings us to the present time. And that's exactly when the Beast was about to break his treaty. You were gathered together for that very purpose, and if God had not been watching, you would have succeeded. But He was watching – watching and waiting. He sent

217

me to you, just as He sent David to the Philistines before, to strike you down, just as David struck down Goliath.'

Amina watched him, knowing he was mad, knowing that something dreadful was to come. What had he meant by referring to 1993 as the year of his great suffering? Had something happened then that might provide a clue as to this man's identity? She racked her brains, but could come up with nothing.

'Tonight,' he went on, 'I asked God what He wanted me to do now. I prayed for guidance, and I opened the Bible, and I read the following verse in the second book of Samuel. "And David commanded his young men, and they slew them, and cut off their hands and their feet, and hanged them up over the pool of Hebron." And it was after that, as God tells us in the next chapter, that David was anointed king over all Israel.

'Reading that verse brought another to my mind, one that I'm sure you all know. You'll find it in Matthew. "Wherefore if thy hand or thy foot offend thee, cut them off, and cast them from thee: it is better for thee to enter into life halt or maimed, rather than having two hands or two feet to be cast into everlasting fire."

'So here we are together at last: the true David, God's anointed king, and the heads of Goliath, the chiefs of the army of Satan, lined up before me like prisoners taken in war. I've heard that your own law says it's right to cut off the hand of a thief, so I guess that's what we'll do.'

He looked towards the back of the room. Ezekiel was standing there, waiting to be called forward.

'Ezekiel! Have you brought the things I asked for?'

Ezekiel stepped into the room. In his right hand, he carried the long axe they used for chopping firewood, under his left arm he held the wooden block on which they rested the logs for splitting. Behind him Zechariah, carrying a small cauldron in which tar had been heated.

He waited until his lieutenant had reached the dais.

'Set it up here,' he said. He looked down at the hostages. 'There are seven letters in the name Goliath,' he said. 'There are seven seals, and seven kings, seven angels, and seven vials, seven heads and seven crowns, seven loaves and seven baskets, seven months and seven weeks, seven priests and seven trumpets, seven bullocks and seven rams, seven spirits and seven stars. So let seven hands be struck off in full view.' He motioned to two of his men. 'Bring four of the prisoners up here.'

CHAPTER THIRTY-EIGHT

Craiguenamanagh Farm
Ballybay
County Monaghan
11 October
0715 hours

Conor Melaugh woke from an uneasy sleep to find a new dawn settling on the fields outside his window. It had not been conscience that had troubled his dreams. He had killed often and sometimes harshly, but after the first death and the short remorse that had followed it, he had known no guilt, whether waking or asleep. He prided himself that he was a soldier in the last days of the longest of wars, a war his father had fought before him and his father before that. No shame and no guilt, then, if a soldier's life brought killing, for in a war none are truly innocent. It was his creed, as much as any priest's.

Yet, since coming to Ballybay he had not spent a night entirely free from unease. It was the boy that troubled him, the boy and the death to which he had sent him, the death which he himself had helped contrive.

That death haunted him still – the manner of it, the sounds of it, the part he himself had played in it – and he found himself needing to know more. He wanted to know who had leaked such highly secret information to his people, and why the soldiers had agreed to stand by while the IRA shot and killed at will. It was such questions that were, more than anything, responsible for his waking sometimes in the small hours, afraid.

He rose and went to the window, and wiped the condensation from the glass with the back of his hand. The window had been left uncurtained, to make the cottage harder to approach by night. A light of any description approaching across the fields would have wakened him.

He looked out onto the long, sloping field that went down as far as the Clancys' two-acre wood. A grey sky and a wet field dotted with mushrooms, and blue hills not very far away taking their ancient shape in the light. He shivered, catching sight of a crow on a rusted harrow, to his left by the stump of a dead tree. His flesh hated the countryside, the cold of it, and the damp, and the grey, still light. He was a city man, a Belfastman through and through. He needed the hardness of streets beneath his feet, not mud and dung and wet grass.

The soldiers had been under orders not to fire, and Conor Melaugh needed to know who had given those orders, and why. There were tears on his face again, thick tears of anger mixed with contrition. He had brought Gearóid Lalor into the army himself, selected him for the ASU, trained him personally. A good wee lad, one of the best. And he'd sent him back to that detachment of British soldiers, knowing full well what was going to happen. His lips pursed and formed a single word, 'Judas'.

He went downstairs and into the kitchen to make himself breakfast. It was freezing cold in the cottage, a miserable hole of a place that he thought the farmer had been using for his cows until recently. He lit the Calorgas heater and crouched down in front of it till it got going. The table was covered with pots and dishes from the night before. A smell of stale food hung in the cold air, unsettling his stomach. He hated living like this, half like an animal, hated the smell and sound and damp feel of it. Right now, all he wanted was to be back in Belfast, asleep in a warm bed with his wife, and the children fast asleep in their own beds in the next room. But he had to settle for a gas fire in the middle of nowhere and a badly cooked breakfast without taste. He wondered how much more of it he could take.

In the cold cupboard, he found some potato farls and a couple of rashers of cheap bacon. The wee girl was due today with his shopping; God help her if she was late. He wasn't supposed to show his face in the village more than was necessary. The locals knew who he was, of course, him and the rest of the ASU, scattered in farms around the township, but no-one would dare inform.

221

The farls and the bacon went together into a frying pan, along with fat that had been on the go for almost a week. There were pieces of burnt food in the fat, but he thought it would last well enough for another day or two. His wife, Bernadette, would have scrubbed the pan out every day. She kept a clean house. Protestants thought they were all animals, that they lived in filth and squalor with outsize families. But Bernadette could have shown the lot of them how to keep house. When he had been in jail, he had thought of nothing else but the smell of their little house, and her in it, the smell of her, and the touch of her skin at night. It had come close to driving him mad, the vividness of his thoughts and the rank odour of the prison all around.

Over the sizzling of the farls and bacon, he could hear the sound of a tractor. The Clancys were at work already, ploughing or planting or whatever it was they did at this time of year. He had passed a few words with them, but they kept their distance. Away from his own streets, he had lost his stature as a hero. Here, he was barely tolerated, little more than a relic of romantic times.

And yet there were men who ploughed here whose fathers had fought the British in living memory. And, thank God, enough young men who still believed in the cause and kept the Tyrone/Monaghan Brigade alive. Although this was the Republic, they were under IRA Northern Command here, and most of them had seen action across the border, in conjunction with ASUs from north Armagh and east Tyrone. Jim Lynagh, the IRA's greatest border commander and the brains behind the ill-fated attack on Loughgall RUC station, had come from near here, from a small place called Tully. Conor had met him once, a couple of months before his death.

He tipped the bacon and the potato bread out onto the last clean plate. Jim Lynagh, his hero, had died in the ambush at Loughgall that May, along with Paddy Kelly, the man behind so many of their most successful operations in Tyrone. This year Gearóid Lalor, a nobody whom he had trained and betrayed, had died in a hail of bullets. And Conor Melaugh kept going, as though there were no justice or meaning left in the world.

There was the sound of a car on the track from the farmhouse. He put down his fork and headed for the front room. The girl never came this early, she had to do the shopping first in

222

Monaghan town. He peered through the narrow window, keeping himself out of sight as best he could. A blue Datsun came round the bend past the hawthorn and drew up outside the front door. Conor breathed out slowly. It was Fintan Mellows, the local intelligence officer.

He let Mellows in. The two men had met three or four times, never for very long. Fintan was the go-between for communications between members of Conor's ASU and Belfast Brigade. He brought them news and instructions, and carried back any requests or complaints. If asked, he would pass on messages to their families in Belfast. It was the only form of contact the Army Council allowed.

They sat at the kitchen table. It was the only warm room in the place, and Conor spent much of his time here, reading. He hated to think of spending a winter in Ballybay, hemmed in by snow and ice.

'Your breakfast's getting cold,' said Mellows. He was a cheerful man, an electrician by trade, a popular figure in the district. A few years ago, he had been the Sinn Féin member on Monaghan County Council. His contacts were numerous, making him an invaluable asset to the cause in his role as intelligence officer.

'I'd offer you a bite,' said Conor, 'but this is all I've got.'

'Go on with your grub. I've had mine. But are you overeating, or is the girl not bringing you enough?'

'I could do with more.'

'I'll see to it. Sure, I'd hate to see you starve.' He laughed. Conor Melaugh was a well built man and showed no signs of diminishing. 'But there'll be no need to bother for a while. You'll be leaving here today. Orders have come in from the North.'

Conor felt his heart miss a beat. Did they know what he'd been up to? Was he being called back for interrogation and punishment?

'What's up?' he asked. He found it hard to keep his voice calm. The bread and bacon lay untouched on his plate.

'Your ASU's to be reformed,' Mellows said. 'As of this morning. A special mission.'

'We're going back to Belfast?' He could not keep the jubilation out of his voice.

'I didn't say that. To tell you the truth, I don't know where you're headed. But the quartermaster's been told to arrange equipment and provisions for a mobile unit. My guess is you're to stay on the move for a while. You'll be OC as before, but Northern Command are sending in someone fresh with overall responsibility for the mission.'

'Did they tell you who it's to be?'

Mellows nodded.

'Maureen O'Dalaigh. I think you know her. She's on her way here already. And I believe she's bringing someone else with her.'

Conor felt his heart trip again. Maureen O'Dalaigh with some-one else. It sounded for all the world like an execution squad. If he had any sense, he'd make a run for it the moment Fintan Mellows left. But he doubted he would get any distance. He was too far from home, without resources, with no-one he could trust not to hand him over.

'You've no idea what it's about, have you?'

Fintan shrugged.

'You know they'd not tell me,' he said. 'The less I know, the better for all concerned. I'll tell you one thing, though – there was a hell of a to-do last night in Belfast. You'll hear about it if you listen to your radio. There was a shootout in Andersonstown. Dezzy McCormick and Con McKearney were killed. But it's not all bad news. Far from it. Over a dozen British soldiers were killed, and a good few wounded. Can you believe it, man?'

Conor stared at him in astonishment. Dezzy McCormick and Con McKearney were far from capable of inflicting damage like that on soldiers.

'Who else was involved, do you know?'

Fintan shook his head.

'It must have been one hell of a shootout. One thing I can tell you, though. Maureen O'Dalaigh's wanted.'

'Maureen? She's good, but . . . a dozen soldiers . . .'

'Well, you can ask her yourself when she arrives. She's due in Ballybay at nine o'clock. You're all to meet up at Joe McCartan's house. I'll pick you up here at a quarter to nine. And I'll see if Joe can fix you up with a better fry than that.'

'Have the others been told yet?'

'No, I'm off to see to that now. Take care of yourself. I'll see you in a bit.'

When he had gone, Conor sat for a while thinking things through. He switched on the radio, but there was only music or light conversation on all the channels. Fintan's news about events in Belfast he had found mildly reassuring. If Maureen was coming here on the run, it was unlikely she had any other purpose in mind.

There was just one thing he had to do before Fintan returned. His family would have to know he was no longer here. He had broken all the rules in telling them of his whereabouts in the first place, but he had wanted to be contactable in case of emergency.

He went out, shutting the door behind him. The phone box was half a mile away, on the road in to Ballybay. Bernadette would be in getting the kids ready for school. He'd make a quick call and tell her he'd be in touch as soon as he could. The main thing was that she shouldn't worry.

CHAPTER THIRTY-NINE

Dawn came a little later to the west coast, hesitant, as though braced for the long journey across the Atlantic. There was a chill in the air, and the scent of rain. Mist hung over Croaghmarhin and the sheer pile of Mount Eagle to the west of Ventry. To the east and north, Brandon mountain stood in the rising sun like another country. There had been rain in the night, and where it now lay the sun sparkled on the bright western slopes. Far out at sea, storm clouds moved in the darkness that was becoming light. Michael Deighan could see for miles in all directions from his vantage point on Clogher Head.

He saw the little boat coming in from Inis Tuaisceart, bouncing on the waves, three men aboard. He had been watching it for several mornings now, and once or twice of an afternoon, coming and going from an island where no-one lived. Tourists, no doubt, like the folk down at the little camp below Ballyferriter. They came to fish, mostly, though he had never seen this lot cast a line anywhere along the coast. Perhaps they went further out or down towards the Skelligs.

He'd had a word with Seán Dearg about them yesterday, and Seán had offered Michael a cut if he could find them and strike a deal. Seán Dearg was a dealer in all sorts of things, and he supplied over half the restaurants in Dingle with the best produce. Crab and lobster from Kenmare, salmon from Sneem, oysters from Galway, *poitín* from a good friend with a still in Connemara, and from his own farm, eggs and milk and bacon.

Michael set off, scrambling down to the narrow road where it skirted the head, hoping to get ahead of them to the little cove where he knew they always landed. For a man of over sixty, he was in good condition. The old legs would do him for a year or two more yet. He chuckled, thinking of the little money he might make if the visitors took him up. Seán Dearg was a man of his word. And there was always the chance that the people on the island would find other little jobs for him to do, things they could not easily do themselves without coming all the way to the mainland. And maybe they'd come back the following year, or send their friends.

Above his head, shearwaters and petrels turned in circles, screaming as they dropped to the water. During his lifetime, he had never been away from this place, not even to Tralee or Killarney, let alone great cities like Cork or Dublin. What attraction was there in those places anyway? Looking round him, he could not understand the young people in every generation who went away and never returned, some to Dublin, some to England, some to America, like their grandparents. Some made great successes of themselves, but he wondered what they lost in the process. And the rest merely exchanged the discomforts of a poor country for the daily grind in London or New York. He had never had much money, and at times he had found it hard going just to find bread for his mouth. But he was with his own people here, he could speak Irish with whom he pleased, and he would be buried at last in a place he knew.

The way down to the cove was steep, but he knew every inch of it. He was there waiting for them when their boat drew up on the shingle. They were dressed alike in black outfits and black woollen hats, and they wore heavy boots. Not sightseers, evidently, but the sort of tourists who took themselves seriously. There was no sign of fishing tackle aboard the boat. They'd be hunters maybe, or mountaineers – that sort of visitor. Well, he thought, they'd have appetites surely.

He strolled towards them, a hand stretched out in greeting.

'*Diá's Muire duit*,' he said. '*Tá an mhaidin go deas.*'

He knew they would not speak Irish, but he thought they'd be flattered that he supposed they did.

'I'm sorry,' one of them said, a tall man with a beard, 'but we don't speak Irish.'

Michael laughed.

'Well, now,' he said, 'and I didn't think you did. But this is the Gaeltacht, and there's money in speaking Irish.' He paused, looking at them in turn. They were hard men, he thought, serious men. 'My name's Michael Deighan,' he went on. 'I'm from Dunquin, just down the coast. I've seen your boat a few times, and I thought I'd introduce myself. I'm a friend of Seán Dearg's, over in Dingle. You may have heard of him.'

The tall man shook his head.

'I'm afraid not,' he said. 'Listen, Mr – ah – Deighan, it's swell to meet you, but we're in a hurry right now.'

'Oh, yes, I understand, I do indeed. You'll be wanting to get on with the hunting, I'm sure. There's little of that on Inis Tuaisceart. Little of anything. It does be hard work on the boat, getting provisions across. Harder when the weather is terrible, though thanks be to God it has been holding up of late. But it's a great pity you don't know Seán Dearg, for he's the man to know in these parts.'

He glanced into the boat. The visitors had brought nothing but a canvas bag and a great tarpaulin. No doubt their guns or traps were under the tarpaulin.

'It's not the fishing you're after, then?'

'No,' said the tall man. 'Look, we really have to go.'

'That's right, that's right. Sure, I'm never keeping you, am I?' He took a step towards the boat.

'Was it Seamus Maguire of Glashabeg you had the little boat from? It is like one of his own anyway.'

'I really don't know who the boat was bought from. I just row it. Now, if you'd just let us get it up on the beach here, then we can be on our way.'

'Are you for coming back tonight?'

'That's the plan, yes. But I don't think . . .'

'Because it's trouble you'll have if that's it. There will be bad weather by later on, and a high wind. From here to Inis Tuaisceart is a hard pull in a bad sea if you're not accustomed to it. And it is heavy you are in the stern, with the bits you are carrying. You would soon sink if a wave was to strike you by the side and fill the sheets. I'll be moving this bag where it can do no harm, and the three of you one to a thwart.'

Before Ezekiel could stop him, the old man had grabbed the gunwale and stepped into the boat. Ezekiel dashed forward.

'Please, you don't need to . . .'

Michael picked up the canvas bag in order to transfer it to the middle section of the little boat. As he did so, he lost his balance,

228

for the boat had not yet been properly grounded. The bag slipped from his fingers and fell across the middle thwart. The top had not been closed. The bag tipped, spilling its contents.

The three men stood stock still, watching the old man. Michael picked himself up, and as he got to his feet, he stopped to replace the bag. It took several moments for it to register. Was it crabs? Small cooked lobsters? And then he saw that what lay on the bottom of the boat was hands. Human hands.

He let out a deep cry and turned, jumping from the boat into the surf, his feet unsteady on the thick shingle. He saw the men watching him without expression.

Ezekiel stepped into the waves and brought the old man out. Michael's mouth opened and closed, but no words came out, in Irish or in English. There were no words in any language for what he had just seen. Had there been an accident? Or were these men doctors, surgeons from America that had come to Inis Tuaisceart to heal the sick?

No, he thought, looking at the men in their black clothes. They were not doctors. They had not come to heal the sick.

'Jesus,' he said, closing his eyes.

'That's exactly right,' murmured Ezekiel as he took the pistol from his pocket and placed it under the old man's grizzled chin.

The shot echoed across the headland and beyond, across beehive huts and oratories and ancient churches, across slate-coloured waves, and shimmered, and died away. Gannets and fulmars and white gulls rose screeching all along the broad shore. And in the silence that followed, Ezekiel drew the boat to the dry sand, and thought of the fishermen on the beaches of Galilee, long ago and far away.

229

CHAPTER FORTY

Office of the Permanent Under-Secretary for Security Policy
Stormont Castle
Belfast
11 October
0830 hours

At first no-one spoke, then everyone tried at once. The DCI sipped a cup of coffee and watched them pass from shock to rage to mutual recrimination. He was not in the business of adjudicating, though there were those who thought it his job. All he wanted this morning was one of two things: a legitimate target or a scapegoat. The others had come to find or make excuses, as usual. He let them go on, thinking it would be good for them to get it out of their systems, whatever it was.

He judged them – if he judged them at all – by a combination of factors that ranged from school ties and accents to their taste in pets and the extent of their marital fidelity or its lack. He had in his early days been a Dollymixture, ploughing the infertile fields of Sloane Street and its environs for what stray seeds of useful information he might uncover, and he brought to his work in the wastes of Northern Ireland a little of that innocent obsession with the trivia and the minutiae of things. Except that he had long ago lost his innocence and now turned his knowledge of other men's minor acts to more exact use. It was, he said, the science of applied gossip.

He had enough information on anyone in the room to crush him very hard should the need ever arise, which from time to time it did, and never more than at times like this, when so many reputations and so many careers seemed to be at stake.

The Under-Secretary sat behind his uncluttered desk, nodding benignly at appropriate pauses. Willoughby, the DCI, noticed that he was doing the *Financial Times* crossword. He hoped it would see him through, and he expected it would. The man's presence at the meeting, like the post he occupied, was largely cosmetic, and Willoughby was glad the present incumbent understood that and made no effort to intrude himself where he was unwelcome. Under-Secretaries who wished to be more than figureheads could be a source of constant irritation. Burrowes had been in the province two years now and not put a foot wrong. Though after last night's fiasco, it was virtually certain his head would be the first to roll. A pity, thought Willoughby, since it might very well stand in the way of the poor man's chances of landing his own K.

What occupied the DCI's thoughts most was the question of which other heads would follow Burrowes's. Was even his own secure? A last-minute disaster could sour a man's retirement. He had seen more than one colleague, all set to enjoy the guerdon of his labours only to see it snatched away by the smallest of miscalculations, the minutest of indiscretions.

He watched them bicker. Would they round on him, make him their scapegoat? Or would they be content with Burrowes, a much softer target, so easily expendable?

All members of the Provincial Executive Committee had been called, and all had turned up. Himself, the Director and Co-Ordinator of Intelligence; Major-General Charlie Wainwright, Commander of Land Forces; Bill Harper, the RUC's Deputy Chief Constable (Operations); and the head of RUC Special Branch, Jim Irwin.

In addition, he had invited Alan Rigby, his Intelligence Controller, who normally operated out of Thiepval Barracks, the army HQ at Lisburn; Andy Kerr, the Special Branch officer in charge of the Tasking and Co-Ordination Group at Gough Barracks; the TCG's army liaison officer, Fred Atkinson; and the Director Special Forces, Colonel Mark Beveridge. Beveridge in his turn had insisted that three of his top people be present: Penrose from 14th Intelligence, Ross from the SAS, and McPherson of the Field Research Unit at HQNI – the three principal undercover operations currently run by the military in the province.

Willoughby sighed and glanced sideways at the photograph of the Queen above the fireplace. It was a relief to him to think she was still there, if not exactly steering the ship of state, at least giving it some ballast. He feared the future, feared a Carolingian state ruled by hippies and New Age peaceniks. They would give Ulster away, take out the troops and send in a detachment of Buddhist monks to chant mantras and ring bells.

'Gentlemen,' he said, laying his coffee cup on the little table so thoughtfully placed by his side, 'we do not seem to be getting anywhere.'

'We're getting somewhere all right,' retorted Andy Kerr. 'We're discovering just what a cock-up that was last night.'

Willoughby looked at him placatingly. Kerr was a good man, a loyal underling, and he needed him in place. But where on earth did they get those grating voices, that wheedling tone that marked everything they said?

'All in good time, Andy, all in good time. I do want your opinion and I will ask for it, have no fear. But we have a more urgent task. Sooner than apportion blame among ourselves, I think we have a duty to the men who died to find their killers. That, I believe, should be our priority. The PM has already told Mr Burrowes here that that is his view also. I take it that we all agree?'

No-one said otherwise.

'Yes, I thought we would.' He let his gaze linger on them. It was less his seniority – which was far from absolute – than his known links throughout the security apparatus that gave him his power here. From 'The Department' he controlled all MI5 operations and, through his network of liaison officers and moles, kept himself on top of everyone else's.

'Charlie,' he went on, turning to the CLF, 'exactly who fed your boys with the tip that sent them in last night?'

'You'll know yourself that a number of PIRA top brass surfaced briefly a couple of days ago, including the woman you're so keen to get your hands on, Maureen O'Dalaigh. On your instructions, all branches started an active hunt for further information.

'Yesterday afternoon around four o'clock, E4 had a tip-off from one of their best touts. It went through the TCG at Castlereagh. 14th Int picked up on it, realized that it could be something big, and passed it on to my staff.'

'What was so good about it?' Willoughby addressed his question to Francis Penrose, the captain commanding 14th Int.

'The word was we could pick up three PIRA hard cases, sir. E4's informant had specified weapons, and there was reason to believe we'd catch them red-handed. The chief draw was Maureen O'Dalaigh.'

'And you had no reason to think you were being set up?'

'I still don't think so, sir. PIRA would never put anyone so senior into a trap. They very nearly didn't come out of it. At least two of their people were killed, and O'Dalaigh only got out by the skin of her teeth.'

'Nevertheless, they were waiting for you.'

'That remains to be seen. They reacted well, but a planned ambush would have to have had a more secure escape route.'

'You say two were killed. I had understood three.'

Penrose nodded.

'Three in all, sir. Desmond McCormick, Con McKearney, and a third man who is as yet unidentified. We don't think he was PIRA.'

'Any ideas who he was?'

Penrose shook his head.

'Not as yet, sir. I have people working on it. A photograph has gone out to all security agencies. We expect a reply within the hour.'

'Very good. Keep me informed.' Willoughby turned to Jim Irwin.

'Jim, I take it you've spoken to your people from E4.'

'Yes, sir.'

'And?'

'It was top quality intelligence. The tout's code-name is Yellow Man.' He glanced round at the others, sensing the incomprehension on the faces of the English present. 'He comes from Ballycastle originally. Yellow Man's a sweet.'

'It's eaten at the Auld Lammas Fair,' said Willoughby. He wondered why Whitehall bothered, really. They were like savages, after all, scarcely weaned from their tribal customs. They ate seaweed and abominable confections and threw bombs at one another. He thought of Cornwall and the gardens at Trellisick.

'That's right, sir. He's been run for over seven years now by Belfast region. My Regional Head there runs him personally.'

'David Cree?'

'That's him, sir. If he was here, he'd vouch for him himself.'

'I'm sure he would.'

'The man's never given David a false piece of information in all the years he's been handled by him. Yellow Man might break your teeth, but he's sweet as honey all the same.'

The DCI threw a withering look at the policeman.

'I'm afraid your tout has broken more than a few teeth this time, Mr Irwin. Assuming that he planted misleading information.'

'The information was fine. It was just incomplete. It should have been checked out thoroughly before setting up an operation.'

Mark Beveridge snorted.

'For God's sake, man. We only received the tip-off yesterday morning. We depended on your assessment of its quality.'

'Which was completely accurate as far as it went.'

'Gentlemen,' intervened Willoughby, anxious to prevent an altercation developing. 'You will have to do better than this. The quality of the intelligence is only part of my concern. Our priority, as I have already explained, is to hunt down and destroy the remaining killers. Now, does anyone have information on this aspect of our operation?'

Wainwright, the CLF, spoke for the first time.

'We still have men working at the scene, Geoffrey. But first indications suggest that only two gunmen escaped.'

'I find that hard to believe.'

'Nevertheless, reports from men involved in the shooting seem to confirm that there were no more than five people in the house. The choppers picked up two people leaving the building. They were tracked as far as a hospital in Andersonstown, after which reports are confused. One helicopter tracked two people leaving the Royal Victoria Hospital after an ambulance from Andersonstown turned up there. They disappeared in the lower Falls.'

'Any idea who these two were?'

Wainwright shook his head. Last night's deaths had struck a fatal blow to his career. He knew he would be leaving soon, under a cloud.

'One was O'Dalaigh, we're confident of that. But her companion could be anyone. Once we get an identification on the third dead man, we may be able to form an opinion.'

'But you must have suspects.'

Again the CLF shook his head.

'None. I'm willing to stake my reputation on it, that he wasn't PIRA. Whoever killed those soldiers last night had done some real fighting.'

'A renegade?'

'Possibly. We'll know more when that identification comes through.'

As if on cue, there was a discreet knock at the door. A secretary came in and crossed the room to the Under-Secretary's desk. Burrowes looked up. The secretary passed him a folded sheet of paper. Burrowes dismissed him, glanced at the paper, and passed it to Willoughby.

'I think this concerns you, Geoffrey.'

Willoughby read it and let it fall onto his lap.

'Well, gentlemen, it seems that the identification has been made. He's on file with the Germans, with their Middle East surveillance unit. His name is Abu Ahmad al-Rikabi, an Iraqi national currently registered for a PhD at Queen's University.'

The DCI looked at them, not quite knowing if he still had control of the situation.

'It would seem that things have started to grow a little complicated.'

CHAPTER FORTY-ONE

Dublin
11 October
0914 hours

Declan moved his head gently, hoping for the best. Everything seemed to stay in place. He tried again, and this time he thought he dislodged something. Only if he sat still could he be sure of relative calm. But that was the one thing he could not afford to do this morning.

The telephone on his desk rang. He ignored it and went on with his relaxation exercise. He was imagining that every muscle in his body was going limp, starting with his scalp and working down. The telephone went on ringing. Each time he got to somewhere around his nose, he thought about Amina and his whole head would go tense again. The telephone rang for the sixth or seventh time. He was just coming down past his forehead. Damn the telephone.

He opened his eyes and lifted the receiver.

'Yes,' he snapped. 'Carberry.'

'Declan? It's Martin Fitzsimmons. Listen carefully, and don't interrupt me. I may be cut off any moment. Ciaran Clark was sworn in as Taoiseach five minutes ago. Almost the first thing he did in his official capacity was to declare your operation illegal. Harker has already brought in a force of SAS troops from the North.'

'What? He can't do that, it's . . .'

'Shut up, Declan. He knows where your operation is holed up. His team is being briefed to go in at this very minute. You'll be told you're acting outside the law and asked to surrender. If you don't do as he asks, he has permission to send an assault force in to the bunker to bring you out.'

'By force?'

'If necessary. Declan, you've got to get out of there fast. Harker won't let you out alive.'

'What do you mean?'

'You'll remember our talk a week ago, Declan, when I told you I thought MI5 might be taking an unhealthy interest in you since your meeting with Austin McKeown. I've been doing some digging around on my own accord since then, and I'm ninety percent certain Harker is the man behind McKeown's murder and the attempt on your life. Last month a British military intelligence officer was killed in Belfast. The name was Wetherell. Does that mean anything?'

Declan felt his head spin.

'Yes,' he said.

'Harker had a full report on Wetherell's death ten hours before his body was identified. Get out of there now, Declan. He won't give you a second chance.'

CHAPTER FORTY-TWO

Stormont Castle
Belfast
0916 hours

'What was an Iraqi doing in the house in the first place? Why weren't we told about him?'

Geoffrey Willoughby was holding his private postmortem on the events of the previous evening. Only his own people were there, all senior MI5 officers on whose tact and judgement he relied. They had a problem, and Willoughby knew that more than just his own career depended on how they handled it.

'We think he may have been there to sell arms, sir,' said Raymond Tolliver, who worked with MI5's K branch, much of whose work now concerned Middle East terrorism. Tolliver was the MI5 officer with special responsibility for a top secret operation known as Scimitar. He had flown in from London that morning.

'You think?' Willoughby did not attempt to disguise the sarcasm in his voice.

'That was the tip-off, sir, that some sort of arms deal was in progress. We've done a check on E4's tout, and we're inclined to agree with their assessment. He provided first-class input, never let them down. His information on last night's soirée was spot-on. He had the names, the rendezvous, the reason for the meeting.'

'Let's stick to the facts, Mr Tolliver. Yellow Man only gave them two names that can be verified.'

'O'Dalaigh was there, sir, we're sure of it. Her prints have been found on a cup and a table, she's not contactable at her office or home today. If there was an arms deal with outsiders, O'Dalaigh would almost certainly have been involved.'

'Very well, three names. Do we know who Yellow Man is?' Willoughby put the question to Alan Rigby. Rigby, who had been at the earlier meeting, was NI Intelligence Controller and the DCI's top-ranking colleague.

'His name is Tobin. Seán Patrick Tobin. Intelligence officer for PIRA Belfast Brigade and intelligence liaison with Northern Command. He's been E3's man since being picked up and questioned at Castlereagh in 1989. Never put a foot wrong from that day to this. The model tout.'

'That's suspicious enough in itself. But if he is so good, why did we never take him over? He sounds too important to leave to the Paddies.'

'No need, really, sir. E3 were cooperative, passed on all he told them to their E4 section, who fed it to the TCG. And the TCG kept in close touch with our Liaison Office in Lisburn. It was all done by the book. Tobin was handled by an inspector from Belfast, a man called Maguire. It seems they got on well. He trusted Maguire, came to depend on him. If he'd been passed on to us, there was a risk he'd have gone sour. We've had too much bad milk in the past, Geoffrey.'

'All the same, I want him brought in. By this evening, sooner if possible.'

Rigby's eyes opened wide. He was a small man with a peppery moustache and cheeks that had been red once but were now fading to an unhealthy shade of copper. His passage through the MI5 hierarchy had never been smooth, and he remained nervous of Willoughby, a man with whom he had never been on good terms. The DCI's suggestion was, he thought, ill-advised. In recent years, relations between MI5 and RUC Special Branch had been deteriorating, and Rigby had originally been sent over from England expressly to help patch things up.

'I think that could lead to bad feeling, Geoffrey. If you don't mind, I think I'd rather . . .'

'Bugger what you'd rather. I don't give a damn whose feelings you hurt, just get Yellow Man in here tonight. We need him to ourselves for once. See he's brought in in good condition and handed over to Malcolm here to interrogate.'

Willoughby turned to a man seated two chairs away.

'Malcolm, get what you can out of the bastard. After last night, he's probably not going to be of any further use, so do what you like with him. Just see he tells you what you want to know.'

Before Malcolm Blake could answer, Willoughby turned back to Tolliver.

'You were telling me about this Arab, Raymond.'

'Yes, sir. Let's see . . . According to the Germans, al-Rikabi had previous involvement with arms deals. It's possible he was in Ballymurphy last night to set up an arms shipment.'

'What the hell are you trying to tell me, man? That the IRA has a love affair going with Saddam bloody Hussein?'

Tolliver shook his head.

'No, sir. I think you may have got the wrong end of the stick. Al-Rikabi was a Shi'ite and an active opponent of the Baathist regime. He fought against Saddam's troops in the south for a while, before fleeing the country. That's why he was watched but never picked up. K branch thought he might prove useful at some point in the future, if the Shi'ites came to power, or we needed to infiltrate certain sections of Iraqi intelligence, or there was another conflict. He'd never been recruited, but he was definitely marked down as someone with potential.'

'And it's your opinion that these Shi'ites have access to sufficient weaponry to make them interesting to the IRA?'

'Definitely, sir. I've spoken with Ronald Calverley at the Metropolitan Special Branch. He's in charge of a special unit monitoring Islamic fundamentalists in this country. It was made an SB responsibility a few years ago. Al-Rikabi's been on Ronald's books for some time now. He says al-Rikabi's people have been receiving high-quality stuff from Iran. And what they don't have, they can get, from there or from Lebanon.'

'And you think they were handing a shipment over last night?'

'No, sir, that's not possible. Al-Rikabi's car was involved in an incident shortly after the shootout. Two joyriders were killed by our side in mistake for O'Dalaigh and the fifth man. We think the youngsters were set up as a decoy. But the car was clean. O'Dalaigh and her companion could never have carried much away with them. In all likelihood, last night was just to arrange terms and maybe look over some samples.'

Willoughby nodded. This was starting to look bad. The government had taken a lot of flak over what he had always considered some very necessary fudging about arms shipments to Saddam Hussein. He knew several of the people involved in the so-called cover-up – decent, honest men every one of them, men who had always served their country well – and he had felt outraged by the drubbing they had received in the press. There had also been a bit of a bad odour about the way the Allies had failed to back Saddam's opponents after the Gulf War, leaving the Shi'ites to take the brunt of the dictator's revenge.

A lot of pinko whingeing, in Willoughby's opinion. What possible advantage would there have been to the civilized world if the chaps in beards had taken over? Just another bloody Iran all set to bugger up our oil supplies again. Saddam may have been a brute, and not a man to invite to dinner with friends, but he was at least a brute who understood how the system worked, unlike the fanatical Johnnies in the marshes who knew nothing but the Koran and how to bugger their wives silly if they didn't behave. At the end of the day, thought Willoughby, you could do business with a man like Hussein. Dirty business, possibly – but since when was keeping your hands clean a criterion for getting things done? The chaps in the turbans wouldn't even do business at all if you had so much as a whiskey and soda on the table.

All the same, the beast of popular opinion was always on the prowl after things like this. If it got out that opponents of Saddam Hussein had been arranging arms supplies to Irish terrorists, sections of the press would start blaming government ministers, pretending they had driven the Shi'ites to it, or something equally bizarre. Willoughby's political bosses wouldn't like that one little bit. Especially not with operation Scimitar and this business down in the South that Harker was handling. This would have to be quashed at all costs.

'I don't want this getting out,' he said. 'There are to be no references to Iraqis in any statements to the press.'

He looked at Rigby again.

'Alan, you'll get on to that, will you? See there are absolutely no leaks on this matter. There were only three terrorists in that house last night – O'Dalaigh, McKearney, and McCormick. Have you got that?'

'It will make it difficult to explain how three IRA terrorists managed to kill fifteen British soldiers, let alone how one actually got away. And there is the possibility that the IRA themselves may make a statement, if only to embarrass us.'

'I think they will prefer to keep the identity of their allies secret for the moment. And it will seem much more embarrassing to us if the public believes they were capable of putting up that sort of fight.'

'That could have a bad effect on morale, Geoffrey.'

'Bugger morale. We'll find an explanation. We pay people to do that sort of thing, don't we? Pay them bloody well, too. They can put it down to a breakdown in communications if they like, I don't bloody care. The chief thing is keeping quiet about this Iraqi business at least until we see exactly where it's heading.'

'I'll do my best, Geoffrey.'

'Do more than that.' He swivelled in his chair. 'Now, Tolliver, what do we know about the fifth man?'

'Well, we . . . We're reasonably sure he came to the house with al-Rikabi.'

'Another Iraqi?'

'Sir, I spent half an hour this morning in conference with Willi Seghers of the German Bundesamt für Verfassungsschutz. As you know, the Germans have been given overall responsibility within Europe for monitoring Middle East terrorist groups. Seghers has evidence that a leading Hizbollah terrorist left Lebanon yesterday and that he passed through Amsterdam en route to the United Kingdom. They do not yet know his identity or his final destination. However, all the indications are that his departure followed closely on a sermon by Sayyid Muhammad Husayn Fadlullah, the clerical leader of Hizbollah in Lebanon. It appears that one of those taken hostage at Castletown was Shaykh Mu'in Usayran, one of Fadlullah's right-hand men. Usayran is thought to have gone to Ireland using the name of Hajj Ahmad al-Madani.

'Seghers is of the opinion that the man who left Lebanon yesterday may have been sent to Ireland to rescue Usayran. When I learned that an Iraqi Shi'ite with close connections to Hizbollah had been found dead in Belfast, I reached the conclusion that your fifth man could have been our Lebanese terrorist.'

Willoughby smiled. A Lebanese angle sounded good. It would draw attention away from Iraq. Maybe they could even put out a story that al-Rikabi had been Lebanese, not Iraqi.

'Thank you,' he said. 'Mr Tolliver, I would like a word with you in private.'

When the others had gone, Willoughby poured two glasses of whiskey and handed one to Tolliver.

'Well,' he said. 'How does this affect Scimitar?'

Tolliver took a deep breath before answering.

'It could ruin everything, sir. Harker must make sure that things are kept under control in the Republic. I'll go straight back to London and start things moving there. We must get Hizbollah to agree before it's too late. Otherwise . . .'

'Otherwise we're all dead, Mr Tolliver.'

CHAPTER FORTY-THREE

Dublin
0917 hours

'Liam, I want you to make direct contact with Harcourt Street right away. Tell them a gang of armed men are about to make a raid on government offices in Merrion Square. Give them this address and make sure it comes up right on their computers.'

Declan turned to the next desk.

'Grainne, get out a call to all patrol cars in the central Dublin area. Same thing – a raid on government offices. Make sure they think it's coming from headquarters.'

'Sir, the patrol cars won't have armed Gardaí. If they come up against SAS . . .'

'Harker isn't a fool. He can't afford a shoot-out at this stage. His men will have very clear orders to back off. They're well trained. Now, get that message off.'

'Sir!'

Dominic Lawlor was manning the security monitors covering the upper levels.

'What is it?' Declan ran across to the bank of small screens showing closed-circuit TV pictures of the shop and the first floor of the bunker. On two monitors he could see men in black Nomex assault suits with anti-flash hoods and gas masks gathered around the inner door that would take them into stage one of the bunker. It felt exactly like a replay of the events at Castletown House. Except that this time he was ready.

'Has that door been secured?'

'Yes, sir.'

'How long before they break through?'

'Depends what they use, sir. Two, three minutes maximum.'

That meant they would be on level one shortly. Declan's team still needed time to put their essential equipment and files together and to destroy any sensitive material before they could make their getaway. Drivers had already been sent to start the vans that were waiting to take them and their equipment out of Dublin. The bunker contained an emergency exit whose existence was known only to the Taoiseach. Pádraig Pearse had told Declan of it in person, and he was betting that Ciaran Clark would not yet know of it.

Declan glanced at the monitor again. Two men had started cutting through the steel door, using portable thermal cutting torches. It was only a matter of slicing through to the lock mechanisms, then they would be in.

He picked up a nearby microphone and flipped the switch on its base.

'Attention! This is a restricted area. You are breaking into a secret government installation without proper authorization. You do not have permission to enter this sector. Please communicate with your commanding officer at once.'

Two of the SAS team conferred together hastily, and one of them appeared to be speaking via his built-in mike to someone outside the building. While this went on, the cutting was suspended. Declan reckoned on getting a minute's extra time at most from his diversion.

Maire O'Brien appeared at the door of the concealed exit.

'The vans are loaded, sir.'

Declan nodded and told her to get ready to leave.

'OK, everyone,' he said, 'this is it. We'll meet up again at Rendezvous One.'

At the door, the British team had started cutting again. Inside, two of Declan's men were covering the door with assault rifles. They would be the last to leave.

The rest of the team hurried into the narrow emergency tunnel. It wound beneath three streets to come out in an underground car park in a back alley off Baggot Street. An external monitor showed only normal traffic outside.

'They're through to the lock, sir!'

'Right, get yourself out of here.' Declan pushed Dominic through the door. On the monitor, he saw the assault team getting

245

into position. One of them was preparing stun grenades. The others were heavily armed.

'Back!' shouted Declan, bringing his two marksmen through and getting them into the tunnel.

The door burst open to the roar of an exploding grenade, accompanied by a blinding flash. Declan, who was wearing ear plugs and had shielded his eyes, paused half a second longer, then pressed a button. As the corridor between him and the door erupted in flame, he ran for the exit, closing and locking the door behind him.

CHAPTER FORTY-FOUR

Craigpatrick
near Mountshannon
County Clare
11 October
1425 hours

Craigpatrick was Pádraig Pearse Mangan's holiday home, some twenty-five miles east of the county town of Ennis, on the west bank of Lough Derg. This was tourist country, where the well-heeled hunting, shooting and fishing set came to make life miserable for the wildlife, or simply to cruise the waters of the lake. Pádraig Pearse's house was a small but expensive hideaway that the ex-Taoiseach had had built early in his political career, within easy reach of his Limerick constituency. The house lay only a few miles from Scarriff, the village in which the great man had been born and raised. It meant he could entertain visiting journalists in comfort before driving them for a picture session outside his parents' two-bedroomed house, as though it were still the family home.

Declan and Concepta had always been free to stay at Craigpatrick, and had often passed weekends and holidays there when Máiréad was small. In recent years, Pádraig Pearse's political needs had overridden all other considerations and kept the house off limits for long stretches at a time; but Declan still had the key.

The team met at a pub in Ennis as pre-arranged. Once they had all arrived, they drove out to Craigpatrick one van at a time. None of them had been followed from Dublin. To tail someone successfully over the deserted back roads of rural Ireland would have challenged the skills of the most experienced pursuer.

Declan was confident that Harker had lost them for the moment. With a little luck, they could go on working for several days longer before it was necessary to make another move. If that happened, he thought, they could hide out in the Burren, a bleak, rocky wasteland in the north of the county, pitted with caves and potholes, the most inhospitable tract of land in Ireland.

Declan had kept one car for himself. While the others went out to Craigpatrick, he drove alone into Mountshannon to speak with Pádraig Pearse's housekeeper, Norah O'Shea. He knew she visited the house at least once a day, to clean and keep the heating in order.

She greeted him as an old and trusted friend; but beneath the welcome he could detect the anxiety of someone who fears that life is about to become uncertain once again. Before going to work for Mangan, she had lost a husband and two children in a drowning accident. Since then, she had built a half-life for herself around the status that being the Taoiseach's housekeeper gave her in and around Mountshannon. That was now visibly threatened. Twenty-four hours ago, she had worked for the Prime Minister of a small but independent nation. Now she did not know what the next news bulletin would bring, or whether her employer might be arraigned on criminal charges and sent to prison.

Declan spoke to her carefully, emphasizing his rank as the head of the country's elite police division. As long as Ciaran Clark did not put out an order for his arrest, there was no reason for Norah O'Shea to know how things really stood with Declan.

'I need your cooperation, Mrs O'Shea,' he said, as though this was one of the private briefings she had relished so much in the old days, when Pádraig Pearse had first put on the mantle of his authority. 'I don't have to tell you that my brother-in-law is in bad trouble. You'll have heard that on the radio.'

'It's a terrible business, Mr Declan, terrible. Sure, the poor man must be in a dreadful state, and him always so careful about such things. His sister will be with him, will she not? And after all that's happened to her and yourself, God help us all.'

'She's down in the country with family, Mrs O'Shea, and I've no doubt Pádraig will be joining her as soon as he can. But I will tell you that I think Pádraig Pearse is innocent of these charges. That's why I've come down here, to carry out a secret investigation in order to establish the truth. I'm convinced we'll find the whole thing has been a fabrication from start to finish. And that's where I need your cooperation.'

'Sure, you know I'll cooperate with anything you suggest, Mr Declan. Will himself be coming down?'

'Not to Craigpatrick, no. He's still being held in Dublin. Everything depends on this investigation. If I can get the proof I'm after, Mr Mangan will go free. The trouble is that the entire operation is unofficial, and it has to remain top secret. If so much as a hint leaked out that I'm down here with a team of investigators . . .'

He paused significantly, letting her own imagination do the rest.

'Let's just say,' he went on, 'that Pádraig Pearse has political enemies, men who would even use my presence here against him. I am, after all, his brother-in-law, and it wouldn't take long for them to work up some sort of story against me as well. That means you must say nothing whatsoever to anyone about my being here.'

Mrs O'Shea nodded vigorously. It was no more than her duty to be discreet, and it would hardly be the first time she had kept her mouth shut about who was visiting up at the house.

'They'll hear nothing from me, sir, you can depend on it.'

'I'm sure I can. But there's another matter in which I need your help. We need provisions for the time we're here. If I were to go into Mountshannon or Whitegate to buy groceries, I'd be sure to be recognized. Do you think you could manage to buy in enough supplies from different places so as not to draw attention? I'll have one of the team drive you round this evening. If anyone asks, just tell them Concepta and a few friends have come down unexpectedly for a few days' holiday.'

It had happened often enough in the past to be entirely plausible. Declan set a time and said he would send Grainne Walsh over.

'God bless you, sir,' said Mrs O'Shea as he was leaving. 'You've not been out of my thoughts these past weeks, yourself and Mrs Carberry. Your daughter was the loveliest girl ever drew breath.'

He stopped her before it got too painful. Coming here was hard for him. Craigpatrick was packed with memories, like a trunk.

'Well, sir, I know you'll get to the bottom of this. If you're in

touch with Mr Mangan, be sure and tell him I was thinking of
him. I lit a candle for him last night in church, and I'll do the
same tonight. Be sure and tell him that.'

CHAPTER FORTY-FIVE

Belfast
11 October
1940 hours

Seán Tobin locked Yellow Man away for the evening. He had learned to live as two people, learned to keep his separate selves as far apart as sanity allowed. If he was to be effective as an informer, he had to be effective as an intelligence officer as well. A slip in one life would irremediably affect the other. Tonight would be spent in McD's listening to the crack and extracting from it the most useful items of information, things he could pass on to his IRA controllers to show he was doing his job. They, in turn, as tokens of their abiding trust, would pass to him details of jobs just done or at the planning stage, some of which he would pass on to Tommy Maguire.

The hard part was that he had come to trust the Protestant, even to like him. At heart, they were very similar. They both liked football, darts, and snooker; they both had children; they watched a lot of the same TV programmes; they even had relations in common, a couple who had mixed and gone to live in England: he was a cousin of Tommy's, she was a niece of Seán's.

He slipped through the pub door and headed straight for the bar. On one wall hung a painting of Máiread Farrell, an IRA activist killed in Gibraltar in 1988, flanked by flags of the Republic and the four provinces. They were all here, all his old friends, people he had known since childhood. All of them knew he was in the IRA, but only a handful so much as guessed his position. Some things it was better not to know. And, of course, with the tightening up of the cell system, you could never be entirely sure that the man on the other side of the pub table, someone you had known since you were wee boys throwing stones at the peelers, was not himself an IRA man.

Jimmy McMenemy was there, at the back table as usual, on his third Guinness by the look of it. Seán took his own drink, a Murphy's, and joined him. He knew Jimmy would be armed. His seat gave him a perfect view of the door and, more importantly, of whoever came through it. Here, as in every Republican area, everyone's greatest fear was that a carload of Loyalist gunmen would drive up outside a bar or a club, automatic weapons loaded, hyped up for a shooting spree. No amount of security cameras could prevent the quick run in, the shoot-out, the getaway. It had happened before, it would happen again.

It was Jimmy McMenemy's job to stop a shooting before it started. He sat in the same place every night, his gun to hand, a clear line of fire to the doorway; but by the time he came to his fifth or sixth pint, it was questionable whether his responses would meet the occasion should a gang of masked gunmen appear.

Seán sat down.

'Good man yourself, Jimmy. Have you seen Patrick this evening?'

'He was in earlier. There's talk of trouble after last night.'

'Aye, I know that. I've a few people to see myself. Andy McAteer said he'd be along later. His wee girl's sick.'

'I heard that. Is she in the Royal?'

'Went in this morning. They're doing a scan.'

'Have they no idea what it is?'

Seán shook his head.

'She was took ill last night, and when the doctor came this morning he had her sent straight on in. I saw Andy dinnertime. He's worried it's something serious.'

'I'm sorry to hear that. She's a nice wee girl.'

Jimmy took a long swallow of Guinness, leaving a thick white smear across his upper lip.

'Speaking of wee girls, how's your Bridget?'

Bridget Noonan was Seán's girlfriend. They had been living together for three years now and were planning on getting married in the spring. They already had a child, a little girl of whom Seán was inordinately proud. Together they made his life worth living.

'She's grand. She's off the night with her sister somewhere. I think they're visiting friends. They might call in later.'

A tall man joined them, Barley O'Brien. He held a large measure of Bushmills in one hand and a copy of *An Phoblacht* in the other.

'Great news about last night,' he said. 'That's sixteen soldiers dead. Another one just laid down his life for England half an hour ago.'

'Has anyone confirmed which of our boys was there last night?' asked Seán.

'I thought you'd know a thing like that,' answered Barley.

'How's that?' Seán did not altogether trust Barley, and would never have admitted openly to him that he was Belfast Brigade's Information Officer, or even that he belonged to the IRA.

'You know fine well,' said Barley.

'I heard it was Con McKearney and Dezzy McCormick who killed them soldiers,' interposed Jimmy. 'Though it's hard to believe.'

'It's more than hard,' said Barley. 'I've heard tell as how there was a third man found dead in the house.'

'He must have been good,' said Jimmy. 'Con McKearney was a hard man, but he was never that good. As for Dezzy . . .'

At that moment, the door opened and two men in suits stepped inside. Everyone stiffened visibly. Jimmy's hand reached under the table. Across the room, another hand pressed a concealed button.

The strangers looked round carefully, unperturbed by the tension they had caused. One caught sight of the little group at Jimmy's table. He whispered something to his companion and together they walked across the room.

'Here you are at last,' said the first man, coming up to Seán. He ignored the other two. His accent was English– educated, but unaffected. His friend joined him a moment later.

'Hello, Seán,' he said. 'Some of your old friends would like to see you. We've got a car outside.' He glanced at Jimmy. 'I wouldn't even think about it, Paddy. Unless you want to join the late unlamented Con McKearney.'

There was that about the man's tone and posture that warned

Jimmy not to risk it. Someone else would be along in a jiffy, he'd let them handle it. He glanced round. Best to be out of here the minute the shooting started.

'Come on, Seán,' said the first man. 'Tommy Maguire's waiting for you. He says you promised him some information about last night.'

Seán looked round. Every eye in the pub was on him, and every eye was hostile. The strangers were not army, a fool could see that. Which left few other possibilities. And everyone knew that it was not the job of Britain's intelligence agencies to pick people off the street or out of clubs for routine questioning.

Seán got to his feet. His legs felt numb, his head was spinning. As surely as though they had fired a bullet into his head, the men in the grey suits had just killed him.

CHAPTER FORTY-SIX

MI5 Holding Centre
Malone Road
Belfast
2110 hours

Willoughby came into the room quietly, like a restless cat who thinks it may find prey. There entered the room with him an indefinable aura of unforced authority. If until now there had been any doubt about who was in charge, Willoughby's arrival sent it packing. He had spent a lifetime learning how to assert himself without raising his voice or wearing loud clothes or invoking petty rules.

It was not a pleasant room. It was not meant to be. Officially it did not exist; unofficially, it was known to members of the Northern Ireland security services as 'The Coffin'. It had no windows, its walls were painted black, its ceiling was a mirror, like a ceiling in a brothel bedroom. Careless analogy might have portrayed the whole house as a brothel, the agents who ran it as pimps, and the touts they controlled as prostitutes. But that would have been to miss the point entirely.

What went on here was not prostitution but gambling. Hard, fanatical gambling to the point of ruin, to death if need be. The men and the occasional woman here bet on a blood sport, one that was played through the length and breadth of an entire province and sometimes beyond. Sometimes they won, sometimes they lost, but they all kept on throwing down their dice until a bomb or a bullet took them physically from the table.

Tobin sat on the floor, his back against the wall, staring ahead like a man who has seen his father's ghost. He was dressed only in underpants. Naked, his skin was pale and pimpled, his flesh untuned. Near him on a chair sat Malcolm Blake, Willoughby's chief interrogator. He and Tobin had spent an hour together. Ordinarily, this would have been just the beginning, but Blake knew that his boss wanted results tonight. He had leaned on Tobin as heavily as he knew how, so far without result.

'Thank you, Malcolm,' Willoughby said. 'Why don't you make yourself a cup of tea? You must be tired. I'd like a private word with Yellow Man.'

Blake looked from Willoughby to Tobin and back again.

'Are you quite sure, sir? I mean, I don't think he's quite ready yet.'

'Don't worry, Malcolm, he'll make himself ready.' He smiled at the man on the floor. 'Won't you, Seán?'

Tobin made no response. Blake shrugged and left. He could monitor what went on from the next room. Willoughby strolled to the chair, turned it and sat down, his arms resting on the back.

'Well, Seán, how has Malcolm been treating you?'

Tobin went on looking sullenly at the floor.

'Come along, Seán. By all accounts, you used to talk without much prompting. You used to be voluble.'

Tobin looked up. He did not know who Willoughby was, he did not much care. But he could tell at a glance that this was someone not far from the top. Higher than he had ever been, and for that reason, more dangerous.

'I want to see Tommy Maguire,' he said. 'He's my handler. It's him I deal with.'

Willoughby shook his head.

'Not a good idea, Seán. We've gone beyond that now, gone far beyond Tommy Maguire and his like. You're in the hands of the big boys now, Seán. The game you've been playing has changed. Believe me, the only hope you have of getting out of this in one piece is myself.'

Tobin looked up at him. The despair in his face was overt and grotesque.

'What the fuck are you talking about, mister? Your fucking apes walked into McD's the night like they fucking owned the place. They picked me out by name and told me I was wanted for information. Jesus, mister, they might as well have told the whole place I was a tout.'

'How quickly you catch on, Seán. That is precisely what was meant to happen. I'm an angry man, Seán, and an anxious one. Something happened last night that shifted all the balances. What is it they say in such circumstances? "All deals are off," I think. The file on you has just been closed. As far as I'm concerned, you are no longer alive. You do not exist. You will not see your girl-friend Bridget again. Your child will be told that you are dead. It is quite likely that, when your friends at McD's spread the word about your extra-curricular activities, Bridget will be asked some very hard questions by some rather nasty people. I wouldn't give much for her chances, would you?'

Tobin said nothing. He knew only too well that the man in the striped suit was saying nothing more than the truth. He looked at him, trying to read his fate in the locked, impassive face.

'Yous've killed me,' he said. 'It's murder what yous've done. I hope yous are happy. I did what yous wanted, I never cheated on yous. Me and Tommy had a deal, and you bastards have broken it. I should've known not to trust the fucking English.'

'Listen, Seán, I'm very sorry things have worked out the way they have. Truly I am. I'd like to have gone on using you. You've been very helpful in the past, and I have no doubt you would have continued to be of use in future. Tommy Maguire thinks very highly of you. We all do. Yellow Man is a legend here.'

Willoughby paused and looked down at the man on the floor. He felt that he could just stamp on him, erase him with a flick of his foot. And that, in a way, was what he was going to do.

'Unfortunately, Seán, things have not quite worked out as planned. As I told you, after last night all deals are off. Last night was out of line, beyond all the limits, and you know as well as I that nothing can ever be the same again. I want you to tell me all you know about the events of last night. Tell me the truth, and you will spend the rest of your miserable life in comfort. Try to trick me, and you will find yourself back in McD's with a label round your neck. I advise you to take what I'm offering. Only a fool would refuse. But . . .'

He looked hard at Tommy Maguire's pet, crouching pathetically in unwashed underpants on a cold, unresponsive floor. Willoughby thought it demeaned him that so much of his own life had been spent in places like this with creatures like Tobin.

Retirement seemed more enticing than ever. And further away than he had thought it twenty-four hours earlier.

'But there is one thing you must understand, Seán. You have exactly three minutes in which to make up your mind. I honestly don't have longer than that to waste on you. I have other business, more pressing than saving a tout's life. Use your three minutes well, Seán.'

He walked to the door.

'You haven't tol' me your name,' complained Tobin. 'I need to know your fuckin' name.'

'Yes, I'm sure you do, Seán. But you don't have time now for social niceties. I'll send Malcolm back in a few minutes. With a tape-recorder.'

Three minutes is not much time. Long enough to boil an egg. Or listen to a popular song. Or run a mile. But not very long to reach a life-or-death decision. Seán Tobin, however, had had ample time in the past in which to think over the very things Willoughby now demanded of him. He had always known that something like this would happen and that, when it did, he would have little choice about which way to go.

The door opened and Blake came into the room. He had a small automatic pistol in his hand, and Seán knew that he would use it if he did not get the cooperation he wanted. Putting a known tout back on the streets was too much of a risk. Touts picked things up from both sides, and a good IRA interrogator could get useful details from a long-term informer like Yellow Man if he had the chance. Far better to do the necessary here, then throw Tobin's body out into the streets and announce his death as another IRA execution.

'Well, Seán, have you had a good think?'

'He'll keep his word, will he? He's to be trusted?'

'Who? My boss? None better. You couldn't ask for straighter.'

'I have to believe you, don't I? I've got no fucking choice.'

'Good. I'm glad you understand that. Now, let's get on with it.'

'Can I have a chair?'

'Later. You can have anything you like later. For now, just take your time and tell me what you know.'

Tobin closed his eyes. He tried to imagine sunny beaches, but all he could see was an unlit alleyway between dark houses. And all he could hear was gunfire in the distance, short and bleak.

'The ASU that did the job back in August,' he began. 'The ones killed your people. It's been put back together. Reactivated – you know? Across the border in Monaghan. I couldn't tell yous where exactly, honest to God I couldn't. Maureen O'Dalaigh's gone there to take charge of them. And she took someone with her, a man, a foreigner. He was there last night. They were both there.'

They spent an hour together, the longest hour of Yellow Man's life. It was a sweet relief to tell the Englishman all he knew, to get it all off his chest, for ever and ever. This was the last time, the last betrayal, the last act of Yellow Man's career. Tomorrow Seán Tobin would be on his way to a new life, under a new name. It made little difference to him where he went, as long as Bridget and the kid were with him, and as long as they spoke English. He laughed at the irony. All this time fighting to get rid of the English, and here he was desperate to speak their bloody language. But then Irish wouldn't get you very far, not even in Ireland.

Blake left him where he had found him, dreaming in a cold dark room of Bondi Beach and the open spaces of the outback. Willoughby was waiting for him next door, where he had been watching the proceedings through a two-way mirror.

'Well done, Malcolm. I think we've got enough. All over for tonight. That part, at least. We shall have to get an operation under way to find our ASU before they leave Monaghan. If a cross-border job is called for, the shorter the distance our lads have to travel, the better. A pity I can't be on this one myself; I'd like to see it all.'

'I could tell the team to make you a video, sir. Of the shootings at least.'

Willoughby shook his head.

'Much too morbid, Malcolm. And it carries risks. If a thing like that ever fell into the wrong hands . . . No, I'll just listen to the verbals and imagine it in my own time.'

'Fair enough, sir. I'll see the job's done properly.'

'It better be. Last night was army – a terrible business and very painful, but army all the same. This is personal.'

'You have my guarantee, sir. A good job. And we'll make sure they know what hit them. And who did it.'

'See they do. And, Malcolm –' He gestured towards the room in which the interrogation had taken place. 'See that's taken care of before you start.'

'All deals still off, then, sir?'

'That's right.'

'He was given promises, sir. We do have a moral responsibility . . .'

'There is no such thing. The term is meaningless. No-one has any responsibility towards a terrorist. If he walks out of here, even under another name, he could do untold damage. He knows of our special interest in Conor Melaugh's ASU. He knows or guesses the men they shot at Malone House were MI5. And he may even know why they were shot. That means he still has information to trade. He may even try going to a newspaper, maybe some rag in Sydney that wouldn't feel a moral responsibility about British state secrets.

'Far better he turns up where he belongs, in some gutter in West Belfast. It'll put a little wind up PIRA and give us some decent propaganda about how they treat their own.'

Blake took the little pistol from his pocket and checked that the safety was off.

'What about the woman, sir – Bridget Noonan? We still have her down the corridor. Is it worth it? Or shall I send her packing?'

Willoughby pondered for a moment.

'No, see to her as well. For good measure.'

Blake nodded and opened the door. The DCI remained, dreaming, not of the barbaric wastes of the colonies, but of a house near Fowey, with a view over the sea. Not even the first gunshot disturbed his reverie.

CHAPTER FORTY-SEVEN

2312 hours

She lay huddled on the rough bed in her cell, listening as the high wind clattered from one end of the island to the other, and off again into the depths of the Atlantic. There were tall seas all around, crashing against the rocks as if in a bid to demolish them. She knew they were on an island off the west coast, but she did not know its name, nor would it have meant anything to her if she had. It was nothing more than a bare rock on the great sea's edge, a place no-one but a hermit or a fanatic could love.

The Lamb of God, he had called himself, the fanatic who held them here. She could think of other names, much less flattering. After the awful session in which he had had those poor men's hands cut off, he had spoken to her. He had told her he had the power to let her go any time she wanted. He had not spelled it out, but she had guessed what the price might be. It depressed her that it should be so predictable, so trite, that even a man who considered himself the son of God could not dream up something a little more original.

That night, she had been far too distressed even to answer. Tonight, she lay listening to the storm, thinking the same thought that had troubled her all day: would he be willing to let some of the other women go in exchange for the favours he wanted from her?

The thought repelled her. But some of the women were in a bad state and getting worse. The sooner they were out of this, the better. If Amina herself were to achieve anything here, she needed as few lame ducks around her as possible. A couple of the women had been trained to fight, the others had spent their lives behind walls and veils. As for the men, she thought it would be much the same.

The wind seemed strong enough to blow the buildings and everything in them into the sea. She almost wished it would. Sometimes, when the wind subsided a little, she could hear one of the hostages, an Iranian woman called Nushin, crying in her cell next door. And, further away, the moaning of one of the men whose hands had been cut off so brutally.

How had anyone ever lived on these barren rocks, she thought, through all those long, wind-buffeted winters, scraping a living from the sea and the thinnest of soils? She thought she would go mad herself if the howling did not stop.

She lay in the darkness and tried to imagine her body as something separate from herself, an unconnected entity. Like a prostitute or a nun or a cancer victim, she strove to create a gulf between herself and her own flesh, to disown what she had previously regarded as her only true possession. She lay in the darkness like a stone, while the storm raged outside. She lay in the darkness listening, waiting from one heartbeat to the next for the sound of footsteps coming to her door. And she had still not decided what she was going to do.

CHAPTER FORTY-EIGHT

Craigpatrick
12 October
0220 hours

It had been a long day. For most of the team, there had been hard work setting the operation up again with limited facilities. They had rewired telephones, created desks from tables and cabinets, run extension leads from the house's few electrical sockets to the bits and pieces of equipment they had managed to bring with them. Computers had been wired up and linked to others, modems had been installed, faxes plugged in and provided with false numbers.

Mrs O'Shea and Grainne had travelled the length and breadth of County Clare in order to lay up adequate provisions without drawing attention to themselves. The result was a well-stocked larder, two packed fridges, and a freezer that would barely close. It looked as though they had stocked up for a siege. Declan clenched his teeth at the thought. A siege was not entirely out of the question.

Everyone was tired, and several of the team had already gone to bed. Myles O'hUiginn was in the library, going through the books there to see if there was anything that might come in useful, and being distracted every so often by a volume on something completely irrelevant. He had already connected his computer to the internet, giving him access to several international databases.

Those lacking technical expertise had been occupied in monitoring Irish and British news bulletins on television and radio. Craigpatrick was equipped with a satellite dish, giving access to

CNN and some European networks. Not that it made any difference who they listened to: all the news was bad.

Ciaran Clark, the new Taoiseach, had publicly admitted that hostages had been taken at Castletown House; but he insisted that the situation was under control, that investigations had already uncovered several important clues, and that arrests would shortly be made. There was a good chance that the hostages might be released in a matter of days, unharmed.

The names of those being held captive were not given. Neither Clark nor the bland government spokesman who followed him – and whom no-one had recognized – referred to the demands of the kidnappers. Nor was any mention made of the death of the Egyptian, 'Abd al-Halim 'Abbud, or the threat to the lives of the other hostages.

There had been an attack on a bus-load of French tourists at Luxor in Upper Egypt, and a statement released by a fundamentalist group, the Jama'a Takfir wa 'l-Hijra, claimed that the assault had been carried out in retaliation for the taking of the hostages. One tourist, a woman from Nice, Madeleine Dubois, had been killed and several others wounded. The coach's police escort had opened fire on the militants, killing two. No-one was prepared to give any reason why a French party had been singled out, and the Jama'a Takfir wa 'l-Hijra had not claimed French involvement in the kidnappings.

The investigation into Pádraig Pearse Mangan's personal finances continued. The former Taoiseach had issued a statement through his Dublin solicitors, Pluck & McCruiskeen, denying the allegations and promising evidence that would establish his complete innocence.

Declan said goodnight to those still awake and went to bed. Pádraig Pearse's room had been reserved for him, though it seemed an inauspicious thing to sleep in the man's bed under the present circumstances. He fell into a heavy sleep almost at once. In his dreams, he was in Lebanon again, running after a man who would not show his face. All the time as he ran, Amina's voice called out after him, but he could not hear the words.

Suddenly, he was wide awake. For several seconds, he did not know who he was. Someone was bending over him in the darkness.

'Mr Carberry, will you get up please?'

It was Dominic Lawlor, dressed in his underclothes.

Declan groaned. 'What time is it?'

'Ten past five, sir. There's a phone call from Dublin. He wants to speak to you.'

'He? Who the hell is ringing at this time?'

'I don't know, sir, I'm sorry. He wouldn't give his name. But he said it was urgent. A matter of life and death.'

'It had better be.'

Declan forced himself out of bed. It was bitterly cold in the unheated bedroom. Outside, the storm was beginning to quieten.

The telephone was in Mangan's study, which meant this had been a direct call on the Prime Minister's unlisted number. Declan, dressed in his trousers and with a blanket thrown round his shoulders, slumped into the soft chair behind the desk and picked up the receiver.

'Carberry,' he said. He'd be lucky to get away without a headache after this, he thought.

'Jesus, Mr Carberry, it's taken me over an hour to find you, so it has.'

The voice at the other end was that of Seamus Cosgrave, Declan's informer.

'Seamus? How the hell did you get this number?'

'Sure, you gave it to me yourself a year or two ago. You were away on holiday, but I needed a number to get you at if there was an emergency. Well, Jesus, Mr Carberry, sir, there's one hell of an emergency now. If you don't help me, I'm a dead man as sure as I'm standing here.'

Cosgrave was speaking rapidly, scarcely pausing between words. His breath, when it came, was snatched and shallow. Declan knew he would not have rung without due cause. Cosgrave was a lot of things, but he was not an alarmist.

'What is it, Seamus? What sort of danger are you in? Have you been rumbled, is that it?'

'Rumbled? Jesus, sure I don't know if I'm coming or going. I stumbled on something I shouldn't have and I panicked.'

'Are they on to you?'

'Yes, I'm certain of it. You said you'd help me if this ever happened. You've got to bring me in. Teresa's going up the walls, she's beside herself. They'll do for her as well if they think she knew and was covering for me. You know that, you know that's what they do. Mr Carberry, sir, you've got to get me out of this, I'm a dead man otherwise and me children orphans. You said I'd be given a new identity, and money to go with it.'

'Calm down, man. Where are you? Are you at home?'

'Home? How would I be sitting at home and them after me? I'm in a phone box in Terenure.'

'All right. Get your wife and children. Go somewhere you feel is safe and leave them there. I'll drive straight to Dublin and pick you up. It should take me a couple of hours. Be in front of the General Post Office at eight o'clock. And for God's sake be there, I can't afford to hang about myself.'

'Jeez, that's an ironic place to pick a man up, Mr Carberry. I'll leave the family with me sister Christine. They'll be all right there till I get them. Should we bring our summer clothes?'

'What?'

'It'll be summer soon in Australia, isn't that right, Mr Carberry?'

'I'm sure it is. Seamus, forget about clothes. Just be at the Post Office at eight. And, before you go, will you tell me just what it is you stumbled across that you shouldn't have?'

There was a pause. Somewhere in the background, Declan could hear a car going past. Then Seamus spoke again.

'Sure, Mr Carberry, I'd be a fool to tell you that. It's me guarantee. It's what you'll come for. I'll tell you one thing, though. It's to do with these foreigners that was took at Castletown a few days ago.'

'Seamus, that's important information. People's lives may depend on it. I'll be at the Post Office whatever happens.'

'Sorry, Mr Carberry. But me life depends on it, and me wife and children. I'll see you at eight o'clock.'

There was a click as Cosgrave hung up.

CHAPTER FORTY-NINE

Ballybay
12 October
0714 hours

Abu Hida put down the telephone gently. He did not cease to wonder at the ease of modern communications. Cities crumbled, entire countries fell apart, the lives of children were snuffed out remorselessly, yet he could stand in a village phone box in rural Ireland and speak to someone he had been with in Baalbek two days earlier. Suddenly, he felt very tired. Tired of fighting, tired of killing, tired of courting martyrdom. In Lebanon, they treated him like a hero, when all he wanted was a wife and children and peace for them to grow up in.

He closed the door and started to walk back to the cottage. A man on the other side of the street stared at him, then looked away. People here knew better than to show too great curiosity about strangers.

As a child he had known nothing but the unrelenting poverty of the south. Later, there had been civil war and invasion. And now the steady erosion of pride and certainty in a world that seemed no longer to care. He still believed in God and the prophet and the holy Imams, in revolution, in the right of the dispossessed and hungry to make a fist with which to strike their oppressors. He still had faith that God would bring justice where there had been none and that it was possible to build a society on earth that was not ruled by greed or poisoned by want or corrupted by gross inequality. He still prayed every day that a time would come when he might set his weapons aside. But in his heart he knew that the killing would never stop, that it would go on until he too fell a victim. And then . . . ? And then there would be more killing, more graves, more tears.

When he reached the cottage, the others were already having breakfast. None of them was in a good mood. Life in hiding had quickly taken its toll. They had grown indolent, self-pitying, nervous. Maureen O'Dalaigh had spent most of the previous day filling them with the fear of God and, more immediately and to greater effect, fear of herself. Today was to be spent in the hills above Shantonagh, the morning in a gruelling round of physical exercise, the afternoon in shooting practice under Abu Hida's instruction. It did not promise to be the best day he had ever spent.

They looked up as he came in. There was already resentment in the air just because he had banned bacon from the breakfast table. His manner made them uneasy. They knew he would tolerate no slip-ups. And they sensed that he would not care if all of them died as long as his own mission was carried out.

Maureen handed him a mug of coffee. She was not wholly easy either. Working with an outsider was proving a strain on her nerves. Army Council had gone against a long-established tradition in agreeing to provide assistance to Abu Hida. Normally, IRA involvement with foreign terrorist organizations was strictly on a guns-for-money or money-for-guns basis. They had turned down more than one request from groups like the PLO and Hizbollah for more active assistance in the form of safe houses or acts of terror carried out in their behalf.

In 1988, while Gerry Adams was in Tehran attempting to negotiate the release of Brian Keenan, IRA representatives had been in Beirut meeting with the leaders of Hizbollah – who had included Abu Hida. Hizbollah had offered to secure Keenan's release in exchange for direct assistance to Islamic terror groups in Europe. Army Council had refused the deal and Keenan had remained a hostage.

So why the shift in policy now? Maureen had not been consulted about the decision to respond to Hizbollah's request, and she failed to see the logic behind it. What would the movement gain from its involvement, after all? A little money perhaps, a lot of arms, probably an opportunity to train recruits at camps in Lebanon or Iran. All valuable enough in their way, but surely not as important to the cause as public goodwill. She knew that getting tied in to other people's politics was a certain way to lose your own followers' support.

The IRA could not control Hizbollah or any of the other Islamic terror groups. People in Ireland still remembered Keenan and the treatment he had received at the hands of his captors in Beirut, even though he had insisted that, as an Irishman, he was innocent of any involvement with the colonial powers. Many Irish families had relations of one kind or another in the United States and thought of America as their second home. Muslim hatred of the Great Satan did not go down well with people who received so much of their financial and moral support from that quarter.

They had spent the previous afternoon and evening going over ways in which to track down the hostages. Feelers had been put out all round the Republic for information that might provide a clue to their whereabouts. Had anyone seen or heard anything unusual, had strangers been seen in places off the tourist track, had there been incidents out of the ordinary? It might take days to get feedback, but Maureen remained confident that, in one way or another, the kidnappers would betray themselves. If they did, she would get to hear of it; she had eyes and ears everywhere, and everywhere people owed her or the movement favours.

Abu Hida sipped his drink and wondered why they bothered to call it coffee. Certainly, it bore little resemblance to the strong, bitter *qahwa* he was accustomed to at home. On the plate beside him was a slice of thick brown bread. He buttered it, imitating the others. He had not yet made up his mind about them.

Conor Melaugh, the OC, was clearly the most experienced and the one to be relied on in an emergency, but he was clearly bitter about something and would have to be handled carefully. Seamus Lenihan seemed capable and intelligent, but Abu Hida did not think he could be wholly trusted. Colm O'Driscoll, the small man with the limp, was the nearest in temperament to himself, but his wife's death and his long absence from his children had both weakened him. Eugene O'Malley, who had played tunes to them the night before on his tin whistle, was the most balanced, but Abu Hida was not sure he could depend on him in a crisis.

They were all very different to the men he knew in Lebanon. He could sense their anger and their commitment, but he sensed that something essential was missing in their make-up. They would choose death, he did not doubt that; but they had no real understanding of martyrdom. They spoke of martyrs, but not as he would speak of the *shuhada'*. For him, martyrdom was a sacred act and martyrs were saints; for them, the glory lay in the defiance the dead offered the English, and in little else. Their own priests condemned the use of violence and regretted the deaths.

There was something else that troubled him, something on which he could not easily place a finger. The dynamics of the group appeared strained, and not, he thought, simply because they had been kept out of action and apart from one another for two months. He guessed it went back before that, quite possibly to the incident that had led to their being withdrawn from active service in the first place. But every time he had alluded to the possible reasons for their move from Belfast, they had clammed up or changed the subject. He would have to tackle Maureen about the topic independently; he sensed that she was willing to be influenced by him and he was sure he could use it to his advantage.

'Did your call go through all right?' Maureen asked. She was at the cooker, frying a batch of potato farls.

'Yes, the line was very good. My friend was as clear as you are now.'

'You never cease to be amazed by that sort of thing, though, do you? The videophone's the next thing. We have one in the office back in Belfast. A grand wee thing if you can ever get anyone to speak to with one of his own.'

She slipped a spatula under a farl and turned it out onto a large blue plate.

'Did your friends have any fresh news about these people you're after?'

'No,' Abu Hida said. 'They know nothing more. Except that the Irish government has now officially admitted that hostages are in fact being held. My friends are pressing hard for details.'

'I don't expect they'll be told much.' She lifted the last farl onto the plate and brought it to the table. The smell of hot fat hung in the cold air.

'That is the way with governments in these matters.' Abu Hida sipped his instant coffee and looked at her. Better to have it out now, he thought, before they went deeper.

270

'It also seems to be the way with your people,' he said.

'Meaning?' She put a fork holding a piece of the potato bread back on her plate, waited for his answer.

'My friend told me that the raid on Castletown was preceded by an ambush of the British ambassador only a few miles away. It was perfectly timed. The ambush was arranged as a decoy, in order to draw off the Irish special forces unit protecting Castletown House.'

'Is that so?'

'My information is that the ambush was carried out by one of your Active Service Units. Do you think that could be true?' His voice was as cold and as heavy as lead.

'I've no idea.' She felt nervous, unprotected. 'That would have been a Southern Command decision.'

'But you would have heard.'

She shook her head.

'Not before an operation. It would be highly restricted information, purely on a "need to know" basis. Afterwards, I'd maybe hear something. But with this thing, it's early days yet.'

He nodded. Perhaps she was telling the truth. He pushed the mug away from him.

'Nevertheless,' he said, 'you see that it introduces a false note into our relationship. If one of your units acted as a decoy for the raid, it's hard to escape the conclusion that the raid itself was an IRA operation.'

The tension round the table was now palpable. Each beat of each heart could be sensed.

'No,' said Maureen. 'It was not the IRA. I'm prepared to swear to that. You may be right about the decoy, and if you are, I'll find out about it, believe me. But there's no way we'd ever take your people hostage.'

She had begun to see, however, that, if this was true, it might provide an explanation for Army Council's willingness to provide help. Had they been tricked into something they now regretted, was Abu Hida's presence here a gesture of apology, a means of avoiding retaliation once word of the decoy got out?

'Perhaps your people thought they could use the hostages as a lever,' Abu Hida said.

Maureen shook her head. The others were watching her, aware that all was not well.

'A lever? Who could we use it on? The levers we need to press are all in London, not the Middle East.'

'There are forces in the Middle East that know how to press levers in London.'

She shrugged.

'Perhaps. All the same, I don't think it adds up.'

'Let us hope not.'

'You have my word.'

He let the assurance hang for a moment, naked, in the fat-sodden air.

'I do not doubt that you know nothing of this,' he said. He had observed the surprise in her eyes, sensed her sincerity in answering. 'But my people will need more than your word. They will require proof.'

'Proof? What sort of proof can anyone give you?' But even as she spoke, she understood.

'Your Southern Command will have details of the people who encouraged them or paid them or forced them to carry out the ambush. Those are the same people who carried out the raid on Castletown House. You have only to give me their names and their whereabouts.'

He paused.

'If your superiors do not make that information available to me, I can tell you that retaliation will be swift and certain. My people will deal with you in ways that the British would not even dare to imagine. Do you understand me?'

She had lost her appetite completely. She looked at him and nodded.

'Yes,' she said quietly. 'I understand.'

CHAPTER FIFTY

Dublin
12 October
0745 hours

As he drove into Dublin, Declan listened to an RTE news bulletin. A coach carrying Hungarian engineers to work on an irrigation project at Aïn Sefra in Algeria had been attacked by mujahidin connected to the banned Islamic Salvation Front; in Dhaka, a Swiss relief worker sent in after the recent floods had been assassinated by a lone gunman; an American journalist, Bill Adair, had been seriously hurt when a bomb exploded outside his Ankara hotel room; and an unconfirmed report had just come in that a group of German workers had been taken hostage in southern Iran.

Retaliation for the Castletown hostage-taking was gaining momentum and threatening to grow out of all proportion in a short time. Declan switched off the radio and slowed down as he came in to Drimnagh.

Traffic was still relatively light, though growing in volume as the early-morning rush-hour took shape. By some skilful navigation through back streets, Declan escaped the most likely jams at the South Circular and Heuston Station. He came into O'Connell Street from the quays and across the bridge. He planned to make an initial pass of the Post Office: if all seemed safe, he would park at the first opportunity, run back for Cosgrave, and get him into the car. After that, he had almost no idea.

The north-bound traffic was moving slowly along the street. Declan kept in second gear. It was almost eight. Cosgrave would get nervous if he was much delayed. The informer could hardly have chosen a worse time to get blown, reflected Declan. Two weeks ago, and he could have mounted a small operation to pick Cosgrave up and send him and his family out of the country as promised. Now, he was in almost as much danger himself. Cosgrave's only hope lay in Declan's being able to persuade Martin Fitzsimmons to do him a favour. If Martin could not or for some reason would not, Cosgrave would just have to go into hiding by himself and wait until things righted themselves. If they ever did.

There seemed to be a hold-up just ahead. Road-works of some sort, as far as Declan could tell. Then, as the cars ahead of him got moving, he saw what it was. A patrolman was directing traffic out into the right-hand lane. The nearside lane was closed off by a Garda car and van. Two Gardaí were cordoning off the front of the Post Office. Declan could hear a siren screaming in the distance and drawing gradually closer.

He did not need to stop to know what had happened. The scene was all too familiar, all too obvious. Cosgrave's killers must have done the job without the formality of a trial. Perhaps the symbolism of an IRA execution in front of the GPO had been too great to forego. It had been from these steps that Pádraig Pearse had read aloud the Proclamation of an Irish Republic in 1916. The passers by then had ignored him and his band of would-be heroes; today, their grandchildren drove past with scarcely a second glance at the latest victim of the republican dream.

As Declan moved away, he could just make out the white sheet that someone had tossed over Cosgrave's body. He recognized the officer in charge, a man called Breathnach; but he decided there was little point in his getting out and asking questions. Whatever information Seamus Cosgrave had meant to pass on, it would have been carried along with all his other secrets, in his head.

There was a chance that Cosgrave's wife and children had not yet been touched. Declan would have to take the risk of contacting them. If Cosgrave had left them with his sister in Terenure as he had intended, they should still be there. Declan did not have the address with him; but he knew the name and the approximate location. He stopped near the Rotunda Hospital and went inside. There was a public telephone in the lobby, with a phone book. The sister was there, under her married name, Mulcahy.

It took him twenty minutes to get to Terenure. Christine Mulcahy lived in a semi-detached house at the end of a cul-de-sac of identical houses. She had married well enough, to a man who could take her out of the drug-infested council estate in the city's north where she and her brother had been brought up. Now, almost thoughtlessly, Seamus had dragged her back to a world in which strange men came knocking at your door before nine in the morning.

'Are you Christine Mulcahy?'

She looked round uneasily. Her husband had not gone to work this morning, in case there was trouble.

'Who's asking?'

'It's all right, Mrs Mulcahy, I'm not here to give you any trouble. I'm a friend of Seamus's.'

'Seamus who?'

'Your brother, Seamus Cosgrave. Look, there isn't time to play games. Are Teresa and the children with you?'

She turned and shouted.

'Tim! Will you come here?'

Declan persisted.

'Christine, will you listen to me? Teresa may be in trouble. You have to get her out of here as soon as possible. Do you understand me?'

A large man appeared in the hallway. Timothy Mulcahy was a plumber by trade, and his hobby was body-building. In one hand he held a length of piping, as if he thought it and his bulk would serve to chase off an IRA gunman.

'My name's Declan Carberry,' Declan said. 'Seamus may have told you about me.'

Tim came forward.

'Just what the fuck do you mean coming here? We're in enough trouble as it is, without you coming here and making things worse. Why don't you fuck on out of here?'

'Listen,' Declan said, 'I don't care what you think of me or what I do or what happened between Seamus and me. The fact is that he was shot this morning and that before he died he told me the people who were after him might come after Teresa too.'

The blood rushed from Christine Mulcahy's face. Her husband took a step towards Declan, raising the pipe menacingly.

'Save your threats for Seamus's companions-in-arms, if they turn up here,' said Declan. 'I'm here to help the family, and at the moment I'm the only chance they've got. Can I come in, or do we have to stand here on the doorstep in full view of everyone?'

Tim Mulcahy did not appear to have grasped the seriousness of the situation. He took another step towards Declan. Christine stepped between them.

'He's right, Tim. For God's sake, let's get inside out of the street. If Seamus has been hit, they'll be looking for Teresa sure as God.'

Declan came in. He had now made up his mind what had to be done. Teresa Cosgrave and her children must be placed somewhere safer than this, somewhere the IRA would never find them. With the limited resources at his disposal, he could think of only one place.

While Christine went in to send the children upstairs and then to tell her sister-in-law the bad news, Declan waited in the hall, watched closely by Tim. The hall smelled of chips. Bright ornaments clung to the walls in no particular order or design, souvenirs for the most part of holidays in the sun.

The big man seemed full of directionless rage. All that body bulk and nothing to do with it but flex deltoids and triceps in competition with others similarly muscle-bound. His body began and ended in itself, muscle for muscle's sake, strength for the sake of strength, or perhaps all for what little vanity a man could snatch in those moments of self-demonstration. If he decided to attack again, Declan knew he could fell him with a single well-placed blow. Brain won over brawn most times, directed training over mere preparation. And sometimes sheer ruthlessness conquered everything, as it had done at Castletown House.

The body-builder stood and glared at Declan, making himself appear larger than he was. Not a word passed between them. Declan suspected that he himself was sorrier about Seamus Cosgrave's little death than his brother-in-law.

A quarter of an hour later, Christine came out again. Her eyes were wet, her voice caught in her throat. Someone had cared for Seamus, then.

'She says she'll go with you on one condition. She wants them dead, the ones who killed her Seamus. You've to promise her that.'

He shook his head. He had half expected it.

'You know I can't promise a thing like that.'

'She says she'll do it herself otherwise, she won't be responsible. Better it's yourself, she says, better it's kept legal.'

'It wouldn't be legal,' he said. 'And you know she wouldn't stand a chance. Not against men like that.'

'That's her condition.'

He closed his eyes. He wanted to make up for the sleep he had lost, to push away the headache he could feel sneaking up on him with a blunt instrument in its hand. If Teresa Cosgrave stayed in order to avenge her husband, she would without question follow him quickly to his grave. The body-builder would never take the children in, Declan was sure of it. It fell to him, then, to face that responsibility. He thought of Máiréad, choked on his own helplessness. There were just so many deaths he could take responsibility for. He opened his eyes.

'All right,' he said, his voice low. 'I promise I'll do what I can. There can't be a guarantee, because there never is in these matters. But I'll do my best.'

A minute later, Teresa, red-eyed and blank-faced, came out of the living room. She was dressed in a red woollen cardigan and a green plaid skirt, neither of which fitted her well.

'Get the children,' she said to her sister. 'It's time we were on our way.'

She looked then at Declan. He could not decide if it was a look of entreaty or hatred.

He took a long, winding route to Killiney, driving at various speeds, taking short cuts faster than was sensible, constantly checking in his rear-view mirrors for a sign that they were being followed. Teresa sat in the front seat with her youngest on her lap; the other five children were squashed into the rear. They sat motionless and stony-faced, knowing that something terrible was happening to them, not yet sure what it was exactly, fearing how it would end.

Teresa did not address a single word to him. From time to time, Declan caught her looking his way, and each time he looked in another direction, unable to meet her eye. He knew she held him responsible for her husband's death, and he guessed that, had it not been for his supposed power to protect her and punish

Seamus's killers, she would have killed him with her bare hands as he drove.

The irony was that he had very little power of protection or punishment to offer her. A death for Seamus's death was almost certainly out of his reach. Even as they circled the white suburbs of south Dublin, Amina faced a threat more meaningless and a death as hard as any Seamus Cosgrave had ever met. Seamus, at least, had gone to his execution knowing the reason for it; Amina might die without even knowing the identity of her killers, much less the true motive behind their action.

They arrived at Declan's house. It was the only bolt-hole he had to offer them, and a very temporary one at that. Concepta might come back at any time. To take them to Craigpatrick was out of the question, and he had not even considered it. In Killiney at least the Cosgrave family should be safe from prying eyes for a few days. And perhaps they would not need that long, if Martin Fitzsimmons could fix up an earlier departure for them – assuming that it could still be done. Declan put the thought out of his head. He would have to cross that bridge as and when he came to it.

He showed Teresa the well-stocked freezer, told her how to operate the central heating, the washing-machine, the dishwasher. She followed him numbly, listening without real interest. The children, still subdued, sat in a rear room looking out over a dull, storm-flattened sea. Declan wondered if they had ever come this far in their lives before. Perhaps the oldest boy could go to the Gaeltacht as planned, perhaps the Brothers would take him in permanently, rescue him from the fate that awaited him somewhere on the drug-dead streets of the city's north.

As he was getting into the car to go, Teresa came out to him.

'He said I was to give you this,' she murmured, pressing a sheet of folded paper into his hand. 'If he didn't make it. I'd have torn it up, only it might help you find the ones that did it.'

Declan unfolded the note and read.

A man caled Aboo Hitter arrived in Belfast two dais ago he's joind up with Maureen O'Dalaigh & is now in Monaghan Cownty with an ASU I dont know were, hes looking for Moslems Is this the one you was after?

When Declan looked up, Teresa had gone back into the house. He folded the paper again and put it into his pocket.

As he came out of the drive onto the road, a man in the back of a small Dublin Corporation van parked opposite pressed the 'send' button on his two-way radio.

'Five to Base. Bird One has left his nest.'

CHAPTER FIFTY-ONE

Dublin
1024 hours

Declan telephoned Martin Fitzsimmons from a phone booth in Bray.

'I can't talk now, Declan. Meet me in half an hour on the Macartney Bridge on Baggot Street.'

Declan drove straight to town and parked on Wilton Terrace. A blue Peugeot drew in several yards away. It had tucked in behind him just past the American embassy, taking over from the black Ford that had been tailing him from Blackrock. They were taking no chances.

Martin was waiting by the side of the canal, dressed in a beige trenchcoat and black scarf. Declan joined him, and they stared at the water for a time. No boats went past. On Herbert Place, a woman walked with a child. A cyclist went past, wearing a grey cape. They were set off from the city here.

Declan showed Martin the note Seamus Cosgrave had left him.

'It doesn't make a lot of sense, does it, Declan?'

'On the contrary, I think it does. I've been thinking about who this "Aboo Hitter" could be. It didn't take me long. His name in Arabic is Abu Hida. He's Hizbollah's top hitman, the very best; or he was when I was in Lebanon. His father is Shaykh Mu'in Usayran, one of the hostages. They'll have sent him to find him and take him out.'

'With the help of the IRA.'

'Could the hostages be in Monaghan?'

Martin shook his head.

'That's one place they aren't,' he said.

'How can you be sure?'

'A bag was left outside the College of Surgeons this morning, Declan. A canvas bag, a sort of satchel. A security guard had his attention drawn to it by a student. No-one knows how long it had been there.

'There was a label tied to the handle, with a typed message: "For the Taoiseach". We don't know if Mangan was intended or Ciaran Clark. Perhaps that doesn't matter. Anyway, the guard thought twice about opening the bag, and contacted the Gardaí. They sent a car over right away. I think they were under the impression that another body had been dumped.'

'And had it been?'

Fitzsimmons shook his head, almost regretfully, it seemed to Declan.

'No,' he said. 'The bag was much too small for that. But I have to tell you that the Garda who opened it is already off duty and undergoing treatment. The bag contained hands, Declan – human hands, all severed neatly at the wrist.'

'Surgically?' Even as he asked the question, Declan felt the bile rise in his throat. What he really wanted to ask was: 'were they a man's or a woman's hands?' But he could not bring himself even to imagine an answer.

'No. The pathologist thinks they were severed by a blow with a heavy, sharp instrument, almost certainly an axe.'

'Has the body been found yet?'

'Not "the body", Declan. The bodies, if there are any. There were seven hands in the bag.'

'Christ Almighty.'

'That isn't seven bodies, though. There are three pairs and a single hand, which would mean a maximum of four bodies.'

'He said one a day.'

'I know. On reflection, we don't know that he has broken his word on that. There might be one body somewhere, waiting to be found. The hands may have been cut from people who are still alive. According to the pathologist, the poor devils were probably not dead when their hands were removed.'

'Who are you using?'

Two men walked past on the other side of the canal. One glanced briefly in their direction, then away again.

'O'Hara. He's got a good team working on it now. But there's not a lot the hands on their own can tell us.'

Declan looked down on the flat, slow-moving water. Wastepaper floated downstream, an old wrapper from a bag of bread. He shivered.

'It's like a sick joke,' he said.

'Yes. Perhaps that's exactly what it is.' Martin paused. 'Declan,' he went on, 'I think you should know that there were no women's hands among those we found.'

What Declan felt was less relief than renewed anxiety, almost unbearable anxiety. He could not rid his mind of a single image: Amina's hand reaching for his that day beside the river, and the warmth of it, and the way it moved gently in his own, completely enwrapped.

'You're certain the hands came from the hostages?' Even a scrap of hope was better than none.

Martin nodded.

'There was a cassette in the bag with them.' He reached into his pocket and drew out a single audio cassette, unlabelled. 'This is a copy I had made for you. I doubt you'll get any more out of it than we've been able to. The voice is pretty clear. American. Texan, according to the boffins. The content's pretty crazy, but it does give some sort of explanation for the business with the hands.'

'Were there any witnesses who might have seen the bag being left at the college?'

'We're interviewing students and staff now, but it's a slim chance.'

'You said something about knowing the hostages weren't being held in Monaghan.'

'O'Hara found traces of salt on the hands and in the fabric of the bag. Sea salt. The bag was saturated with it. O'Hara is sure they're being kept at the coast. It narrows down the search considerably. And it rules out places like Monaghan.'

'Well, it's only three and a half thousand miles of coastline or thereabouts to search, now, isn't it?'

Martin smiled.

'You're forgetting your country's heritage, man. Did you never read Peig Sayers or any of that lot in school? Has it not occurred to you that they could be on an island?'

282

'I'll give that some thought.' He paused. Now he had come this far, he had to be sure it was worth going on. 'Tell me, Martin, should we be keeping on with this? Surely it doesn't matter now who finds the hostages, so long as they're found. The thing between Harker and myself – well, that's a different matter, it can wait.'

'I'm not so sure, Declan.'

'What do you mean?'

Martin hesitated.

'Let's keep moving, Declan.'

They started walking along Herbert Place, in the direction of Huband Bridge.

'Declan, have you ever heard of a thing called the Scimitar Network?'

Declan shook his head.

'Nor had I until yesterday evening. I couldn't work out why it was so important for MI5 to take control of this business. There are obvious reasons, of course, but I didn't think any of them were enough. And the more I looked at what Harker was doing, the more I became convinced he was playing for time. I started to get more interested in Harker than in the hostages.'

'Did you, now?'

'Harker has been communicating with his boss in Belfast the long way round, via a secure link-up in the British embassy. It took my lads till seven o'clock last night to find a way into the system. It's still imperfect, but I've been able to tap several messages. In three of them I came across a reference to something called Scimitar.

'Now, that sounded somewhat Middle Eastern to me, so I thought I should ask around, see if it meant anything to people in the know. Within Europe, responsibility for collating intelligence on Arab terrorist suspects rests with the Germans. So I thought I'd ask some of my German friends if this rang any bells with them. But before I tell you what one of them told me, I'm going to have to explain something you may not know.'

He paused. They had come to Huband Bridge now, and were starting back down Percy Place.

'In March 1990,' Martin went on, 'after the reunification of Germany, department heads in the BfV started restructuring their counter-intelligence operations. From now on, Allied intelligence agencies that had been treated as friendly were to be considered as foreign; there were proposals for the mounting of operations against the USA, France, and Britain. That was only natural, considering the number of operations the people in question had already been carrying out on German soil.

'At the end of 1991, electronic installations in Western Germany that had been under American, French, and British control, were taken over by the Germans. But they didn't just get hardware: they found ways to tap into files that had previously been closed to them.

'The man I spoke to last night was Helmut Kuchler, an assistant director of the Bundesamt für Nachrichtendienst, their foreign intelligence service. I asked him what Scimitar referred to, and he told me.

'During the Gulf War, the Americans and British ran an important espionage network inside Iraq. The network was known as Scimitar, and it was set up to run a highly secret operation known as Project Babylon. Quite simply, Project Babylon was designed to locate and destroy a top secret installation at which a form of sarin nerve gas was being developed, together with the means of delivering it. All the Allies know is that, like sarin, this is a binary gas, that it is reputed to be a thousand times more powerful than the formula on which it's based, and that it is still in production.

'Apparently, Scimitar was successful. A report reached a CIA tracking station in Saudi Arabia that the site had been identified and mapped, and orders were given to get the agents out. An SAS team was sent in for this purpose, but the Scimitar agents never turned up.

'It was assumed that Scimitar had been blown and the agents – sixteen in all – killed. But soon after the war ended, word began to leak out that they had been captured and moved to various locations around the Middle East. They are now being held hostage in five different countries, by different extremist groups. Unlike previous hostages, their presence has been kept a secret from the public. Their families believe they've been killed in covert operations, and nobody else knows they exist. But they're being used as levers to negotiate the release of terrorists. The British and the Americans want them out, Declan – they want them out very badly indeed.'

They stopped. Two lovers passed, hand in hand. Traffic went by on Baggot Street.

'Are you telling me . . . ?' Declan began.

'That was all my German friend knew.'

'But you say Harker and Willoughby are involved in this.'

'Yes.'

'They couldn't have set up the conference, Martin. That was Pádraig Pearse's own initiative from the start, I know it was.'

'No doubt about that, Declan. Though I reckon he may have been influenced at a later stage as to whom he should invite. Or, more probably, Ciaran Clark was.'

'Jesus, Martin, it was a godsend to them. Once we'd set up the conference . . .'

'The CIA and MI5 moved in. And now they have their own hostages.'

'While they negotiate the release of the Scimitar agents, Harker stretches things out down here.' Declan paused, thinking. 'They won't have used their own people for this. Too dangerous if anything went wrong. I'd guess it's an independent group that can't be traced back to any intelligence agency. In that case, how does Willoughby control the hostage-takers?'

'MI5 have their own man with them. Willoughby referred to a communication he'd had from him two days ago. Declan, you aren't going to like this.'

'I don't understand.'

'The go-between is a man called Peter Musgrave. I think you already know of him.'

A close silence tightened round both men. Traffic and passers-by and a radio blaring near at hand were all consumed in it. Declan closed his eyes, and for a moment he was in the ice-cream parlour again, staring into the eyes of his daughter's killer. And the face became a photograph in a file, a photograph with a name and an identity.

Martin Fitzsimmons put out his hand and squeezed Declan's arm.

'Declan, I can get you out of this. Not easily, but there are ways. A new identity . . .'

'You can't pin an identity on a dead man, Martin. I have to go on with this.'

'Is it the woman?'

'Amina? How'd you know about her?'

'God, Declan, sometimes I think you were born yesterday. It's in your file.'

Declan shook his head. Thinking of Amina, he realized that he'd not been in touch with Concepta since going underground. He wondered how she was coping on her own.

'What matters isn't in any file, Martin. Take care of yourself. I'll be in touch.'

'Declan . . .' Martin reached out a hand holding a card on which a number had been scrawled. 'I don't know how long I can keep you in touch with what's happening at this end. They're tightening security across the board. If you need help and I'm not contactable, use this number. You don't know the man, and you won't need his name. Just tell him who you are and he'll do what he can.'

Declan took the card and slipped it into his pocket.

'Thanks, Martin. Keep your nose clean. I'll send you a postcard from the seaside.'

Martin watched as Declan walked away, crossing the road to Wilton Terrace. He'd left his own car on Haddington Road. As he turned to go, he saw the lovers coming back, still hand in hand, engrossed in one another, and he thought of Declan and the lover he had found only to lose again. He smiled at them, and the girl turned slightly and smiled back. He did not see the knife in her free hand, but he felt it like something burning as it entered his stomach and cut him open to the breastbone. There was no time to understand. The last thing he saw in his mind as it closed was her pretty face and the smile on her lips. And then he drowned in blood.

CHAPTER FIFTY-TWO

Security Liaison Office
Thiepval Barracks
Lisburn
12 October
1418 hours

Malcolm Blake thought the old man was looking rough. He had been up all night and much of the morning, working with Rigby and himself on the new operation. The key obstacle to their success was the lack of detailed information regarding the whereabouts of Conor Melaugh and his ASU. 'Monaghan' was far too vague.

Willoughby had not the remotest intention of notifying the authorities in Dublin that a Northern Command ASU was active on their territory. That could make an operation of the sort he had in mind unworkable, simply because of the increased military and police presence they would meet in the area. But without on-the-spot reconnaissance it would be very hard indeed to get intelligence of the quality they needed. Operation Kickback seemed doomed from the outset.

They needed a breakthrough, and they needed it quickly. At fourteen-eighteen hours, they got it.

A communications analyst working at the US National Security Agency's monitoring station at Menwith Hill in Yorkshire, had logged a call from the Irish Republic to Baalbek in Lebanon between 0709 and 0714 hours that morning. The call was recorded and details sent as a matter of routine to K Division at Britain's GCHQ in Cheltenham, where it went onto the desk of one of the sixty staff handling Irish communications.

All communications between Ireland and the Middle East had been scrutinized since the raid on Castletown House, and this one was passed straightaway to MI5's T Branch at Thames House. A second copy had already gone from Menwith Hill to the secret US Middle East Collection Ten unit known as MC10.

Late that morning, a tape-recording of the call was played through by an Arabic-speaking Middle East affairs specialist from K Branch, but it was not until shortly after two o'clock in the afternoon that details trickled through to MI5 Northern Ireland and were passed to Alan Rigby.

Willoughby sat down. His face was grey from lack of sleep and his bad temper was beginning to show.

'What have you got? It had better be good.'

'It is good,' said Rigby. 'A telephone call was made yesterday morning to a number in Baalbek from a small town in Monaghan, Ballybay. The recipient was Ihsan 'Abbas, a member of Hizbollah's national council. K Division are not yet sure of the identity of the caller, but there is a strong possibility that he is Abu' l-Fath Muhammad Usayran, better known to our counter-terrorist people as Abu Hida.'

'Say that in English.'

'A hitman, Geoffrey. Their best. When you read the transcript, you'll understand. He's come to rescue one of the hostages. The ASU's been put back on the road as back-up. Maureen O'Dalaigh's holding his hand. We've got them, Geoffrey. The nicest little package there ever was.'

CHAPTER FIFTY-THREE

Craigpatrick
12 October
1545 hours

The journey back west had passed without visible incident. While Declan had been busy talking with Martin Fitzsimmons, a small homing device had been fitted behind the rear bumper of his car. The vehicle that followed him to Clare never approached closer than within a mile, and though he used his rear-view mirror diligently, and took unexpected turnings, and waited round bends for the car behind to pass, he was at no time aware that he was being tailed.

Grainne Walsh was waiting for him in the long garden at the rear of the house, watching the late-afternoon sunlight shift and change on the lake waters. She had found it a hard day keeping the team's morale high in Declan's absence.

'I'm sorry,' he said, sitting on the bench beside her. 'It was very important.'

'Dominic Lawlor told me you had to get an informer out of trouble.'

'That's right.'

'And did you?'

He shook his head. Out on the lake, a heron flashed in a pulse across dim waters. Had Seamus Cosgrave ever set eyes on a view like this even once in his dark life, wondered Declan. Had he ever smelled air as fresh? Seen sunlight so perceptible? Heard so much birdsong gathered in a single place? Fished in a deep lake, walked on wet grass that was not littered with broken bottles, made love in a pine wood? He and his like were all trapped in viciousness and despair and envy, concrete and debt and unlovely, breaking things. How desperately he must have wanted a new life.

Grainne understood the shake of Declan's head, knew the end that awaited all informers, the guilt their handlers inevitably felt when it came. It had happened to her twice. The second man's wife had killed herself and her family in despair. After that, Grainne had refused to do one-on-one handling again.

Declan told her about Cosgrave's ill-spelled note, the reference to 'Aboo Hitter', the link that had been made with Maureen O'Dalaigh. She nodded. It had started to make a warped sort of sense.

'I think this man was in Belfast two nights ago,' she said. There had been further news of the gun battle at Andersonstown, and Liam Kennedy had been able to extract clearer details from various sources in Dublin, using a secure modem and an up-to-date password supplied by Martin Fitzsimmons. Grainne told Declan what they had learned.

'The gun battle has a hitman's mark all over it,' she said. 'But it may have been a serious mistake. The British won't leave a stone unturned in order to run him to earth. He may not find it as easy as he thought to get to the hostages. If MI5 are looking for him, they'll know he's there the moment he shows his hand.'

'They aren't after him,' said Declan. 'They're after O'Dalaigh and the ASU.'

He explained about the ambush at Malone House, about MI5's need for revenge. But he did not tell her about Austin McKeown or the connection to the attempt on his own life.

'This complicates things,' Grainne said.

'It gives us an extra chance to find the hostages. If we can locate Abu Hida, he may be able to lead us to them.'

'What if he gets there first?'

'He may be able to do the job for us.'

Grainne looked at the lake and back again.

'What if his job is to kill them, not to set them free?'

'You think you're clever, you think you're smart, you think God smiles on you. Well, I'm not clever and I'm not smart, hell no, but I know you're all full of shit.'

The voice rang through the library like a child's voice in a church, sudden and out of place. Declan could sense at once the unease it instilled in everyone. They listened with the barely polite distance of men and women for whom religion had never been a matter for unnatural excitement or outrageous sentiment. Each one of them was the product of Ireland's Catholic educational system, and even if most of them had long ago lost their belief in the supernatural realities of their faith, none would have thought for a moment to replace it with the excesses of Protestant fundamentalism.

Myles O'hUiginn sat hunched in a corner, seemingly more interested in his own thoughts than in the ravings of a Texan preacher. But he alone followed the drift of the sermon, he alone saw significance in the allusions, in the eccentric use of biblical quotation.

'Hell, that's why I was sent. To break the seals on the book. To unloose the seven seals on the seven scrolls. "And I saw in the right hand of him that sat on the throne a book written within and on the backside, sealed with seven seals. And I saw a strong angel proclaiming with a loud voice, Who is worthy to open the book, and to loose the seals thereof?"'

The expression on the professor's face changed. He was no longer abstracted, but seemed like a man coming awake after a long sleep. The voice went on, proclamatory, triumphal, self-congratulatory, and the longer the voice spoke, the more troubled the look on Myles O'hUiginn's face became.

'In the story of David and Goliath, we know that the army of Israel is an antitype for mankind and the Philistines an antitype for the forces of Satan, just as the Assyrians in the book of Isaiah stand for the United States and the two tribes for the Branch of David.'

O'hUiginn almost shot out of his chair.
'Holy God,' he said.
'What's wrong?' asked Declan, pausing the tape.
'It's nothing, Declan. Jus . . . He just confirmed something I had only suspected till now. Go on with the tape. I want to hear how it ends.'

They listened to the complex explanation of the prophecy from the Book of Daniel, again only O'hUiginn following the preacher's train of thought.

'Tonight, I asked God what He wanted me to do now. I prayed for guidance, and I opened the Bible, and I read the following verse in the second book of Samuel. "And David commanded his young men, and they slew them, and cut off their hands and their feet, and hanged them up over the pool of Hebron."'

The sermon continued to its by now foregone conclusion.

'I've heard that your own law says it's right to cut off the hand of a thief, so I guess that's what we'll do.'

But the tape did not end there. The tape continued to play as Ezekiel set up his axe and block on the podium, as the four selected hostages were brought to the front, as the first blow of the axe rang out into a great silence. Only the terrible cry that followed the blow prompted Declan to stand up and, with a shaking hand, switch off the machine. No-one said a word. No-one could bear to look at his or her neighbour. They sat like that for a very long time.

At six o'clock the telephone in the study rang.
'I'd like to speak to Declan Carberry.'
'This is Carberry. Who am I speaking to?'
'We've never met, but I think you know my name. This is Anthony Harker.'
Declan did not respond at once. The bite and crunch of the axe were still in his head, inexpungible, and the cry that had filled the library until it had been snapped into silence.
'Yes,' he said finally. 'I've heard of you. What do you want?'
He did not know how Harker had found him; there were so many ways, and what did it matter which one they had used?
'You've done very well, Mr Carberry. The Irish government has every reason to be proud of you. You have served them generously. I am much struck personally by your integrity and resourcefulness. I admire you.
'But what's the point of going on any longer? The cabal that instructed you to act independently has been dissolved. Your

brother-in-law has resigned his office and is now a private citizen again. Seán Roche has taken early retirement. Eoin Ceannt has been dismissed. Martin Fitzsimmons is dead.'

'What?'

The bare statement hit Declan like a blow to the stomach.

'He died this morning in what the police are treating as a revenge killing. Someone stabbed him to death just off Baggot Street, by the Grand Canal. Apparently he was seen talking to an unidentified man a little earlier. The police are putting together a description.'

There was a short, deliberate pause. Declan felt his flesh crawl. He bit his lip hard.

'Go on,' he said.

'If anyone's to blame for this illegal operation, it isn't you or your team. You were asked to undertake a mission by your superiors, you had no choice in the matter, you thought you were acting for the best. The Taoiseach has asked me to tell you that the situation has now changed and that you should consider your previous orders rescinded. For the present, you'll be reinstated in your post as head of the Special Detective Unit. But I can assure you privately that, as soon as this hostage business is over, there will be promotions to several senior posts. You shall have first choice.'

'And if I refuse?'

'I really can't believe you'd be that stupid, Mr Carberry. You have no viable option. If you truly want to help the hostages, you'll be of far greater use working with us than against us. We need your expertise and experience. There's nothing you can do on your own. Even if you found the hostages – what then? What can you do for them? You have no army, no police force, no hostage rescue unit at your disposal – just a handful of desk officers. In the end, you'd just have to hand your information over to us, to allow us to mount a proper rescue operation, or to negotiate from a position of greater strength.

'So why not do it now? Why not accept the inevitable and stop playing this silly game?'

'This silly game, as you call it, is at least one I can play under rules I understand, with fellow players I can trust.'

'Are you saying you don't trust your own government, your own Prime Minister?'

'You're not the Taoiseach, mister, and so far you're the only person I've spoken to. To be honest, I'm not even sure Ciaran Clark is entitled to the office in any legitimate sense. The fact is that I don't recognize Clark's authority or yours. Or MI5's, for that matter.'

For all his bluster, Declan knew that what Harker said was true, and that he was skating on very thin ice indeed. He had no right to jeopardize the careers, perhaps the lives, of the men and women working with him. And Harker had not been wrong to say that the hostages stood a much better chance if the operation to find them was fully co-ordinated and linked to well-trained, properly-equipped military units. The legality of Ciaran Clark's rise to power or the propriety of MI5's presence in the Republic were mere sideshows beside the central drama of freeing the hostages and bringing their abductors to justice.

But he also knew that Harker was working to a hidden agenda. The business of the hands showed that, whoever was in charge of the hostage's immediate fate, it was not MI5. Willoughby, Harker, and their superiors could afford to let a few Muslims die or be mutilated, if it helped put extra pressure on the people holding the members of the Scimitar network. But Declan was beginning to think that they had entered into an unholy alliance with someone operating to a very different agenda indeed, someone whose voice they had just listened to, someone who would kill all the hostages if it suited him.

Under the circumstances, his own operation was as vital to the safety of the hostages as it had ever been. The others would have to take their chances, of course: he would offer them the choice of going on or taking Harker's offer. But he himself would continue the search, even if he had to do so alone.

'You can have my resignation,' he told Harker. 'I'll write a letter tonight and fax it to Mr Clark in the morning.'

'You misunderstand me, Mr Carberry. That is not an option. You will work with me, or I will have you placed under arrest. There are no intermediate positions. The same condition applies to every member of your team. Those are the only options I am prepared to consider.'

'Then you can go to hell.'

There was a long silence. Declan expected the other man to slam down the phone, but he did not. When Harker's voice came again, it was no longer soothing, no longer gentle. All the affability had gone, as when a cat, stretching, unsheathes his claws and looks round slowly, scenting prey.

'You still do not understand. If there is a hell for creatures like us, then you, not I, are travelling in that direction. I am not speaking from Dublin, but from a mobile phone no more than a thousand yards from where you are now. Craigpatrick is surrounded by an SAS unit acting under the authority of your own Ranger Wing. They have received direct orders to kill anyone attempting to leave the grounds. You have half an hour in which to talk the situation over with your colleagues. If you do not come out at the end of that period, the SAS have instructions to enter the house and take you by force. And I think it only fair to warn you that any attempt to resist, however token, will be dealt with ruthlessly.'

CHAPTER FIFTY-FOUR

Ballybay
1805 hours

It had been a long, punishing day, and it was far from over.
Weapons had been brought in earlier from Dublin and stored in
a nearby cache. The evening had been set aside for familiarization
and training in the use of the third-generation light intensifiers
with which the guns would be fitted and the thermal imaging
devices capable of seeing through smoke, mist, and light undergrowth. No-one would go to bed until midnight or later – much
later if they proved slow to learn.

During the morning, and again in the afternoon, Abu Hida had
earned the grudging respect of the ASU. At his request, Maureen
had told them nothing of the siege in Andersonstown. Nor had
he said a word about his life in Lebanon, the missions he had
been on, the men he had killed. He had simply set out into the
countryside with them, through dark woods, across swollen
rivers, to the tops of steep hills. And all the time he had pushed
them harder than they had ever been pushed in their lives.
Pushed to run, to remain still, to hide, to break cover, to fire, to
hold fire.

He had never raised his voice, never asked them to do what
he did not do first. At first they had been reluctant to follow him.
But as the day wore on, their shame at being left behind had
grown, and in the end they had tried everything he had asked.
And where there had been no verbal reproaches to punish their
failure, now there was only praise for each small achievement.

They were in the kitchen, devouring their first meal since
breakfast. No-one spoke. Abu Hida took only bread and cheese.

Maureen had gone to the village to make a phone call. Abu Hida found himself missing her. All day long she had outperformed the men in the group, and at the end of it she had seemed almost untouched by her exertions.

There was a sound of footsteps on the path outside. Abu Hida got up and went to the window. Maureen was coming towards the house, and as he watched her coming up the path, he felt a surge of certainty rush through him: she had the information he had been hoping for. There was a spring in her step that had not been there earlier, when she had set off.

As she came through the door he knew it was true. He could see a light in her eyes, a light of triumph that he had seen a few times before, when she had caught up with him or mastered a difficult task he had set her.

How he regretted the exigencies of his life, the confinement of all emotion to the struggle and its demands. He could see so much in a woman's eyes, read what lay unread behind the veil. Maureen O'Dalaigh had never covered her face with a piece of cloth, but she had learned how to wear a different sort of mask, how to hide behind false smiles, expressionless features, the long, bitter stare that gave nothing away. But he could read deeper than that, he could reach out and all but touch the raw emotion that lay so close to the surface. Triumph and fear and excitement and – he admitted it – lust. And the regret in him was like a stone, pulling him steadily earthwards.

'They found a body on the Dingle peninsula,' she said, slamming the door behind her. She was there now, facing him, her eyes alive. She had brought him what he wanted, and in return she might hope to have him for herself.

'An old man,' she said, 'by the name of Michael Deighan. A harmless old soul by all accounts, one that did odd jobs about the place and never got in anybody's way. They found him on the beach below Ballyoughteragh this morning, his brains blown out.'

'Well, sure old men are meddlers,' said Conor Melaugh. 'He could have been shot for a hundred reasons. We'll need more than an auld fella with his head blew in.'

'Shut up, Conor, and listen, will you? There are strangers on Inis Tuaisceart. Americans, or so the locals say, though they've seen little of them. They bought a load of supplies in Dingle early in the summer. Said they were a church of some sort, that they'd

297

come for a retreat. The locals say they were friendly enough, but kept to themselves once they got to the island. All men, no question of impropriety. They were left alone: people in those parts respect retreats, they're part of their own culture. As far as anyone knows, they're still on the island praying; but from time to time a few will come ashore in a boat and drive inland. They keep cars near a cove facing the island.'

'Where is this place?' Abu Hida was eager to see it on a map. He sensed a rightness about it: an unnecessary, violent death, strangers who kept to themselves, frequent trips inland.

Maureen found a map of Ireland and spread it across the table, clearing cups and plates away to make room.

'Here,' she said, pointing to the south-west, to the Dingle peninsula. 'Here is where the old man would have been found. Just south is the cove where the cars are kept. And this is Inis Tuaisceart.'

Abu Hida nodded. An island just off the coast. It was an ideal spot.

'Are there many people on the island itself?' he asked.

Maureen shook her head and explained what had happened to the Blasket islanders. Abu Hida smiled inwardly. It made a pattern, he sensed the coherence of it deep down. He would have chosen just such a place himself.

'We leave tomorrow,' he said. 'At dawn.'

CHAPTER FIFTY-FIVE

Declan put down the phone. His hand was shaking. He took a deep breath and made an effort to steady it. His heart was racing, his mind hurrying to keep pace with it. For over a minute, he sat still at Pádraig Pearse's heavy old desk, thinking quickly through the possibilities.

The easiest thing was to go along with Harker; Declan was sure his team would all have promotions and any little bonuses they might ask for. They'd risked enough, and were now embroiled in something none of them had bargained for. At the price of silence, he himself could probably ask for and receive any one of several government posts. Maybe even Ciaran Clark's old job. Or an ambassadorship somewhere like Paris or Washington, or as representative to the UN in New York. There was nothing Harker and his friends could not do. And the new Taoiseach could afford to be generous.

He was almost cynical enough to consider it. After all, he had lived close enough to government circles to know what went on, had been narrowly enough involved with the world of intelligence to know that his refusal to cooperate would make little or no difference. The fate of the hostages would be decided – had already been decided – by men more powerful and more cynical than himself. And if he could ensure that their calculations involved Amina's release, it was all one to him. If he wanted, he could just retire and go somewhere with Amina. It was what he most wanted. The world could take care of itself.

On the other hand . . .

He opened the door. Grainne was waiting in the next room.

'Get everyone together, Grainne. As quickly as possible.'

A few minutes later, the entire team had gathered in the library. Declan glanced at his watch. They had twenty-five minutes left in which to make their minds up.

'Liam,' he said, 'I want you to get in touch with the Search-and-Rescue unit at Shannon airport. Use radio, not the telephone. Use an SDU emergency code. Tell them we need a Dauphin to pick up one or more passengers from this house twenty-five minutes from now. Say it's an emergency, that there are people in need of urgent medical help. They've done it before, they know the routine.'

When Liam was gone, Declan went to the front of the room.

'You'll have guessed by now that something's up. I've just had a phone call from Harker. He knows where we are and what we're doing, and he wants us to stop.'

He went on to tell them the main points of his conversation.

'So there it is,' he said. 'I think you can take him at his word. You're all free to go, with no stains against your records. It's worked out better than any of you could have hoped for.'

'Why the helicopter?' asked Dominic Lawlor.

'It's for anyone who wants to use it. If anyone wants to leave, they'll be dropped wherever they want to go. I don't recommend it, but I think the option should be left open.'

'Are you taking it, sir?' Grainne asked.

'Yes.'

'You don't trust him?'

He shrugged.

'I trust him to carry out his promises as far as this unit is concerned. You were brought into this business by the ex-Taoiseach and leading members of the security services. There's no blame in that. Harker has no reason to wish any of you harm. Quite the opposite. You could be useful to him.'

'But not you?'

He shook his head.

'No,' he said, 'not me.'

Grainne looked hard at him. There was something he wasn't telling them.

Liam Kennedy came in.

'They're on their way, sir. They wanted authorization, and I gave your name. I hope that wasn't a mistake.'

Declan shrugged.

'Too late to worry about that now. How long before they get here?'

'Fifteen minutes. A single Dauphin as requested.'

'Good. Go outside and get ready to illuminate the helicopter pad. The light switches are in a box by the kitchen door. Don't do anything until the 'copter's right overhead.'

'We can't all get out in a Dauphin, sir.'

'I know that, Liam. I'm not expecting everyone to go. Now, get on with it.'

Liam left. A tense silence fell on the room. It lasted half a minute, then a voice broke in from the back.

'Tell me, Declan, could this hostage crisis have any connections with an American intelligence agency?'

Myles O'hUiginn was on his feet. He had the little cassette in his hand. Declan thought he seemed agitated.

'Myles, this is no longer your concern.'

'You brought me here, Declan. You asked me to do a job. I'm still doing it. I asked you if the business we're involved in could have any links with the FBI. Or the CIA perhaps. Well, could it?'

Declan hesitated, then nodded.

'The answer is yes, almost certainly.'

'I see.'

Myles remained standing, pensive and ill-at-ease.

'Declan, can you make contact with the FBI? Can you do it without their knowing what's going on? There's something I have to find out.'

'I don't know. It's possible. It depends on what you want to know.'

O'hUiginn lifted the tape.

'I'll play this again for you later, Declan. It may not mean much to you on its own, nor to anyone else who's heard it so far. What I can tell you is that it reveals the identity of the kidnappers.'

'It's too late to worry about that now, Myles.'

'No, it isn't, Declan. Not when you know who this is, what he's capable of.'

'All right, then — who is it?'

'There's just one problem, Declan.'

'Yes, what's that?'

'The person on this tape, the one giving the sermon . . . As far as anyone knows . . .'

O'hUiginn's normally confident voice trailed away.

'Yes? What's wrong, Myles?'

'Until this evening, I would have been prepared to swear that he was dead.'

CHAPTER FIFTY-SIX

Craigpatrick
1826 hours

The helicopter landed minutes before Harker's deadline ended. It was an Air Corps 365F, one of a new shipment bought with EC funds as part of a scheme to reduce shipping fatalities off the Atlantic coast. Blades still turning, it sat on the small illuminated pad at the bottom of the garden, from which Pádraig Pearse had often taken off for unannounced visits to the capital or some provincial centre.

Declan ordered the lights switched off. Darkness returned, quick and heavy. Most of the team had decided to take their chances with Harker and Ciaran Clark. There was, in any case, little for them to do now that the operation had been blown. All the goodbyes had been said.

The others ran for the helicopter and were already boarding by the time the SAS unit could react. Declan reckoned that they would think twice before opening fire on an unarmed Search-and-Rescue craft. Not even Harker would find that easy to explain away.

Declan went to the front of the helicopter and produced his identity papers. The pilot stared at him.

'Look, whatever your name is,' he said, 'will you tell me just what the hell's going on here?' He was a young man, a year or so out of the helicopter school at Baldonnel. 'I've just had a radio intercept from a Fiannóglach patrol. They wanted to warn me off, but I said it was an emergency. I can't just ignore . . .'

'Look, this *is* an emergency. We need to get out of here fast.'

'The message we received said I was to pick up people with

injuries. As far as I can see, the whole lot of you are fine. If you want me to fly you out of here, I'll need authorization.'

'Will this do?' Declan asked.

As he spoke, he produced a pistol from his inside pocket.

'You're going to be in a lot of trouble, mister. Your people have no authority to commandeer an Air Corps craft.'

'I'll take care of any trouble. All I want you to do is fly this thing.'

At that moment, the radio burst into life.

'SAR 248, this is Captain Loughran of the Ranger Wing. You are in a restricted zone under military surveillance. I require an explanation of your presence. Over.'

The pilot reached for the transmitter button, but Declan leaned in front of him and switched it off.

'I want this helicopter in the air now,' he said. 'You can tell the Fiannóglach whatever you like.'

The pilot hesitated a few seconds more, then, grasping the simple fact that the man with the gun was in the cabin and the Fiannóglach patrol outside, he turned the engine to full throttle.

'Close the doors,' he said, 'and strap yourselves in.'

Moments later, they were in the air.

'Head due north to begin with. And switch off your exterior lights — I don't want anyone tracking us visually. If you can keep below radar level, so much the better.'

'Jesus, man, those are the Slieve Aughty Mountains up there.'

'Forget the mountains. Stay with the lake as far north as Portumna, then take the road west for Loughrea. That'll take you through a gap in the hills. If you keep on due north from Loughrea, you'll cross a road heading east and west. It'll take you east over the hills to Ballinasloe. I'll give you further instructions when we get there.'

While they had been at Craigpatrick, Liam had set up three separate back-up sites with cars and equipment. If they were still in place, they could pick up what they needed and head on to another hideout. The question was, where?

Several factors restricted their choice. They dared not spend too much time in the air: before long, a combination of ground radar and military aircraft would track them down and force them to land. That meant they would have to keep behind hill cover and head for the nearest back-up location, just outside

Ballinasloe. From there, they could head in any direction, but Declan did not want to stray far from the coast: if the information Martin had given him was correct and the hostages really were being kept near the sea or on an island, it would be a mistake to head inland.

Outside, the night thickened. Without instruments, they would have crashed long ago. From time to time, the lights of a remote farmhouse winked at them, then were hidden behind a fold in the land. Beneath, the lake glistened in the grey light, a dull, unpolished rippling that seemed to go on forever. And then, in a single leap, it flashed and was gone. They were over the land now. And Declan knew that, somewhere, hands were reaching out for them.

They landed east of Ballinasloe, at the edge of deep woods. The silence after they touched down was astonishing in its complexity, as though the entire countryside had been struck dumb. Declan imagined small creatures in the fields and hedgerows, shivering in the darkness as they held their breath.

They managed to slide the helicopter underneath the branches of the outermost trees. It was not perfectly hidden, but would be invisible from the air. Liam disabled the radio and homing signal. The pilot was left in the cabin, tied up with a length of the thick rope used for fixing a line to a drifting vessel.

'I'm sorry about this,' Declan said. 'But it's in a good cause. Believe me.'

The young man said nothing. He watched them walk away into the night, heading for their rendezvous. He did not know exactly where it was, but he didn't think they would get that far. With only a little effort, he raised his knee and pressed the button on his chest that activated a homing device built into his suit. It beeped quietly in the darkness, regular and reassuring. Someone would be along soon.

CHAPTER FIFTY-SEVEN

1920 hours

They headed north-east on the N6 as far as Athlone, then turned east and finally south towards Tullamore. There they crossed the Grand Canal and headed on down into Offaly and Tipperary, the road turning with them through half-glimpsed fields. Declan reckoned that they had got clear of Ballinasloe with little time to spare. The helicopter would have been tracked somehow, the SAS squad sent after them.

A second car had gone west into Galway, driven by Dominic Lawlor. They would meet up again, if at all, at Desmond Castle, south of Limerick. Declan could only guess at Harker's resources. He and his people might very well know by now the registration numbers of the cars Declan's team had laid by for just this emergency. But Tim O'Meara had surrounded the purchase and disposal of the vehicles with more misleading information than Ireland had shrines to the Virgin, and there was a good chance that discovery was still days away.

Declan drove a deceptively old Volvo estate whose engine was as well tuned as that of a brand-new Mercedes. Tim did not just pick his cars up off a scrap heap, even if first appearances suggested otherwise. In rural Ireland, a new car would have attracted attention, but a serious breakdown in the wilds would have spelt trouble of another sort.

In the car with him were Grainne, Liam, and Myles O'hUiginn. The three men were dressed as priests, Grainne as a nun, wearing clerical outfits provided for just such a contingency. It was an obvious disguise, but none the less effective. Ireland is not England or even France, a priest or a nun is still a common sight, and country people still defer to the cloth. They carried well-forged papers identifying them as members of an African missionary order on a fund-raising drive. Their presumed destination changed every few miles, each time they turned or bypassed a likely town.

As he drove, Declan had time to think over what Myles had told them. There would be opportunity later to go over in detail the evidence that had given Myles the idea in the first place. But if he was right – and his confidence was considerable – Amina was in much greater danger than Declan could ever have imagined. There was a man in Washington who might be able to confirm or disconfirm Myles's suspicions, an old friend who owed Declan several favours. Once they had found a place for the night, Declan would try to make contact.

They passed through a tunnel of trees, on a road without end or beginning. In the darkness, the occasional lights of isolated farmhouses spoke of a long, aching loneliness, the desperation of wet fields. There was little fun out there, he thought. And only three traditional ways out: the priesthood, suicide, or drink. Women became nuns or mothers, and spent long lives uselessly sitting behind the windows of cold rooms, dreaming into the darkness, dreaming of God knew what.

In the countryside, it was hard to find a place where a small group like theirs arriving unannounced at a late hour would not draw attention. Declan thought of several friends with whom they might stay, but rejected all of them; it would be unfair to turn them into accomplices who might be arrested for helping them. He and the others were outcasts and criminals now, wanted by more than just the police – he had to keep that fact constantly in the forefront of his mind.

There was a Garda checkpoint just outside Templemore, and another near Thurles. They passed through each time by virtue of their cloth, but Declan knew that not all patrols out tonight would be local Garda units ready to nod at a black suit and a starched collar. They had to get off the road soon.

Suddenly, Declan remembered a Sunday outing he had made with Concepta and Máiréad several years before. During their drive, they had visited Ballynahow Castle, a circular fortification built by the Purcells in the sixteenth century. To get inside, it had been necessary to obtain a key from a nearby farmhouse, and

Declan now recalled that the farmer offered bed and breakfast. It was out of season, but he was sure they would make allowances for a party in holy orders.

He took the Nenagh road and turned right at a petrol station. The castle was a mile further, the farmhouse a mile and a half again. Declan stopped the car and got out, taking Liam with him. They spent fifteen minutes under the bonnet, getting the engine into less than perfect order. When it was done, they drove on to the farmhouse.

The door was opened by a teenaged girl dressed in clothes that might have been fashionable twenty years earlier, though 'fashionable' was probably stretching things a bit. She gaped at them, as much, surmised Declan, because they were human beings as because they were priests.

The girl seemed to respond to neither English nor Irish, and Declan had started to despair when a larger woman, dressed almost identically, materialized beside her.

'I'm terrible sorry, Father, but the girl is shy in front of strangers. Is there anything I can do for you at all?'

Declan explained how they had got lost on their way to Cashel and that their car had engine trouble. Someone had told them bed and breakfast might be available here. Could they stay the night?

The woman seemed unsure for a moment. She only did the bed and breakfast in the summer, she explained. There was little in the house to feed them all. But, under the circumstances . . . If word ever got out that she had turned three priests and a nun from her door, and them in need of shelter . . .

Grainne was given a room to herself, while the three men had to make do with one between them, with a double and a single bed.

'There's just one thing,' Declan said, returning to the kitchen after he had helped the others stow their things. 'We need to make a couple of phone calls. They're important, or I would never ask.'

'Sure, that's no trouble at all, Father. You can use the phone in the parlour if you like.'

'Well, I should explain that these are international calls. They may turn out quite expensive. If it's all right with you, I'll time them carefully and leave the correct money.'

The woman, whose name, she had said, was Mrs Kavanagh, seemed dubious for a moment. Her husband was out drinking in Ballycahill and would probably not be back until much later. On the other hand, the work of the church was of the utmost importance. If her neighbours ever heard that Peggy Kavanagh had refused a priest the use of her telephone . . .

'And I'll need privacy,' Declan went on. 'There are certain matters, confidential matters . . . I'm sure you understand.'

To Peg Kavanagh, confidentiality and priests went together like cows and milk. She knew well the sanctity accorded the confessional, and she did not doubt that all communications of the priesthood deserved the same respect.

'Of course, Father,' she said. 'We know how to keep a secret here as well as anyone.'

She led him to the little back room that served as the parlour and left him with the phone.

Declan reckoned that there was little risk in the call. Telephone traffic between Ireland and the United States was heavy, especially at about this time of night, when folk still awake in Ireland might hope to reach their relatives just returned from work. Harker would have no reason to expect Declan to contact anyone in the States, and a routine trawl of transatlantic calls would show nothing of especial interest.

He used Conrad Lee's home number in Washington and prayed he was not on weekend duty or away for any reason. The phone rang several times, then a girl's voice answered.

'Lee residence.'

'Hi,' said Declan. He guessed the speaker to be Louise, the youngest child, whom he had never met. 'Is that Louise?'

'Yes. Who is this?'

'This is a friend of your father's. I'm ringing from Ireland. Is he at home?'

'He's here. But he told me I should always ask for a name.'

'Tell him it's from Ireland. He'll know who I am. But, Louise, could you do something for me? Could you ask him not to use my name when he answers? He'll understand.'

'OK, I guess.'

Half a minute later, Conrad's voice came on the line.

'You in trouble, Denis?'

'How'd you guess?'

'I guessed because you asked me not to use your name, and because heavy things are going on over there, and because I hear rumours that we are getting involved in some way. And you are ringing me.'

Declan had first met Conrad Lee in Lebanon, when Conrad was serving with US military intelligence in Beirut. They had worked closely together for a time. Later, Conrad had joined the FBI and had spent time in London as part of a liaison team working in Europe. During his tour of duty, he had spent several weekends and vacations in Ireland as Declan's guest.

'Conrad, you are perfectly right. I am in trouble, big trouble. But I want you to believe me when I say I am on the side of the angels.'

'You haven't asked me how the kids are yet.'

'How are the kids?'

'Fine. Michele asked me last week when we were going back to Ireland. She misses her uncle Denis. How are Máiréad and Concepta?'

'Concepta's fine. She's in the country with family.'

'Has Máiréad started college?'

Declan shut his eyes. A wave of pure loss rose up from nowhere and washed through him, leaving him naked and aching inside.

'No, she . . . Máiréad is dead, Conrad. She was shot a few weeks ago. I . . . Please don't ask me to go into this now.'

There was a long silence. Conrad had been very attached to Máiréad.

'Christ Almighty, Declan. Oh, I'm really sorry. That's just the most terrible thing. I don't know what to say. Is this . . . Is your reason for ringing connected to her murder?' Shocked by what Declan had told him, Conrad had used his friend's real name.

'Yes, in a way. I can't go into the details, don't ask me. The thing is, I need some information badly, and I don't know of any other way of getting it except through you.'

'Will this help find Máiréad's killer?'

'It could do.'

'Then you can have anything you want, provided I can get it. What do you need to know?'

Declan told him. Slowly, carefully, without drama.

'Are you serious?'

'I've never been more serious in my life. We think he's holding the hostages somewhere on the coast.'

'He can't be. He's dead.'

'Nevertheless.'

'All right, I'll do what I can. Have you got a number where I can reach you?'

Declan gave him the number at the farm. It made no difference. If the call was being traced, they had the number already.

'There's just one thing, Conrad. When you ring back, a woman will answer, a Mrs Kavanagh. Can you tell her you're ringing from the Vatican and that it's urgent? Ask to speak to Father MacLogan.'

'Father MacLogan? The Vatican? I won't ask why. Do you want me to speak in Italian?'

'I doubt it would do you any good. Just make it convincing.'

'Very well – I'll ring you back once I have something to report. But I don't think I'll come up with anything.'

'Just try. That's all.'

'Good luck. And take care.'

Declan replaced the receiver. He made a note of the time and calculated how long the call had taken. It seemed almost laughable to think of him, the head of Ireland's key intelligence agency, reduced to calling colleagues on farmhouse phones and counting the cost per minute.

The others were in the kitchen eating a substantial meal that seemed to have appeared from nowhere. Conversation was somewhat stilted, though Myles, with his knowledge of religious matters and his contacts in the Dublin hierarchy, was doing more than his share to convey the correct impression.

Grainne looked up as Declan entered, and he knew at once that something was wrong. The others sat silently, on hard chairs, side by side. Mrs Kavanagh was slicing bread.

'Mrs Kavanagh's just been telling us the news,' Grainne said. 'Isn't that right?'

The big woman looked up.

'There was a flash just now on the radio,' she said. 'You would hardly credit it, would you, but there's terrorists loose between here and Ballinasloe. Terrorists! Sure, that's a thing they have in the North, not down here, where we do be peaceful folk going about our business. They say there are Gardaí everywhere, looking for them. I'm dreadful worried Pat will run into trouble on his way home. He'll be that full of drink, he won't know what's happening.'

Realizing she had put her foot in it, she glanced round hastily.

'Not that he takes that much drink himself. But now and then he does like to go for a pint or two of stout. And to see his friends.'

'Mrs Kavanagh says there's some good news, though,' Grainne added.

'Oh, indeed. Well, it is a relief to hear it, that the Rangers have found and shot several of the gang anyway. A carload of them, headed west. The Lord alone knows what they were up to in these parts. Sure, there's nothing for them here. Nothing at all.'

CHAPTER FIFTY-EIGHT

Ballybay
2045 hours

He went to the village as he had done before, to make the call to his contact in Baalbek. His father would be free tomorrow, *insha' allah*. And if God did not will it? He did not concern himself with that.

'On an island, you say?'

The line was poor tonight, the satellite in a bad position. There was a sense of terrible distance, a bleakness that had not been there the first time. Every now and then he could hear his own voice bounced back at him. All that immensity, he thought, and we speak of our squabbles and old hatreds. He felt lost.

'A place called Dingean,' he said. 'In English, they call it Dingle – that is what you should look for on the map. There is a peninsula, then a scattering of islands. No-one inhabits them. It's a perfect place. One I would have chosen myself.'

'Not so perfect if you found them.'

'I would not have made the mistake they made.'

'Can your group do the job? Are they ready?'

'Not as I would like. They've never been well trained. But they are dependable, I'm sure of that. If necessary, I can use them as decoys while I rescue the shaykh.'

'You have to get him off the island.'

'Don't worry, I've thought of that.'

'And the rest of your mission?'

'We shall see. The shaykh is my first priority. Only if he is safe will I go on with the rest.'

'And if he is not safe?'
'Then he will die revenged.'

The darkness was woven with threads of deeper darkness. As he walked back to the cottage, trees and bushes and hedges laced the edges of the road. There was an air of melancholic dream about this countryside. The richness and greenness of it were almost unbearable to him, and its darkness depressed him like the inside of a prison. There were no stars, the sky was closed and leaden, he felt cut off from the realms of light, the celestial country of the Imams and the angels. All imagination, he thought, no more than stories to capture the minds of boys and peasants. But he wanted to believe in it all the same, a realm beyond the moon where nothing changed, where a day lasted a thousand years, where the women were eternal virgins, where the only tears were tears of joy.

He walked on, drawing closer to the cottage, and as he did so he noticed a subtle change in the atmosphere, so imperceptible at first that he dismissed it as nothing more than the effect of his low spirits. But as he came into the path that led to the building, its lights barely visible through a network of trees, his previous impressions of unease grew to certainty. The stillness and the silence that held the night were too intense. Last night there had been birds and small animals in the woods and fields. Little sounds, but unmistakable. Tonight, nothing stirred.

And then he heard a sound on his left, sharp and singular, the silence on either side of it raw, bleeding, like skin freshly whipped. He knew what it was at once, it was a sound he had lived with all his life: a rifle bolt being drawn back.

He neither slowed nor quickened his pace. If there were armed men in the grounds, they would be waiting for him and the others to be together inside the cottage, they would not shoot him separately out here and alarm the others. And if they were planning a raid, they would almost certainly wait until their targets were asleep. He went on walking, never really afraid, knowing that all the time the barrels of guns were pointing at him and that all it would take to kill him was the slight pressure of a man's finger on a trigger. He reached the door and went inside.

Lenihan, Melaugh, and O'Driscoll were sitting at a low table, playing cards, using matchsticks for stakes. Eugene O'Malley was sitting in a corner, playing softly on his whistle, music that seemed almost familiar to Abu Hida, poignant and moving. In the short time he had spent with them, he had begun to understand how little like the English these Irish were. He greeted them and went into the kitchen.

Maureen was there, cleaning a pistol on the table. She looked up and smiled as he came in.

'How'd it go?' she asked. 'You get through all right?'

'Just like before,' he said, at the same time frowning and motioning to her to follow him into the sitting room.

The others looked up from their game. Abu Hida switched on the television and turned the volume up until it was loud enough to drown out anything he might say. He stepped close to Maureen and whispered sharply in her ear. They might have parabolic microphones outside, pointed at them.

'We have visitors,' he said. 'I don't know how many.'

'British bastards.'

'How do you know they're British? This is Irish territory, isn't it?'

She nodded.

'Yes, but those won't be Irish soldiers outside. If they're waiting to make a sneak assault, they mean to kill us. The British would do that, but not the Irish. They'd try to arrest us.'

'Whoever they are, I think they're waiting for us to make a move or go to sleep. Tell the others to go on with their game. They should try to behave normally. You'd better come upstairs with me.'

While Maureen relayed the message, Abu Hida took a night-vision scope from the box that had been sent from Dublin. Turning the television down to a more normal level, he preceded Maureen to the top of the stairs. They stopped outside the door of one of the two front bedrooms.

'They'll be watching the house through sights like this,' he whispered. 'I need you to cover me while I return the compliment. Go into the room, but don't turn on the light. Look as though you're feeling tired – that shouldn't be difficult. Don't look through the window or show you suspect anything. Start undressing, and once you've undressed get into bed. Take your time. I want them to keep their eyes on you.'

'You want me to do a striptease for those bastards out there?'
Her face was flushed, her anger almost tangible.

'I'm sorry, I don't understand. "Striptease"?'

'Forget it. You'd never understand. Will they see much through those things?'

'Enough to keep them interested. Don't make it look as though you're aware anyone is there. If they think we know they're there, they'll attack straight away.'

'What'll you be doing while this is going on?'

'Watching them. Counting them.' He paused. 'Are you ready?'

'You'll not breathe a word to the others about this. Do you hear me?'

He nodded.

'Let me get down,' he said, kneeling. On all fours, he looked up at her.

'Switch off the landing light,' he said, 'and go inside. Remember, you're very tired. Too tired even to switch the light on or close the curtains.'

She switched off the light and opened the door. It was dark in the room, except for the red glow that came from the votive candle in its glass in front of a picture of the Sacred Heart. In spite of the darkness, it felt as if she were just about to go on stage. She imagined a sea of faces outside in the darkness, eyes fixed on her, hushed, their breath caught in their throats, their mouths dry. Slowly, she walked into the room. Abu Hida crept behind her, low down. When she was sure he was inside, she closed the door. She had slept here the night before, but the room still had a sour, musty smell, as though it had been empty for months or even years.

The bed was positioned so that she could sit on its edge and still be seen through the window. She walked towards it, shoulders slumped, head bowed. He had been right, she did not have to act. The long day had genuinely worn her out. As she sat down, she saw him inch his way towards the window, keeping below the level of the sill.

She pulled off her jumper and tossed it down on the floor carelessly. He was at the window now, moving up slowly into position, the night-vision scope in his left hand. She undid the top button of her shirt. Half of her felt silly, as though performing for a crowd of little boys, crouched below with their guns, come to stalk a hard Irish bitch and forced instead to watch an unexpected erotic interlude.

The other half felt aroused at the thought of undressing here, in the dim red light, only feet away from him, at the possibility that he would look round and catch sight of her, that he too would be roused by her nakedness. She undid the next button. The air felt cold against her skin. In the dimness she could barely see him, bent at the window. Her own breath was louder than anything else in the world. The red light lay on her skin like a dark film of blood.

He waited. They would not all be watching yet. Slowly, one by one, they would turn their eyes on her. Word would get round. He could sense them out there, lying or crouching in the grass, behind trees, in the shelter of bushes, their cold muscles cramped, their nerves taut, their night glasses turned on the silent house, watching, listening. Behind him, she undid the third and fourth buttons.

'My shirt's half-way undone,' she whispered. 'Can they see me yet, do you think?'

'A little more and I can move,' he answered. A careless image of her hand moving against her breast flickered against his mind's eye. He shut it out, clenching the night scope, preparing to move into position.

She finished unbuttoning the shirt front and let it fall open. She was nothing but a slut, she thought, displaying herself for men she had sworn to kill, men who had killed friends of hers, SAS murderers, the scum of the earth. She unbuttoned the cuffs and peeled the shirt off, an arm at a time.

'My shirt's off,' she said, keeping her voice low. If someone came up from downstairs, what would they think . . . ?

She let the shirt fall and reached behind her back to unfasten her bra.

Now, he thought, now they have their eyes on her, now I can move. He raised the glasses a fraction over the sill. Would he have used a Muslim woman like this? he thought. Would he have asked one of his sisters, one of the *'Ara'is al-Damm*, to strip naked in front of a squad of Israeli soldiers, in order to distract them? He knew the answer, knew he could never have asked it. And yet he would have had no hesitation in sending any one of them to her death, to walk into the squad of soldiers smiling, carrying a bomb. Was this not noble too, what he had asked Maureen O'Dalaigh to do?

She let the bra fall to the floor. It did not seem to matter much what happened outside. All she really wanted was for him to turn, to cross the room to her, to touch her, to make love to her, to be her lover. She sat slumped on the bed, her breasts naked and untouched, wondering how, in all honesty, she had ever stumbled into this war, this warped peep-show in which everyone was naked at last, watchers and watched alike. She lived among a naked people, in a land where everyone was watched.

He had the scope against the windowpane now. His heart was beating faster than it should have been. He imagined her, naked to the waist. He heard the bump as first one shoe, then the next was dropped to the floor. Shutting out the images that crowded into his thoughts, he pressed his eyes to the glass.

The scope could provide a light gain of up to eighty thousand times. With it, he could recognize a man-sized target at up to three hundred metres in starlight. Tonight, visibility was much poorer, but he only wanted to establish the positions of the nearest ambushers. Slowly, very slowly, he began to scan the ground nearest the cottage. There was a sound of bedsprings creaking behind him as Maureen got to her feet. He continued scanning.

Maureen stood sideways to the window, thinking that to face it would seem too blatant, too much like a performance, that it might create suspicion. She unzipped her jeans, pulled one leg off, then the next, hopping unsteadily on one foot as she did so. She had not thought what she would do once she was naked. Dance for them? Bow and leave the room, go to a back room and start all over again?

He saw the first man, flat against the grass, his face turned up towards the window, watching through a single lens scope. On the ground in front of him lay an assault rifle. On his back was a rucksack with the rest of his equipment. His face was blackened. He lay still as a stone.

She rolled her pants over her hips. As a child, she would never have dared undress in front of a religious picture or the image of a saint. Now, the red light with its double meaning brought back feelings of shame she had thought long buried. And with them a rush of excitement she had last felt as a teenager with her first boy.

318

The second figure was behind a bush, the third behind a low mound. They seemed to glisten in the strange, monochrome glow of the night scope. Trees, bushes, snipers – all seemed unreal, as though etched into a night that was really blank underneath, a world that was not there at all. Only the cities of Jabulqa and Jabulsa existed, high above the clouds, eternally renewed.

Her pants fell to the floor, and she stepped out of them.

'I'm naked now,' she whispered. She wanted to tell him, she wanted him to know. 'Shall I get in the bed?'

'Go to the bed, lie down for a couple of minutes, then get up as though you've forgotten something. Come to the window, look out, then close the curtains.'

She did as he said. The red light in the darkness had quite sapped her of volition.

He counted seven in all. There would be more at the sides and the back, probably others positioned further out. Whoever they were, they were coming in for the kill. And he could tell that these were not raw squaddies sent out to patrol wet streets, but men who had lain in ditches long before this, men who knew exactly what to do and how to do it. He doubted very much if he and the others could outshoot or outwit them.

He sensed her beside him, then heard the swish as she drew the curtains. The cloth fell between his lens and the window-pane. He switched off the scope and took his eyes away. His vision was unfocussed after the strain of looking through the scope.

'Are there any there?' she asked.

He felt his heart race suddenly, knowing she was naked.

'Yes,' he said. His voice sounded unreal. The word had been hard to squeeze out. His throat was dry. He realized that he wanted her very badly. As he stood, his eyes started to adjust to the thin red light that touched the edges of the room's darkness. A little of it lay on her skin. The rest was imagination and desire. She was only inches away from him.

'You'd better get dressed,' he said. 'We may have to make a run for it.'

'I've done with running,' she said. She stepped towards him. He did not move.

'I have to find the island,' he said. 'That's what I came here for.'

She was right in front of him now. She knew he wanted her.

One hand took his and lifted it to her left breast. He caressed it blindly, then her right breast, then her belly and her hips, and she felt herself give way. She reached out to pull him towards her.

'No,' he said. He had never had to fight so hard in his life before. He knew that, if he lost, it was certain death. He pulled away, leaving her hands empty. Wretched, aching, he ran to the door.

'Put on your clothes,' he said. 'I'm going outside. I'll try to find a way through. We need the weapons from the cache.'

She watched the door close, heard his feet like a curse on the stairs. Above the bed, the little red light winked like a malevolent eye. She felt so naked, stripped right down, stripped past flesh and bone. Above the bed, Christ opened his chest to reveal a paper heart. It was the heart of a phantom; but it was not beating.

CHAPTER FIFTY-NINE

Abu Hida paused only long enough to tell the others what was happening. He turned the television on again and gathered them round the set.

'Stay inside,' he said, 'and keep your weapons with you. The ones you have here are too light to keep off a serious assault, so I'm going to bring back heavier guns from the cache. I'll have to go on foot, and it may take me some time to get clear of the area. On my way back, I'll take a car from the farm and drive in. Whatever you do, don't open fire on me.'

'How will we know what the bastards are up to?' Conor asked.

'You won't. None of you knows how to use a night-vision sight well enough, so it's a waste of time trying to outsmart them that way. Better to send somebody upstairs to listen for any sign of movement. The rest of you should stay down here and continue talking. Put the television off once I've gone.'

'Shouldn't one of us come with you?'

'No, he'd only hold me up or worse. Wait here. I won't be above an hour.'

'How do we know you'll come back?' Colm asked.

'You don't,' answered Abu Hida. 'But I swear by the blood of Husayn that I will do all I can to rejoin you. You have my word. But first of all, I have to get out of here. Eugene, I want you and Colm to help me. Come to the back. I'll show you what to do.'

As they got up to go, Maureen appeared in the doorway. She looked pale and drawn. Abu Hida wanted to take her to him, to tell her he was sorry, that he had wanted her, that he still did. But he said nothing and did nothing. They looked at one another for several seconds, then he went past her into the hall, followed by the others.

From his bag he took a black sweater and a special forces-style black balaclava with only eye-holes and a slit for the mouth. He slipped them on, then pulled over his head a set of Nova night-sight goggles. The single lens gave him a bizarre, alien appearance. On his hands he wore a pair of thin black gloves. He carried no gun, but in one pocket a Peskett close-combat weapon, a British special forces device from the Second World War. It had a knob at one end which could be used as a bludgeon. If a button at the other end was pressed, a long spike popped out to serve as a very efficient dagger. Pulling on a tiny metal ball at the bludgeon end drew out a long metal cord for use as a garrotte. It was all he would need.

'Colm,' he said, 'you're a smoker. I want you to go through the back door and leave it open. Take out a pack of cigarettes and light one, then walk to the right, to the far side of the kitchen window as though you've just gone out for a smoke. Make it look natural.

'Eugene, once he's in position, go into the kitchen and switch on the light. Once you're inside, fetch something and go out again. Don't leave the light on for more than five seconds.'

'What's the point of all that?' asked Colm. He thought the Arab was getting too clever for his own good. And he didn't place any weight on the blood of whoever it was he'd said. The Arab was getting himself out and that was it.

'He's taking advantage of the light, Colm,' Eugene said. 'Any fool could see that. They'll have their eyes on you, the light going on will blind them, then it'll be off again before their eyes can readjust. Isn't that right, mister?'

Abu Hida nodded. He hoped it would work. There was a slope to the side, one that lay the wrong way for the ambushers to use; he could be there before they had a chance to see him move. Unless, of course, someone vigilant had been placed further back to cover the side. He was staking everything on their having left the blank wall unwatched, on the assumption that no-one would go in or out that way.

'Are you ready?' he asked.

Colm nodded. He took a packet of Players from his jacket pocket.

'If thon bastards shoot me,' he muttered, 'you're fuckin' dead.'

Abu Hida smiled faintly. It was an old joke, even where he came from.

Colm opened the door and stepped outside. Abu Hida crouched low, out of sight. He heard Colm's footsteps on the gravel outside, then silence as he stopped. Moments later, the kitchen light went on.

He crawled out, lying on his belly, going fast across gravel, then onto wet grass. The grass helped. Behind him, the light went out. Any second now, he thought, he might be shot. Or, if they wanted to retain the element of surprise, he would find himself set on silently by one or more of the men lying in wait in the darkness.

He got to the slope and threw himself flat against it. Moving would be easier from here. If they had not seen him crawl away from the house, they would not be expecting movement from the slope. He could get to the first proper cover in about twenty seconds, from there into the trees in another ten. He wished there had been a chance to spy on the ambushers stationed at the rear, to know their distribution.

When more than a minute had passed in perfect silence, he slid over the top of the slope and began crawling towards the first bush. With the help of the goggles, he could see the land ahead. A watcher lay some twenty yards away to his right, and he thought there might be another on his left, fifteen yards or so down.

At the bush, he stopped to draw breath. It was going well so far, but he had a long way to go, and in the woods he could be on top of someone before he knew. Not only that, but the undergrowth would prevent him moving on his belly.

The best way in lay between two ash trees. He crossed the open ground slowly, fighting back the instinct to stand up and run. Inch by inch, hugging the ground, pressing his body flat against the grass, he slid towards the trees. He remembered crawling like this across a stretch of rubble-strewn roadway in Beirut, at every moment expecting a burst of machine-gun fire from the Palestinian-occupied building opposite. And in the south, crawling at night under the noses of the Israelis, passing a look-out tower outside Bent Jbail.

He was almost there when he saw the watcher. Judging by his posture, the man had not seen him. But he would do if he went much further. Abu Hida scrabbled on the ground until he found

323

a stone. It would not be easy to throw it without drawing attention to his position; but he did not have to toss it far.

It skimmed the surface of the grass for about ten yards and fell rattling to the ground a little to the watcher's right. Abu Hida saw the man turn, and as he did so crawled the last remaining feet that separated him from the trees.

He made up his mind what to do next, knowing that, if he did not secure himself, he would not be so lucky next time. Moving forwards several feet, then turning left, he swung in a gentle arc in behind the man at the edge of the trees. The ambusher had investigated the noise and found nothing. He was not equipped with a night-sight – his chief function out here, after all, was simply to wait until orders came through for the raid on the house.

Abu Hida waited until his quarry had calmed down and was again motionless against the tree he was using for cover. A little closer and he could hear him breathing. He kept his own breath under tight control.

And then in, his left hand covering the man's mouth, his right bringing the Peskett round behind and low down, pushing the sharp spike up at least an inch into the man's anus.

'If I press this any further,' he whispered, 'it is long enough to disembowel you. You will die slowly and painfully before your friends can get you to hospital. The slightest attempt to get free or draw attention will make me use it. I have killed men with it before, I can do it again. Do you understand me?'

The man, stiff with pain, nodded vigorously.

'Good. All you have to do is tell me where your colleagues are. Not all of them, I'm only interested in those in this section of the woods. Just numbers and approximate locations, that's all. Be quick. I'm fighting against time and you are in my way.'

The man, half choking, nodded again. Slowly, Abu Hida withdrew his hand, pressing the Peskett in harder as he did so.

'You fucking Irish bastard,' the man grunted.

'I am not Irish and I am not a bastard. You have three seconds.'

'All right, just stay cool. And go easy with that thing for God's sake. There are three others in this sector. Units F, G, and H. F is twenty yards to my right, G twenty to my left. H is further back, about midway.'

'Is he the last in the circle?'

'Yes. There's a back-up van further out. But the three I told you about are all between here and the road.'

'Thank you,' said Abu Hida. He removed the Peskett, but still held the man by the chin. The slightest careless movement, and he knew the other would turn the tables. He would have liked to leave him, but he knew he could not.

'You know I can't just leave you,' he said.

'Then get it over with.'

The point of the Peskett fitted under the man's chin. Abu Hida held it steady there for a moment, then jabbed upwards with all his strength. He felt it hit the top of the skull, held the man hard against his shoulder, hand on mouth, until he stopped kicking. It seemed to take forever until all movement ceased and Abu Hida could lay his victim on the ground. He forced himself not to think of the wife and children the man probably had somewhere, sitting at home, unaware of all this. It got harder every time not to think of it, not to feel regret. He removed the spike and pulled it back into the handle of the Peskett.

Abu Hida could not be sure the man he had just killed had been telling the truth. He must have known he was going to die, whatever he said. But the pain of the spike entering his bowels should have prompted a little honesty.

He moved on through the woods, moving with great caution, setting his feet down each time as though on the finest glass. A twig could give him away, a poacher's snare, the slightest thing. In the night-sight, the woods seemed haunted, the trees lit with a green, phosphorescent light. They seemed to go on forever, drawing him in deeper to a world that had no sound and no colour.

Watcher H was where the dead man had said he would be. Abu Hida gave him a wide berth.

Abu Hida came out onto the road. He knew approximately where he was, he had thought it out carefully in advance. Taking off his boots, he began to walk quickly in his socks, making no sound on the road's tarmacadamed surface.

He had been at the arms cache only a few hours before, and the way there was still imprinted on his memory. The lane to the O'Farrells' farmhouse appeared on his right. He went down it, then over the low gate into the field where the guns were kept beneath a thorn bush.

He took all he could carry, slinging them over his shoulder by their straps until he was quite weighed down. Two boxes of ammunition were all he could manage.

The pick-up truck was there, where he had seen it earlier that day. He threw the guns and ammunition into the back, climbed in, and played with the wires under the dashboard until the old engine burst into life. By the time the first light went on in the farmhouse, he was on the road again, headed back to Craiguena-managh Farm.

He had a simple choice, of course, and every second of the way he pondered it. Rejoining the ASU meant the end of his mission and the loss of his own life for people he scarcely knew, for a cause that was not his own cause. If he left them to their fate, he would still have a chance to find the place called Dingle, to track down the island where the hostages were being kept, and to rescue Shaykh Usayran. Rationally considered, it was his duty to choose the latter course. But he had given his word. He had left in order to bring help, and they had watched him go.

Maureen O'Dalaigh had played the whore for her enemy in order to give him cover. And, more than that, she had offered herself to him, naked, without guile, helplessly, and he had turned away from her, almost with contempt. He owed her something for all that.

He did not think that getting to the farmhouse would be difficult. They had no reason to stop anyone driving in, indeed they would welcome new arrivals as an addition to their prey. There were no milkmen or postmen at this time of night.

But the minute he neared the entrance, he knew something was wrong. A van was parked at the turning, with two men beside it. He drove past, round the bend, then pulled in to the ditch and stopped the engine. In the silence, he could hear gunfire. The assault had already begun.

Jumping out, he grabbed a handgun and a SPAS-12 shotgun, loaded them, and ran back to the turn, pulling the night-vision goggles back into place.

The van was still there. As he came up, he heard shouts. Coming down the path were two more men, dragging someone between them. It was Maureen, struggling to pull free, but limply, without real hope of escape.

326

He jumped into the ditch, waiting for the men to come nearer. They dragged Maureen to the back of the van and forced her to climb in. Abu Hida waited until she was inside, then raised the shotgun and fired twice. The two men dropped and lay still.

A third man appeared from the front of the van, his sub-machine gun poised to fire. Abu Hida shot him in the head.

'Maureen!' he shouted. 'Stay where you are!'

He crept out and rolled across to the rear right wheel of the van. If others had heard the shooting, they would be here soon. Beneath the van, he could see the legs of the fourth man, taking cover at the front. Taking aim between the wheels, he fired once, blowing half the man's leg away. Standing, he walked to the front of the van. There was another shot, then he returned to the back.

'Where are the others?'

'Half of them are dead. Conor's the only one holding out. He's at the back. You can do nothing for him.'

He knew she was right.

'Get in the front,' he said. 'We're getting out of here.'

CHAPTER SIXTY

Inis Tuaisceart
13 October
0048 hours

She remembered something her father had told her once, years before, when she was a teenager, seventeen years old and suffering her first real heartbreak. They had gone to their villa in the Shouf Mountains for the weekend, as they did quite often in those days, before the civil war. A week before, her boyfriend Hamid, a first-year student at the University of Beirut, had dropped her for another girl, a plump girl from Sidon in his class, studying agriculture.

She had spent much of the time alone down at a nearby lake, refusing to eat, speaking in monosyllables, darting angry looks at her parents. When in the house, she had closed herself in her room, only to come out hours later, red-eyed and morose.

Her father had found her at the lake on the Sunday afternoon. It had been a fine day in early September, more summer than autumn, with a gloss of sunshine across the surface of the water, like paint spilled on glass. Now, lying on the rough bed in her cell, she could see the sun lying indolent on the wide lake and hear her father's voice coming to her softly across the reeds.

They had talked for hours that day, and he, without prompting, had discovered that she had been sleeping with Hamid, the first man she had thought she loved enough to make that commitment. She could never have told her mother. Liberated though she was, she belonged to a very different generation that had only just emerged from behind the veil. She would have disapproved, would have made a scene and gone on making one for weeks.

328

For all her brittle femininity, her mother had always lacked the empathy that women are supposed to possess more deeply than men. Amina had known from an early age that her mother was a basically selfish woman, and that if she needed comfort or understanding, she should turn to her father first.

He had made no scene, as many Arab fathers would have done, had not threatened her, had not even commented on the loss of her innocence. He had just listened to her reflections on the unfairness of love, the treachery of men, the immensity of the loss she was feeling. Like her, he had been surprised by Hamid's casualness, for he had considered him a likeable young man and genuinely fond of his daughter. He had reassured her that she was beautiful and managed to make her laugh by suggesting that the despicable Hamid had selected his latest conquest in preparation for a life spent growing olives.

'It's not the pain that matters,' he had told her at last. 'There'll always be pain, for Hamid or for someone else. Whether they love you or not, you'll always know some sort of ache inside. The important thing is to keep the pains separate, not to let them build up until they've become a single thing, something so big you can't cope with it.'

She had known even then that he had not loved her mother, that he had never loved her. Their marriage had been arranged, and love had never grown out of it. When she was younger, it had mattered to her, the sense of formality and often open grief between them. Now, at seventeen, contemplating her father's misery from the exalted heights of her own unhappiness, she thought she understood for the first time a little of the reality he lived.

And today, so many years later, with Hamid long forgotten and the names of other lovers burned onto her flesh, pain upon pain, scar upon scar, none of them separate now; today, despite having all that behind her, despite the knowledge of her love for Declan and the abruptness of their second separation, the burn and ache of it, she knew for the first time a pitch of misery that drowned out everything else, that wiped all that other, delicate, whimsical pain into oblivion. She lay on her hard bed, beyond tears, wishing Declan were here, wishing he could just be with her, not to rescue her, as in her earlier fantasies, but to listen to what she had to tell him.

Except that this was something she knew she could not tell anyone, not even him. That was why it hurt so badly, knowing that it was hers and only hers, in all its density and depravity. The things the American had done to her, had made her do, were like burrs wrapped tight against her nerve-endings, she had only to think of them to experience the pain again and again.

It was not that he had raped her. She had expected that much, prepared herself for it, like a woman in a prison-camp or a town under siege. That was humiliation, but it was something she could live with. Thousands of women lived with worse. It was not that he had hit her when she had argued with him, tried to make him see reason. That was anger, and in time the weals and bruises would fade.

But he had tried to thrust his mind on her. He had spoken to her out of the innermost recesses of a puzzled and diseased heart, and she felt sick and contaminated. She knew that he wanted more than her body, that he wanted her mind and soul as well, and she knew that he had his ways of taking them. All that night he had kept her awake, pouring out his most secret thoughts, uncovering his most private feelings. After his men had taken her back to her cell, she had fallen into a tormented sleep, and woken sweating and in tears. She had not dreamed once of rescue.

She rolled over on the bed. They would take her back to him tonight, he had promised. She prayed she would be ready for him. That afternoon, she had spent time with one of the other women, the Iranian called Nushin. Nushin wore her *chador* at all times, refused to let so much as a lock of hair peep through the hem. But underneath it, to keep her hair in place, she wore a long clip with a steel pin. She had already told Amina that she had it, that she was keeping it in case it might come in useful one day as a weapon.

Amina had told her what she wanted it for, and why. Not everything, she could never tell anyone that, but enough. Nushin had not hesitated to pass the pin over.

'I shall pray for you,' she had said. 'Hazrat-i Fatima will look after you.'

'Thank you,' Amina had answered. 'Pray that I'm given strength. That's what I need most. Not physical strength. The strength to do it.'

330

But now, lying awake in her cell waiting for the sound of the guards' footsteps, she began to wonder what she needed the strength for. To kill him while he pawed at her? Or to kill herself when it was done?

CHAPTER SIXTY-ONE

Washington
12 October
1334 hours local time

For a long time after hanging up, Conrad Lee sat looking at the scribbled notes he had made on the pad by the telephone. He wanted to take the paper and crumple it into a little ball, and throw the ball away. He'd let a couple of hours go by, then ring Declan back and tell him it was nothing but a crazy story, that he'd found nothing. But Declan Carberry was a very close friend, and his daughter Máiréad had been one of the best kids Conrad had ever met.

'Jean,' he called out, stepping into the kitchen, 'I've got to go in to the office.'

His wife turned from the cooker.

'Oh, for heaven's sake, Conrad, surely not on a Saturday. Who was that? Ritchie? Is he asking you to cover for him while he goes off hunting again?'

Conrad shook his head.

'I'm sorry, honey, but I've got to go. A friend's in trouble, bad trouble. Maybe I can help him out, I don't know.'

'The Halperns are coming for dinner this evening. It's too late to cancel.'

'I'll be back by then, don't worry. This won't take long. I promise.'

Jean sighed. She'd been married to the FBI too long to think there was any point in arguing.

'Make sure you are. And don't forget you promised the kids a trip tomorrow.'

*   *   *

332

As a Deputy Assistant Director with the FBI's criminal investigative division, Conrad had access to most of the Bureau's on-line files through his own office Macintosh. The incident Declan wanted him to look into had taken place in 1993, the trial had been in 1994, a lot of appeals were still working their way through the courts. In theory, all the files should be available. He found them in a single folder, six hundred and seventy-five separate files, under the single ID code MF (multiple felonies) 1793B (1993) – WS, followed by their individual serial numbers. They ranged in length from a single page to several hundred.

He began to skim through them in no particular order: depositions, reports from the Federal Bureau of Alcohol, Tobacco, and Firearms, FBI reports, evidence collated by the Texas Department of Public Safety, the Dallas District Attorney's Office, and the Texas Rangers, eye-witness statements, statements made by survivors, psychiatric reports, forensic evidence from the Tarrant County Medical Examiner's Office and from the FBI's own laboratory in Washington. It was a small mountain, more than he could have guessed.

He kept on like that for over two hours, getting nowhere, growing more and more frustrated. Declan could not be right, and Conrad was increasingly sure he was just wasting a Saturday afternoon ploughing through masses of evidence that all added up to the same thing. He had almost decided to drop the whole business and get back home to his family when he ran slap into a brick wall.

He'd been trying to open a forensic evidence file from the Tarrant County ME's Office when a flag appeared on the screen telling him that access required special authorization. That seemed odd. Three files on, it happened again.

Returning to the main folder, he asked the computer to list how many of its files were open access, how many restricted to his rank and above, and how many needed the highest level clearance. Six hundred and twenty-one files were open to the public; another forty-seven were classified closed to anyone below the rank of Deputy Assistant Director; and seven were closed to anyone but the Director of the FBI in person.

He knew it would be impossible for him to enter any of those files without direct authorization or the password. Even if he knew enough about computers to hack his way in, the slightest error could trigger alarms that would bring armed security guards from every direction. It was beginning to look as though the case he had opened was locked up tighter than anything since the Kennedy assassinations.

Just as he was about to switch off and go home, an idea came into his head. He picked up the phone and rang Archives, located in the basement.

'This is Lee in CI. Can you tell me if you still store a group of files coded MF 1793B (1993) – WS 1 to WS 675?'

It took less than a minute for the records clerk to check.

'I've got them all here, sir. But you should be able to access them through your desktop.'

'I need to look at some photographs. They never scan the way you want them.'

'Ain't that true. OK, sir, they're here when you want them.'

Conrad replaced the receiver and dug out his desk copy of the week's duty roster. The present archivist would be checking off duty in an hour and a half. Since it was a Saturday evening, demand for archive material was light, so one man handled the entire section.

He took the elevator to the basement and checked out six of the files restricted to his own rank. Returning to his office, he used his computer to create a printed label identical to those on the files. A little fiddling with fonts and print sizes got him perfect results in a matter of minutes. He printed out a single label on the nearest laser printer and slipped it onto one of the files he had borrowed. When it was ready, he rang Jean and said she should apologize to the Halperns and start dinner without him. She didn't say anything, but the quality of the silence that followed his explanation left him in no doubt that it would take him several months to repay this one. He replaced the receiver and waited for the evening shift to change downstairs.

He gave them fifteen minutes extra to be on the safe side. When he approached the desk this time, he saw a new man in charge, a kid who looked as though he might be fresh out of Quantico, young enough to be awed by Conrad's seniority. Taking a deep breath, he approached the unsuspecting clerk with the air of a man who knows how to pull rank.

'Where's that damn fool gone who gave me these files?'

'Jones, sir? He's gone off duty, sir.'

'Well, isn't that convenient for Mr Jones. Take these files back, boy.' He handed over all but one file. 'But this one here,' he went on, waving the doctored folder in the young man's face, 'is the wrong file. Now, what the hell do you think I do up there, son? Write poetry?'

'I'm sorry, sir. What number should it have been?'

'Hell, that's the right number, but that isn't the right file. Just bring me whatever you've got to right and left of it, and let's see what we've got.'

The unhappy clerk took the file off into the pneumatic stacks. As soon as he left, Conrad checked that no-one else was near, then got hold of the register in which the file numbers had been noted down against his name and signature. The file he had just returned had originally been MF 1793B (1993) – WS 625; Conrad altered that to MF 1793B (1993) – WS 626, a change of only one digit.

When the clerk returned, he looked more unhappy than ever. He was carrying a total of four files, one fairly thick, the others of average size.

'I'm sorry, sir, there seems to have been some sort of mix-up back there. I've got WS 624 here, and WS 627, but I've also got what looks like another file numbered WS 626, same as the one you've got.'

'Show them here, let's see what kind of tom-fool mistake those idiots have made this time.'

He made an act of glancing through each of the files, then thrust 624 and 627 back over the desk.

'Those are fine.'

He then handed back the file he'd doctored.

'That should be 625, not 626. Get it seen to.'

'Yes, sir.'

Then, taking the Top Secret file WS 626, he thundered, 'And this is the damn file I originally asked for! Jesus, boy, does anyone round here ever get a simple thing right anymore?!'

Seeing the Top Secret flash on the file, the clerk made as if to check Conrad's authorization. Glancing down at the register, however, he saw that Conrad had already presented his pass to see file MF 1793B (1993) – WS 626. Asking for the authorization a second time would only mean more trouble. He smiled and watched Conrad stomp away.

Back in his office, Conrad closed the door and sat down to read the file he had so underhandedly extricated from the archive. Ten minutes later, he knew two things: first, that Declan had been right, and, second, that his own life was in danger if anyone knew he had read the file.

He also had what looked like the ten-figure key that would give him access to the other seven files. Bringing the folder up on his screen again, he clicked on the next closed file and tried the number. Like a dream, the flag disappeared and he was in.

It took him another hour to work out what had been done, and how. He sat for several minutes afterwards, thinking, trying not to think. He knew what had been done, and how – but not why.

He lifted the phone and rang the number Declan had given him. A woman's voice answered sleepily, and he asked for Father MacLogan.

'Who's that?' she asked, a little suspiciously.

'I'm ringing from the Vatican,' he said, 'it's very urgent, I have to speak to him.'

The woman's voice grew a little breathy.

'Well, of course, your excellence; I'll fetch him at once. Don't hang up, now.'

Declan came on a minute later.

'Denis MacLogan here.'

'This is Conrad.'

'I thought so. Well?'

'The answer is "yes".'

'I see.'

Silence. A hollow sound, as though space winds were booming off the satellite. Then Conrad spoke again.

'Is he in Ireland? Is that why you wanted to know?'

'Yes,' answered Declan. 'I think he's the one holding the hostages.'

Silence again, as though all the time lags and the spaces between words had come together to form a single emptiness in space.

'Do you want to know the details?'

'If you think they could be important.'

'Yes, there are some things I think you should know. Denis, I don't know the full story. This is just what I've been able to piece together from some secret files I was able to break into. It's incomplete.'

He paused, and he could hear the sound of Declan breathing on the other end, heavy and uneven. It was early morning in Ireland. Declan was in a great stillness.

'Denis, I guess you know what most of us know. Back in 1993, the FBI laid siege to a compound out near Waco, in Texas. The blockade lasted fifty-one days, and it ended suddenly on the nineteenth of April, when our people moved in with CS gas and the whole shooting-match went up in flames. Close on eighty people were shot or choked to death or burned alive, all of them members of a religious sect known as the Branch Davidians, an offshoot of the Seventh Day Adventists. Their leader was a man of thirty-three called David Koresh, real name Vernon Wayne Howell. He was later identified as one of the victims. That all sound familiar?'

'Absolutely. That's what I read in the papers here.'

'It's the official version, Denis; but it sure as hell isn't the truth. Let me tell you what really happened out there. The night before the siege ended, Koresh spoke on the telephone for around three hours with a man called Joshua Babcock. Ever heard of him?'

'No, never.'

'Don't suppose you would over there. He's a big-time fundamentalist preacher down in Texas. Owns his own TV station, got churches all over, runs missions to Africa and Asia. Very powerful in right-ring evangelical circles here. He's getting on in years now, but he still makes his Sunday-morning appearances on TV, and he keeps close contact with a whole network of people with influence: businessmen, congressmen, state senators, lobbyists. The president doesn't like him, and, to tell you the truth, I don't either. He wants to see America ruled by his own narrow views, and he likes to use his money and his voice to bring that about. He's got strong views on abortion, homosexuality, the dissemination of what he calls "dangerous books" in schools and colleges, and a whole host of other subjects.'

'I've got the picture. Over here, they're known as bishops.'

'OK, just so you know who this is. For some reason, Babcock wanted Koresh out of the compound, and he did a deal with some top people in the FBI to help get him out.

'Seems there were tunnels dug underneath the compound, lots

of them. Most of them were short, like they just wanted to dig deep and hole up underground till the apocalypse was over, or the war, or whatever they expected. Only, it looks like one tunnel was longer. A lot longer. Forensic reckon the only way into it would have been from Koresh's own bedroom. That's how they managed it.'

'OK, it could have been done. But you said yourself a body was identified as Koresh's. And that was agreed at the inquest, wasn't it?'

'It was. But it still wasn't Koresh's body. The work was carried out by the Tarrant County Medical Examiner's Office, who brought a team of pathologists over from Fort Worth. They said they'd never seen so much destruction to bone or tissue as on the bodies from the ranch. When they were through, the inquiry was moved to the FBI's forensic science lab here in Washington.

'Koresh was supposed to have been identified by his teeth. He'd had two missing since the age of fifteen, and that corresponded to the jaw of a body found in the communications room at the ranch.

'But now it looks like there was some tampering with the evidence. The teeth were removed somewhere between Fort Worth and Washington, around the time there was speculation in the press that Koresh might have escaped after all. The body with the missing teeth was a different height. Nobody bothered carrying out a DNA test on it, unlike most of the other bodies. It wasn't Koresh. He was already drinking coffee with Josh Babcock out in New Kadesh, a Christian settlement in the New Mexico desert.'

'You've done a great job, Conrad. I'm grateful to you.'

'There's just one other thing, Denis. I don't know if it's important. But, earlier this year, a top official in the FBI received a request from CIA headquarters at Langley, asking for Koresh to be passed into their keeping. Does that mean anything to you?'

The wind passed through the emptiness of space like an animal prowling for food.

'Yes,' came back Declan's answer. 'It makes perfect sense.'

'Would you care to tell me? I need to know what I'm handling here.'

'No, you know too much already.'

'I figured that myself. You going after him?'

338

'Koresh? I've been on his trail for four days now, though I didn't know who he was until now.'

'Take care when you find him. I've looked at some of the psychiatric profiles here. They say he's capable of just about anything.'

'They must have been crazy to use him.'

'Who? The CIA?'

'Them and some other people I know.'

'Maybe. Depends what they wanted him for. He'd have been perfect as a front for an operation that had to be deniable. The Man Who Never Was.' Conrad paused. 'Take it easy, Denis. Don't turn your back on him.'

'I won't. Thanks again, Conrad. I'll be in touch.'

The line was disconnected. Conrad replaced the receiver. He sat for a while, just staring at words on the screen in front of him, words that no longer seemed to mean anything. And it wasn't just the words that had lost meaning.

CHAPTER SIXTY-TWO

Inis Tuaisceart
13 October
0715 hours

Sunday morning, the light bent and broken over stone, the sea spent on the shore, birds in the distance above the mainland, turning and turning in ever tighter circles before widening out once more in a clamour of white wings, sunlight above the hills, and a dark wind rising out at sea.

Here on the island, the Sabbath was over. Not the mainland Sabbath of mass and lunch and Sunday papers, but the seventh day, the true Sabbath, God's resting-day, presided over by the Lamb of God in person. There had been hymns for the faithful, and Bible study, and a sermon for the unbelievers, without translation or apology.

David Koresh had been on edge all day. Once, white with anger, he had struck a hostage who had dared interrupt his sermon with a verse of the Qur'an. Later, pacified, he had sung softly to his followers, accompanying himself on guitar, the Prince of Peace.

Now, as the morning strengthened, he stood by the shore alone, gazing seawards. Feeling the wind in his hair, he looked up at the sky, where clouds were skidding past rapidly. No-one, he thought, had seen in the sky the things he had seen: angels with wings the size of mountains, and trumpets, and beasts with one and two and five and seven horns, red and purple and golden raiment stretched from horizon to horizon, and blood in a golden cup poured out, whole cities set with precious stones, riders on dark and pale horses, armies, the face of the living God.

He covered his eyes with his hands and wept. No man alive had seen what he had seen, no-one knew the things he knew or could unfold the secrets he held in his heart. And yet – last night, when he had gone to the Arab woman's bed for the second time, she had turned on him, attacked him, slashing his chest and stomach again and again with a sharp object, until he had kicked her off.

He had been covered in blood, the bedclothes had been soaked in it. His blood, the blood of the Lamb. She had tried to kill him and had nearly succeeded. But she would be punished, he would see to it himself. He shivered, remembering the ferocity of her attack, the betrayal in her eyes. To attack the Son of God, someone who had seen the towers of New Jerusalem, God's anointed – surely that was the most heinous crime of all.

He heard footsteps behind him. Ezekiel was there, calm, possessed, understanding. Last night, he had bathed his wounds and applied ointment to them.

'They're all assembled, David. We're just waiting for you now.'

'There's no rush. Let them wait. Come here.' He beckoned to his friend to join him on the rock. 'Tell me what you see.'

Ezekiel sat beside him.

'See? The normal things,' he said. 'Waves, some seabirds, clouds in the sky. What do you expect me to see?'

'Nothing. You have not been blessed with sight, with true vision. Would you want it if I could offer it to you?'

Ezekiel shook his head slowly, watching the black waves beneath them.

'I don't think so,' he said. 'It only seems to cause you pain. I couldn't bear that, to see things as they really are. I'm not strong enough for that. None of us are.' He thought of his wife Mary, burning like a torch, her arms outstretched, and the wall of flame between them. Of his children, Sarah and Rachel, screaming for him, and the wall of flame like a barrier of ice. He had seen enough of things as they really were.

'I wasn't strong,' said Koresh. 'But God opened my eyes all the same. Didn't ask if I was ready, if I wanted to see or not. Just opened my eyes. Strength and weakness are all one to Him.'

'Nevertheless, I wouldn't want to be a prophet.'

'That's wise of you. You would see things you'd wish you'd

never seen. Hear things no-one should hear. Day and night you'd be watching and listening.'

'What can you see today?'

'Today? That it is very close now, very close indeed. A matter of days, or hours.'

'As little as that? Don't you know exactly?'

'He won't tell me. It would be dangerous, He says. Only when the moment is on us will I be told. But it is very near. Today, tomorrow – the day after at the latest.'

'Everyone will die?'

'Everyone but His chosen ones.'

'By fire?'

Koresh shrugged. He continued staring at the empty sea.

'I don't know,' he said. 'Perhaps. He has not yet made it clear.'

Ezekiel shuddered.

'And it will be the beginning of the end of all things?'

'God will leave nothing alive on the face of the earth. You've read the prophecies, you know what He intends to do.'

There was a long, peculiar silence. Ezekiel shivered in the growing wind. It was very hard to do God's will.

'They're waiting for you,' he said. 'The woman is ready.'

Koresh got to his feet. The pain of the wounds was sharp and lacerating still. Even small movements anguished him. He clenched his right hand and unclenched it slowly. A Biblical verse ran through his mind again and again: 'Vengeance is Mine, saith the Lord.'

CHAPTER SIXTY-THREE

County Tipperary
0816 hours

They had left the guest house as soon as it seemed reasonable to do so. Declan wanted to ring the number Martin had given him, but he preferred to do so from a public call-box. They stopped at the first lay-by and changed their priestly garb for that of farmers. Liam had a fresh set of number-plates that would correspond to those of a car of the same description owned by a farmer in Ballyporeen. The car, suitably mud-splashed by now to pass as a farmer's vehicle, had plenty of petrol in the tank and was running well again. They decided to head for Clare, and, if stopped, they could say they were on their way to the matchmaking festival in Lisdoonvarna, now drawing towards its close. If they weren't one sort of celibate, they could try their hands at being another.

They found a call-box at a place called Cullen, near Limerick Junction. The others stayed behind in the car, plotting different routes west, while Declan put through a call to the number Martin had given him. It rang seven times before there was an answer.

'O'Toole's Bar.'

'I was given this number by Martin Fitzsimmons. I need your help.'

'I'm sorry, sir, but I think you have a wrong number.'

'This is Declan Carberry. I'm ringing from a call-box.'

'Why didn't you say so earlier? You've taken your time to get in touch. Did you know Martin is dead?'

'Yes, I heard yesterday. Do you know how it happened?'

'They followed you both to the bridge. One of them stabbed

Martin, and now Harker's on your back like the devil himself.'

'How secure is this line?'

'Oh, secure enough. What can I do for you?'

'I know who's holding the hostages, and I think it's just a matter of time before he kills the lot of them. I need to know if anyone has had any leads.'

'There's been another body, a man from Syria. He was found this morning in a church in Cork, St Anne's no less, the one with the bells. On the altar, from what I understand.'

'That's no good to me.'

'I didn't think it would be. I do have one thing, though. A phone call was made early Saturday morning from a town in County Monaghan to a number in Baalbek, Lebanon. A tape recording was made at Menwith Hill. One copy made its way to GCHQ, another to the US MC10 unit. The GCHQ copy went direct to MI5 and was immediately buried. But somebody at MC10 made a mistake and forwarded a copy to C3, together with a translation. That copy has already been destroyed, and all trace of it obliterated from the records, so you'll just have to take my word for what it says.'

'I trust you. Go ahead.'

One minute later, Declan was back in the car.

'Inis Tuaisceart,' he said. 'He's holding them on Inis Tuaisceart.'

'Babcock's a sane lunatic,' said Myles. They were heading towards Dingle now, still keeping to the side roads and losing valuable time because of it.

'Why would he want Koresh?' asked Declan. Liam was in the front, driving, Grainne was napping.

'I'm not entirely sure. They have a lot in common, although Babcock's more mainstream. There is one thing, though. Babcock published a book a few years back. It was a big seller in some parts of the States. Bible prophecies interpreted, the end of the world in our lifetime, Jesus is coming any day now – pretty standard stuff, as I recall. But it did have one significant feature: Babcock thinks Islam is Satan's weapon against the Christian West.

'Babcock's a thinly-veiled racist. His church is predominantly white lower-middle class. He's an anti-Semite and has strong views about Catholics. Communism was his great hate until the

344

collapse of the Soviet Union. But since then he's been preaching that Islam is the principal weapon in the devil's armoury and has been since the seventh century. Everything else is just a side issue.'

Declan nodded.

'That certainly explains why he might get mixed up in a business like this. But it still doesn't explain Koresh.'

'I was just coming to that. This book of Babcock's is called *The Seven Seals* – a reference to the seals in the *Book of Revelation*. Now, this was one of Koresh's main preoccupations too. He was writing a commentary on the true meaning of the seventh seal during the siege. It's supposed to have been destroyed when Ranch Apocalypse went up in flames. But supposing it wasn't burned. Supposing it was carried out instead by Koresh. It could have been what Babcock was after.'

'And as long as Koresh went on writing it, he'd be safe. Babcock would see he wasn't touched.'

Myles nodded.

'And then,' Declan went on, 'one day a man turns up from the CIA and says "We need someone to help us settle the account between ourselves and those Muslim fanatics out there".'

'I think that's right. I also think Koresh will have had a group of his own followers with him by then. There are stories that Babcock had arms stored out at his New Kadesh settlement, and that he'd been training survivalists and others to protect him and his church from the forces of Satan.'

'Come the Day of Judgement.'

'That's right, Declan. Come the Day of Judgement.'

They stopped in Tralee, for food and a chance to stretch their legs. There had been more checkpoints, at Tipperary, Bruree, and Newcastle West; not Gardaí, but soldiers, men who looked twice before waving them on. Declan was surprised they had made it this far. Harker wanted them badly, and he would find them in the end, they all knew that. It was just a matter of when and how.

'If Abu Hida knows where the hostages are,' Declan said to Grainne, 'he must be on his way there already.' They were drinking coffee in a small café in the square. There were few other customers. Myles and Liam had gone out to buy provisions. The

345

staff seemed bored, caught in a time-warp that condemned them to live forever in 1962, vaguely aware that the world outside had moved on, even in Tralee.

Grainne nodded, biting into a sandwich. The bread was good, the filling mostly coleslaw.

'Where did you say he rang from?' she asked.

'A place called Ballybay. Somewhere near the border.'

'In County Monaghan. I know of it.'

'It's a bit of a distance away,' said Declan. 'But we lost a lot of time last night. Abu Hida would have left soon after he made the phone call. The people he's with will have contacts in the Dingle area.'

'What do you think he plans to do?' she asked.

'If he has back-up in the form of an Active Service Unit, he may try to get onto the island, launch some sort of attack, pull his father out.'

'Could he do it? What would he be up against?'

'Professionals. Koresh may be crazy, but his people are well trained. I saw them at work at Castletown. They were good. Very good. I wouldn't give much for the chances of an IRA unit trying to take them on. On the other hand, Abu Hida's very good himself. In all the years of the civil war in Lebanon, there was no-one like him. He knows better than to storm in like that. He'll check out the island, assess the opposition, then wait until the right opportunity comes along.'

Grainne pondered. She sipped her coffee, tasting the slightly rancid milk that had been poured in it.

'I think we should find him,' she said.

'Who? Abu Hida?'

She nodded. The coffee was going cold. She could not drink it.

'Find him,' she went on. 'Before he goes to the island. Talk to him, persuade him you can be useful to him, you can help get him and the hostages out of Ireland.'

'I don't know I can help him.'

'Oh, come on, sir. If you could get them off Inis Tuaisceart, you could have all the television crews in Ireland round you inside the hour. Harker could do nothing about it. You're an important man, your brother-in-law was Taoiseach.'

'I don't know. You could be right. It might work. But I'm not sure Abu Hida would leap at the opportunity.'

'Tell him what Harker's up to, the whole thing. Once he knows the risk he'd be running without you, he'll listen to reason.'

Declan shook his head.

'It could backfire. Once Hizbollah know the remaining hostages are safe, the Scimitar network could be shot in reprisal for the ones Koresh has killed.'

'Try him. In return for your help, he does what he can to persuade his own people to release the Scimitar agents. By-pass MI5.'

Declan shrugged.

'It might work. If he doesn't shoot me first.'

'You don't have to meet him in person first time. Send a message. Tell him what you know. He's not a fool, he'll see the sense of doing a deal.'

Declan thought hard. Perhaps she was right, perhaps Abu Hida and he might come to an agreement. He would make a pact with the Devil if it helped get Amina out of David Koresh's clutches and brought him within striking distance of Peter Musgrave.

Before leaving, Declan made a phone call. Tommy Murtagh had given him his private number at Curragh Camp, and told him to call if he needed help. The phone was picked up on the first ring.

'Murtagh.'

'Tommy, it's me. Can we talk?'

'We can, but keep it short.'

'I need your help. Badly. I know where the hostages are and who's holding them. It's a job for a Hostage Rescue Unit, but things are going on behind the scenes. They won't let your men in until it's too late, if at all. I'm going in myself if I can, but I need some back-up.'

'I can't ask any of my men, not without official permission.'

'You won't get it.'

'Surely . . .'

'Believe me, Tommy, Clark won't give it. This is deeper than you think.'

There was a silence.

'All right. I'll come myself. I can promise you that, at least. Where do you want me to go?'

'Dunquin, on the Dingle peninsula.'

'I'll be there.'

347

CHAPTER SIXTY-FOUR

0914 hours

Harker told his driver to stop the car. They were in the middle of nowhere, on a road between two towns with ridiculous names, places so small they should never have been on a map at all. In its ruralness, Ireland reminded him of parts of France, but there were no vineyards here, no chateaux, no unexpected cathedrals, precious little sunshine. He hated the Irish, despised them for their parochiality, their bigotry, their lack of any real sophistication. And here they were suddenly at the heart of the world, barbarians become the hosts of the most delicate of entertainments.

As though by a miracle, the car telephone was working. He dialled a number in Dublin and got through immediately.

'News?'

'We just received a report from a place called Thurles, sir. They spent the night at a farmhouse and moved on this morning. Carberry and three others, dressed as priests and a nun. Still no reports of a sighting, though.'

'Keep me posted. They're still to be shot on sight.'

'Yes, sir. One thing – Carberry made a phone call to Washington last night and received one early this morning. The person he spoke to used his real name once by mistake.'

'Do you know where to?'

'The first was to the home of an FBI official, Conrad Lee. The second was from Lee, out of FBI Headquarters.'

CHAPTER SIXTY-FIVE

Inis Tuaisceart
0917 hours

'Bring her to the front.'

David Koresh had not known such a sense of power since his days at the Mount Carmel ranch. People loving him, fearing him, adoring him, loathing him – it gave him a sense of personal completeness. He needed the hatred quite as much as the adulation. The truly godly, he had preached often, are despised and rejected of men. They had crucified Jesus, stoned his apostles, burned his saints. Those whom the world adores, pop stars and sports heroes, politicians and movie queens, are never truly loved. When they fall from grace, they fall forever, for all they have and all they are is a sham. Michael Jackson had fallen, O J Simpson had fallen, even Jim Bakker and Jimmy Swaggart had fallen.

He, on the other hand, though his name had been dragged through the mud and his photograph published throughout the world as the quintessence of evil, was in reality purer than ice or fire.

Amina tried to pray, and could not. There was too much of God in this place. The day before her ears had been deafened by the singing of hymns and the voice of David Koresh praising his Creator and himself in equal measure. She could see the block set up on the stage, and the axe lying beside it. Her attempt to strike back had failed, and now she was going to pay for it.

At first she had thought it was to be her hands, as with the others; but as she stepped onto the stage, Ezekiel stepped forward and tied her hands behind her back, and she knew that it was worse, much worse.

'Kneel down,' said Koresh. He was dressed in jeans and a dirty tee-shirt, his hair had not been washed in weeks, his chin was heavily stubbled.

She looked hard into his face. She had made up her mind not to ask for mercy, but it felt such a cheap thing to let herself be killed by a man like this, for so little reason.

'Kneel down,' he repeated, pointing out the place. She did not move. Ezekiel came behind her and placed his hands on her shoulders. A sharp push forced her down. The block was in front of her. It seemed absurd, like some medieval fantasy. All this would stop, she thought, as the axe falls, and I will wake up in bed with the sun on my face.

Koresh stepped to the front. Without speaking, he removed his tee-shirt, revealing the wounds Amina had inflicted on him. They were red and caked with blood. None of them had been serious, he had never been in any real danger, but they looked deep and painful, clearly inflicted in the course of a frenzied attack.

'This is her work,' he said. 'I offered her God's body, and she wounded me. I offered her the true communion, my own flesh and blood, and she tried to stab me to the heart. When I was on earth before, I let them flog me and hurt my head with thorns and hammer nails into my hands and feet. But today I shall not be crucified. Today, those who persecute me shall perish instead.'

He paused and looked round the room, at the blank, bearded faces, each struggling with his own fear. Had they guessed the truth by now, that they would all perish, that the time of destruction was at hand?

'I remember,' he went on, 'back home in Texas, I used to watch a lot of television. One day, I was watching this programme, it was to do with the war in the Middle East, and I was interested because I visited Israel once, and I know Armageddon will start out there. And in this programme, they showed how in Saudi Arabia they execute people by cutting off their heads. There wasn't any film, because they don't allow people to film that stuff; but they'd done some drawings of how it looked, and I thought how awesome it was, because it reminded me of the Old Testament and how God dealt with the wrongdoers back then.

'I remembered how Jael, the wife of Heber, cut off the head of Sisera. And David slew Goliath, as I already told you, and cut off his head, and took it before Saul. And how Judith went into the tent of Holofernes and made up to him, then sliced his head off with a sword.

'Well, I don't have a sword, but I have an axe, and I reckon my axe will do the job as well as anything.'

He turned to Amina. Her entire body felt numb, as though each of her senses in turn was shutting down. Before this, she had thought that memories would race through her brain, that all times and places she had known would be present almost simultaneously; but nothing like that had happened, every moment passed with leaden feet, every word was stretched out, as though played at the wrong speed, every breath seemed to last a day or a week.

'If you keep real still,' he said, 'I'll take care not to miss. That way it'll be over in one blow. But if you wriggle or try to dodge, I'll miss your neck, and we'll just have to start again.'

He nodded to Ezekiel. Carefully, Ezekiel knelt down beside Amina and, taking her head in both his hands, he forced it down to the block.

'I've talked to him about this,' he said, 'and I can't budge him. Just do what he says, keep still, and you won't know a thing. I sharpened the axe this morning. He's strong and the axe is heavy. Heavy and sharp. Is there anything you want to say to anyone?'

She tried to answer, but her tongue would not work. There were a million things to say, all the things she had thought and never said, but it was too late.

'I'll pray for you,' he said.

She managed to look up.

'Pray for yourself,' she said haltingly. 'You're the one that needs it.'

Ezekiel took his hands away and stood up. He looked at Koresh, silently pleading with him to stop now, but his leader showed no sign of relenting.

At that moment, there was a shout from the middle row of onlookers. Koresh and Ezekiel looked round. An old man was on his feet.

'This is evil!' he shouted in English. 'Is not justice. She has wounded you, you kill her. Where is justice? In Qur'an, God is called Merciful and Compassionate. *Al-Rahman, al-Rahim*. Where is your mercy, your compassion?'

'Make him sit down and shut up,' said Koresh.

But the old man kept speaking, he would not be quieted.

'If you want kill, kill me. I am your enemy, not this woman. I am old, have less time to live, is more just.'

Among the hostages, those who spoke English realized what the old man was saying. They turned in their chairs, shaking their heads, calling to him in Arabic not to be so foolish, to sit down and accept what was happening. But nothing would budge him.

On the stage, Koresh seemed flustered. He had not planned for this. The old man in his strange, foreign clothes was obviously a figure of some respect among the hostages. His offer threatened to turn the tables, to expose Koresh's own weakness and cowardice.

Now, the hostages nearest the old man were letting him push past them and into the aisle. Everywhere, there were murmurings. The guards on either side of the room were growing uneasy, fearing some sort of rebellion, a rising that might have to be put down violently. The old man was in the aisle now. One of the guards took him by the arm, trying to force him back to his seat.

Then, from the stage, Koresh called out.

'Bring him here,' he said.

There was a moment's confusion, then the guard understood and led the old man down to the front of the room.

'Come up here.' Koresh was desperately trying to regain command of the situation.

The old man stepped slowly up to the stage. He was thin and stooped, his limbs moved arthritically, yet he walked with composure and dignity. Below, no-one spoke now. A silence was growing that was more than mere silence.

'What's your name?' asked Koresh.

'I am Shaykh Mu'in Usayran. A Muslim and the son of a Muslim. What was to me from God I now return to Him. You may have my life in return for the woman's life. It is fair exchange.'

'Why are you doing this?'

'It is Muslim's duty to help do what is good and stop what is evil. This is an evil thing.'

Koresh deliberated. He had seen the reaction to Usayran's offer, sensed the dismay among those present. By now, they all understood what was happening, people had passed on messages in Arabic from row to row. If he did not kill the old man, they would be relieved. He would have given them hope. They did not care

352

if the woman died, but one of their leaders in her place – that would be a great blow.

'Very well,' he said. 'You can have your wish.'

He turned to Ezekiel.

'Take her back to her cell. See she's chained up. I haven't finished with her yet.'

When Amina, still shaking, had been led from the stage, Koresh faced Usayran. For a moment he looked into the old man's eyes, but what he saw there was so unexpected and so uncompromising that he had to look away. Not reproach, not fear, not anger – none of the things he might have looked for. But compassion, as though the old man knew what devils walked through David Koresh's mind.

Ezekiel was there again, waiting at the foot of the steps.

'Let's get this over with,' said Koresh in a quiet voice, as though speaking only to himself.

CHAPTER SIXTY-SIX

County Tipperary
1023 hours

'There's no-one,' Maureen said. 'We're on our own.'

They had left the van at a garage belonging to a Republican family in Cavan. Over the next few days, it would be stripped and carted off in pieces for scrap. The garage had given them a car, a Ford Sierra, and the papers to go with it.

They were in a narrow lane off a side-road in Tipperary, going over a map they had bought at a stationer's shop in Birr. She was explaining the layout of the coast and the islands, as far as she remembered them. It had been several years since her last visit, she did not know the area particularly well.

'You mean you have no people there at all?'

She shook her head.

'No, of course we have. Kerry's always been a Republican county, ever since the Civil War. Terrible things were done back then, and memories are long in the West. But we have no ASUs, no-one with proper military training. We still recruit in the region, but it's not like Donegal or Monaghan, there's no need to keep fighting units at the ready. Most of the volunteers are moved on, either to the North or across to England.'

'This isn't what I planned for,' he said. 'Your people and mine made a deal. The IRA is being paid handsomely to provide me with assistance. I need proper back-up. I am not in a position to negotiate with the hostage-takers, so I have no choice but to take Shaykh Mu'in from them by force. Now you say there are only two of us.'

'We'll have help with supplies and so on. Accommodation,

equipment, boats – whatever they have down there. But it would take time to send another ASU from the North. The team we had should have been perfect. They weren't on active service when we heard you were coming. That was why it was possible to make them available at such short notice.'

'Then why the raid last night? Because of us? Because of what happened in Belfast?'

She shook her head. They had slept very little the night before, and she was tired. Hours of driving had worn her down, with the constant dread of turning a bend that would lead them straight into the arms of a police or army patrol. There had been Gardaí checkpoints, which she had avoided by taking side-roads; but she was sure the Brits had tipped off the authorities in the South and that they were on the lookout for them.

'They were MI5,' she said. 'Undercover troops trained by the SAS in Hereford, but run by MI5's Northern Ireland office. They wanted the ASU. Not you, not me, just the others. Mind you, they'd have been happy as Larry to get us into the bargain, we'd have been a terrific catch for them, dead or alive. But it was the fellows from Belfast they were after. And they wanted them just one way: dead.'

'Why? Why risk a raid across the border to kill a team not in active service?'

She might as well tell him, she thought. He would have guessed by now that it was revenge, he came from a culture in which that was perfectly normal. And, in any case, she reckoned he had a right to know.

'It was back in August,' she said. 'Some leading MI5 men were visiting Belfast to set up a deal with the Loyalists. The plan got to the ears of some people in the British army, who weren't very happy about it. They've been having talks with our people, trying to reach an agreement that will let them take their troops home. We set up an ambush. The army stood aside while our ASU went in and shot the people from MI5.'

'And MI5 were there last night because we brought the ASU to life again? That's what alerted them, isn't it?'

'I guess so. I don't believe in coincidences. We may never know just how they found out where we were. But, yes, it was something like that.'

'I can't complain then, can I?'

She shook her head.

'Not really. But you weren't to know, we never told you.'

'That's all right. But you're willing to go on? Even after last night?'

'What, the shooting?'

He shook his head.

'No, not that. What I made you do. In the window, in front of all those men. It was wrong of me, I . . .'

'It was the right thing. I'd be dead if you hadn't got out and come back the way you did.'

'And after . . .' He hesitated. He did not have the words. He had never spoken of such things to a woman. The formalities of desire.

'I know what you mean.' She looked straight at him. He would never know how much he had hurt her, she would never tell him. 'It isn't important. You did what you had to. If you'd stayed, we'd both have been killed. You did the right thing.'

He reached out a hand and touched her cheek. She closed her eyes, almost flinching. Small tears formed beneath her eyelids.

'Not right,' he said, 'just necessary. But you know that I wanted you.'

She leaned forward, and he took her and cradled her against his shoulder.

'Did you?' she asked. She could not stop the tears rolling down her cheeks. 'Did you?'

'I still do,' he said.

CHAPTER SIXTY-SEVEN

Dunquin
County Kerry
1217 hours

Dunquin sits on the end of the Dingle peninsula, with views to the sea and the long-abandoned Blasket Islands. Inis Tuaisceart lies almost exactly five miles away, directly west.

Declan found them lodgings in Kruger's Pub. He and Grainne registered as man and wife, Myles and Liam also shared a room. Once they had put their bits and pieces away, they went down to the beach.

Liam still had some of the equipment he had brought from Dublin, including a powerful Simrad binocular telescope that would work equally by day or night. With its help, they could see the island, a small heap of land rising from the sea, with a low coast on its eastern side. There were buildings here and there, and once or twice they saw people walking in and out of them. But in itself it was a promising sign, that the island was definitely inhabited.

'Liam,' said Declan, 'your Irish is better than mine or Myles's. I'd like you to go back to the village and have a chat with some of the locals. Buy them a few rounds of Guinness, tell them your father was a Blasket islander, say you knew Peig Sayers and Tómas O Cromthain personally – but find out what they know about whoever that is over there. Where they land on the island and here on the mainland, how many they think there are: you know the sort of thing we need.'

'They may not be talkative.'

'You're a Kerryman yourself, you can loosen their tongues.'

'Well, I'll try. But it may take time.'

When he was gone, Declan spoke to Myles.

'Myles, I'd like you to find a car and make your way back to Dublin. We need to make contact with Pádraig Pearse. He's not without resources even now. I'll write you a letter for him, and I'll give you a list of other people I'd like you to speak to. You have to tell them what you know about Koresh, what he's capable of. I'll do what I can at this end, even if it's just to keep an eye on things from a distance. But you've got to convince the right people that an assault on the island could lead to disaster.'

'We don't know the hostages are there yet.'

'I know. But I intend to get onto the island to find out. There's bound to be diving equipment for hire. You can keep in touch through the pub.'

'I'll do my best, Declan.'

'Good man. Go and find a car. Ask at the pub first, they'll know the most likely person. I'll see you there in half an hour.'

When Myles had gone, Declan and Grainne sat together on the beach, glancing from time to time at the rough outline of Inis Tuaisceart far out at sea.

'It's too far to swim,' she said.

'I know that well enough. But there are boats in and out of here all day long. I can row close in the dark, then swim the rest of the way.'

'Then you'll need someone with you. I can handle a boat. It's too risky on your own.'

He hesitated, then realized that she was right.

'All right,' he said. 'But I'm going on to the island alone. If I'm not back after a specified time – say, two hours – you're to row back alone. That's my condition. If we're both lost, it cuts down the chances for everyone else.'

She agreed reluctantly.

'If Abu Hida gets this far,' she asked, 'where do you think he'll go?'

Declan shrugged.

'It depends. If one of the ASU was with him, he might be able to make contact with some local Republicans, get help from them.'

He stood up. The sky above still held a threat of rain or worse. On the beach, waves fell hard against bright wet rocks. Seaweed moved in deep pools without sound. A light mist rode over Inis Tuaisceart.

'That's it,' he said. He turned to Grainne, his eyes bright. 'All we have to do is find who the local IRA men are. Even if all the ASU are dead, Abu Hida is bound to have contacts in Belfast. They'll put him in touch with their people down here. If he's here at all, that's where he'll be.'

Back in the pub, Liam was playing the Kerryman for all it was worth, speaking in broad West Munster Irish, ordering drinks all round. '*Tabhair dúinn dhá ghloine fuiscí, mas é do thoil é,*' Declan overheard him say, getting two more whiskeys for a couple of old fellows sat hard in by the bar.

He left Grainne chatting to the publican's wife, and stepped into the saloon. His own Irish was bookish, learnt at great cost in school. But here in the Gaeltacht, English marked a man and made the winning of trust that much harder. They needed local information badly, and Liam had to have support in his efforts to get it.

'*Dia's Muire duit, a Liam!*' he said, taking a chair from a nearby table and drawing it up to Liam's.

'*Dia's Muire duit agus Pádraig, a Declan,*' answered Liam. 'Can I get you a drink?'

Declan nodded.

'I'll have a Murphy's,' he said. A glass was ordered and brought. By then, Liam had made the introductions. Declan shook hands with the other men round the table. They were old men mostly. He guessed they would have known Michael Deighan.

'Liam,' he said, leaning over, 'would you mind coming outside? I'd like a quick word with you.'

'Sure, you haven't had your stout yet.'

'It'll keep. Come on, this is important.'

Apologizing for the interruption, they left the old men to their drinks. Outside, Declan walked down the little street with Liam.

'Liam, do you think you could break into the police computer using your laptop? You have a modem.'

Liam frowned.

'Jesus, Declan, it's not as simple as that. They'll have changed all the passwords. It could take hours. If I make a mistake, they'll be on top of us before we know what's happening. What do you need to know?'

359

'I need the name of at least one IRA informer in or near Dunquin. Someone who'd know if Abu Hida made contact. And I'd like to know what makes our man tick, what I can use to make him sing to me.'

'It's a bird you want, Declan.'

'I'll be content with an informer.'

Liam sighed. It could be done, but it would mean taking a risk.

'Don't worry,' he said, 'I'll get you one.'

CHAPTER SIXTY-EIGHT

Jean hadn't spoken to him since he got back, but Conrad sensed she was starting to thaw a little. As she was clearing the breakfast things away, he told her about Máiréad Carberry. Jean had known her from a visit they'd made to Ireland one year. They'd spent a month together with the Carberrys, half in Killiney and half at Craigpatrick.

'You should have told me before this,' she said. 'I'd have understood.'

'Not when you had guests, that wouldn't have been fair.'

'At least I'd have known what you were doing, why it was so important. Is Declan in any danger?'

'No, he's quite safe.'

The children came in just then, Michele, who was thirteen, and Louise, who had just turned six. Michele would remember Máiréad, Conrad thought; but he didn't want to tell her until he knew more about what had happened. She'd ask questions, and he didn't have the right answers.

'Everything's packed, Dad. We won't get there in time for lunch if we don't leave right now.'

'OK, sweetheart, we'll be out in a minute.'

They were all going to Williamsburg for the day. It was the kids' favourite drive; each time they went, Michele decided she was going to be an historian. Unfortunately, her grades in history never quite matched the aspiration.

'Michele, which car did you put the things in?' asked Jean.

'In Dad's, just like you said.'

'I thought we were going in your car, honey,' Conrad put in. Jean drove a Volvo estate, which was more useful for days out.

'I'm sorry,' she said, 'but with your unforgivable behaviour last night I forgot to tell you that the Volvo's got a transmission problem. It's sticking in second. I'm going to take it in to the garage tomorrow. We'll take your car today.'

'OK, but I'll have to get some gas on the way out of town.'

'Come on, Dad, it's late!' shouted Louise.

Conrad ran to pick her up, swung her under one arm, and carried her to the car laughing.

The children got in. Jean locked the front door, her thoughts still fixed on what had happened to poor Máiréad. Shot, Conrad had said. Was the war over there spreading South?

She got into the passenger seat.

'Sure you wouldn't like me to drive, dear?'

'You can drive back.'

He looked round.

'You kids got your belts on? OK, here we go.'

He turned the key in the ignition and the engine leapt into life. They rolled out of the drive and set off.

They'd been driving on Highway 95 for several minutes when Jean first started feeling drowsy. She pressed the button to wind down her window. Nothing happened.

'Honey, my window's stuck. Could you roll yours down to let some air in? It feels real stuffy.'

Conrad pressed the button on his door. The window stayed where it was. She was right, he thought, it was feeling stuffy. By that time, the gas had penetrated the whole of the car's interior.

'Michele,' Conrad said, half-glancing back, 'our windows are stuck up front. Could you open one in the back, please?'

Michele tried one side, then the other.

'They're both stuck, Dad. Hey, can we stop, I'm feeling kinda funny. And Louise is falling asleep.'

'Watch out!' Jean caught the wheel just in time as Conrad swayed, almost driving straight into the path of an oncoming truck.

'Better pull in, we're all . . . falling . . . asleep.'

The gas was odourless and tasteless, and it kept on coming. There was enough in the little canister to fill the car twenty times.

The next truck, the truck that killed them, was going too fast.

When Conrad swerved for the last time, the other driver didn't stand a chance.

When the rescue team finally arrived to cut their bodies from the wreckage, the gas had entirely dispersed. There was not a trace of it in or around the car. Later, the canister that had held it would find its way into a garbage pail in a garage belonging to the FBI's motor vehicle examination centre.

CHAPTER SIXTY-NINE

David Koresh washed his hands carefully. There was little fresh water on the island, what they used – and used sparingly – came mostly from rain butts placed at intervals through the yard. Fortunately, there had been plenty of rain since their arrival, and they still had enough filters to let them use most of what they had for drinking. The hostages were rationed to one litre each per day, with sea water for their washing and religious ablutions. There had been some fuss at first, but Koresh had settled it by threatening to make them drink the salt water as well.

He came out of his private bathroom to find Zechariah waiting for him.

'Have they settled down?' he asked.

Zechariah nodded.

From the men's cells nearby came the sound of voices raised in prayer, some angry, some sad, some frightened.

'They're praying hard,' Koresh said. 'I guess old Allah just doesn't listen.' He smiled at his own joke and turned to Zechariah.

He crossed the room to a small refrigerator and took out a Coca Cola.

'Want one?' he asked, holding it out to Zechariah.

'No, thanks.'

Koresh closed the door of the fridge and opened the can. He drank half of it and wiped his lips.

'Sir, you said you wanted to see me.'

'That's right. We need to talk. Sit down.'

Koresh finished his Coke and put the empty can down on a

table. Zechariah sat down, watching him. He never knew what way things were going to go. The execution of the old man had been sickening, and he was still trying to see the wisdom in it. He guessed he'd have to do a lot of praying himself tonight.

'Zechariah, when we came here you did a job for me. While Ezekiel was away planning the raid and bringing back the hostages.'

'Yes, sir.'

'Who knew about it other than yourself?'

Zechariah fidgeted. He never liked being this close to Koresh.

'Munro and Peters. We buried the charges together, fifteen each, twenty pounds a charge.'

'Just the three of you?'

'That's right.'

'You've told no-one else? Ezekiel, for example?'

Zechariah shook his head. He had long curly locks that flopped over his forehead and caught the light.

'No-one. You told me yourself, and I made sure Munro and Peters understood.'

'Fine.' Koresh fetched himself another Coke. He was coming to the end of his supply, but he guessed it didn't matter much now.

'Last time,' he said, returning to his seat, 'things went a little wrong. A lot of people escaped. The Lord did not receive His due sacrifice.'

'That's true.'

'A lot of people died in vain. Can I have your assurance that when I press that button it'll leave no-one alive?'

Zechariah licked his lips. He felt hot and uncertain of himself. The direction of the conversation made him uneasy.

'When that lot goes up, sir, they'll see this island erupt back in America.'

'Well, it may still come to that, Zechariah; it may still come to that. Thanks for reassuring me. Will you find Munro and Peters and ask them to pay me a visit?'

'Yes, sir. Now, sir?'

'As soon as you find them.'

Outside, Ezekiel slipped away down the corridor and past the cells containing the male hostages. He hadn't heard everything, but he had grasped enough. David wasn't going to be content to wait on God's will to usher in the apocalypse; he was going to start it himself. And from the look of it, it was going to be tonight.

CHAPTER SEVENTY

Dunquin
1413 hours

'He's called Lynch. Patrick Thomas Mary, aged fifty-five, a school-teacher. He lives in Ballyferriter. Married with seven children, all girls, the eldest two with husbands. His father fought against the Free Staters in the Civil War. An uncle was involved in the Maga-zine Fort raid in 1939. He joined the movement himself when he was seventeen and has been a treasurer for Sinn Féin in Kerry ever since.'

Liam passed the printout he had just prepared to Declan. They were alone in what was now Liam's room: Myles had found a car and set off for Dublin.

'Yes, I've heard of him. But he doesn't sound as if he'd be much use to us,' said Declan. 'Too loyal.'

'Now, don't be in such a hurry, Declan. I hadn't finished. It seems our Mr Lynch was a greedy man. Spent a bit on the races. He was by all accounts a regular visitor at the meetings on Ross Road. Apparently, he lost a lot of money, but with seven children he needed more. So he dipped his fingers into the pot. And went on dipping.'

'For how long?'

'He'd been at it for ten years when C3 first came across him. That was in 1986. And not just Sinn Féin money. IRA funds as well, some of them from America.'

'How'd he get away with it for so long?'

'He was very nearly found out just before they got on to him. If they hadn't done, he'd have been dead long ago. One of Martin Fitzsimmons's men, Denis Laverty, saw what was happening and offered him a choice: be found out or act as an informer. He's been on an allowance ever since. It helps him keep the books straight, and it supplies us with all we know about the IRA in Kerry.'

'I take back what I said. He's the very man. Have you got an address?'

'It's there in front of you.'

'Well, then, get the car out and I'll give you a letter to take round to Ballyferriter.'

They did not have to wait long. Abu Hida and Maureen O'Dalaigh were expected any time. Liam left the letter and a phone number. Shortly after five, Maureen rang the pub and asked to speak to Declan.

'Is this true?' she asked.

'Yes,' he said. 'We have to meet. Even if you decide to act on your own, we have to talk things over. I can help you, I promise.'

'From what I hear, you're as much outside the law here as we are. What possible help can you be?'

'I can get your friend out of Ireland, him and anyone he wants to bring with him. As for yourself, it's too early to say. But I won't hand you over.'

'What if he says to hell with you?'

'That's his prerogative. But I'd think he was a fool. It can't do either of you any harm to meet. We already know where you are, we can pass on the information without damage to ourselves. Things could become uncomfortable.'

There was a brief pause. Declan could hear a whispered conversation.

A man's voice came on.

'They'll meet you in half an hour's time. There's a stone circle just south of Ballyferriter. You can't miss it. If you're driving from Dunquin, take the road to Teeravone and go on through. It's off the road about half a mile along, before you get to Ballyferriter itself. See there's no funny business. There'll be somebody watching you the whole time.'

The Dingle peninsula is littered with the past. The ruins of monasteries and oratories, beehive huts and stone circles, ring forts and Celtic crosses abound everywhere. The Saint's Road runs from

Kilmalkedar to the top of Mount Brandon and St Brendan's Oratory. Here, more than anywhere else, the visitor can see for himself why Ireland was once the shining light of the Christian West, the home of culture and learning when the rest of Europe was in darkness. It seemed a fit setting for the meeting between Declan and Abu Hida.

Grainne and Maureen accompanied them, waiting at a distance while they talked. There was no need for an interpreter. A low mist had come in from the sea and settled around the stones. The countryside was silent. No-one passed. As the two men talked, it grew dark. Night was coming. Ghosts gathered in the circle of standing stones, the pagan and Christian dead, the famine starved, the victims of invasion and war. In 1580, just a little north of here at Dún an Oir, a band of Munster rebels had been massacred by English troops. Men, women, and children had all died, among them Italians, Spaniards, and English Catholics. The air was thick with sudden death.

Declan and Abu Hida talked for a long time. Finally, they shook hands. Grainne saw Declan come towards her out of the mist. His face was serious, his eyes troubled.

'We've decided to get Amina and his father out. If we can rescue one or two others, all to the good. He thinks that, if we can put even a couple of hostages on television, it will force Clark's hand. We're going across tonight.'

He rang Tommy Murtagh when they got back to Dunquin.

'Tommy? We're going in tonight. Are you still game?'

'I'll be there. I've got a score or two of my own to settle.'

CHAPTER SEVENTY-ONE

Dunquin
1815 hours

Declan sipped his orange juice and put the glass back on the table. He'd have preferred a whiskey, but not with the business that lay ahead of him. Liam and Grainne each had mineral waters. They were sitting in a private room in the pub.

'Well, Liam, your exertions earlier today have paid off. One of the old men claims to have known your father. His name is Cearbhall O'Hannrachain.'

'Never heard of him.'

'Maybe not. But whether or not he knew your father, he did know Michael Deighan quite well. Well enough to be bitter about his death. A lot of people round here feel the same way, he says. I asked him about the people on the island, and he told me something of interest. Cearbhall O'Hannrachain has a sister who lives in Clogher, a short step north of here. Most evenings he cycles over there. The road passes near the coast, towards Clogher Head, then in again to Clogher itself.

'Our Mr O'Hannrachain says he has seen lights on the beach below the head several nights in a row. He thinks someone comes ashore from Inis Tuaisceart and drives off in a car, headed inland, towards Dingle.'

'The bodies and the hands,' said Grainne.

'Yes, I think so. And I think perhaps Michael Deighan stumbled across them, maybe during the day. I suggest we go on up to Clogher Head and keep watch. If there are lights, we head down to the beach and pick up whoever lands and whoever is there to pick them up. Some gentle questioning should tell us all we need to know about the set-up.'

'I wouldn't be so confident, judging from what Myles says.'

'It's worth a try. Let's get our friends from Ballyferriter. They should have the equipment by now anyway.' He glanced at his watch. 'We've no time to waste.'

They met on Clogher Head, hooded figures like witches meeting for their Sabbath. Declan had spent an hour with Tommy Murtagh, explaining what he knew about Koresh. Tommy had brought extra weapons and, more importantly, expertise.

Abu Hida had been as good as his word. Through Patrick Lynch he had been able to obtain a boat, a locally-built rowboat that would take them to Inis Tuaisceart. He had the weapons he had taken from the cache at Ballybay. They would be kept in waterproof bags until needed. He went through the details of what he had brought with Tommy, and together they made an assessment of their strengths and weaknesses.

Declan described in as much detail as he could the circumstances of the assault on Castletown House: the tactics used by the raiders, their dress, their equipment, their weaponry. Abu Hida listened carefully.

'It makes our task all the more formidable,' he said. 'They will not be easily fooled.'

'No. But I think their efficiency may be undermined by their religious zeal.'

'I would not depend on that. My people are zealous, but we are not poor fighters on that account. The mujahidin in Afghanistan pushed the Russians out. Zealots, Mr Carberry. Fanatics. Whatever you wish. But an efficient fighting force for all that. Don't underestimate these people because they pray.'

'Yes, I see your point. Then we can only assume that we'll be up against tough opposition.'

'Only if they know we're there,' said Tommy. 'The thing is to get in and out again as quickly as possible, and be as far away as we can before they can organize a response. It'll be much easier if we know what to expect.'

'It may be a long wait,' Declan said. 'We don't know that anyone's due to cross to the mainland tonight.'

'Then we just go on waiting.'

Declan kept watch along the strip of coast south of the head. From time to time, Abu Hida would relieve him, positioning himself behind a large rock from which he could see right along the coast as far as Blasket Sound, where Dunmore Head reaches out a hand towards the Great Blasket.

'How old was your daughter?'

'She was eighteen last May.'

'She was beautiful?'

'Yes. Very beautiful.'

'And you loved her?'

'Yes, of course.'

'You love your wife?'

'No,' said Declan, surprised by his candour with a man whom he had once considered his enemy.

'That is a pity. A man should love his wife.'

'Fate isn't always kind. Are you married?'

Abu Hida shook his head. Along the coast, small banks of mist still drifted in from the open sea. The lights of fishing boats bobbed on the dark water of the Sound.

'I have chosen *jihad* above comfort,' he said. 'The path of God is not for married men.'

They went on watching. Grainne and Maureen took turns to watch the coastline north of the head, as far as Sybil Point, in case anyone tried to make a landing there instead. Liam and Tommy watched their rear and went over the problems affecting communications.

'When this is over,' said Declan, 'if we're still alive, I can help you get out of Ireland along with Shaykh Usayran and anyone else you may want to take. But I can't do anything about Maureen. She can take her chances, but I can't protect her. She's an Irish citizen, but the British can claim a right to her as well.'

He had noticed earlier how Abu Hida and Maureen were together, sensed the undercurrent of desire and affection that passed between them. He clung to it as a means of humanizing them for himself, for he knew that otherwise he would find it difficult to accept them as allies.

Abu Hida said nothing in reply. It was still too soon for him to know what he really felt for Maureen. Love was not a word that had ever figured commonly in his vocabulary.

'Look!' he said. 'Down there.'

Declan took the glasses from him. On a flat beach just north of Dunquin, the headlights of a car were flashing.

CHAPTER SEVENTY-TWO

0026 hours

By the time Ezekiel saw the lights, he had already rowed about a quarter of a mile off course. Usually he could depend on the village lights of Dunquin to give him his general direction, relying on the car to bring him in to the beach; but tonight the frequent patches of mist made navigation more difficult. He pulled round, rowing hard towards the lights, and wishing as always that he could use the engine when approaching or leaving the mainland shore. It was out of the question, of course, but the rowing did slow things down, and he felt tired and depressed tonight.

The shaykh's head lay under a seat, wrapped in burlap. It lay more heavily on Ezekiel's heart, troubling him with disloyal thoughts. He was unable to free himself of the image of the old man, getting unsteadily to his feet in the knowledge that he was sealing his own doom. Nor could he erase the old man's face as he stared at his killer with such equanimity. Could these all be the devil's spawn, as Koresh maintained? He found it hard to reconcile the old man's Christian fortitude with the cruelty of his death at the hands of someone he believed to be the son of God.

He also found it hard to refresh his shrivelled loyalty to the man he had considered God for so many years. Knowing that David planned to kill everyone in the compound brought back the most painful of memories. The sight of fire and the sound of children's voices calling for help. And if they all went to hell, all those Muslim men and women, would they be there for all eternity calling for help?

That was what David taught, it was what Ezekiel himself had believed for years. But he thought of his own children in flames, and he thought of them enduring that pain for another hour, another day, another week. And he thought of Jewish children who had gone to their deaths in the concentration camps. They'd never heard of Jesus, they'd never had a chance, but God had punished them all the same, God was burning them for having been born Jews at the wrong time and the wrong place.

The boat crunched onto the shore and he jumped out, thrusting the disloyal thoughts away. Ramon switched off the car lights and came down the narrow beach, ready to help pull the little craft further up the slope, above the reach of the tide. Ramon was Mexican, one of several immigrants who had joined the church in recent years. He had served in the Mexican army in a communications unit, and Koresh had given him the task of keeping a base open on shore. He lived in a small caravan in the campsite at Carhoo, just above Dunquin.

'A terrible night,' he said. 'This mist make my bones to hurt.'

'You could always try rowing to Mexico,' said Ezekiel. It was a regular joke between them. 'It's right across there.' He pointed out to sea. 'You just have to point the boat in the right direction and get David's blessing.'

'Not to joke about such things, please.' Ramon was one of Koresh's most dedicated followers, utterly loyal to the man who had rescued him from deportation back to a life of poverty in Mexico.

They got the boat settled and the oars properly stowed. Suddenly, a bright light erupted in the darkness and flashed in their faces, blinding them.

'Stay absolutely still!' came a voice from the darkness at the top of the beach.

Ramon whirled. He always carried an Uzi pistol in his belt. Now, pulling it out, he started firing wildly, unable to see straight or aim. But firing towards the light was enough. Several bullets hit Liam in the chest and shoulder, bringing him down and sending the light bouncing across the sand.

A second light flared, picking Ramon out. Abu Hida raised his own pistol and shot him twice in the head. The Mexican fell and lay still.

The sound of gunfire rolled out to sea. Back in Dunquin, people looked up from whatever they were doing and exchanged glances. On the beach, the silence that followed the shooting was protracted. No-one spoke. No-one seemed to breathe. Then, slowly, sounds began to creep back out of the darkness. Waves shattered on the shore. Someone's feet crunched the shingle as though it were broken glass. From far away, the sound of a car engine drifted through the night. But what everyone heard most clearly was the sound of liquid bubbling in Liam Kennedy's chest as he struggled to breathe.

Declan bent down beside him, holding his head with one hand from below.

'Hold on, Liam. We'll get you up to the car. It's not a long drive to Dingle. They have a hospital on the west of the town. They'll look after you there.'

'Don't . . . be . . . a bloody . . . fool, sir.' Liam spluttered, choking on blood. 'Be . . . a . . . waste of . . . time.'

'Lie still, Liam, and try not to talk.'

'Make . . . no . . . difference . . . Finished . . . anyway . . .'

In the light of the torch, Tommy knelt and peeled back Liam's shirt. A glance told them he was right. It would be a wasted journey, one he would not survive.

'We were . . . in the . . . right, sir . . . weren't we? . . . Be sure . . . to tell . . . the wife . . . I never did . . . anything wrong.'

'It was all for the best, Liam. To save lives. You were appointed by the Taoiseach himself. I'll be sure to tell her that. They'll give you a medal.'

'The fuck . . . they . . . will . . .'

Declan looked down, then up at Tommy. He shook his head. Declan closed his eyes for a moment, then reached out and put his fingers over Liam's eyelids, the left, then the right, closing them. Only the sound of the sea now, falling on the dark, pebbled beach.

Abu Hida and Maureen had already dragged Ezekiel to the road. He had not resisted. When Declan and Grainne got back to the car, he was sitting in the back seat with Maureen, staring ahead, as though at some darkness beyond the windscreen that only he could see.

'He's dead,' said Declan, getting into the driver's seat. Abu Hida was in the front passenger seat beside him.

'I'm sorry,' said Abu Hida. 'You've lost a lot of your men.'

'He wasn't just one of my men,' snapped Declan. 'He was a friend.'

'I understand. Believe me.'

'Do you?'

Abu Hida looked round, puzzled by the sharpness in Declan's voice.

'We have to get out of here,' he said. 'Someone will have heard the shooting. The police will be poking their noses in before long.'

Declan started the car. As he eased it into gear and prepared to leave, a voice came from the back seat. Ezekiel was leaning forward, agitated.

'The head,' he said, 'the old man's head. I left it in the boat.'

Declan cut the engine. He felt giddy, almost paralysed. Slowly, he turned round.

'What did you say?'

Ezekiel stared at him, a shadow within a darkness to which he was blind. Maureen grabbed him by the shoulders and shook him.

'What did you say, you fucker? What did you say?'

'Leave him,' said Declan. The man was not just frightened, there was something more, something Declan could not properly grasp. Hurting or threatening him would only drive him deeper into whatever it was.

'You said something about a head,' said Declan, 'that you had left it on the boat. What did you mean?'

Ezekiel stared into the darkness, struggling to make sense of things none of the others could see.

'I had to deliver it in Dublin. He wanted me to leave it in a church.'

'A head?'

'He cut it off. In place of the woman's. The old man volunteered.'

Abu Hida leaned across from the front.

'What old man? What was his name?'

'I don't know. A foreign name. They all sound the same.'

'No,' said Abu Hida. 'They do not.' He turned to Declan. 'We'd better take a look in the boat.'

They walked together back down the beach. The waves had not parted from the shore, the mist still lay along the surface of the sand or stretched, ectoplasmic, across the rocks. Their feet dug deep into the shingle in sharp, shuddering bursts.

The boat lay tilted along the border dividing sand and shingle.

Using their torches, they found the burlap sack. Abu Hida lifted it out gently while Declan played the light on it.

Carefully, Abu Hida unfolded the edges of the sack from the top of the head, then pulled the burlap down. The face was covered by blood-stained hair and beard. Cradling the head in his left hand, he drew them away.

Declan saw him sway, saw his face contract in pain, saw him close his eyes to shut out what he had just seen. And then out of nowhere there came a cry so heart-broken, so forsaken, so heavy with a lifetime's grief, and the grief of all the lifetimes that had gone before it, that Declan had to put his hands to his ears to shut it out. He saw Abu Hida sink to his knees, holding the severed head tight against his chest, swaying in his bereavement like a child torn from its mother, weeping into the mist and darkness, howling in his despair.

And Declan stood and watched, and glanced from time to time up the beach towards the spot where he and Tommy had left Liam Kennedy under a blanket. He thought of men and women he had known in Lebanon, all victims of Abu Hida and his friends, all dead; and their killer here, bowed down with the grief of his father's death on a beach at the end of the world.

Looking up, he heard the sea fall against the beach, and he saw the darkness multiplied. Out there on an abandoned rock was the only person in the world he loved. He saw Amina's face as it had been the last time he saw her, minutes before the raid. And he wondered if she was still alive or whether all that awaited him on Inis Tuaisceart was yet more grief.

CHAPTER SEVENTY-THREE

Ballyoughteragh
0050 hours

In a quiet spot near the golf links below Ballyoughteragh, Declan talked with Ezekiel. It took a long time to go through it all with him, but Declan was sure that persuasion would succeed where pain would have brought contempt and silence. Ezekiel was not afraid of the things that frightened ordinary men. The Day of Wrath was very close, perhaps only hours away: what would a day's torture matter, set against eternity?

'What's your name?' Declan asked.

'Ezekiel.'

'Like the prophet?'

'That's right. He gave me the name, bestowed it on me.'

'Who did? David?'

'That's right. Who are you? How do you know about David?'

'I'm a policeman, that's all. I want to help you. And I want you to help me rescue the hostages you took . . .'

'I know who you are,' Ezekiel broke in. 'You're Carberry. You were with that woman the night before the raid, the Arab woman, the one David wanted to kill.'

'Amina. Is she all right?'

Ezekiel nodded.

He wanted to ask more, but time was pressing.

'What were you called before he gave you the name Ezekiel?'

'Jay,' Ezekiel replied. 'Jay Johnson.'

Declan motioned Tommy to his side and whispered quickly to him.

'Tommy, get hold of Myles. Tell him we're holding one of

Koresh's people, a man by the name of Johnson, Jay Johnson. Ask him if his database has anything on him, something we can use.'

'I don't have a number.'

'He's staying in Máiréad's flat in Ballsbridge. I gave him the key. Here's the number.'

Declan wrote it on a piece of paper and went back to questioning Ezekiel. The man seemed almost intoxicated. It was hard to pin him down. He would answer no questions concerning the set-up on the island. Every time Declan glanced at his watch, valuable time had gone by.

He was on the point of giving up and handing Ezekiel over to Abu Hida, when Tommy came back.

'I've just come off the phone with Myles,' he said. 'Jay Johnson was at Waco. He was one of the Mighty Men, Koresh's personal bodyguard. It seems he managed to get out after the fire started and was arrested. Somehow or other, he got parole. He never showed up again. He had a wife and children: they died in the fire. The wife was called Mary, the little girls were Sarah and Rachel. Sarah was four, Rachel was two.'

Declan went back to Ezekiel. Above their heads, the night thickened, as though stirred by a great hand.

'Why didn't you tell me about your wife, Jay? Or about Sarah and Rachel?'

Ezekiel looked at him as though into a deep well, one in which he might drown himself.

'You know a lot,' he said. 'You know too damned much.'

'I had a daughter too,' continued Declan. 'She was shot less than a month ago, in Dublin. In an ice-cream parlour. She'd just told me she was going to have a baby in five months' time. The man who shot her was the Englishman you've got on Inis Tuaisceart, the one who communicates with Harker, keeps the deal intact.'

Ezekiel looked stunned.

'Deal? What deal?'

Declan frowned. Surely Ezekiel must know what Koresh was up to. But the question had sounded genuine.

'You don't know?'

Ezekiel shook his head.

'David brought Musgrave in because he knew ways of tapping

380

official communications. We need to know what's really going on with these negotiations.'

'How'd he get hold of Musgrave?'

Ezekiel shrugged.

'I'm not sure. David was in England a few years ago, he made a lot of friends. Musgrave used to be with military intelligence or something.'

'Not used to be, Jay. Is. Or, to be precise, he is working for MI5.'

Declan went on to tell Ezekiel all he knew. About Musgrave. About Harker. About Scimitar. When he had finished, he asked him again, 'Tell me about Mary and the children.' Ezekiel told him then, without hesitation. It was the first time he had talked of them to anyone since the inferno.

From there he went on to tell Declan all he needed to know. How the compound was set up, where there were guards, what sort of arms they carried, where the alarms had been set. It seemed to Declan that Koresh had relied more on his arrangement with Harker than on an elaborate defensive arrangement. If they could get through the outer perimeter of guards whose function was to watch the approaches to the island, they could easily get inside the compound itself.

Ezekiel drew a rough map, on which the guardroom, cells, sleeping quarters, and kitchens were all shown. He told Declan where Amina was being kept.

They had just about finished when Ezekiel sat bolt upright with his eyes wide and staring. He had remembered Koresh's talk with Zechariah.

'What is it, Jay? What's wrong?'

'He isn't going to wait. It's obvious now. He has explosive charges under the compound, and he's going to set them off. It's what he intended to do the first time, at Waco. This time he means to do the job properly.'

'Calm down, Jay, and tell me exactly what you know.'

Jay told him about the conversation he had overheard. And about his own talk with Koresh early that morning. When he had finished, Declan left Ezekiel tied up and went to join the others. From where they sat, they could hear the sea rising and falling against the shore. Carefully, he told them everything Ezekiel had said. No-one uttered a word.

Declan turned to Abu Hida.

'I realize,' he said, 'that you may not wish to come. Your father has been murdered. I'm sorry about that. And I'll understand if you say you want to leave now and go back to Lebanon. I'll still help you get out. I'll give you names and addresses of people to go to. Your own people have their own resources. Perhaps they'll be able to help you take Miss O'Dalaigh out with you, if that's what she wants. But I've already made my own mind up. I'm going across tonight.'

Abu Hida's voice came from the darkness, low and unforced.

'I will come with you,' he said. 'My father was not my only reason for coming. There are others whose release would mean a great deal to my people. Even if I can only secure the escape of one or two, it will be something.'

'And the others?' asked Declan. 'What about them?'

'I cannot help them all.'

'Had you no orders concerning them? Some of them are your enemies. Perhaps you would rather see them dead. I don't want you with me if that's how you feel. If you have orders to kill them.'

Abu Hida shook his head. A shadow gesturing in the dark.

'Yes,' he said, 'I do have such orders. But I can choose to ignore them. If I kill them, I am no better than the man you have just told me about, the man who struck off my father's head. Pretending to be God, killing because he is filled with hatred of himself. If I come with you, it will be to rescue those I can. Believe me.'

'I believe you.' Declan turned to Maureen.

'What about you? This isn't your fight.'

'Mister,' she said, 'for years now I've been arguing that the IRA is the only legitimate military force in Ireland. From what I hear, the Brits have all but taken over down here. Captain Murtagh here seems to be the last independent Irish soldier left. So this is my great chance to prove my point. This is as much my fight as yours.'

Declan knew there was no point in arguing. In any case, he needed all the fighters he could get, legitimate or illegitimate no longer seemed to matter. At the moment, he was in no position to sit in judgement on Maureen O'Dalaigh.

'Tommy?' he asked.

Murtagh nodded.

'At the moment, I'm about as legitimate in the eyes of the Republic as Miss O'Dalaigh. I can't go back, so I may as well go ahead.'

'Grainne?'

'Count me in. I'm in the same position as the rest of you. And I wouldn't like to think Liam died just so we could pack up and go home.'

They started to head back down to the shore, where their boat waited. As Tommy passed him, Declan took his arm.

'Tommy, can you get Myles for me? I need to ask him something.'

Tommy patched him through on his military mobile.

'Myles? This is Declan. Listen, I need to know something. Your gut reaction, that's all. Koresh has the compound mined. Would he do it again? Would he blow himself and dozens of other people to pieces just to set the Day of Judgement going? Does that make sense?'

There was a long pause. When Myles answered, his voice was barely recognizable.

'If he had the means to do it, Declan, he'd blow the world to pieces. He thinks he's God. And he thinks it's time for the end of everything he created.'

CHAPTER SEVENTY-FOUR

Near Inis Tuaisceart
0236 hours

The island of Inis Tuaisceart is an inverted triangle in shape, with its longest side facing north-west. They came to it the long way, setting out under power from a beach to the north of Clogher Head. There was room in the boat for five more.

Out past the head, the waves were high and the darkness brooding and terrible. No lights were visible on the mainland; it was as if it had sunk behind them, silently, a vast land mass dropping like a stone beneath grey waves. Clouds covered the sky. There was no moon, there were no stars by which to navigate. A storm was rising out at sea, a winter storm, born in the mid-Atlantic.

The greatest danger was that, in the darkness, they might over-shoot and miss their way entirely. They dared not risk going in close to the island with engines running. There were no lights on Inis Tuaisceart, and even with a mile and a quarter of coast on which to strike, Declan knew it was not impossible to be pulled out past the island by a strong current and to head into the open sea. The morning might find them adrift in heavy seas in a small boat.

They cut the engine. Tommy was navigating, using a marine compass and a battery-operated radar.

'Get the oars out now,' he said. 'This current's strong enough to drag us all the way past.'

Declan and Abu Hida unshipped the oars and slipped them into the rowlocks. There was about a mile to row. At least, thought Declan, if they got off the island again, they would be able to use the motor all along.

Grainne sat in the prow, scanning the darkness through the Simrad telescope. Ahead of them lay nothing but white-capped waves. The sea was growing choppy, but at least the wind had driven the mist away.

The pain in his neck and shoulders reminded Declan that he had not had a headache all day. He could not recall when he had last done such hard physical work. Behind him, Abu Hida pulled smoothly, his breath coming and going in long, measured lungfuls.

'Shhhh! Stop rowing.'

Tommy was leaning forward, one hand to his ear. Without the sound of the oars, they could hear the waves dashing against the sides of the little craft. For what seemed an age, they drifted in silence.

'What can you hear?'

'Shhhh!' Then, abruptly, a muted cheer. 'That's waves breaking on rocks, that is. A lot of waves. And some bloody big rocks. You can start rowing again, boys. Inis Tuaisceart's straight ahead of us.'

They landed twenty minutes later, on a narrow shingle beach in a small cove. Above them rose a high cliff wall. Declan and Abu Hida sat hunched forward for a while, recovering their breath, letting their arms regain their strength.

They beached the boat carefully, tucking it well into the cove. Abu Hida and Tommy distributed the weapons they had brought. The Arab carried, in addition to a Franchi assault rifle, a Mossberg Bullpup shotgun, two pistols, and his Peskett. He also carried a light crossbow, equipped with a powerful night-sight, and a small supply of bolts.

Climbing carefully and in total silence, they reached the top of the cliff. There were boulders here to shelter behind, while Grainne scanned the landscape ahead of them. A stiff wind blew uninterruptedly across the flat, scarred surface of the land. Almost nothing grew here. It was hard to believe that men and women had once lived out their whole lives on this desolate, unforgiving rock.

'There,' Grainne whispered. 'That must be St Brendan's Oratory.' She passed the telescope to Declan, indicating the approximate spot. He looked for a while, then nodded.

'The rear lookout will be positioned a little to the left,' he said.

'If our friend back there was telling the truth,' said Abu Hida. He asked for the telescope. For over five minutes, he lay watching through it. At last, he sighed and turned to the others.

'This has to be done in silence,' he said. 'There are two of them. Leave them to me.'

Leaving his other weapons, he took the telescope and his crossbow, together with the pouch of bolts, and slipped off into the darkness.

He returned in half an hour. Without a word, he gave the telescope back to Grainne.

'Now we can go forward,' he said.

He led them into the darkness from which he had just come, his nimble feet finding the surest paths between the rough, weathered rocks. They were going down now, towards the low-lying eastern coast of the island. It was here that Koresh had established his compound, on the site of an old smallholding.

As at Waco, so here he had erected a watchtower, as much for its symbolic as for its practical value. Ezekiel had warned them about it, telling them that the guards positioned in it were equipped with night-vision scopes, and that they were vigilant.

They saw the tower, about forty feet high, then the little cluster of buildings huddled at its base. From behind a clump of low rocks, Grainne established that there was only one guard. Most of the time, he looked out across the expanse of land dividing the compound from the shore, as though expecting an attack from that quarter. But from time to time he would turn his night scope in their direction.

Tommy lay down beside her. They were about two hundred and fifty metres away.

'I can take him from here,' he said. He brought out a Steyr SSG sniper's rifle, fitted with a Kahles Hella eight-power low-light scope. The gun also carried a Blind Pugh device, which could project a black spot onto a target. Unlike other similar targeting devices, which use red dots, the Blind Pugh remains invisible in darkness.

Tommy aimed carefully. The rifle had been suppressed, but a succession of shots might be heard inside. Letting out his breath, he waited until the man turned to face him, presenting an easier target. His finger tightened on the trigger. It would be difficult to get the shot right, there was a risk that the unstable cross-winds might throw the bullet wide. Steadying himself, he dropped the spot until it lay on the centre of the man's face. An inch either way would still put the guard out of action.

The shot sounded outrageously loud in the silence. Grainne, watching through the Simrad, saw the guard jerk and fall. She kept her eyes on the tower until she was sure he would not move again. Tommy was already watching the entrance to the main block, where the guard's dormitory lay. He let a minute pass, then two, then three. No-one came. The shot had not been heard.

They had already talked over their plans. From here on, they would proceed in silence, unless an emergency forced one of them to break it.

The compound consisted of four buildings. The largest, on the north side, was the former barn that served to house both the hostages and their keepers. Ezekiel had described the inside for them in detail. A central aisle divided into cells, the eastern end kept separate for the women prisoners, with its own toilet and showers. Along the northern side of the building, separated from the cells by a narrow corridor, was the dormitory for Koresh's bodyguard and, on its eastern end, his private quarters. To the south, without a dividing corridor, were the kitchens and the dining hall. A guardhouse stood at the western end of the cell block, opposite the one entrance.

To the south of the main building stood a square cinderblock shed in which were housed the men's toilets, showers, and wash-basins. The prisoners were taken there two at a time every morning and evening. Next to this stood a small radio hut, manned at all times to receive any communications that might come from Ramon on the mainland. East of this was the armoury. The watch-tower stood in the corner formed by the armoury and the radio hut.

Judging by Ezekiel's description, the fabric of the building itself would not withstand much force. They had decided to effect an entry by breaking down part of the kitchen wall, on the side furthest from the dormitory. From there, they would make their way through the dining hall and into the short corridor that ran past the guardroom and the cell block. If they could overpower the guards on duty there, Abu Hida and Maureen would locate and free four of the hostages, taking their names from a list supplied to Abu Hida in Baalbek. They would not know who was

387

dead or alive at first, but they expected to be able to move through the list quickly and have their four men free in a matter of minutes.

Meanwhile, Declan, Tommy and Grainne would head down to the women's quarters, overpower the guards there, and find Amina. As for Musgrave, Declan still had not made up his mind what to do about him.

It was pointless even to consider releasing the other hostages. There was only one other boat on the island, which would take five at the most. By the time they found it, the rest of the body-guard would have been roused. In all likelihood, there would be a massacre.

Once they had the five hostages they had come for, they would make their escape while Abu Hida and Tommy covered the dormitory. They would have to get everyone across the cliff and to the boat before an alarm was raised. Once on board the boat, they had a better than even chance of making it to the mainland unhindered. The others would have to take their chances, but it was possible that Koresh's band, knowing their hideout had been discovered, would abandon the island, leaving the remaining hostages behind. More likely, Declan admitted to himself, that David Koresh would instigate his night of the apocalypse first.

Coming in from the west, they kept the ablutions shed between themselves and the main building. Ezekiel had mentioned the risk of their running into perimeter guards, whose task was to patrol the grounds every half hour or so. Each step had to be taken with the utmost care in order not to make a sound. With Abu Hida leading, they crept in single file along the south flank of the outhouse. As they reached the corner, he raised a hand, cautioning them to stop.

An armed man was walking slowly towards them, patrolling between the armoury and the shed. They could let him go by, hoping that he would not see them in the lee of the shed wall. But once he turned the corner, if he chanced to look up, he would notice that all was not well in the watchtower.

Abu Hida unsheathed a long knife. He waited until the man had gone past, then stepped out behind him. No hesitation. No second thoughts. Just a step forward, one hand reaching for the man's chin, the other poised to cut his throat. He grabbed the chin hard, pulling back and upwards, preventing the guard from crying out. There was a moment when the man might have broken free, then the moment was gone. Abu Hida's hand descended in a short, crisp arc, the blade caught then sliced through the throat a full two inches. Close up, the sound of choking was an abomination, something best forgotten. But even feet away, there was nothing to break the silence. Abu Hida released his grip and dragged the limp body back into the shadow of the shed.

They rounded the corner, crossed the east flank of the out-house, and reached the main building. It was just as Ezekiel had implied it would be: old stone, thinly mortared and poorly repaired. Abu Hida set to work with the Peskett, ramming it between the stones to loosen the mortar. It was essential that the hole be made carefully, in order to prevent stones higher up collapsing. Tommy worked beside him with a small trenching tool. From time to time, Declan shone his torch on the wall, to enable them to decide which stone to move to next.

It took half an hour before the hole was large enough to crawl through. They slipped inside, one at a time. The kitchen was silent.

'Ready?' asked Declan. He drew a pistol from his belt and fitted a suppressor to the barrel.

At that moment, someone switched on the light.

CHAPTER SEVENTY-FIVE

Dublin
0240 hours

Myles got out of bed shivering. Something had woken him. A noise? Bad dreams? He'd hardly been sleeping well. So far, his efforts to contact Pádraig Pearse Mangan had been met with little success. Of the other people to whom he had spoken, only one or two had taken what he had said with any seriousness. And now Declan was suggesting that Koresh was about to repeat the holocaust at Waco.

There was a draught coming from somewhere. The window must have been left open. He crossed to it and pushed the sash down hard. Beyond the glass, the city lay sleeping without thought. If the world were to end tonight, Dublin would slip into oblivion without a murmur. He was about to turn back to bed when everything went insane.

The first man grabbed his arms and pulled them hard behind his back. The second stepped in front of him. He did not see the plastic bag, but he felt it as the man pushed it over his head, and he could not escape it as it pressed in, cold and clammy, against his skin, hugging his cheeks and forehead, bowing inwards at the curve of his open lips. It took him two minutes to die. He did not go without a murmur, but it made no difference: oblivion was still oblivion.

Anthony Harker stood at the water's edge. Darkness beyond. Darkness in all things. Tiredness washed over him like water. He heard a footstep on the cobbled quay.

'Message from Dublin, sir.'

Harker turned to see Christopher Sheldrake standing next to him. Sheldrake was second-in-command of the SAS team he had been holding on standby here at Ventry since early evening.

'Have they taken care of that business yet?'

'Yes, sir. The message is from the unit that carried it out, sir. They found a note on the table by his telephone. Thought you should see it straight away. This is a verbatim copy I took from them, sir.'

Harker took it from him as they walked back a little to the first streetlight. It was brief but to the point.

Phone message 0205 am. Declan thinks Koresh may be planning another conflagration. He has the place mined. His own people are going in. God help us all.

Harker crumpled the message and tossed it into the darkness, over the water.

'Tell your commander to get his team ready. I want him to take out the raiders and put the hostages under their own control. Warn him that the raider leader has mined the compound and may be contemplating mass suicide. And tell him Carberry and his team are already on their way there.'

CHAPTER SEVENTY-SIX

0335 hours

Harry Ferguson had been with David Koresh since 1989, three years before the business at Waco. He was an Englishman, an architectural student from Birmingham who had gone to the States for the summer vacation one year and never returned. His family were Seventh Day Adventists, and when in the States he had made contact with a church in Tyler, Texas. That had eventually brought him into contact with the Mount Carmel organization. He had listened to Koresh's Bible classes, been impressed, and stayed. In 1993, he'd been on a mission trip to California, and so had missed being trapped inside the ranch when the AFT agents and then the FBI had surrounded it. A lot of his best friends, including several other British Davidians, had either been burned in the fire or were now serving time in jail.

Harry liked to eat. He had a good body and looked after it, keeping his calories high but his fat low. During the night he generally liked to have a high-protein snack. Ezekiel didn't like the men keeping food or drink in the dorm, so Harry would get up a bit after midnight and head for the kitchen.

That night, when he flicked on the switch, he had the worst fright of his life. It was also the last. Five intruders, all dressed in black body-armour, with balaclavas pulled down over their faces, all armed.

Declan saw him open his mouth to shout. His reaction was instinctive. The suppressed gun was already in his hand. He raised it and fired, almost without aiming. When he looked again, Harry was on the ground, kicking and clawing the air. The bullet had entered his mouth. Abu Hida bent down and finished him off with the edge of his knife. He looked up and saw Declan staring at the dead man, saw the momentary look of remorse on his face.

'This is not a game, Mr Carberry,' he hissed. 'You did not shoot him in fun, I did not finish the job for pleasure. Remember that, or we shall all be dead before the night is through.'

'He wasn't even armed,' whispered Declan.

'Then feel bad about it later. Not now.'

Abu Hida extinguished the light and moved to the door. He took shelter against the wall beside it. The others followed suit, pressing themselves against the other side. Grainne could feel her heart thumping as though each beat were set off by a tripwire. Minutes passed. No-one came. Abu Hida opened the door slowly. The dining hall was in darkness.

They slipped through quietly. Declan knew that they were more exposed here, that sounds would carry straight to the ears of the guards in the next sector. Maureen flashed her torch once, to show the way to the door. Her breathing was tight, she felt a sense of panic, knowing that they had passed the point of no return. It would not be easy to get out of here again, through those two dark rooms, through the hole, back to the cliff, pursued every inch of the way.

Abu Hida opened the door. He guessed that the man Declan had shot had come to the kitchen for food, and that his colleagues would be expecting him back any minute. No-one would be surprised to see the door open.

They came into a dimly-lit corridor. According to Ezekiel, they would turn right here. A few paces would take them to the guardroom. A single door led into it, and another out again, into the cells. Ezekiel had told them to expect two guards on duty here, and another two at the entrance to the women's section beyond.

They came to the door. Abu Hida hesitated, his hand on the knob, waiting for the others to group themselves around him, Declan and Tommy on his left, Grainne and Maureen on his right. The door opened to the right, so Tommy would be first in, then Abu Hida, then the others. Once in, they would have to capture the guards quickly. All it would take would be a shout, a finger on an alarm button, a shot, and they would be surrounded and picked off. Declan remembered the ruthlessness with which Koresh's men had swept through Castletown House. He nodded once. Abu Hida threw the door open.

Not two men, but six, gathered round a table, reading books that must be Bibles. Tommy ran to the right, turning as he did so, lifting his pistol. He saw one man rise, caught a glimpse of Abu Hida entering, moving to the opposite corner, then a second man rising, Declan coming through, Grainne and Maureen following him, a third man getting to his feet. Maureen closed the door.

'Put your hands on your heads,' commanded Declan. He prayed they would obey orders. He felt the muscles tense all along his arm, down into his hand, felt his fingers tight on the gun, knew that, if they did not do as he said, his hand would start to shake.

One man raised his hands. A second jumped for Declan. Declan felt his hand knocked sideways, strong hands clamped round his neck, tightening. His vision started to go crazy, lights flashed in front of his eyes, it was like being pushed under water. And then, mercifully, the pressure loosened. He opened his eyes and saw a man's face inches from his own. An ugly, distorted, struggling face, with gaping mouth and popping eyes. And then he saw the blood and the terrible wound opening in the throat, and he was staring into a dead face and pushing a dead man away from him.

Abu Hida released the garrotte and let the guard's body slump to the floor. Declan took several deep breaths and looked round. Grainne and Maureen were herding the five remaining guards together against the rear wall.

Maureen took a roll of packing tape from a pouch on her waist and unpeeled a length. Pressing it over one man's mouth, she wound it about his head several times before tearing it and fastening the end. She repeated this on the others. Tommy and Abu Hida found rows of handcuffs hanging on one wall and used them to fasten their prisoners' hands behind their backs.

There were keys in a box on the wall near the door leading to the cells. Abu Hida took out several bunches, noted the numbers on the tags, handed a set to each of the others, and used a key on his own set to lock the door through which they had entered. When he had satisfied himself that they were secure, he opened the door to the cells and led them through.

They closed and locked the door behind them and started to walk down the aisle between the cells. Declan wanted to start opening the doors to release as many of the hostages as they could, but Abu Hida warned him that they would have to deal with the guards in the women's section before they could do anything else.

They had reached about half way when, without warning, the door to the women's quarters opened. Two men in fatigues came out, each holding a sub-machine gun pointed at the intruders. They threw themselves to the ground as a burst of rapid fire raked the corridor. A bullet took Declan in the left arm, knocking him sideways as he hit the floor. A second and a third hit Maureen in the waist and upper left thigh. She screamed with pain and rolled sideways in an attempt to avoid being hit again.

Abu Hida was already on the ground and rolling as the first bullets started to hit the walls and the cell doors. The guards paused, checking to see what damage they had inflicted, who remained a threat, who was out of action. In the brief moments before they recommenced firing, Abu Hida knelt and got off five rounds with the assault rifle. They were more than enough. The heavy Glaser rounds made up for any inaccuracy there might have been in his aim. The side of one guard's head disappeared in a cloud of blood, the other lost an arm and most of his chest.

Abu Hida checked that they were dead, then ran quickly to where Maureen lay bleeding on the floor.

'How bad is it?'

'I'll live. Two hits, but they both went through, I'm sure of it. There are some field dressings in my bag – get them for me.'

He found the dressings and threw one to Grainne, who was kneeling by Declan. Tommy was covering the main door. They could hear the sound of voices nearby, then feet running. From the cells came shouts and cries, frantic questions in Arabic and Persian, hurried prayers.

Grainne pressed Declan's dressing in place, then turned to Abu Hida.

'Leave her to me,' she said. 'You'd better start getting your friends out.'

He nodded and passed the packet of dressings to her. Getting to his feet, he ran along the rows of cells, calling loudly in Arabic, trying to make himself heard above the racket that had broken out.

'Shaykh Hasan al-Najafi! Can you hear me? Are you there? Mulla 'Ali Shirazi. Can you hear me? I've come to take you out of here. Answer me.'

Out of the cacophony that surrounded him, he distinguished two answering voices. Precious moments were lost finding the right keys. There was a sound of banging on the outer door, raised voices, running feet. Abu Hida tried one key, then another. At last, he found one that fitted the first door. A deep thudding began as the bodyguards started to break down the first guardroom door. He was at the other cell now, trying key after key. The thudding resounded through the building.

At last, the first two hostages were out of the cells, looking bewildered and frightened. Abu Hida told them to join the others at the far end, then started shouting another name.

'Hajj 'Umar Fadlan. Can you hear me? Answer me. This is Abu Hida. I've come to take you out.'

There was a dreadful crash. The sound of feet on the guardroom floor. And now the thudding started on the inner door.

A voice answered from a cell at the back. Abu Hida ran to it, fumbling among the keys. The thudding grew louder, and with it the sound of wood splitting. A man stumbled out of the cell, pale and ill-looking, barely able to walk. His hands were missing, and the stumps wrapped in layers of blood-stained bandage. Abu Hida helped him to where the others were waiting. He felt a terrible anger in him at the sight of Fadlan's wrists.

'We have to go,' urged Declan. 'They'll be through the door any second now.'

But Abu Hida ignored him, turning back and shouting the name of the fourth man on his list. By now the other hostages had worked out what was happening, and were calling loudly for him to open their cells too, to take them, to have pity on them.

''Ali Bouslimani! Can you hear me? 'Ali Bouslimani!'

'He is dead,' shouted one of the freed hostages from the back.

Abu Hida could hear the hinges of the door groaning, the wood shattering in places. It would give way in a matter of moments. He had a fifth name, that of a man who had once taught him *hadith* in a school in Beirut, a man he admired deeply.

He looked round. Tommy was still guarding the door. Declan and Grainne were helping the others into the room beyond. Declan looked up and caught his eye.

'I will have to close this door,' he shouted. 'I have no choice. Do you understand? I have to close and lock it. Leave him. It's too late. Tommy, for God's sake get out of there!'

Abu Hida made up his mind. He rushed back to where he had left the bag containing his Mossberg. Taking out the shotgun, he chambered two 7mm rounds of tungsten alloy buckshot and handed the gun to Tommy. While Abu Hida went back to the cells, Tommy took several steps towards the door, aimed, and fired twice. The heavy rounds were capable of penetrating steel plate at one hundred and fifty metres. They blasted straight through the wood. Horrific cries erupted on the other side.

'Shaykh Ubayd!' Abu Hida shouted. 'Where are you? Shaykh Ubayd!'

An answering voice came from the middle of the aisle. Abu Hida ran to the door and started going through the keys. As he did so, he looked round. Declan was about to close the door.

'Go!' he shouted. 'I will at least set him free. I gave my word.'

Declan was torn in two. Amina was in the room behind him. Grainne had found her and was already going through the keys that hung on the wall of the women's sector. She would be free in moments.

But he could not leave either Abu Hida or Tommy to die. He bent and picked up the sub-machine gun that had been dropped by one of the guards.

There was a crash and the far door, weakened by Tommy's shots, broke in half. Declan ran forward and very calmly fired through the opening while Tommy did the same from the other side.

Abu Hida pulled the cell door open, and Shaykh Ubayd staggered out.

'Hurry!' shouted Declan. 'Get behind me. Through the door! Tommy, cover them!'

As they passed him, he fired a second burst, a long, chattering roar of bullets that emptied the magazine. Throwing the gun down, he turned and ran after Tommy and Abu Hida, slamming the door shut behind him.

CHAPTER SEVENTY-SEVEN

0342 hours

Peter Musgrave ran from the radio hut as fast as he could move. He could hear the shooting from the main compound, and guessed that Carberry and his self-appointed hostage rescue unit had arrived on the scene. It would be satisfying to finish what he had started with Carberry, and to take his revenge for the wounds he'd received in the shooting at the ice-cream parlour. But the orders that had just come from Harker had to take priority. If he didn't find the little shit first, David Koresh was going to blow this place to kingdom come.

He guessed the cult leader would be in his own quarters, and he guessed that was where he would have the lever or button or whatever it was he planned to use to trigger the explosives. There was no point in trying to find the charges themselves: if the entire place had been mined, there would be dozens of them at the very least, and finding them in the dark would be far from easy.

He skirted the ablutions block and made for the entrance on the western face of the main building. The growing wind was singing in his ears, disorienting him. Reaching the door, he dashed inside to find a scene of chaos.

One of Koresh's bodyguards was holding the door that led through to the cells. He almost fired on Musgrave, pulling his gun away only at the last second.

'Where's David?' Musgrave demanded.

'In his room.'

'Is he alone?'

'There are two guards on the door. He's praying: no-one's allowed in.'

'To hell with that. I've got an important message for him.'

Musgrave turned off into the corridor that skirted the guards' dormitory and ended at the door of Koresh's quarters. At the door, two guards were waiting at the alert, weapons at the ready. Recognizing him, they relaxed. He was not one of them, but he'd been around from an early stage of the operation, and they knew he enjoyed Koresh's confidence.

'What's going on out there?' one of them asked.

'I don't know. Looks like somebody's broken in. Government troops maybe. Look, I've got to speak to David. It's urgent.'

The other guard shook his head.

'Can't let you in,' he said. 'I'm sorry, but David gave strict orders he wasn't to be disturbed. He's in deep prayer right now.'

'I don't care if he's got Jesus Christ in person in there, I've got to see him.'

The guard shook his head.

'Not till he says it's OK.'

Musgrave swore, turned, and began to walk away. At five paces, he spun, Browning Hi-Power in hand, and got off two clean shots before the guards knew what was happening. They slumped to the ground and lay still. They had been well trained, but Peter Musgrave had taken his lessons in an even harder school.

He opened the door and went inside. Koresh was on the other side of the room, on his knees, mumbling prayers. He did not register Musgrave's presence at first, but continued praying as if nothing out of the ordinary was happening. Musgrave had to hand it to him, he was as cool as a field of cucumbers.

From nearby, the sounds of shooting and yelling penetrated to Koresh's little sanctuary, but he seemed blissfully unaware of them. On the floor beside him, lay a small black box from which a thick wire ran to the wall and then beneath the floor.

Musgrave eased himself forward, frightened lest the smallest incautious movement or the premature betrayal of his presence should provoke Koresh into grabbing the box and conjuring up the private doomsday for which he was even now no doubt obtaining permission from his God or himself – if there was any difference. A clear shot to the head would remove the threat.

The Englishman adopted a firing stance and raised the gun, aiming at Koresh's temple. Suddenly, God's emissary stopped praying, turned, and looked directly at him.

Half a second later, Musgrave felt the cold tip of a gun barrel graze the skin of his neck.

'If you shoot him,' said a controlled voice behind him, 'you'll be the next to die. And then I'll take the box and finish the job myself.' It was Zechariah. Musgrave had helped train him in the days leading up to the raid, and he knew that, of Koresh's inner cohort, he was by far the most ruthless.

He lowered his gun, and as he did so Zechariah reached from behind and snatched it from his hand.

'Take a seat, Mr Musgrave,' said Koresh, rising from his kneeling position. 'Your job here's over. Just relax now, and wait. I've been speaking to my Father. It's time to bring this old creation to an end and build a new world in place of it. God be praised.'

Amina was waiting for him outside the door of her cell, cold, lost, inarticulate with rage and fear and helplessness. She could not embrace him, could not touch him with her hand or mouth, but she wanted him for herself, to take her away from here, no knight in shining armour, but a lonely man on a lame and shambling beast.

'You took a long time,' she said.

He smiled and put his hand on her cheek and held it there until he felt the blood move in her skin. There was no need for words. Their eyes said everything that was needed.

'Which way are Koresh's quarters?' Tommy asked, not wanting to interrupt, but knowing time was short.

She pointed to a narrow door in the side wall.

'That door leads into a short corridor,' Amina said. 'At the end of it, there's another door into his bedroom. That leads into his study.'

Declan looked at her.

'How did you find that out?'

She did not stumble in answering, or take her eyes from his.

'I was taken there,' she said. She felt no guilt, that would never be at issue between them, Declan was not a fool. But a terrible grief lacerated her, knowing that she could never tell him all the truth, and that his not knowing would always be a separation between them greater than seas or ranges of mountains.

The main thing would be speed, figured Tommy. Even a few

seconds delay would enable Koresh to run or, infinitely worse, make his final decision and take them all with him on his last great journey.

At the door, a deep thudding started.

Abu Hida stepped across to them. He pointed to the wooden partition at the other end of the short corridor.

'In there is the kitchen,' he said. 'I think we can break through, but we should be prepared for a reception committee. Get them all together, I'll do what I can.'

'We have to stop Koresh first,' said Declan. 'Tommy, are you coming?'

Tommy nodded. As he did so, Amina went to Abu Hida, speaking to him in Arabic. She had known immediately who he was, although she could hardly guess how he came to be here as Declan's ally.

'Give me one of your guns,' she said. 'I know the way through, what to expect.'

'Can you use this?' he asked, holding out the Franchi assault rifle.

'You know I can, Abu Hidda.' The name she gave him was a play on words. Abu Hida meant 'Father of Isolation', but the form with a doubled middle letter came from an entirely different verbal root and meant 'Father of Wrath'. It was how he was referred to by the Lebanese security forces. He smiled and handed her the rifle.

Tommy used one of his own weapons, a Remington 870 12-gauge slide-action shotgun, to blow the lock. He slid a fresh round into the chamber and kicked the door open. A six-foot-long corridor led to a second door. Declan and Amina followed, Amina whispering a description of the bedroom to him as they went. As they stood by the door, she gave Tommy a quick run-down of what he might expect to find inside.

But no warning would have sufficed to prepare either man for the sight that met them on the other side of the door. Tommy blew part of the jamb away with a single shot and the door swung back. They rushed in, Tommy first, then Declan, followed by Amina, for whom the room held nothing but the most awful memories.

They halted, mouths open at what they saw. The walls and ceiling were covered with coloured photographs. Pictures of fire in all its incarnations: fireballs, infernos, conflagrations, bonfires, bush fires, firestorms, funeral pyres, autos-da-fé, suttees, hells, lakes of fire, pits full of flame, heretics at the stake, their eyes agape, houses burning like torches, entire families at the windows, burning, crematoria, their open mouths bulging with flames, men burning in the caul of flame-throwers, Buddhist monks in the act of self-immolation, Dresden in torment, Coventry searing the sky, paintings of the damned, scorched and screaming, cars and trucks erupting with fire, racing cars exploding, the burnt faces of fire victims, black and inhuman, grinning with bright white teeth, whole torsos charred and blackened, the limbs twisted, barely recognizable, Joan of Arc incandescent, a Persian martyr, his flesh pierced and filled with burning candles, Giordano Bruno in the Campo dei Fiori, wreathed in light, children running from soldiers, their hair in flames, like halos round their heads, Vietnamese villages, hut upon hut a dwelling of fire, palm trees drenched with petrol, cocooned in yellow and red, oil wells across Kuwait, red flames set against black smoke, bonfires of books surrounded by students waving swastikas, Ranch Apocalypse, like a forest of flames, banners of smoke proclaiming God across the proscenium of the sky. Not an inch of wall had been left empty.

No-one breathed. The fires seemed to sear their throats and creep down to their bellies. They stayed for only moments, but in that time they were burned through like crêpe paper.

Amina pointed out the door to the study. Tommy got in place, Declan stood facing him, they counted down from three with fingers, and Tommy smashed the door open with his boot.

Zechariah was standing, facing the door, his pistol at the ready. As Tommy came through, Zechariah got off three shots, and Tommy's rush became a stumble, then a skid. He crashed at Zechariah's feet, and another three shots finished him.

Declan rolled into the room and was on his feet, gun at the ready. As Zechariah raised his pistol, Declan fired on automatic, leaving a line of bullet holes across his chest. The American stood mute for a moment, as though waiting for a sign, then bellowed 'Jesus!' and pitched forward across Tommy.

At that moment, Declan caught a movement with the corner of his eye. He turned and saw David Koresh with his arms upraised, the black box in one hand, his finger poised above the button. A second burst of fire lifted Koresh and threw him backwards against a chair. The box dropped from his hand and bounced on the floor. Declan ran across, grabbed it, and used a knife to cut straight through the wire. Now, even if another of Koresh's bodyguards were to find it, they could not easily trigger the explosion.

'Declan!' Amina's voice from the other side of the room alerted him to danger. He turned and saw her. Musgrave, hidden behind the door, had ambushed her as she entered, disarmed her, and grabbed her round the neck.

'Drop the gun!' he shouted. 'Now! Or I'll break her fucking neck.'

It was only then that Musgrave recognized Declan. His eyes widened, and he smiled.

'Well, well. Mr Carberry. Isn't it a small world. My apologies for what happened last time we met. I'd no intention of killing your lovely daughter, but you reacted too quickly.'

'Let her go,' said Declan, knowing Musgrave would not.

'And have you shoot me? I'm not such a fool. Now, drop the gun.'

Declan knew Musgrave had the training to break Amina's neck exactly as he threatened, with a simple twist of the arm. He dropped the gun.

'Kick it away from you!'

Declan did as he ordered. Musgrave started to back towards the door that led into the dormitory corridor. There would be no-one there now, he reckoned, and once outside he could dump the woman and make his getaway. Slowly, forcing Amina to bend with him, he crouched down and picked up the Franchi with his free hand. She squirmed, but he had her fast. They shuffled back to the door. There was nothing Declan could do. From the room beyond, Abu Hida was calling urgently for them to rejoin him. Declan could hear the sound of wood splintering.

Suddenly, there was a great cry of pain. Musgrave went shuddering backwards, letting Amina free. The hair-pin she had been given by Nushin was embedded in his thigh, two inches of hard steel. After her attack on Koresh, she had simply fastened it back in her hair, and no-one had thought to look for the weapon there.

Choking, she stumbled away from him. He found the pin

and pulled it out. Despite the pain, he had not dropped the Franchi. He lifted it, aiming directly at her head. Declan shot him once in the stomach and once in the throat. He did not apologize.

CHAPTER SEVENTY-EIGHT

Declan and Amina raced back to the room where the women's cells were to find the door buckling under the strain of whatever battering ram was being applied to it.

Seeing them come, Abu Hida lifted his shotgun. Pointing it at the wall, he fired several rounds, each time placing a shot in a pre-arranged position. Picking up a heavy chair that had been used by one of the guards, he began to smash at the weakened wood between the holes he had created. The wall gave in seconds, leaving a hole big enough to climb through.

There was a splintering sound behind them. Declan looked round. Someone had taken an axe and was using it to break down the upper panels of the door.

'Hurry up!' he said. 'Get through the hole. Maureen, show them the way out. Head for the cliff.'

Abu Hida reloaded the Bullpup. The door shattered with a final blow from the axe, caving in. But no-one appeared in the opening. Moments later, someone opened up with a machine gun, peppering the wall and throwing plaster and wood chips into Abu Hida's face. He replied with four rapid rounds, tearing away what remained of the door. The machine-gun fire paused.

Maureen and the man without hands had got out. There were still three hostages, Amina, Declan, and Abu Hida to go.

And then, in the lull that followed the shooting, they heard a bewildering, unexpected sound. A helicopter, moving in rapidly. And a second, and a third.

Declan and Abu Hida exchanged glances.

'Harker,' said Declan. 'The bastard followed us after all.'

'I think we should get out of here before they land,' answered Abu Hida.

The Davidians had heard the choppers too. Declan could hear someone barking orders, feet running in all directions.

They got the last hostages through the opening. Maureen and Amina were already at the gap in the east wall of the kitchen, helping everyone through.

Declan ran up to them.

'Take everyone down to the beach on this side. I'll bring the boat round and pick you all up.'

Maureen gestured towards the helicopters.

'What about them?' she asked. 'They'll have friends landing by dinghy. We have to go out the way we came in.'

Declan nodded. She was right. They might have landed already and be on their way here.

'Get going,' he said. He looked round for Abu Hida. 'I'll hold the rear. You go ahead to cover the others.'

'I should stay here,' Abu Hida said.

'It makes precious little difference. But you have a night-sight on your weapon. I'd prefer it if you acted as escort.'

There was no time to waste. In the sky to the east, three flares went off simultaneously.

As the file of released hostages moved off, Amina ran back to Declan.

'Don't stay long,' she said. 'There's no need, they'll soon be busy with Harker's crowd.'

'Don't worry. I'll give it two minutes, then follow you. Once you're clear of the compound, they won't know which way you've gone.'

He caught up with the others as they stumbled through the darkness, heading west away from the compound. Behind them, they could hear the sound of firing.

The hostages had to be coaxed and helped through the night. They had to stop every now and again to rest or to let Maureen use her compass. At the compound, the shooting continued.

'That's it,' shouted Maureen, pointing into the darkness. Declan could just make out the shape of St Brendan's Oratory, a Celtic ruin that was the only real landmark on the island. They were almost at the shore.

Suddenly, out of nowhere, they heard the sound of a

helicopter. Then it was there, coming down right in front of them. Maureen got everyone down, then watched it land about thirty yards away. A door opened and a soldier jumped out, face blackened, rifle in hand.

One of the hostages, Shaykh Ubayd, got to his feet. No-one had explained to him, he misunderstood who and what the men in the helicopter were. He stood up and started to walk towards them, smiling, unaware. The soldier started to raise his rifle.

'It's all right,' said Shaykh Ubayd, 'we're hostages. We . . .'

Maureen was on her feet, running towards him.

'No!' she shouted, 'no!'

She threw herself on the shaykh as the soldier opened fire, knocking him to the ground and winding him. Rolling, she wrestled the Steyr AUG from her shoulder and half rose, trying to find the soldier in the dark. But he had already seen her fall. Taking aim through his night scope, he fired a quick burst. The bullets caught her in the neck. She was dead before her body rolled back across Shaykh Ubayd's.

Abu Hida cut the soldier in two, firing from the hip with the Bullpup. And as the man fell, Abu Hida reached into a pocket and drew out a grenade. A second man appeared in the door of the helicopter. Abu Hida drew the pin, tossed the grenade, and threw himself to the ground. Seconds later, the helicopter erupted in a ball of fire.

They reached the clifftop clinging to one another, like a party of schoolchildren gone astray in the wilderness. No-one spoke, as though speech would have conjured up demons from the dark, as if there was nothing to add to Maureen O'Dalaigh's last, impassioned negative.

Abu Hida had left two aluminium ladders at the cliff's edge. They found them after a short search and began the descent. It was not far to the beach. Only Hajj 'Umar Fadlan found the descent really hard; like a fireman, Abu Hida took him across his shoulders and climbed down with him and set him in the boat. All around them, unseen, high waves pounded against the rocks.

He heard the sound of helicopters, a dull, pounding racketing that shook the compound and brought back painful memories of an earlier encirclement. His head ached, and if he moved too much, whole parts of his body cried out to him in pain. He had been wounded, pierced, crucified again. Opening his eyes, he remembered being shot. Everything in the room was spinning, as though caught up in the rotors of the helicopter and whirled round. He closed his eyes again briefly, then opened them carefully.

Near him on the floor lay the wire that God had given him to trigger the first blast on the trumpet of Judgement Day. Someone had cut the box from it and tossed it out of reach. He put out his hand and held the wire, but it was useless, the apocalypse would not be so easily bidden. He felt nauseated and weak from loss of blood. Across the room, he could see Zechariah spread-eagled over the body of a stranger, and past them Musgrave, his Judas.

He wanted to sit up, but the pains in his chest and stomach made it almost impossible to move without losing consciousness, and he knew that was the one thing he must not let happen. Everything swam when he turned his head. Terrible heat and terrible cold alternated across his skin. He felt a fierce thirst, as Jesus had done on the cross, but there was no centurion here to wipe his lips with vinegar raised on a sponge.

He twisted, and as he did so noticed a lamp on the table beside which he was lying. An idea started to form in his darkening mind. Reaching out his right hand, he pulled the lamp from the table with a jerk. It fell to the floor, smashing in a dozen pieces, and he pulled what was left of it towards him. Cutting his hands as he did so, he removed the broken bulb and switched the lamp on. Carefully, holding the bare wire of the detonator in his left hand, he smashed the top of the little lamp until its wiring was exposed.

The door crashed open and a black-faced soldier rushed in, rifle poised. He saw Koresh on the floor, bleeding, his arms outstretched in a grim mockery of Christ on the cross. The first soldier was followed by another. They scanned the room, alert for danger.

David Koresh smiled up at them, and as he did so his right hand clasped the bare wires in the lamp, making the connection.

The boat moved out into the Atlantic, lifted and tossed by the swell. Declan and Abu Hida had to pull hard to get the craft past the breakers and into the open sea. Then a current took them and they rowed with it. They came to the northern corner of the island and straightened the boat, heading directly east in order to land just south of Clogher Head.

And as they pulled away, doomsday came to Inis Tuaisceart. Facing forward towards the island, Declan and Abu Hida saw it in the fragment of a second that separated it from the blast: a sphere of light brighter than the sun. After it came the explosion, rolling like the end of the world across the water. When they looked again, it seemed as though Inis Tuaisceart was on fire. The echoes died out slowly across the waves and a black silence filled the entire world.

David Koresh had found his Day of Wrath at last.

CHAPTER SEVENTY-NINE

Dublin airport was packed. Students were returning to Trinity and UCD, parents with children in boarding schools were taking late holidays together, businessmen and women were starting the Christmas rush.

Abu Hida's plane was due to leave in half an hour. In a few minutes the flight would be called and he would go through the gate. A friend of Pádraig Pearse's had supplied him with the passport and papers of a Greek businessman. He would arrive in Athens that afternoon and fly straight to Beirut.

'Tell them everything about Inis Tuaisceart,' said Declan. 'That Harker sanctioned the raid, that the raid triggered the explosion, that fundamentalist Christians were behind the hostage-taking, and that MI5 and the CIA were using them. Your people know about Scimitar, and they'll have been approached already about a deal.'

Ciaran Clark was already peddling a shopful of lies to cover up what had really happened. The hostages had died as the result of an unfortunate accident involving heating fuel. Irish troops had done their best to locate and rescue survivors, but none had been found.

The true identity of the hostage-takers had not been revealed, not even to the extent of describing them as, for the most part, American citizens. There was already talk of a Muslim splinter group from Lebanon that had sent agents to Ireland. Any day now, the 'real' culprits would be named and identified as Arab terrorists operating out of Beirut or Cairo or Tripoli.

Inis Tuaisceart had been closed to visitors. No-one could get near, not journalists, not television crews, not the representatives of the governments whose citizens had been taken hostage and died in the explosion, not lawyers working for the families of the victims. A team of forensic scientists was busy identifying the remains. And tidying up.

'My own people will believe me,' Abu Hida said. 'And they will be able to persuade the Arab governments. There will be evidence, once people start looking in the right places. But we may never be able to make any of this public. Anything we say will be dismissed as Muslim paranoia, the ravings of people with a grudge against the West.'

Anthony Harker had vanished. He would pop up again somewhere else, Declan knew, his hands washed of all that had happened in Ireland, as though he had never been there at all. And one day a man very like Peter Musgrave would turn up at Declan's door.

'Just tell them what you know,' Declan repeated. 'When the time is right, I'll get involved, I'll testify before any tribunal you please.'

'They're going to reinstate you,' Abu Hida said. 'You'd be jeopardizing your career.'

'Career? I hardly know what that means.'

'Take care,' said Abu Hida, taking Declan's hand.

'You too. We'll meet again, I'm sure of it.'

Abu Hida shook his head.

'Perhaps. But I have no desire to return to Ireland. You will have to visit me in Lebanon.'

'It's what I intend to do as soon as things are settled here.'

'You'll need to make it soon, or you won't find me.'

'You mean to leave? I thought it was your home, that you wanted to settle down.'

The Arab shook his head.

'I don't think you understand, Declan. They will find me sooner or later. A year, two years. It will not be long.'

'Find you? Who?'

'I can't say exactly. But when it is known that I rescued four hostages, all sympathetic to our cause, it will be said that I left the others there to die.'

'You couldn't have saved them all anyway.'

'Who knows? All we know is that they are dead. That too many people died for nothing.'

Declan said nothing. A woman's voice announced that the Athens flight was now boarding from Gate Five.

They embraced.

'Remember,' said Declan. 'Tell them everything.'

Abu Hida smiled and turned away. Declan watched him until he had disappeared, then walked to the café, where Amina was finishing a cup of coffee. He bent and kissed her, then sat down. Her flight to London left in half an hour. From there, a Middle East Airlines jet would take her to Beirut. She would arrive before Abu Hida.

'Will they believe him?' Declan asked.

She nodded.

'I think so, yes.'

'It won't be easy to make anything stick. We need proof. By now they'll have dumped every file they ever had, created new ones, forged letters, invented cover stories for everyone involved.'

'Yes. But it won't be easy. There's a lot to cover up, and we have plenty of witnesses.'

They went on talking until her flight was called. It made things easier, pretending that they were just colleagues, chatting before the end of a business trip. But as she picked up her flight bag, Amina turned to him.

'You promise you will come this time?' she asked.

He nodded.

'When Concepta's fully recovered,' he said. 'I can't rush her. Máiréad was all she had, really. And the raid affected her badly.'

'I don't want to wait another fifteen years,' Amina said.

'It won't be that long,' he said. 'I promise.'

Her flight was called for the last time. At the gate they kissed, a long kiss, then broke apart and went their separate ways again.

Concepta was waiting for him in their tall white house above the bay. It was October, and the sea below was huge with waves. Teresa Cosgrave and her children were gone, their tickets to a new life in Australia paid for by Pádraig Pearse Mangan. The house belonged to Declan and his wife again, and to Máiréad's shade, still restless, still afraid. Concepta was in the dining room, at a tall window overlooking the water, gazing down and far away. Hearing him come, she looked up and smiled.

'Have your friends gone?' she asked.

'Yes,' he said in a quiet voice, the voice of a man beginning to grow old. 'They've gone.'

'Come and sit here with me,' she said, 'come and sit and watch the sea.'